# Venturing into the desert...

"She doesn't have a stitch of clothing on!" exclaimed Sheriff's Deputy Ben Rodriguez. He pushed a couple tourists out of the way to get a better look at the shapely woman riding the prancing white horse down the main concourse of the Arizona Renaissance Faire. The arid desert wind blew her long blonde hair about, but not enough to suit the deputy.

—*A Time for Steel*

He ate my two-headed rattlesnake. I know he did, even if I can't prove it.

That rattler was about my top attraction after the tic-tac-toe playing chicken. The trouble with the chicken is the way the computer chip rigs the game. Tourists drop in a quarter to against play the chicken, which pecks at a button. They make their move, the chicken plays and gets a kernel of corn and so on until it comes down to crunch time. The bird-brain actually beats most of the tourists, but when it's going to lose, the computer chip in the mechanism cheats so the chicken always wins. It takes most folks a dollar or two to figure out they can never beat the increasingly plump refugee from KFC.

—*Me and Mr Jones*

A flash. A flash of skin. Seductive, colorful, forever changing. You long to reach out and touch the woman's delicate skin but you know better. The emoto-dyes, the emotion-activated dyes injected beneath her skin, would alter the eddying dyestuff design you find so beguiling.

—*All the Colors of Life*

# Is not for the faint of heart.

# Stories from
# Desert Bob's
# Reptile Ranch

## Robert E. Vardeman

Walkabout Publishing • 2008

Walkabout Publishing
S.D.Studios
P.O.Box 151
Kansasville, WI 53139
www.walkaboutpublishing.com

Cover painting copyright © 2008 Terry Halladay
Cover Design and illustration by Stephen D. Sullivan

ISBN: 978-0-9802086-8-9

## Dedication

Words are not enough to thank you for taking Chris and me into your heart and family. But here's a try at it. This volume is lovingly dedicated to

Fred Saberhagen

# Contents

# Introduction

I never wanted to write short stories. For that matter, I never wanted to be a writer. I am a product of the Cold War, growing up in the '50s amid bomb shelters and *On the Beach* and Khruschev pounding on a desk at the UN promising to bury us. I can remember exactly the moment of Kennedy's assassination (high school chemistry class), I can also remember the precise instant I learned of *Sputnik* (standing in the cafeteria line at Jonathan Wainwright Elementary School—5th grade). This decided me to be a nuclear physicist.

I eventually ended up in solid-state physics research for Sandia National Laboratories, working on bomb stuff and other useful things like an RTG to power spacecraft (such as the Viking Lander). One thing led to another, I was accepted to work on a PhD at UC Berkeley, but I got sidetracked.

Geo. W. Proctor was a reporter for the *Dallas Morning News* and had always wanted to be a fiction writer. "Let's coauthor a story," says Geo. before I went to California. A short story. It was fun. It sold. There was a feeling of accomplishment unlike anything I had felt before.

I reconsidered getting that PhD when I sold a fantasy novel three months later. And then a science-fiction book followed. And a spy book.

But that short story? The magazine folded before it saw the light of day. Payment on publication. Oh well, says Geo., there are other markets.

My very first short story appearance was in a Spanish language magazine, *Nueva Dimension*. I never got paid, not one thin peseta. But I was published. Shortly after came publication in an Australian magazine, *Void*, of a story I coauthored with a friend, Dick Patten. We bought a pitcher of beer with the money (we had to kick in from our own pockets for a tip). I don't remember the year, but it was around 1977. Not only did they misspell my (pen) name on the story, they misspelled the title, too. But the story was alongside others by Ed Bryant and A. Bertram Chandler!

Another story sale to Ed Bryant for his *2076: The American Tricentennial* was coauthored with a friend in Denver, Jeff Slaten. In the inimitable way of the publishing world, this anthology was postponed until 1977. You know, the year *after* the Bicentennial. The next sale of any import came to Andrew Offutt for his *Swords Against Darkness III* 1978 anthology. Another Krek story (see also: "The Opal Egg" reprinted here), this one sat alongside stories by Ramsey Campbell, Manly Wade Wellman, Poul Anderson and Geo. W. Proctor.

Oh yeah, Geo. called to tell me our story (the first one we had done together that never got printed) had sold again. Payment on publication.

I hit a stretch of novels, Nick Carter Killmasters along with fantasies under my own name in the early '80s.

Geo. let me know our story wasn't going to be published. The magazine had gone out of business. But ours would have been in the next issue. Not to worry, he said he'd send it out again. He did a few years later. To the New Orleans World SF Convention for their tabloid publication to be handed out to attendees. Payment on publication.

It never happened. The tabloid didn't get funded or the gray space aliens ate it or something. No publication, no payment. We decided to put the story in the trunk, having driven three publications out of business. The name of the story? "A Killing in the Market."

Since then I have had decent luck with short stories, primarily to original anthologies. Jean Rabe, editor of this collection, has graciously bought several of my stories, along with "The Coins of Darkun" in the Popcorn Press volume (now, like the volume you are holding, in a new Walkabout Publishing edition), *Pirates of the Blue Kingdoms.* Check it out. Great stuff between those covers, and I don't mean only my story. Steve Sullivan and Jean have done a great job inventing a rich tapestry of a world to set stories.

Now, sit back and enjoy the mixture of horror and fantasy, whimsy and ad copy, comics and SF, assembled here for your pleasure.

Robert E. Vardeman
Albuquerque, NM
2007

# Godfire

*Netzines were new to me back in February of 1994. I saw that Tre Chipman was looking for stories to be published on-line only for his WayfarerOnline site. He had some cool stuff on gaming and I sold him a fantasy story that became my first ever e-submission.*

Nuos scrambled to the top of the jagged rise and stood for a moment, staring at the lush green valley twisting and turning through the Gleon Mountains, the Backbone of the World. He sucked in a deep breath, letting his chest expand fully as he took in the thin, high-altitude air. It tasted sweet and good, but carried a distant hint of sulfur to it. The scent of growing grain and animals—and people—quickly pushed away the acrid odor and made him feel just a tinge of homesickness, more for the contrast than the similarity he experienced.

The young man saw a winding trail down the face of the bluff dropping so precipitously in front of him. Like an agile mountain goat, he went down the rocky trail until he reached the valley floor. For the first month of his Journey of Proving he had wondered at the ancient ritual requiring all newly christened adults to leave the coastal area and explore inland. Now he knew the reasons for the temporary exile from all that had been familiar throughout his life. He had never been cut out to be a fisherman. Ocean salt spray did not excite him as it did so many of his friends. Worse, he had never stopped getting seasick when his father and uncles took him out to cast their immense fishing nets.

The Journey of Proving was supposed to broaden his view of the world and allow him to learn what he could not in the tight-knit coastal fishing villages. But he was supposed to return and share his newfound knowledge and experience with others, to inspire younger children and to win the approval of the adults with tales of his daring adventures.

Nuos loped down the green valley, his feet crushing tender blades of grass. He felt more at home here than he ever had seafaring. As he savored the intoxicating air and listened to the buzz of insects lacking so near the ocean, he knew why fewer and fewer of those taking their Journey returned of days. Had they crossed the Backbone and found this paradise?

And stayed?

As he intended doing?

Cattle grazing in broad pastures lowed as he passed. He chucked a rock at a skulking gray wolf, scaring it away—for the moment—from a tender young lamb that had strayed from its flock. Nuos took the time to chase the youngling back to relative safety, though he knew the wolf's hungry look would bring it around again after he left.

That was the order of things. On his Journey, he had come to enjoy fresh meat almost as much as the wolf. He was as likely to eat the lamb if it survived, having developed quite a liking for mutton.

Nuos found a deeply rutted road and let his instincts run wild. He knew which way town lay. Turning so the sun beat warmly on his tanned face, he started jogging, his long, powerful legs devouring the distance as hungrily as the wolf might its prey.

He slowed when he saw people toiling in the freshly plowed fields. They looked prosperous, well dressed and with homes that were to be envied. Nuos had grown up in a shack that leaked during every storm and whined like a thing alive when wind twisted through the crevices in the walls.

Nuos came to the edge of town and saw real wealth, decent structures and well-fed, well-dressed men and women going about their business. From under a shade tree beside the road came a sturdy man with a keen eye and long stride.

"Good day to you, young sir," the man greeted him. He wore broad leather straps crisscrossing his chest. A sheathed rapier dangled at the left hip and at the other rested a short dagger. The man spoke in a friendly tone, no hint of threat or of being threatened by a stranger.

"And to you, sir. I'm a traveler with a yearning to stay in your fine township, at least for a while. Do you welcome outlanders?"

"I'm town constable, Povel Antar, by name. If your intentions are honest and you can support yourself with a useful trade, I welcome you."

Nuos was impressed with the amity shown by the constable. He had passed through much larger towns where the law was interested only in harassing him.

"I doubt fishing is much of a profession to pursue here, not from the small streams I have seen, but I have other skills that might prove profitable."

"And what might those skills be, son?" asked a tall, whipcord-muscled man who had been handsome beyond belief before some accident—or fight—had scarred half his face. The man came up from behind Nuos, unnoticed until he spoke.

"Nuos, sir. My name is Nuos. If it does not intrude on an existing business and take away money from someone needing it, I know sail making and boat building."

The tall man looked at the constable and laughed. "We have no need for those skills." He eyed Nuos more carefully. "I see you are no stranger to work, for all your good looks. Your hands are callused, and those arms have seen long hours of work. Have you ever worked as a smith?"

"Sir, I know a great deal about the art. My uncle is a blacksmith, and he taught me much."

"Do tell," the man said, eyebrows arching. He exchanged quiet words with Povel Antar. The constable looked distraught, but finally backed away.

"As you say, Hawtho. But he is so—"

Hawtho motioned the constable to silence.

"We recently lost the town smith. The job has gone begging since no one here is skilled in metal-working. You could stay a day or a lifetime, depending on your skill."

"I'm good and work hard, Lord Hawtho," Nuos said, recognizing in the man's tone and the way the constable deferred to him a hint of nobility.

"Lord? You jest! No one is called lord in Fdys. I am town mayor, but it is an elective post and one which carries too much work and too little respect. Isn't that so, Pavel?"

Nuos watched carefully. The constable's mouth curled into a smile that was natural and honest.

"You wanted it, more than I did the post of constable. Young Nuos, do you want to be constable? You can have the position for the taking!"

"Is it so terrible?" Nuos asked.

Both men laughed. "It is too terrible," Pavel Antar declared. "It is boring. Nothing happens in Fdys, or at least only rarely. Two nights ago, Banch got drunk and smashed up Black Ryn's inn. He hadn't done that in almost a year, but then he was upset. His last daughter married a man he does not like and moved down the valley to another town."

"That's all the trouble here?" asked Nuos, astonished. More than once he had been in a fight to save his own life. Deepwater sailors from along the coast ported at his village and took out their frustrations on fishermen they considered landlubbers—and worse, they unleashed their passions on the village women, willing or not.

"Not all, alas," said Hawtho. "There is—" The words were cut off as the ground began trembling. Nuos tried to take a step and was thrown down forcibly. Reaching out, he grabbed double handfuls of grass, as if this would keep him from bouncing around like a grain of corn dropped into hot oil. He popped about, thrown off the ground and then smashed downward as the earthquake ran its course. Both Hawtho and Pavel Antar had similar trouble keeping their balance on the gyrating, suddenly treacherous ground.

The temblor passed quickly, though to Nuos it seemed to linger an eternity.

"All along the Backbone we have these quakes," Hawtho said, dusting himself off. "I have heard they are not as severe elsewhere, but this is our home. No reason to leave because the ground shakes now and again."

"And I can see why you would not want to leave, sir," Nuos said. Running down the road toward them came a young woman so lovely she took away

Nuos' breath. Long dark hair fluttered like a daring war pennant away from her tanned oval face. Her bee-stung lips parted in worry as she rushed to Hawtho.

"Father, are you hurt?"

Hawtho touched his scarred face as if to be sure it was still there, then he shook his head. "I am unhurt, Aria."

"Thankfully," she said, heaving a deep breath that caused her ample breasts to rise and fall. Nuos knew it was impolite to stare, but he could not help himself. Aria was too beautiful.

She turned bright emerald eyes to him, and Nuos' heart almost skipped a beat. Or was it a new earthquake? Aria's smile shook him with its openness, its friendliness, the half-stated invitation for more than friendship.

"My dear, allow me to introduce Nuos. He is passing through, or perhaps we can persuade him to stay and replace old Thalon."

"You're a blacksmith?" she asked, her eyes wide with admiration. "Such muscles, yes, of course, but you're too young to know the trade."

Nuos puffed up at her compliment. "Not so young. I am an adult." He held back telling her that he was on his Journey of Proving. He was an adult—barely. But he was still eligible for all rights and privileges of an adult, including entering into marriage. At that moment, he doubted he had ever seen anyone lovelier or who he had more seriously considered to be his wife. The women of his village were coarse of body and language, and nothing like Aria. He was coming to appreciate Fdys more and more.

"I see that," she said, her green eyes moving down his powerful body. If another had eyed him that way, it would have made Nuos uneasy. He flexed just a bit to impress Aria.

"What happened to your town smith, this Thalon?"

Hawtho and Antar exchanged a glance, and then the constable said, "Take a deep sniff. Brimstone. He was working at his forge up in the foothills during an earthquake. We're not sure what happened, but he died."

"An avalanche?"

"Worse," Aria said seriously. "His forge fire. It ran wild, out of control, and burned him to death."

"That's unusual, though strange things happen during earthquakes." Nuos tried to be agreeable, but he was not certain how peculiar things might be during earthquakes. He had endured hurricanes and water spouts at sea but never an earthquake before this day.

"Will you stay at Thalon's house? It was undamaged in the earthquake that killed him," Aria said. "His house is near ours."

"Aria," Hawtho said sharply. "Let Nuos make his own way and don't push. You're getting to be as bad as your mother."

"Why don't you join us for dinner? Mother wouldn't mind another at our table," Aria said, ignoring her father.

"I—" Nuos found himself speechless.

"Good!" Aria cried, settling the matter.

\* \* \*

Nuos felt as if he had lived in Fdys all his life. Hawtho's wife Zia had prepared, for him, a feast. From the way they ate, Nuos guessed this was an ordinary meal and that they had not gone out of their way to impress him. Such consideration would have been wasted, even if they had tried. He had eyes only for Aria, and she for him. And once, he thought he felt her bare foot running up and down his leg under the dinner table. It might have been his imagination or a small animal or—

It had been her foot and the promise in that fleeting, intimate touch excited him.

After dinner Hawtho took him up a winding path into the foothills to a nearby house that seemed more like a palace to Nuos.

"Yours, should you stay," Hawtho said, pointing to the house. "Thalon's smithy is out back."

"The house is splendid," Nuos said. He rubbed sweaty palms on his pants legs. "I can hardly believe a town blacksmith lived so lavishly."

"We are a rich community," Hawtho said, "and Thalon gave much to it."

They went to a large, dark building. The heavy scent of sulfur made Nuos' nose wrinkle. The instant he entered, he felt the raw power in this shop bestowed by the curiously dancing flame in the forge. As if drawn by invisible strings, Nuos went to it and peered over the edge into the heart of the fire. He felt as if he was being pulled into the center of the world.

"The earthquakes opened the fissure and released this...godfire," Hawtho said. "A skilled smith can work iron into something more."

Nuos looked around the shop and saw what Hawtho meant. Lacy filigree necklaces and bracelets of black iron dangled from wall hooks, next to keen-edged shiny swords. Other parts of the shop showed where Thalon had forged wagon tongues and steel bands for a wheelwright. Nuos ran his fingers over the steel and felt how expert Thalon had been.

"His loss must have been great. I am not this skilled."

"Try," urged Hawtho. "Do something."

"Now?"

Even as he spoke, Nuos felt the urge to plunge iron into the flame, shape it, turn it into steel and anneal it and create. So he did. Stripping to the waist, he began working, slowly at first, then with greater confidence using the raw materials left by the dead smith. The flame became a part of him, giving just the right amount of heat and carbon precisely when he needed it. He banged and stroked and toiled and then quenched the steel knife blade he had made.

In the light of the surging godfire, Nuos held high the gleaming blade he had forged.

"It will hone down into a knife even Thalon would be proud to call his own," Hawtho said. The man clapped Nuos on the back. "Welcome to Fdys."

Hawtho left, but late in the night Aria came to him. Delightfully.

* * *

For a month Nuos labored, spending long hours at the forge, making whatever anyone in Fdys asked of him. But in the few free minutes he had, Nuos fashioned an intricate ring of gleaming steel, the ring he would give to pledge his troth to Aria.

The fire—the godfire—seemed to approve and lent elegance to his skill as he worked. So intent was Nuos that he did not hear Hawtho and Pavel Antar enter the smithy.

When he did see them, he jumped guiltily.

"You startled me," he said, feeling as if they had caught him in some unworthy act. He had not asked Hawtho yet for permission to marry his daughter, but Nuos thought the man would agree. He brought so many commissions that he had to know how prosperous his future son-in-law would be.

"You have done well," Hawtho said, beaming. "Your skill surpasses even Thalon's."

"You are too kind, sir," Nuos said. Then he saw Pavel Antar's furtive glances, eyes averted, as if the man was embarrassed. Or frightened. Outside stood a dozen other men from Fdys. Nuos had worked iron and steel for all of them and all had complimented his ability to use force and fire in precisely shaping the metal.

"You enrich Fdys with that skill, as Thalon did," Hawtho said. "We are prosperous because of you. We sell your work the length of the Gleon Mountains, trading for what luxuries we lack here."

"You lack little."

"Because of you we lack nothing," Antar said, shuffling his feet. "We need you. It's hard finding anyone who can use the godfire, much less make art out of iron."

Nuos started to thank the constable and then saw the man meant more than he said.

"What's going on?" he asked, fearing his affection for Aria, and hers for him, had somehow insulted Hawtho.

16

"We cannot afford to lose someone who is only passing through on their Journey of Proving," Hawtho said, moving away from the constable.

"I would stay! I want to—" Before Nuos could proclaim his love for Hawtho's daughter, Pavel Antar blindsided him by swinging a thin iron rod that caught him on the right knee. The sick crunch of breaking bone was quickly drowned out by Nuos' scream of pain. Clutching his damaged knee, he fell. The constable swung again. This time he broke Nuos' other knee.

Then the men of Fdys came in and finished the job of permanently crippling him so he could never run away and leave them without a skilled blacksmith.

* * *

Nuos stared at the circular mark carved into the palm of his hand. He had grabbed the ring intended for Aria when the constable had attacked him and had clutched it so hard that it left a permanent imprint. Nuos moaned as he reached down and used a hand to move his crippled legs. He had been able to run all day, and now he could hardly support himself on those mangled limbs. The broken bones would never heal.

He looked up when Hawtho came over to him.

"You should get to work. We need a shipment of sword blades by the end of the week. A war is brewing to the south, and we want to be primary suppliers for the Onlonians. They have been most generous trading with us for their fine woven rugs."

"Make them yourself," Nuos said, fighting down his pain and anger.

"You are the skilled one," Hawtho said. "If you do not do as you are told, you will starve. You will never again sleep in that fine bed—the one you have shared so often with my daughter."

Nuos glared.

"I had hoped Aria's charms would hold you, but I saw the wanderlust in your eyes whenever you spoke with her. You would have convinced her to leave with you." Hawtho shrugged. "I hope you see we could not permit that. Fdys needs the metal goods you make." The man turned the scarred part of his face toward the dancing flame. "The earthquake that permitted that magical fire to come forth has been our salvation. You have no idea how we struggled in poverty before it burst forth and lent its magics to Thalon's steel."

"Aria was part of the scheme to keep me here?" Nuos asked, his heart as cold as the godfire was blistering.

"We all do our part. For the good of the community."

"But it's my steel that brings in your wealth," Nuos said angrily. "And now you're going to use it in a war." The idea repulsed him.

"Thalon felt the same way. He did this to me." Hawtho touched the scar on his face. His expression hardened. "What you're thinking is obvious," Hawtho said, shaking his head. "Is it some defect in all blacksmiths?"

"What do you mean?"

"When he found he could not fight his way to freedom, Thalon tried to cut back on production. If starving you does no good, we will begin removing more and more of your legs until there's nothing left below the waist." Hawtho pointed to a corner of the forge room. "That platform, the one with rollers on it. Thalon had to use it in his last days."

"Before he killed himself?" Nuos asked bitterly. He was not surprised that Hawtho silently confirmed what he had already deduced. Thalon had committed suicide rather than keep producing weapons like some slave, some crippled, humiliated slave.

"We can chain your waist so you cannot jump into the godfire," Hawtho said, almost offhandedly.

"If you can find a smith to forge the chains," Nuos shot back. To his surprise, Hawtho laughed.

"You have a wit, son. I like you. It's too bad you would have wandered."

"I wouldn't have," Nuos said sullenly. Hawtho laughed at him and left without another word, leaving the young man to his pain and self-pitying misery. Nuos only looked up when a shadow crossed the threshold and he saw Aria.

"I heard what they did to you. I'm sorry, Nuos. I didn't know."

"You knew," he said, not trying to hide his hatred. "You were part of their scheme."

"No, I—" Aria ducked when he threw the ring he had fashioned with so much love at her.

"Get out, get out and stop lying to me."

She started to say something more, and then turned, wiped at her eyes and left. For a brief moment, Nuos wondered if Aria had known. Then he went back to work. His belly growled, and the prospect of the townsmen crippling him even more drove him to finish the sword blades.

\* \* \*

"You are slowing down," Pavel Antar said. "We need more steel dagger blades."

Nuos glared at the constable. He wanted to drive one of those sharp-tipped knives into the man's foul heart, but he could not cross the forge to reach Antar. The constable had chopped off an entire foot when Nuos had refused to work for two days.

"Would you have me become like Thalon, despising you with every beat of my heart?"

"You already do," Pavel Antar said uneasily. "It does not matter. What does matter is shipping the weapons so we can collect our due."

"My due," corrected Nuos.

"The town's," Pavel Antar said fiercely. "I don't like this, but Fdys needs your skill and you would have denied it to us. Get to work!"

Furious, Nuos shoved his hand into the godfire in an act of defiance. For a second he felt only coolness, then heat that turned to utter pain invaded his hand and arm and mind. Shrieking in agony, he yanked back.

"Thalon did the same thing," the constable said. "To no avail. Get to work or we won't feed you this week."

The constable stalked out, but Nuos hardly noticed. He stared at his hand, the one that had entered the flame. It was uninjured when it should have been charred, or at least blistered. Curiously, the fire still burned inside his hand. Nuos held the hand up appraisingly and felt inspiration flood him like some heady wine. He turned to the forge and began working expertly, hammering and heating with greater skill than ever before.

The fire within his flesh gave him a mastery of iron and flame that had been lacking before. And the godfire that had invaded him continued to spread, to burn brighter, to glow until Nuos thought he could no longer endure it.

But he did. Until he changed.

Nuos noticed how the skin of his hand turned prickly and began shimmering as if he stared at it through a guttering flame. The warmth spread up his arm and into his body and consumed him. Totally. It flooded his being and took possession of his mind and carried him away from the prison of his crippled body.

A puff of evening breeze came through the smithy's open door and, like a spark, Nuos burst into a full blazing fire. His entire body was consumed in a brilliant flash. Nuos screamed and arched his spine, throwing his head back and yowling in pain. As he writhed, he felt himself caught by the wind and whirled about like a column of rising smoke. He spun away from the forge, then passed through the godfire and became one with it.

For an eternity he hung in the dancing flame, drawn downward into the burning heart of the world. Nuos knew that Thalon had already passed this way, but he could not. Not yet. Nuos fought, jerking about until he became a whirlpool of fire that separated from the godfire and blasted from the smithy into the dense, dark night.

Nuos tried to give voice to a cry of triumph. He was free! He had left behind his crippled body and now soared like a bird, flying into the air, sailing on the wind faster than any clipper ship.

19

Reaching in front of him, Nuos saw how he had changed. Free of his maimed body, yes, but changed. His flesh had become a silvery fire that burned with eye-searing intensity. He tired to change his direction and found he was prisoner to the vagaries of the wind, his inferno of a body lacking substance.

Nuos cried in anguish and sent long streamers of fire leaping from his nostrils and mouth and eyes. Then he stopped fighting and allowed the night wind to carry him to Fdys. From house to house Nuos flittered, reaching out and lightly touching the roofs and walls and people as they rushed out to see what brought such blinding light to a moonless night.

In less than ten minutes, the entire town was ablaze. And Nuos was carried in the direction he longed for most.

He gusted through the night to Hawtho's home. Nuos tried to control the anger and hatred he felt, then gave in to his rancor. He curled about into a tight ball of dancing fire and darted for the front door just as Hawtho emerged.

"What?"

The man's question went unanswered. Nuos forced himself into a parody of human form, a body shaped in fire rather than flesh.

"Know real misery," Nuos hissed. "Share mine." He reached out with both arms and embraced Hawtho as a long-lost brother. The man burst into flame like a dried log. The stench of burning flesh filled the cool night air, but Nuos could not smell it. He was no longer human.

He was fire. Godfire.

"Father! No, no!" cried Aria, coming from inside the house.

Nuos whipped about, ready to embrace the faithless woman. But he could not. She wore the ring he had fashioned for her.

He reached out, gently, carefully, and laid his forefinger on her cheek. Aria shrieked in pain as her flesh charred. Then Nuos shot upward, caught on a strong gust of wind and was carried toward the forge and the godfire blazing there.

He twisted and turned and flowed to the fiery pillar in the middle of the forge. His mind dimmed, and the Siren's call of the godfire drew him inexorably now. Hatred gone, all human emotion seared from his soul, Nuos arched up and then drove downward into the maelstrom of fire, consumed totally.

\* \* \*

"Nuos, Nuos," called Aria, stumbling along the path to his smithy. She had followed her lover's flaming trail marked in the night by cascading sparks until she reached the smithy in time to see him consumed whole by the godfire.

"Come back, don't leave me," she sobbed. She touched the brand he had placed on her cheek and knew he could have killed her as he had her father. "I loved you, I truly did."

The woman stepped closer to the forge and reached out, her hand nearing the column of flickering godfire. Aria yelped when she burned herself. She drew back and cradled her injured hand. Realization came slowly, but it came.

Aria took off Nuos' ring, kissed it and then threw it into the godfire where it exploded in a spectral burst she would remember forever as the colors of love.

# A Time for Steel

*Medieval jousts. Chivalry. Damsels in distress and knights on white chargers. Such is the lure of the Renaissance Faire. My son and I had gone to the Ren Faire in Phoenix for years, using this as an excuse to visit friends and take a special spring break. But it was such a good excuse. The performers (such as Don Juan and Miguel) were superb, the attractions (Tomato Justice) astounding and the hurly-burly atmosphere delightful. How could I turn Jean Rabe down when she put out the call for stories set at a Ren Faire? (When we went down to Phoenix around the time I submitted the story, I gave a copy to Mike Stackpole, who worked in details from mine into his—this is a coherent universe, milords and ladies. So, if you enjoy "A Time for Steel," you'll probably love Mike's "Brewed Fortune." Buy a copy of* Renaissance Faire *and check it out, along with the rest of the tales inside.)*

"She doesn't have a stitch of clothing on!" exclaimed Sheriff's Deputy Ben Rodriguez. He pushed a couple tourists out of the way to get a better look at the shapely woman riding the prancing white horse down the main concourse of the Arizona Renaissance Faire. The arid desert wind blew her long blonde hair about, but not enough to suit the deputy.

"What?" asked his partner. Jason Hardin almost dropped the huge turkey leg he was gnawing on when he caught the merest flash of slanting afternoon sunlight against creamy white thigh. "She can't do that!" he exclaimed, moving in his partner's wake to get to the front of the crowd gathering to watch the unclothed spectacle.

The woman laughed and waved cheerily, giving them just enough glimpse of skin under her flowing hair to let everyone know she wasn't wearing a body stocking. She was naked. Entirely.

Hardin cursed the day the Pinal County sheriff had assigned him and Rodriguez to police the Renaissance Faire with more than its share of weirdoes and freaks. The immense crowd, more than twenty thousand people jammed into the thirty-acre re-creation of a medieval village, proved less of a chore to police than the semi-permanent resident vendors and actors. Hardin had never quite gotten into the spirit of the Ren Faire, although he knew that Rodriguez was continually ooh-ing and aah-ing over the displays and performances, the wares and the clever costumes.

None of it made a lot of sense to Hardin, in spite of numerous eager participants explaining to him that the people wanted to relive the Middle Ages, but with running water and CD players for their folk music.

"There she goes!" he cried, breaking through to the front of the crowd in time to see nothing but the golden cascade of hair draped decorously down the woman's back and over the white charger's hind quarters like some silky blanket.

"Wow," Rodriguez said.

"What are you doing just standing there?" demanded Hardin. He towered over his shorter partner, but Rodriguez was ten years younger and in better shape. Hardin started to throw down the turkey leg he had been eating for a late lunch, then decided against it since it was all he'd had since breakfast at six a.m. Let his partner chase her down.

"What do you want me to do?"

"That's public lewdness. We've got to arrest her."

Rodriguez laughed. "Can I order a line-up? I wouldn't mind seeing a lot of these babes without clothes. But identifying her's not going to be easy."

"You weren't looking at her face," guessed Hardin, standing on tiptoe to see which way the horse had gone when it reached the main concourse. From there, the naked woman could have gone any of four ways. He thought she would leave behind a wake of curious bystanders, but it was as if she were nothing more than a drop of water in a vast ocean. She had vanished quickly, and no one in the crowd was inclined to keep staring after her. As odd as that seemed, too much else competed for their attention.

"Nope," Rodriguez agreed cheerfully, "but she has a cute little rose tattoo. I was looking there." He pointed to a spot on his groin, then moved his finger down a bit more. "Maybe lower. I'll have to—"

"We're supposed to enforce the law," grumbled Hardin. Sometimes he didn't understand Ben. His partner looked at this as a lark, a plum assignment, while he saw it as an inch away from a living hell when there were real crimes being committed throughout the county. The sheriff was investigating a murder twenty miles out in the desert, two other deputies were after a major league drug dealer, and here he was chasing a naked woman for public indecency. It wasn't right, and it made him mad.

"If you cut through and go around, you might get to the concourse faster," Ben suggested, but Hardin was already squeezing between booths selling turkey legs, steak on a stake, and lemonade.

Hardin popped out behind the vendors and coughed as a cloud of dust enveloped him. The last bulldozer rattled away from the artificial lake gouged into the sun-baked ground. The lake was almost full, foot-high waves breaking against the sloping shoreline as the wind picked up, as it always did around sundown. The dozer had merely added a final touch to the far shore and was being loaded onto a flatbed trailer. Hardin had asked the faire director, Pita Hewell, about the lake and had been told they intended to have a Viking boat display and some simulated sea attacks on a mock castle tower as program items later in the faire. Possibly some of the crowd might like to go along for the siege.

Anything for a buck, he thought in disgust.

Hardin skirted the lake and turned back into the main concourse when he heard a whistling sound, quickly followed by, "Drop the turkey leg!"

His sense of danger was acute enough that he tossed the half-eaten meat in one direction and dived in the other. The whistling sound turned into ferocious flapping. A peregrine falcon caught the meaty leg before it hit the ground. Hardin landed hard, rolled and sat up, fumbling for his holstered service revolver.

"No, wait, don't!" came the same voice that had warned him. Hardin quickly shifted his gaze to a man dressed in medieval jerkin over a blue silk doublet and sporting a well-worn, heavy leather glove on his left hand. "I warned everybody about eating during the show."

"Show?" Hardin asked, still pumped from the nearness of flashing claws strong enough to rip off his arm.

"The birds of prey show. No raptor's quicker on the attack than the peregrine." The bird handler made certain Hardin wasn't going to draw his pistol, then rushed back to the elevated grass area of Falconer's Heath and thrust his gloved hand into the air. The falcon landed with enough force to stagger the burly man.

Hardin got to his feet and brushed himself off, glad the crowd gathered for the bird show was more intent on the falcon than the damn fool deputy who had almost been the predator's dinner. He hurried to the middle of the concourse and looked around.

The crowd had swelled, pouring in for evening events. A half dozen shows ran simultaneously, including the hunting birds. Ventriloquists, sideshow blockheads, jugglers, more dancing and singing acts than Hardin could tolerate—and all obstructed his view enough so that he couldn't find the Lady Godiva wannabe.

"Officer? You're a real policeman, aren't you?" asked an older woman.

"Yes, ma'am," he acknowledged. "A sheriff's deputy."

"I want her arrested!" the woman exclaimed. "I've never seen such a thing."

Ben Rodriguez came up in time to hear the complaint.

"We never have, either," Hardin said, looking fiercely at his partner, silently warning him not to speak. "Which way'd she go? Lady Godiva?"

"That way," the woman said. "I hope you catch her. Why, there are children in the crowd. This is supposed to be wholesome entertainment."

"Yes, ma'am," Hardin said, glaring at Rodriguez some more. His partner grinned ear to ear. "You head that way, Deputy Rodriguez," he said pointedly. "I'll check the jousting arena."

He had been told to stay out of sight as much as possible. The public wanted to know they were safe, but a constantly patrolling uniformed deputy took away the festive air. At least the sheriff hadn't insisted he wear a silly costume. Hardin shuddered at the thought of a Robin Hood cap with a jaunty feather stuck in it.

Angling to the side of the concourse, he moved past some of the audience-participation booths. One that intrigued him was simple enough, but the mechanics verged on a scam. A guy stuck his head out of a hole in a wall and insulted the crowd. For a few bucks they could buy tomatoes to throw at him. The part that irked Hardin was the man passing over the tomatoes. If they gave him a large bill, he made certain to lay their change in a puddle of tomato juice. No one took it and shoved a soggy wad of one-dollar bills into his pocket. They bought more tomatoes to throw. Hardin had counted more than $800 an hour going across that counter.

He shook himself and tried to remember this was a modern-day sideshow without all the freaks and geeks of days of yore. At least not all of them. There were glass-eaters, people dressed as chickens, and executioners, and others Hardin had not wanted to identify. He took a moment to jump onto a crate and look around. Lady Godiva had vanished from the earth, as if she had never existed. He considered letting the matter drop. Then he knew he couldn't. She had gotten away with her ride once. She'd do it again, thinking the laws of the twenty-first century somehow had been nullified in this bubble of the Middle Ages.

To the east lay the jousting arena and stables for the knights' horses. Just the place to find Lady Godiva. Hardin kept a low profile but hurried to the climbing wall and went through the fake castle portal to the arena, and turned left to the stables. A grin came to his face.

"Gotcha," he said, spotting the white horse Lady Godiva had ridden. His excitement died when he saw the horse standing alone in a stall. The saddle was draped over the stall divider and a long blonde wig hung over it. Hardin picked up the wig and saw the wearer had left a bit of herself behind.

"Red hairs," he said, thinking hard. He had seen this particular, peculiar color before. The grin returned to his lips. The magician's assistant! Merlin the Magnificent was on stage now. It wouldn't take much to match his assistant's hair to this strand. Hardin picked up the wig and turned to leave.

He went cold inside when he saw the armored body, partially covered with straw, in the stall opposite Lady Godiva's horse.

The deputy knew then that this nothing duty had become more. Much more.

He carefully made sure that the man was dead. A single savage slash had cut through the light armor he wore, severing his right arm. Shock had probably set in and the man had bled out on the spot. But the stroke that had sliced through arm and armor had been prodigious.

Hardin backed off, pulled out his walkie-talkie and let Rodriguez know what had happened. Then he used his cell phone to call the sheriff and get an investigative unit dispatched.

It was well past sunset by the time the body had been removed and the sheriff had gone, leaving behind several detectives to carry on the investigation. But with twenty thousand visitors, the crew seemed overwhelmed. Rodriguez stood close to his partner and spoke in a low tone.

"What aren't you spilling, Jase?" he asked.

"The sword beside him wasn't his," Hardin said. "It doesn't fit into his sheath. I tried. What blood's on the blade got there after the death stroke. I think he was killed with his own sword."

"And the killer took it with him?"

Hardin nodded.

"So why not tell Gizmo and his boys?" Rodriguez spoke with contempt of the detective unit under Deputy Gizzarello. "Afraid they'll grab the glory? Like usual?"

"I don't care about that. I want the murderer, and Gizzarello's not asking the right questions of the right people," Hardin said. "This guy's part of the show with the fake king and his court."

"Yeah, the king's champion. So?"

"He was also a vendor when he wasn't in the show. He was a metalsmith, sold chainmail, swords, and daggers at a booth on the main concourse."

"Gizmo'll get there eventually. There's something else," Rodriguez said, urging his partner to tell the rest of what he suspected.

"I think Lady Godiva might have seen something. The time of death is close enough to when she rode into the stable."

"You sure she's Merlin's assistant?" Rodriguez asked eagerly.

"No looking for the tattoo," Hardin cautioned. "Unless it comes to her being a suspect in the murder."

The two made their way through the increasingly chilly Arizona desert night and came to the stage where Merlin had performed. The audience was half gone, those lingering were fumbling out a dollar or two to put in the jester's cap being passed by the redheaded assistant. Hardin looked from the strand of hair taken from the wig to the woman. He was no judge of dyes and what women did to their hair but it was close enough.

"Officers," greeted the magician, putting away the last of his stage tricks. A tall, thin man with a wispy beard, Merlin was younger than his costume suggested. He took off a pointed cap festooned with mystical symbols, dropped it on the small table to the side of the stage, and ran his hands through longish brown hair. He looked tired from his performance, but Hardin thought there was more to the sharp-eyed gaze that fixed on him. He tried not to shiver as Merlin the Magnificent bored into his very soul with those gray eyes of his.

"Your assistant was seen this afternoon," Hardin said, holding up the blonde wig. "She left behind one of her own hairs."

Merlin chuckled and relaxed. "Rachel is quite a handful," he said. "I'll talk to her about her, uh, riding apparel. Like the rest of the Rennies here, she sometimes takes odd jobs during her breaks. This might not have been the best way of making a few extra ducats."

"I didn't mind," Rodriguez piped up. Hardin silenced him with a cold look.

"Most of the crowd wouldn't, I suspect," said Merlin. "The male half. She's a bit on the wild side."

"Why don't you and Deputy Rodriguez come to a meeting of the minds on this?" Hardin asked. "I need to attend to some business." He glanced in the direction of the porta-potties.

Merlin laughed and said, "Some things remain constant up and down the corridors of time."

Hardin let Rodriguez lead the magician away so they could talk to Rachel, but he didn't go to relieve himself. Instead, he went behind the stage and found Merlin's gear. Something struck him as wrong about the man. He had been too relieved that the law wanted to discuss Rachel's naked riding—relieved because he didn't have to address some other matter, Hardin guessed. Depending on what he found, Hardin might have a suspect in the knight's murder. The magician could have killed the knight for putting the moves on his assistant. Jealousy was a decent motive for murder.

A quick search of two boxes and a huge trunk unearthed a dozen well-read volumes of Arthurian legends and an expensive leather-bound personal diary. Knowing this was an illegal search didn't stop him from flipping through the pages. A diary, nothing more. As he leafed through the pages, he noted something odd. The first page was dated almost five years in the future. Every subsequent entry came closer to the current date, as if Merlin was Japanese and worked from the back of the book forward. But that couldn't be right, because a quarter of the journal's pages were blank from this morning's entry to the last page and everything was penned in precise English.

He read a few of the entries, and then quickly replaced the book when he heard Rodriguez and Merlin returning to the stage.

"I do have to get my equipment stored, Officer."

Merlin looked around, startled, when Hardin stepped on stage.

"Did you know a man named McLeod? A metalsmith?" asked Hardin. Again, he saw the flash of emotion that didn't mesh well with the question.

"He's done work for me. For most of the performers. McLeod's a talented artisan."

Merlin was as tense as a man can get without bolting in fear.

"He was killed this afternoon."

"His sword," Merlin started. "I mean, he was making a sword for me."

"There was one beside the body. It wasn't the murder weapon. Your assistant had just finished her bareback ride when he was killed."

"Rachel doesn't know anything about it. She would have told me."

"About the stolen sword or the murder?" asked Hardin, taking a shot in the dark and hoping to get additional information from the man. He read the answer on Merlin's face. He was upset that McLeod was dead but more upset about his sword. Hardin could come to only one conclusion. Merlin knew the murder weapon was his sword.

"Tonight is a full moon," Merlin said unexpectedly.

"I suppose. So?" asked Rodriguez.

"Let's take a ride, you and Rachel," said Hardin. "We can go to the district HQ and get a full statement. I'm especially interested in this sword McLeod was making for me. Was it sharp enough to slice through armor and bone?"

"It's a special titanium alloy," Merlin said distantly. He looked east where the moon poked a thin sliver above the Superstition Mountains. "Yes, it's full tonight."

"Come on," Hardin said, reaching to take the man's elbow. "Get his assistant, Ben." Rodriguez hurried off to find Rachel but Hardin hesitated. Merlin was tall and gaunt and didn't look as if he had the strength to push open a door, but Hardin found it impossible to move the man along, even with the special come-along grip police used.

Hardin tightened the punishing grip but Merlin still didn't budge. He stepped back to get out his cuffs, then blinked. The deputy looked around in surprise and saw...nothing. Merlin had been there one instant and gone the next.

"Ben, he's skipped!" he shouted to his partner. "Keep an eye on his assistant."

He hardly heard Rodriguez's quick acceptance of looking after the magician's sexy assistant. Hardin thought Merlin might go back to his equipment. He saw the curious journal where he had left it. On impulse, he picked it up and tucked it into his broad leather belt. Then he did a quick mental inventory of the items and decided nothing was missing. Wherever the magician had gone, it wasn't here to pick up anything incriminating.

Even as that thought crossed his mind, Hardin was making his way behind the shops and to the stables where McLeod had been killed. The deputy ducked under the yellow tape marking off the area as a crime scene. The criminalists' work was done, and they wanted everything left intact should they need to go over the area again, but two uniformed deputies who should have been more attentive looked away—past—Hardin as he went by.

"Has anyone come in?" Hardin asked the new-hire whose nameplate was hidden by his crossed arms. The deputy ignored Hardin. "I said, have you seen anyone in here recently?"

When he got no reply, Hardin grabbed the deputy's arm and squeezed hard. He might as well have not bothered for all the response he got. Hardin ran his hand in front of the deputy's eyes. The man wasn't asleep. He simply didn't notice. His attention was focused somewhere else.

So was his partner's, and nothing Hardin did roused them.

Hardin shook his head in amazement. It was as if the pair had been bewitched. He went into the stables and stopped dead in his tracks when he saw faintly glowing green footprints leading to the rear. Hardin dropped to one knee, took out a pencil and poked at a print. Whatever fluoresced didn't come off onto his pencil. Somehow, he doubted the footprints had been here while the criminalists were working the scene.

He started to put the pencil back in his pocket, then thought better of it and dropped it. He followed the tracks to the stall where McLeod had been killed. It took several seconds for him to make sense of it.

"I'll be damned," he said. It was as if the killer had dipped both feet in the glowing green ichor, then tracked it around as he killed McLeod and finally left. The trail was so blatant even the two insensate guards outside should have been able to follow it.

The tracks led out back of the stables, then turned toward the artificial lake. Hardin pulled out his walkie-talkie and told Rodriguez what was going on.

"Meet me at the lakeshore," he said.

"Want me to bring Rachel along?"

"This might get dangerous," Hardin said. "Keep her away from trouble."

Hardin heard his partner's laugh and knew what it meant. Rodriguez wanted to see how much trouble Rachel could be, but he joined Hardin in a few minutes.

"All's quiet on the lake front," Rodriguez said as he strode up. Then he saw the green footsteps. "That looks like the perp stepped in a bucket of green paint."

"Come on," Hardin said, anxious to follow the trail. He worried that it might fade. "Watch out while I—"

A loud splash in the lake drew both of them in the direction of ripples moving away from the center.

"What was that? A fish jumping?"

"Look," Rodriguez said. A silvery flash in the light of the full moon was all they saw.

"Bare skin," Hardin said, not sure of his identification. "Could your Lady Godiva be skinny dipping?"

"No way. She's back at the stage. I told her to wait there."

"If she's mixed up in a murder, you think she'd do what you said?" asked Hardin.

"More likely to hightail it than to go skinny dipping by moonlight. Maybe that was Nessie."

Hardin cut off a retort. His partner might be right. Or partly right. The Renaissance Faire management always looked for new attractions. A mechanical sea monster might fit the bill.

"It looked more like a woman's hand and arm," he said finally.

"The trail's starting to fade, Jase," his partner pointed out. "We'd better get onto it right now. If it's Rachel out there swimming stark naked, I can deal with it later."

Ben was right. The trail was vanishing as Hardin stared at it. He got a sighting on where the tracks cut back toward the main concourse and ran for the spot, rather than following step by step. Hardin pushed his way through patrons clustering in front of the shops and booths. None of the fair-goers took notice of the fiery footprints—they might have thought it was part of the overall show.

The tracks led across the fortuneteller's green to a shop selling chainmail and other metal implements. A CLOSED sign dangled outside.

"McLeod's booth," he said under his breath. "Come on, Ben." He made certain his service revolver was handy, the leather strap holding it firmly in his holster pulled free, then advanced. Two men were arguing inside.

He recognized one voice immediately as the stage magician's.

"You don't know what you're talking about," the other voice sounded.

"You killed him, Birmingham. Don't deny it. You can't lie to me!"

"Because you're the Merlin?" came the contemptuous reply.

"Yes."

Hardin sprinted for the booth and tried the door. Locked. He heard scuffling sounds inside.

"Police! Open up!" he shouted. The struggle between Birmingham and Merlin grew more intense. Hardin heard metal clashing against metal. With daggers, maces and swords on display, it was nothing short of a miracle that one of them wasn't already dead. There were too many weapons a desperate man could use.

Hardin kicked hard and the door sagged. A second kick tore it from its hinges with a screech of nails pulling free of wood. He jumped into the shop, pistol leveled. Rodriguez followed, his pistol ready for action, too.

"Drop it or I'll shoot!" Hardin went into a crouch, both hands steadying his revolver, and aimed at Merlin. The magician held a sword like he knew how to use it.

"You've got this wrong, Deputy," Merlin said. "Birmingham's the one who killed McLeod."

"McLeod was making the sword for him," Birmingham said, holding a pair of daggers, the one in his right hand sporting a foot-long blade and the basket-hilted main gauche in his left was even longer. "He wanted to cheat McLeod and they fought. He killed my boss!"

"Drop those toad stickers," Rodriguez said, moving around beside his partner. The muzzle of his semiautomatic was pointed at Birmingham.

"He's lying. He killed McLeod for the sword," Merlin said. "I followed his tracks here."

"The green glowing footprints?" Hardin couldn't figure it out. "What caused them?"

Birmingham's feet suddenly glowed a brilliant emerald, causing him to hop about as if they burned.

"You bewitched me, like you did the sword! I should never have taken it!" Birmingham was a smallish man, and he moved fast. Rodriguez—and the bullet from his 9mm Glock—was faster. The report filled the small shop with a deafening sound that momentarily diverted Hardin's attention.

Swifter than any man should move, Merlin threw down his sword and grabbed a long black display case from behind the counter. Hardin responded to the movement, turned back and fired instinctively. But he shot at empty air. Merlin had vanished, as he had before.

"Cuff him. I think we've got our murderer," Hardin said to his partner. Birmingham grunted as Rodriguez rolled him over on the floor and grabbed his wounded arm, forcing it back so he could apply handcuffs.

Hardin vaulted the counter, skidded and stopped at the rear door before peering out with a quick out-in look. He didn't want the magician slicing his head off, because he was certain the case held another sword. Whether it was the one Birmingham claimed was bewitched didn't matter. It was probably the cause of the murder.

Hardin had seen fancy craftsmanship during his few weekends at the Ren Faire, jewelry selling for more than he made in a year, expensive crystal goblets and even woodcarvings he wouldn't have minded displaying in his own home. An expertly crafted sword might be worth a young fortune—and worth killing to get.

His quick peek assured him Merlin wasn't laying in ambush. He darted out and looked around, wondering where the man might have run. Something drew Hardin toward the lake. Long legs pumping and lungs straining, he made his way along the alley behind the shops and burst out onto the path leading to the lake. He saw a dark shape ahead, at the lakeshore.

"Merlin!" he cried when he recognized the magician. "Give it up."

"Birmingham is the killer," Merlin called. "My fate is worse. And better."

Hardin ran along the unlighted path and stepped into a pothole. With a grunt of pain, he twisted his ankle. Pain lanced up into his knee, but he wanted Merlin in custody. Not only was he a material witness, Hardin had questions. Other questions.

He felt the magician's journal grating against his belly, where he had tucked the book into his belt.

"You won't be arrested. We need you to testify."

But his words seemed muffled. Crawling a few yards, he clambered to his feet and hobbled along in time to see Merlin open the dark case. The magician began a low chant that ate away at Hardin's nerves. Merlin held the polished steel blade high above his head so that moonlight ricocheted off its gleaming length.

A splash sounded far out on the lake. Hardin saw ripples expanding outward from...a hand. A woman's hand rising from the depths.

Merlin adroitly spun the blade about, caught its hilt and then sent it cartwheeling high into the air. Every rotation caused a unique, unnameable color to reflect from its steel, as if moonbeams were being torn apart by an eldritch prism.

"Hold Excalibur well, Lady," Merlin said, "until the time is nigh for its return."

The hand surged high and deftly caught the sword before vanishing without a ripple into the lake.

"Merlin, that was evidence." Hardin limped up, not sure what to do. He tried to fix the location of the sword in the lake. Somehow his eyes had tricked him into believing a hand had grabbed it. Merlin had only tossed it into the water to keep it from him.

"The sword will be returned, many years before now," Merlin said cryptically.

Hardin stared at the man and doubted his eyes. There was something unearthly about him, as if distinct edges were blurred and he vanished into the distance across a heat-shimmered desert.

"Stop," Hardin barked. "Your journal!" He pulled it out.

"Thank you," Merlin said softly, taking it from him. Hardin's fingers refused to close tight enough to prevent the removal.

"Jase! You okay?" called Ben Rodriguez.

Hardin turned to see his partner running along the path.

"Be careful. There're holes in the path that'll trip you up." He turned back to Merlin. He caught his breath. Merlin stood at the stern of a boat silently gliding across the lake.

"Is he in the boat?" asked Rodriguez, coming up, not even breathing hard. "You want me to fetch him? I got the sheriff to send a half dozen more officers."

"What boat?" Hardin asked.

The lake was still, no sign of movement anywhere except occasional insects dipping down to the surface for a nocturnal drink. The boats to be used for the Renaissance Faire mock battles were docked to one side.

"Where'd he go?"

"Back in time," Hardin said. "Our time. For him our past is his future."

"Huh?"

"McLeod must have been one hell of a fine swordsmith," Hardin said, letting his partner help him back along the path.

"We've got a picture of it. Birmingham's spilling his guts, but he's trying to cop an insanity appeal. The sheriff's trying to get him to shut up until he can get a lawyer."

"Insanity? What's he saying?"

"He says that was King Arthur's sword and that the stage magician was the real Merlin."

Hardin thought about this for a moment, and smiled. He had never expected to see such a turning point in history. Or perhaps it was more properly a nexus. A crossroads? Metallurgy was a science now. Coupled with Merlin's spells and the ambiance of a Renaissance Faire, the most important sword in history had been created—and passed backward in time to await the man destined to wield it.

# Tony and Archie

*Back in the dim mists of 1987, my good friend Gordon Garb (computer guru and Hollywood mogul whose work includes graphics for the stars in* Last Starfighter *and producing the indie zombie movie* Stink of Flesh—*watch the DVD, buy the novelization that I wrote!) suggested I get in touch with Lex Nakashima, who was launching a series of comics. Lex wanted something offbeat that could run in six panels—call it a single page of contained story. This is my contribution, but the project never got off the ground. So "Tony and Archie" never...evolved.*

[frame 1]

(Tony, a lumbering blue brontosaurus philosopher, is sprawled in the middle of a swamp. On a tree limb above is precariously perched Archie, a pterodactyl who isn't too bright. All around the swamp desert sand encroaches.)

Tony: What's wrong, Archie?
Archie: I dunno. Been bored. Feel like...changing.

[frame 2]

(A small ferret-like mammal is sitting cross-legged on a large egg in the background, a straw stuck through the shell. It is slurping loudly at the contents.)

Tony: Let's go to the jungle and try to pick up some babes.
Archie: Don't wanna move. Wanna change.

[frame 3]

(A volcano spews huge clouds of dust into the air in the distance.)

Tony: You mean evolve?
Archie (bobbing head): Maybe. Why not?

[frame 4]

(A glacier in the background is pushing down from the north.)

Tony: You're out of your tree! We never had it so good!
Archie (flapping long, leathery wings, looks skeptical): Wanna fly. Soaring is no fun anymore.

[frame 5]

(A fiery comet flashes across the sky and impacts in the distance.)

Tony: Look at how much energy you save. We're successful. The most successful ever!
Archie: Wanna fly without having to fall off a cliff first.

[frame 6]

(Two monstrous horned, armor-plated dinosaurs in the background are entwined in vain attempt to mate.)

Tony: Wait for a gust of wind. We've got it made, man. Don't even think of evolving.
Archie (mumbling to self): Still wanna. Be nice having pretty feathers.

# The Opal Egg

*My first US magazine appearance came in the Winter '78 issue of* Sorcerer's
Apprentice, *Liz Danforth editing (well, Ken St Andre was officially the editor but
Liz bought "Brother to Ghosts.") It was such a nice experience I sold SA this story
for the Summer of 1982 issue. By this time, Liz was the editor. "The Opal Egg"
explores the background of one of my favorite characters in the Cenotaph Road
series, Krek.*

The broadsword gleamed brightly as it rose and plummeted onto the
exposed helm. The victim of the fierce blow staggered and fell to his knees. He
dropped his own sword into the dust and gestured defeat.

"Halt, my king, stay your mighty blow!" cried an onlooker to the mock
battle. "Lord Bren has suffered much at your hand this day." Morven's lips
curled back in a sneer as he mouthed the words. That blow had been innocuous.
A swordsman of Bren's ability could have deflected it easily and retaliated with
a deadly cut to the neck—could have, if his opponent hadn't been the king of
the realm. Only a fool bested his liege lord in a practice session of no real
importance.

"Ha!" cried King Balint, rubbing his arthritic shoulder. "A good fight. You
do well, Bren, but remember to use that shield. You allow too many blows to
reach your helm. That'll be your death in real battle."

"True, my king. Thank you for the lesson." Bren bowed his head, both in
obeisance and to hide the smile on his lips. He glanced up and silent
communication flowed between him and Morven. Once, King Balint had
battled and bested all the knights. Once. Now the winds of time blew cold and
chill past his thin frame. Even his mind lacked its former agility. Without
Morven and the other advisors to the realm, Balint's far-flung amalgam of petty
baronies would have split apart like an overripe fruit years ago.

Morven took the sword from the old man's hand and said, "Your Majesty
has done well, as he usually does in battle."

"Battle? You call this lover's tryst a battle?" Balint snorted. "The Battle of
Tymen, now that was hard-fought. Hard won, too," he said, drifting into the
endless corridors of his memories. It had been a noble battle, that one. Tymen
marked the rise of his fortunes forty years ago. A barbarian from a distant land,
he had hired on as a mercenary to aid the rebels intent on overthrowing the
Duke of the Outer Reaches. Overthrow the duke he had done, and more.
Expert swordsmanship mixed liberally with shrewdness for manipulating others
had brought him a throne. Balint remembered those days with fondness. Now
the accountants ruled. The bureaucrats perpetrated ordinance after bewildering

ordinance in his name, and he had scant knowledge of what those meaningless proclamations accomplished.

The old days. Those were better, the king knew. Battles. Subtle alliances. Intrigues. Bold policies. His favorable marriage to the defeated duke's daughter Lyesa had given him the legitimacy needed to pacify the commoners and make nobles take heed.

King Balint. It hadn't happened overnight. It took almost twenty years, but he was still in his prime then. Now the twilight of senility crept through his mind, fogging it, bemusing it, making him the laughingstock of his own men, the son of men who had supported him so long ago.

Morven cleared his throat and said softly, "The council requires your presence, sire. Many new ordinances are to be passed upon."

"Eh? Speak up, damn you, Morven. Always whispering." Balint stiffly bent forward to shed his chainmail like a snake losing a layer of dead skin. He managed to get into his doublet without much posturing.

Morven walked half a pace behind Balint to the chambers of state. Once he would have taken this position as a matter of deference to his liege; of late he had to guard against the king's stumbling. A fall might kill the old man. If that happened before the marriage between his son and Princess Adara...

"What manner of nonsense worries us today?" demanded Balint, sitting on his throne and reaching into a huge chest to withdraw an oversized egg glittering internally with a faerie light. The old man's rheumy eyes drifted over the surface, tracing out the lovely patterns in the huge egg. The major axis of the egg matched the span of the king's forearm. The distance through proved greater than twice his hand's width, and the surface gleamed like the finest fire opal ever mined.

"Sire, please, your attendance is required. A new sanitation system is proposed for the community of North Goodland. Our engineers say..."

Morven's voice faded as Balint became more and more engrossed in the flittering fireflies of brilliance inside the eggshell. He held it close and pressed his ear to the cool smoothness, as if listening. Balint smiled and nodded absently, then turned his own lips toward the egg and whispered a reply to the phantom voice from within that only he heard.

At Balint's right, Baron Zesiro said, loud enough for all to hear, "The king's mind is truly gone."

"Silence," snapped Yucel. "He is still king!"

"King? In name only. We rule, Yucel, and well you know it. Who drafted those plans for North Goodland so they wouldn't drown in their own excrement? You!" Zesiro leaned back and pointed at Balint. "He even thinks Duke Darvin will attack through the mountains. Pah! That is the most difficult route of all. If that upstart pretender to the throne wants to attack Strongkeep, he must assemble his men on rafts and float them down the Tymen River. In no other way can he muster the force required to break us. And yet he insists we bleed our treasury white by arming the frontiers facing the el-Liot Mountains. Pah!"

"The king," said Yucel, "is a strategist second to none. He has won more battles than the lot of you put together!"

"Aye, that he has—twenty years ago. You, Yucel, are the oldest of the council. You remember the brilliance, but times change and the realm today is different from his heyday. Look at him. He mumbles loving words to a present given him by some itinerant peddler. He is senile." Zesiro slumped in his chair, arms crossed over his broad chest.

"I fear Zesiro is correct in his appraisal of the Darvinian problem," said Morven. "Since other matters have been dispatched, what is the feeling of the council on this question? Should we assemble our forces in the foothills some weeks' travel away as our king suggests or do we use our men to build water traps for likely invasion down the Tymen River?"

"The river."

"Traps in the water, aye!"

"I second that. The river!"

Around the table went the vote until it came to Yucel. He shook his balding head and pounded his fist on the table. "Nay! The mountains! We must guard the mountains as our king decrees."

Morven smiled without humor as he said, "Fourteen in favor of barricades and fortifications on the River Tymen. One opposed. The motion carries."

"But the king!" protested Yucel.

Morven glanced at the old man, billing and cooing to the opal egg, and snorted in contempt. He didn't bother answering Yucel's challenge. He rose and left the chamber, the others following. Balint hardly acknowledged their departure.

"So the battle was decided by little more than the proper placement of a small troop of men," Balint explained to his egg. "On such things are great victories dependent."

The egg gleamed in the ray of sunlight lancing through the open window. Balint stroked the shell, his gnarled fingers curiously gentle when handling the egg. If any had been present to hear what followed, they would have known sorcerous powers were at work.

The egg spoke.

"Are you so sure this Duke Darvin will attack through the mountains?"

"Aye," Balint said vehemently. "He is shrewd, that Darvin. Much like I was in earlier days. It would not surprise me if he studied every battle I fought and won, perhaps even giving the ones lost special attention. Such a march would aim a massive force directly at the throat of the kingdom. Strongkeep would fall within a day."

"What of this Zesiro and his contention Darvin will come by river?" The entire egg shivered visibly at the mention of the river.

"The river is too easily defended. Darvin knows that."

"I agree. The thought of being sprinkled with even a drop of water is repugnant." The egg shuddered again, a tiny crack appearing down one side. "Only Yucel supports you in council. Why not remove the others?"

Balint sighed. "Many times I've considered this, but they do well in the boring routine of kingdom. Never could I properly deal with the paperwork and petty decisions. They lack imagination, but they are good men for their jobs, if they aren't required to think."

"I personally think you should eat them."

Balint laughed at this barbarism. "Nay, my appetite is not so large that I could devour fourteen of them. Is yours?"

"No. Truth to tell, I know only slightly of such things. Vague memories transmitted to me through the ages. Oh, what does it matter? Since I was stolen, nothing has gone well. I am blind and virtually deaf and without a friend in the world."

"I am your friend. Don't I speak to you every day?"

"True, but you are senile."

Balint laughed as he stroked the egg's surface. "I may be, but I am all you have."

"Such is my sorry lot in life. Although I am hardly deserving, is it possible I might be returned to the mountains from which I was stolen? You are king and such a minor task is within your feeble grasp."

"I shall take you to the el-Liot Mountains myself!"

"All the way?" asked the egg.

"It will be difficult," admitted Balint. "I will leave Yucel as regent since Istuwan is incompetent and Adara, lovely Adara who reminds me so much of her dead mother, lacks majority."

"Morven would marry his son to her and thus rule the realm by default," said the egg. "I overheard."

Balint gestured away the problems and called for his squire. Balint, egg, and squire left for the mountains at sunrise the following day. Only Yucel was on hand to bid them farewell.

\* \* \*

"They are after me. I know it," quavered the voice inside the egg. "They are evil, and I am helpless..."

"It's not you they seek," said Balint. "I do so wish my squire hadn't taken flight, though. He was a useful lad for doing menial chores. But those brigands were rather fearsome." He chuckled. "I think I handled them well, even if I do say so myself."

"They do not seek to eat me?"

"No, no, they were after a few coins and nothing more. I may not be the swordsman I once was, but I can still swing a blade. And they must have been deterred by my silver-tongued claims."

"They thought you a crazy old man. Their clans demand protection of such," the egg said.

"Nonsense." Balint snorted indignantly. He knew the egg was probably right. His shouting and boasting of being king had made the brigands laugh. He looked at his tunic and noted for the first time that the royal coat of arms embroidered on the front was obliterated by mud stains.

"Where do we find the lower passes in which you expect to sight Duke Darvin's army?" asked the egg. "I feel I should know, but I was stolen before full consciousness came to me. I know so little." The tone turned self-pitying. "Not even fresh from my egg and already a failure. How will I redeem myself?"

"You provide me with companionship when others of my own realm desert me," said Balint. "After this adventure I shall make you—"

"Halt!" The word roared and echoed down the rocky gully they traversed. Even the partially deaf Balint snapped around.

"Who orders a king to stop?" he demanded, pulling his sword free from its sheath. The action took long seconds of fumbling.

The mighty voice roared again, "Leave! We do not want your kind in these hills." A spider larger than a peasant's hut leaped to bar his path. Balint's horse reared and threw him. The king lifted himself on one elbow and gaped at the monster. It towered twice his height atop the eight hairy legs flexing with sinewy power. Huge mandibles capable of slashing a man in half clacked ferociously. He grabbed for his sword, knowing he had no chance against this ferocious mountain arachnid.

"You shall be my dinner!" bellowed the spider, advancing with a rolling gait. Balint scuttled away, unable to rise. He pulled himself into a sitting position and noticed the fate of his precious opal egg.

It had fallen from his grasp and had broken apart on the rocks.

"Murderer!" cried Balint. "My friend is killed!" He had no firm idea what had lived inside the egg, but he had come to cherish that creature.

The giant spider hesitated, turned and looked at the egg. A coppery leg reached out and rolled the shattered eggshell into the sun for closer examination. Balint saw the creature stiffen in rage.

"Kidnapper," accused the spider. "I, Kral-wilk'nek'niik, Webmaster of the el-Liot Mountains, will devour you slowly for your heinous crime!"

"Is all this wrath because of me?" came a scared, tiny voice.

Balint gasped at the large spider sitting on a nearby boulder—large by normal standards. The furry beast's body was the size of a dinner plate, and its legs stretched out to span a distance equal to a strong man's shoulders. Compared with the towering monster blocking the path, however, it was a midget.

"You live! Are you of this egg?" demanded the huge spider.

"I am unhappily the same. My eyes adjust now to the light, and I see you are as I, though a trifle larger."

Seeing that the large spider had relaxed noticeably, Balint ventured to speak. "This egg came into my hand by a scurrilous trader. When the egg began speaking, I answered. Was this wrong?"

"Krek!" cried the huge spider, ignoring the human totally. "You have returned to the web of your birthing."

"Krek?" the baby spider asked. "That sounds like a fine name, one befitting such as I, but who—"

"I am Kral, Webmaster of these mountains. You are my first hatchling. When you were stolen, I despaired. Now you have returned."

"Krek?" the smaller spider said again, as if savoring the taste.

"Krek-k'with'kritklik," said Kral, now shivering with joy.

"I like it," said Krek. "The name fits nicely. Noble, even regal, and it rolls well off the palate."

"A name befitting a future Webmaster. Not that I intend to die soon, unless my mate finds me."

"You hide from her?"

"Naturally. I have little desire to be devoured. At this moment, she is occupied with tending others recently hatched."

"Siblings?" Krek sounded hurt at the idea of others sharing the web.

"Yes, but not of noble birth as you are."

Balint started to speak.

"Silence, or I shall eat you now," snapped Kral. Balint pressed into cold rock as Kral clacked heavy mandibles under his nose.

"In all fairness," Krek said, "this human brought me back. He is my ally. I was weak and he aided me."

"Then he deserves the protection of my web," Kral said solemnly. With less belligerence the spider added, "I apologize for wanting to devour you. I have had much on my mind, and it makes me fretful."

"Quite all right," Balint said, painfully using his sword as a crutch to stand. His shoulders ached with arthritis and his fingers stiffened from being wrapped so tightly around the hilt.

"Are the other puny humans your friends, too, Krek? I like them not, but all tell me I am too intolerant of my hatchlings' friends."

"Others? From the north?" asked Balint, now on his feet.

The huge spider bobbed his head. Balint walked slowly to the rock where Krek stretched his newly freed limbs. With a startlingly springy leap, Krek perched on the king's shoulder. Balint felt the bristly fur of the spider's legs against his face. He flinched slightly, and then decided this didn't look good, not when Kral stood only a long pace away.

"These are enemies," Balint said carefully. "Krek and I journeyed to the mountains to stop them from...from annoying you. I'm sure the humans passing into these mountains provide no end of misery for you and your kind. Didn't they steal Krek, after all?"

"They did," agreed Kral. "You would stop these annoying humans? It would be good to attend to web repair again." Kral hissed like a venting fumarole. Balint hoped this was nothing more than a spiderish sigh.

"A treaty between your web and my kingdom can be worked out," the man said, warming to the task. It had been years since he had been allowed to negotiate a real treaty. Yucel told him that Morven and the others were more adept. Balint doubted that yet acceded to his old friend's wishes. But it did take the zest out of being king not being able to barter destinies and trade promises over the treaty table.

"Krek?" asked Kral. "Will these humans honor such a pact?"

"Balint is honorable. The others in his kingdom are less so."

"They can be dealt with," Balint said hastily. "We can provide guards at all roads into the mountains. Perhaps you require some small product of ours to make your lives easier?"

"There is a gummy substance humans manufacture which makes excellent bonding for snare webs," said Krek. "I have not made such webs, of course, but memories flood my mind now. The strands hold prey well but break loose from rocky moorings. This human substance bonds well between web and rock. We could trade them some of our lesser silks. Their cloth is so coarse." Krek's claws tightened on Balint's shoulder and wrinkled chainmail under his tunic. Balint didn't correct the spider's mistake.

"Can you stop Duke Darvin?" he pressed, his ancient heart hammering. A treaty welded together now and a war averted swayed in the balance. Balint felt years younger with Krek sitting on his shoulder. No longer useless, he fulfilled the true destiny of a king.

"Naturally," said Kral, somewhat disgusted. "A few humans cannot stand to a mountain arachnid."

"How few? How armed?"

"Not more than five thousand," Kral said. "They wear those silly carapaces of metal."

"Breast plate," muttered Balint, conjuring the picture of a major army moving steadily through the mountains. Such a force would rip the guts from his kingdom. "Are they into the mountain passes?"

"Less than two hours' travel from here."

The baby spider said, "Are you doing anything important this afternoon, Kral? Besides leaping out and frightening these frail humans?"

"No."

"Why not turn these other humans around and send them back to their web? I could hardly do it," said Krek, jumping up and down on Balint's shoulder, "but for a mighty warrior such as yourself, it should be simple."

"Of course." Kral paused a moment before adding, "I might get several of the others to aid me. Perhaps your mother would join us. She needs some activity away from the web and your siblings to get that notion of devouring me out of her head."

Kral turned and loped off, not even casting a glance back at Krek and his pet human. Balint found himself hard-pressed to maintain the pace on foot. But he did. Dignity demanded it, even if the other royalty were overgrown spiders.

\* \* \*

Balint saw Duke Darvin's camp and stood in sheer awe. If anything, Kral had underestimated the size of the force. Ten thousand armed men, with supplies and horses, spread across an entire valley. Only his blurred vision prevented him from taking a more accurate count.

"But the numbers, Krek. Darvin has an army!"

"So?"

Balint studied the placement of the troops that the spiders would face. He nodded slowly as he realized Duke Darvin had copied a position he himself had employed successfully on many occasions. Not many weaknesses, and overwhelming strength in all areas where a human assault could be mounted. Balint carefully pointed out the failings of Darvin's position to Krek. The tiny spider absorbed all this with equanimity. When Kral loped into view, Krek clicked and squealed rapidly, possibly pointing out all Balint had said or passing judgment on the silliness of humans. Balint didn't know or care. He was too excited at the prospect of battle.

He only wished he could lead a force of his own men against the duke. To be in the saddle again, under streaming banner, sword swirling brightly in the sun. He sighed. War was for young men, and he was no longer young. All his thrill must be vicarious, but the excitement was nonetheless real for that.

He watched the force led by Kral sweep into the valley. Fully twenty of the monster spiders bowled over the guards before they could recover from their shock at the sight. Then came carnage. The nightmarish spiders snapped and clawed through the center of Darvin's camp, juggernauts of prodigious power. The battle became confused, diffuse. Balint no longer followed the course as the spiders spread out to pursue individual fighters.

Once, a man clad in full battle regalia charged up the hill where Balint stood. The king pulled free his sword, lowered the facemask of his helm and waited. His heart pounded as it had in olden days and his hands no longer ached. He was transformed, he was a man forty years younger. As he engaged the soldier, he howled in glee. He fought hard, his muscles responding smoothly, his joints lubricated with virile youthfulness. Each cut he made was perfect, exactly on target. He beat back his attacker, forced him to his knees, and then dispatched him.

And turned to meet another knight attacking from the flank. Balint's blade leaped to the fray. He parried the double-handed broadsword and beat harshly at his opponent's blade. A leg betrayed him then, and he fell to his knees. A swift, powerful block prevented the knight from decapitating him—and then Balint saw his ally.

Krek had ridden throughout the fight on the top of his helm. Now the spider jumped and covered the Darvinian soldier's vision ports. The man shrieked and dropped his sword to pry loose the spider. Balint's blade drove upward under chainmail and into the man's groin. He died instantly.

Krek pranced back and preened, saying, "That will show them. I think I killed him nicely."

Balint blinked twice when he saw that Krek's baby mandibles had torn through the thick steel of the gorget and severed arteries in the throat. Whether his own thrust had killed or Krek's had done the trick, he could not say. He was willing to give the credit to the spider.

"A powerful pair we make," agreed Balint, leaning on his bloody sword, panting. His joints now exacted their toll and stiffened on him until he moved in agony. For the brief fight, it had been worth it. He looked past Krek into the once peaceful valley. Darvin's army was in rout, only a few rallying to the duke's flag in a vain attempt to continue battle.

"I would parlay with Darvin. Can you arrange it, Krek?"

A high-pitched squeal echoed through the valley, cutting past the din of battle, and was answered by a slightly deeper screech from below. In a few minutes, a man dressed in full plate armor was dragged to Balint's feet and unceremoniously dumped.

Duke Darvin rolled agilely and came to his hands and knees in the heavy armor. He raised his head to a strange sight. Balint stood, helm under arm, smiling. The king had a replica of the deadly arachnids perched atop his head, as if this were quite normal.

"Balint?" asked the fallen duke, unsure.

"Krek, help him from his armor." The spider leaped from the king's head and landed on the duke's back. In less than a minute, powerful mandibles had opened the man's armor and left him standing like a lobster without a shell.

"Are you willing to deal with me, Duke Darvin?" asked Balint, once Krek had regained his position on his head. "Your troops are defeated; mine hold the field."

"Yours?" the dazed duke asked. "I underestimated you, King Balint. I knew you were wily. No ordinary assault down the river would have worked. I studied your strategies and decided a quick attack through the mountains would work. I never thought you...the spiders...this is too much! Name your terms of surrender."

"I think you will find them generous, Darvin, perhaps too generous for a brash youngling like you. But tell me, did you copy that battle formation from my own fight at the battle of Tymen? You were brilliant in adapting it to the circumstances here. I—" and Balint forced Darvin to suffer through reminiscence from an old, garrulous and lonely king.

\* \* \*

"This is madness!" exclaimed Morven. "Such a marriage is absurd!"

Yucel smiled wickedly as he said, "You have no choice. The marriage will take place and this realm will be united with Darvin's. Princess Adara has already left to prepare. She seems well pleased with the match. Especially considering her alterative." Yucel smiled even more as Morven uncomfortably looked away, his plans for personal power shattered.

All eyes turned to Balint, dozing on his throne. He snorted and stirred slightly, feeling content to let his advisors lament his decision. He had ordered two companies of armed men to establish entry points along the foothills to prevent more humans from blundering into the el-Liot Mountains. It was a true bargain. The mountain arachnids benefited, but his kingdom benefited more having such powerful allies guarding the high approach to his realm. Also, he had seen the "lesser" silks Krek had sent; the merchants danced all night over the profits to be made from this trade. A worthless glue in exchange for the finest of silks. Trade. That was the essence of being king, to be able to negotiate successfully.

With a battle or two along the way to keep the joints limber.

Balint snorted as he turned in his uncomfortable chair and decided his other machinations were nothing less than brilliant, too. His advisors cared little for Duke Darvin, especially Morven now that his reprobate son had no chance of marrying Adara. But the young duke had a spark of ingenuity that reminded Balint of himself when he was younger. With Darvin slated to assume the throne, Balint need not worry about a capable heir. His kingdom would not suffer. And soon there would be a young prince to dandle on his knee. He smiled at the thought.

"But King Balint," came Zesiro's plaintive voice, "this duke is unable to administer his own duchy. He asks for our advisors!"

"A trick," muttered Morven. "He will kill them."

"No," said Balint, opening tired eyes. "He truly wishes to ally with us. Perhaps you, Zesiro, might show him how to properly tax his people."

"An entire duchy, undertaxed. Virgin territory," muttered Zesiro. "Yes, very well, sire." Zesiro leaned back, smiling at the promise of tax revenues flowing into the coffers. He would support this Darvin. For a while.

Morven protested but the other advisors slowly turned against him. As Balint drifted off to sleep, he wondered if Krek might not be right. Perhaps he should devour Morven. His appetite was large enough for just one advisor.

# Kill Me Two Times

*Voodoo, magic and zombies have always held a macabre fascination for me. I wrote this in July, 1998 for an anthology that was closed by the time I got around to sending it. Another plus for e-submissions. Immediate gratification. Immediate delivery. Another theme was wrapped into this that I've done in other ways (notably in the Magic: The Gathering anthology* Distant Planes *in "Festival of Sorrow"). What is to be done when you cannot take revenge because the object of your hatred has the impudence to die too soon?*

"This will be expensive and...dangerous," the chocolate-skinned Yvette Bell said in a husky, conspiratorial whisper. She made a gesture in the air in front of her, then crossed herself quickly, as if one might protect her if the other failed. Steve Parman had no time for such theatrics.

"If there's enough money, can you do it?" he asked pointedly. He felt the pressure of time working against him. The slender thread he clutched at so frantically slipped away faster and faster. All chance of getting Adrienne back would be gone if he didn't act decisively.

"I deal in love potions, in winning the woman you love," the woman said. "This is...unusual." Yvette Bell stood amid a rustle of silk and spun, her long skirt billowing as if a hidden breeze blew past her. "It is unusual, and I have seen much, so very, very much. I am the great grand-daughter of Marie Laveau!"

"But you can resurrect the dead? Your powers are strong enough?" He almost threw her out of his house when she crossed herself again, as if this warded off evil spirits. Mixing voodoo and Catholicism wasn't unknown in voodoo circles, he had learned. Expecting anything more from Yvette Bell only distracted him. Parman had spent a great deal in the past week just locating this *café au lait mama loi* who claimed to be descended from the greatest of all the voodoo high priestesses. He didn't care if her mother was Marie Laveau and her father the Pope. He needed her arcane powers. If they existed at all.

"What you get back from the other side will not be your woman," Yvette Bell said, looking just a little sly, as if she could dupe him out of even more money. "This unholy animation of the body can be done, but of the soul? That is beyond my power to command. A zombie will return to you, a corpse animated by the faintest ray of soul-light. And then?" She shrugged expressively, causing a ripple in her silk blouse from shoulder to trim waist. "The danger is not in what this almost soulless creature might do. The danger is in" —again she lowered her voice as if speaking aloud would bring down the wrath of God— "possession. Demons are eternally vigilant for such a *returned* creature."

"I don't want a demon," Parman said. He licked his dry lips, and then came to a decision. "Can you also do the exorcism so only the part that is—was—my wife remains in her body?"

"I can," the voodoo priestess said uneasily, "but the body! It will come back as it is now, not as it was." She stared at him with eyes wide. Parman wondered if the fear he felt was radiating from those dark brown eyes or if it boiled from within his own breast.

"Once more with her, even if it is only a few minutes," Steve Parman said anxiously. "That's all I want. To talk to her, to let her know all I wanted to say and..." He swung around guiltily when the doorbell rang. Too damned many people came by to offer their hollow condolences. Parman shot to his feet, pointing toward the kitchen. "Out the back way. When can we do this?"

"Tonight, midnight, the dark of the moon. I must get—"

"Yes, yes, tonight at the grave," Parman said, torn between the ringing doorbell and dealing with the voodoo priestess' demands for the ceremony. "Here, take this. There will be even more if you're successful." He shoved an envelope thick with money into her hands. She hurried off, mumbling to herself.

Steve Parman took a deep breath, composed himself, then went to the door before the two men there could ring a third time. Parman didn't have to see their proffered badges to know they were policemen. He had dealt with too many in the past week. It wasn't their cheap suits—one was dressed rather expensively—or the bulges of their sidearms or even the battered, too-nondescript car in his driveway. It was their attitude, a combination of "we're tired of all this" and "fuck you" that he recognized immediately.

"I'm Detective Sergeant Toricelli, and this is my partner, Detective Walsh." Toricelli stood an inch taller than Parman and wore the expensive suit. He peered down a long, thin nose, giving the effect of a bird of prey studying its prospective dinner. His partner Walsh was shorter, dressed in a brown suit that might have come off the rack at a discount house, and he looked half asleep, as if he had been on duty two hours too long.

"What can I do for you?" Parman asked brusquely, still annoyed at being interrupted. He had so much to do, even if Yvette Bell prepared all her magical potions and conducted a good ceremony at midnight. So much more needed doing before then.

"If you got a minute, we need to clear up some matters about your wife's death. Can we come in?" Since they were already halfway inside, Parman stepped back and silently ushered them down the narrow hall into the living room. He paused a moment, wondering if the lingering jasmine perfume of the voodoo priestess would prompt any questions from the policemen. They seemed not to notice. Walsh kept wiping his running nose with a cheap cotton handkerchief, and Toricelli reeked of cigarette smoke.

"What's the trouble?"

"Well, might be nothing, Mr. Parman," Toricelli said, flipping open his small spiral notebook and scanning it. He needed reading glasses from the way he peered at the crabbed writing in the notebook, but didn't put on a pair. Parman wondered if the man was too vain or if he simply glanced at the book to lend an air of authority to his questions. Either reason was an irritation because of the time it wasted.

"Can I get you something to drink? Coffee? I can make some—"

"No need, Mr. Parman. We won't be long," Toricelli said. Walsh wandered about the room, fingering expensive knickknacks Adrienne had bought over the six years they had been married. Parman started to object, then sank into a chair, trying to make himself small and insignificant so they would discount him. The less he complained the sooner they would be gone.

"Now," Toricelli went on. "There's no question about the wreck being an accident. Two different witnesses, the truck driver fell asleep and admitted it— poor son of a bitch is still torn up over it, you know—and physical evidence shows where Villanueva swerved to avoid the truck and lost control. No chance in hell of getting out of that wreck alive, either of them."

"Air bags," Parman said weakly.

"Not in a Ferrari. At least, not in this one. Vintage model. You ever see it?" Toricelli peered at Parman. "Bright green. English racing colors, somebody told me."

"No, I never saw the car. Or Villanueva. I let Adrienne handle the family finances. She said she had met a new banker who wanted to show her some investment property."

"Strange time to go see it, don't you think? Ten o'clock on a Saturday night?"

Parman shrugged. He was past reaction and felt numb. Living on adrenaline as he had since Adrienne's funeral when he had gotten this idea left him drained. So many people to meet, so many to question, and all to hire Yvette Bell for tonight. Tonight and Adrienne.

"You think she might have been having an affair with Villanueva?" asked Walsh. The question hit Parman like a hammer blow.

"I...I don't know. She had just met him."

"Two days before," Toricelli said, pretending to look at his notebook again. "That checks out."

"What is the problem? You said it was an accident. People saw it." Parman felt anger boiling up now, replacing numbness and even his previous irritation. "What department are you two from?"

"Homicide," Toricelli said. "There's nothing to worry about, Mr. Parman. Really. But an odd coincidence makes the questions necessary."

"What coincidence?"

"We found an elaborate bomb under Marcos Villanueva's bed."

Parman sat and stared. No words came. He shook his head and tried to deny it, but nothing slid past his lips.

"Real pro job, we think. A contact was made from spring steel. One person on the bed, nothing. Two bouncing on the bed gives enough weight to force the sides of the spring together. That would close a circuit and detonate enough explosive to blow Villanueva and whoever was with him to Kingdom come."

"Why are you telling me this? Do you think I had anything to do with it?"

"No, no, not at all. You see, we have reason to believe Villanueva was laundering drug money, maybe from the Cali cartel. He skimmed, he was marked for death. This isn't their usual way of getting rid of people ripping them off—a drive-by with lots of lead flying sends the message better. But this might be their doing. We traced the explosive to a theft last month at a construction site downtown."

"The Gracie Building? The one they are going to blow up?" asked Parman.

"Good guess. 'Cept they implode the building, they don't blow 'em up," said Toricelli. "You ever see any of these men with Villanueva or your wife?"

A fan of photos was thrust in front of him. Parman leafed through and handed them back.

"I don't remember seeing any of them since I never met Villanueva. If my wife knew them, she never introduced them to me." Bitterness at the unfairness of her death twisted him up inside. If he didn't get closure tonight, he might have to live with his grief and anger forever.

"Thanks, Mr. Parman. Doubt we'll be bothering you again. Don't get up. We'll find our way out."

Steve Parman listened to the front door softly latch, stared at the far wall of his living room without seeing anything, and said softly, "Adrienne."

\* \* \*

Parman forced himself to breathe. The stench of the cemetery was more in his mind than his nostrils. Worse, he could not get the idea out of his mind that he was wasting money and precious time dealing with the voodoo priestess. For some reason Yvette Bell appeared more nervous than he was—if she failed, all she lost was the balance of the money he had promised. He lost his only chance to see Adrienne one last time.

He wiped dirt from his hands. Opening the grave had been backbreaking work and had taken him far longer than he had anticipated, even though the dirt had not yet compacted over her coffin. But his part was done. Now it was up to Yvette Bell, all decked out in her fancy clothing and fetishes hanging from her neck and the gris-gris placed around the area to ward off evil spirits.

Black candles at the four corners of the gaping grave burned slowly down into white ones, the flames sputtering for a fleeting moment as the wick shifted from death to life. Salt trails laid to ward off the demons that might come swooping in if the resurrection occurred shone white in the guttering candle light. Parman closed his eyes and wondered if he ought to pray. He wasn't sure he knew how any more—or to what god. So much rode on this. So very, very much. His life.

"I begin," the woman said. She looked up from where she knelt at the headstone. She glanced at him, then into the grave. The coffin remained securely sealed. Yvette Bell rose and began her slow, sinuous dance, the Calinda, once banned and once danced only by men. Yvette shook and shimmied sensuously as she circled the grave, her belle-belle swirling about her.

As she moved, she sang.

> Jump bullfrog, your tail will burn.
> Take courage it will grow again.
> Dansé Calinda,
> Bou-doum! Bou-doum!

Her high, clear voice raked across Parman's brain like a sharp knife blade. He jerked with every inflection, with every emphasized syllable. The voodoo priestess switched from English to Creole French and danced faster, her arms flailing in the air wildly. The tempo picked up, and Parman felt himself being dragged along with the beat.

"Should I open it? The lid?" Parman asked, shaking off the uncomfortable feeling of being caught up in something stronger than he was. He felt the need to do something, anything, to take back control of his senses. He ran his fingers over his coat pocket, feeling the hardness there. Adrienne had to come back to him, she had to! If only for a few minutes.

"No, if she becomes one of the undead she will open the coffin of her own power. This is the way, but she will be not the one you remember."

"She was fucking embalmed. I know," Parman said, losing his temper. "Get on with it. Every minute counts."

The woman turned her face to the sky. Heavy clouds moved across the bright stars, giving a darkness matching that of the grave. She shuddered, then closed her eyes and began scattering the fragrant herbs and shining potions, doing this and that until she got back into the rhythm of her chant.

Steve Parman was not certain when he began to feel the power, not the power of Yvette Bell's chant but real power welling up from the ground, coming down from the sky, oozing from the grave. There was a definite shift from the mouthing of meaningless syllables to a curious, crazy sense that flitted just beyond his understanding. The power mounted to the point Parman staggered away from the salt-ringed grave. His eyes slipped inexorably from the voodoo priestess to the mouth of the grave.

He had not thought of the grave as yawning. Now he did. Without moving it changed subtly, widened in his perception and made him look against his will into the pit. There had been dark before. Now there was a blackness so intense it hurt both eye and soul.

"Adrienne," he whispered. She felt so near.

A creaking noise like nails pulled reluctantly from old wood sounded. Parman jumped when the voodoo priestess swung past him, her skirt brushing his hand in a feathery touch. He hadn't thought it was possible but the chocolate-complected Yvette Bell had turned a deathlike white. Her hand fluttered at her mouth and tears ran down her cheeks, pulling at her heavy mascara until it appeared as if some evil creature had clawed her face savagely.

"It...it worked," she said in amazement. "I have never done this thing before. And never again will I do it! A zombie. I have brought back your wife, but you must hurry. Demons. I feel them. All around. They flock like hungry crows and come to feed on this unnatural flesh. I cannot hold them back long."

Parman stepped up and shone a flashlight into the grave. The lid of the coffin lifted slowly to reveal Adrienne Parman—or what remained of her. The embalming had left her looking gaunt and pale. How Parman hated it when some fool inevitably had said at the funeral, "My, doesn't she look natural."

She had looked dead then. Now she looked worse. The guttering candles burned low and no longer cast their heavy musk over the cemetery. All he could smell was the decay of his wife. He positioned a video camera and turned it on, the cone of light from a floodlight pinning his wife-zombie in its hot center. The videocam whirred as it began recording.

"Steve?" came a voice worse than glass grinding into his soul. "Steve, I saw you. At...at I can't remember. You were—"

"There is no time," the voodoo priestess said urgently. She tugged at his arm. Parman saw the fear in her and knew how close to feeling panic himself. "Give me my money. Minutes only remain in this reanimation."

Parman pointed behind him at a briefcase leaning against a nearby tombstone. The woman raced for it, clutched it to her breast and then left him alone with his Adrienne.

"We don't have much time, my love," he said, trying to control the emotion welling up inside like an artesian spring and threatening to overwhelm him. He wanted to turn off the floodlight and not look at her face—but he couldn't. It had been so beautiful once, that face. Now it sagged, and here and there worms had gnawed holes in the carefully formaldehyde-preserved flesh.

He jumped into the grave, balancing precariously against one side to keep from falling into Adrienne's coffin. Parman positioned himself so the recording camera was above him. He did not want to miss a single instant of this by carelessly blocking the lens with a shoulder or his own head in a moment of obsession.

Parman reached into his coat pocket and clasped the hardness resting there. His fingers sweat and slipped on the handle. He stared at Adrienne, trying to tell himself this repulsive zombie was really his wife, with all her feelings and emotions and memories.

"Do you remember how you died?" he asked.

"Marcos," she said in a jagged voice. "He swerved to miss the truck. Then pain, so much pain."

"How long?" he asked.

"Pain, so long," she moaned, reaching a hand toward him. A gobbet of flesh fell off.

"Not your pain, you stupid bitch!" he screamed. "How long have you been cheating on me? Marcos wasn't the first. And the real estate agent before him. He wasn't the first either. You fucked anything that moved, and I hated you for it. How long, Adrienne? How many men were there I didn't know about?"

"Steve?"

His hand moved like lightning. The knife swung through the cramped space of the narrow grave, sharp edge coming down on Adrienne's bony wrist. The hand severed cleanly and dropped back into the coffin where it quivered with its pseudo-life, a finger pointing up at him.

"You cheated on me and I knew it and couldn't stop loving you. I hated you and loved you and wanted rid of you but couldn't bear the idea. God, how fucked up I was!"

"Steve—"

"I brought you back so I could make you suffer like I have!" he shrieked. Parman hacked and slashed with the razor-edged blade, taking off Adrienne's shriveled arm at the shoulder. It was like boning a chicken. Then he drove the tip repeatedly into her flaccid belly. It was curiously satisfying, even if no blood gushed from the deep cuts. If she had been alive, any one of those gashes would have been fatal, but there was no need to worry she would die. He could indulge himself because she was already dead but could still suffer. He shoved the blade in and twisted, cut and moved it about until most of her abdomen fell free. She flopped about spastically, supported by her spine and little more other than the animating spell.

"I was going to kill you and Villanueva together. I knew about you from the first time you went to bed with that Latin lover. A month ago I put together a bomb. I was going to kill you and the real estate agent in bed together, but you dumped him for Villanueva!" Parman laughed hysterically. "The police think it was a drug deal gone bad. I didn't know anything about that. But you cheated me by dying in the wreck. Now I'll have my revenge."

He swung the blade again, taking off her other arm. Then he began working on her legs, those long, trim legs that once had been such a turn-on for him. Now he panted in exertion as he reduced them to little more than chipped bone.

"Are you suffering? Do you know what is happening to you? Can you feel it? Do you know I am hacking you apart? Suffer, damn you, suffer."

"I—" Adrienne's voice cut off when he viciously chopped at her throat, severing her head from the remainder of her decaying body. The head landed with a dull thud in the coffin, face staring up at him. Her voice came in the same ragged way it had before.

"You'll pay," she said, the words now slurred and distant. Little of her reanimation time remained, spurring him to an even greater rage.

"I hate you with every ounce of my being," he said, kicking at her head. The toe of his shoe sank into her face, the bone yielding and snapping. Then the head bounced around inside the coffin like a soccer ball in a goal. "Nobody cheats on me like you did. Nobody makes me feel like shit."

How long he kicked he couldn't remember, but his leg began to cramp from the exertion. Panting, sweaty, he pulled himself from the grave and sat on the edge staring back into the coffin. Desecration. He had desecrated his wife's corpse.

And it felt damned good.

Steve Parman brushed some of the protecting salt from his hands, turned off the video camera, and then began shoveling the dirt back into the grave, not even bothering to close the lid on the coffin again. He took delight in every shovelful of dirt crashing down onto what remained of Adrienne's once proud body. All he hoped was that she was still animated so she would know the terror of being buried alive.

Or buried as a zombie.

It took a half hour to finish filling in the dirt, then he went home to celebrate.

\* \* \*

His hands had stopped shaking by the time he slammed the front door behind him. Parman then let out a whoop of glee.

"I sent you to hell in style, bitch. You won't be cheating on me any more!" He opened the nylon case and took out the videocam, popped out the tape and shoved it into the VCR on top of his television. "I can watch you get yours any time I want," Parman gloated. He waited impatiently as the tape rewound. He pressed the PLAY button and a dim, grainy picture began unfolding on his big screen television. Parman clicked it off, an idea coming to him.

"A drink. Celebration! Where's the good stuff?" He went to the liquor cabinet and rummaged in it a few minutes until he found the bottle at the back of the shelf. The Bottle. Four Star Cognac. Hennesy. The best he could afford and perfect for his commemoration of Adrienne's infidelity.

Parman poured the aromatic amber fluid into a large snifter and sat in his favorite chair. Comfortable, he used the remote to turn on the VCR again, savoring the memory of the voodoo priestess' ritual that had not been recorded, the rigmarole that would bring out Adrienne's zombie. Then the tape showed the open grave.

"Yeah, baby," Parman said, sliding forward to the edge of his chair. He took a stiff drink, his eyes fixed on the way Adrienne rose from her coffin—and how he hacked her to pieces. His heart beat faster as he watched and relived the revenge. Parman rewound and watched it through again. And again.

He tugged at his collar when he began to get too hot. Then he realized his collar wasn't fastened. He put down the snifter and wiped sweat from his face.

"Too much excitement for one night," he said, but his throat began to burn, to constrict, to cut off air. Parman gasped for breath. He half rose, then fell to his knees. The TV began to fade, darken, and the sounds he had captured on the tape of the voodoo priestess and Adrienne's voice and his own condemnation of an unfaithful wife echoed into the distance, replaced by a steam engine roaring in his ears.

A dark tunnel crushed in on his sight, but Steve Parman was past caring about blindness. His lungs strained and his throat broiled and his belly felt as if it would blow up.

"Wha-what's happening?" he groaned, the words jumbling in his throat.

At the end of the tunnel Parman saw a growing dot of light, of fire, a roaring, dancing, blazing, blistering fire. He reached out for it only to recoil in terror.

"Did you enjoy the brandy?" came Adrienne's mocking voice. "I hated you as much as you did me, dear Steven."

Steve Parman tumbled through space and past time and fell into searing agony, realizing the worst had happened. He and Adrienne were destined to spend eternity together. In Hell.

# At the Bentnail Inn

*Charles L. Grant had a great original anthology series going with his Greystone Bay stories, a mythical New Jersey seashore town where mythic and horrific things happened.* Doom City *(1987) was the second excursion into the foggy terrors. Any hint that the following story has Twilight Zone overtones is entirely intentional.*

"Be careful, Larry!" cried Anna Wexler. "You're driving too fast."

"It's this damned road," Larry Wexler grumbled. "Winds all over and the fog. Damn the damn fog. Can't see a damn thing."

"Stop swearing," Anna said sharply. She settled back on her side of the car and stared straight ahead into the white veil of fog, hands folded primly in her lap. "You know I don't like it when you swear."

Wexler said something too low for the woman to hear. She turned, a strand of neatly coiffured auburn hair falling from its place. "What did you say?" she demanded, her voice brittle.

"You wouldn't want me to repeat it. Not if you don't want me swearing." Wexler cast a quick look at his wife, fuming. The road had been made by some demented highway engineer, each curve designed to insure that he'd lose control in the fog, no matter how slowly he went. And for what?

Larry Wexler snorted and hunched over the wheel, trying to concentrate but finding that his anger mounted too much. His wife wanted this vacation. Such a nice little harbor city, she'd said. So quaint.

Greystone Bay.

Wexler couldn't have cared less. His business was in ruin, the creditors circling like vultures, their beaks clacking at the idea of ripping apart his life work—his life. His oldest daughter had run away from home twice in the past year. And now Anna wanted to "get away from it all" and take a second honeymoon.

As if six days in an-out-of-the-way spot would mend all that had gone wrong in their fourteen-year marriage.

"There," Anna said suddenly, jarring him from his trance. "There's Plummer's Run."

"There's a damned cemetery," Wexler murmured, but he guided the car expertly along the narrow lane, the fog lifting as if in silent tribute to those laid in the ground. Droplets of moisture on granite tombstones caught the headlights and reflected it back as if the eyes of the dead opened.

"There's Port Street. Head down it," Anna said, her voice completely neutral. She reached forward and touched the AAA tour book on the dashboard. "The Bentnail Inn will be off on the right. There!"

Wexler cursed again as he missed the rough cobblestone lane. The side of the car scraped a building ancient before the Civil War and broke the door handle. He stopped and peered out the window. Opening the door might be a problem. But Wexler didn't think he could convince his wife to turn around, go find a nice Holiday Inn near a service station and spend a civilized night.

"This is it. Bentnail Lane. The bed and breakfast is at the end."

"In the middle of the bay," he said. The fog had again pulled misty white fingers across the small town, making every new doorway and alley a surprise.

Larry Wexler found the Bentnail Inn's sign outlined by the twin headlight beams. It didn't do much to bolster his sagging spirits. The sign had been assaulted by saltwater and storms until the lettering all but vanished. Only the rusted and bent nail driven through the center of the rotting wood gave any hint about the dilapidated building's identity.

"I suppose we can leave the car here," said Anna, craning her neck and peering into the fog. "I don't see a parking lot."

Wexler said nothing. He gingerly opened the door. The outer handle fell off and sent clattering echoes down the silent lane. He kicked the offending handle under the car. He wanted nothing more to do with it. He wanted nothing more to do with any of this second honeymoon or the sickening "quaintness" Anna found so desirable.

"I'll see if there's anyone inside," said Anna. "You'd better get the bags. I don't think there's a bellhop." She stood erect, shoulders back, chin up, and went through the fog like the Queen of England preparing to knight a hero.

Wexler pulled their luggage from the trunk and dropped the heaviest bag—Anna's—to the ground to close the trunk lid. As he reached up, a tiny, almost imperceptible scratching noise made him spin about.

For an instant, out of the corner of his eye, he caught sight of a man dressed in rags, scrabbling in the gutter to find a discarded cigarette butt. But as quick as Wexler was in turning, the apparition proved faster and faded into the fog.

"Damned bums are everywhere," he grumbled. "Even in a jerkwater place like this." He hefted the luggage and wrestled it inside the Bentnail Inn lobby, where he dropped it and stared.

The outside hadn't hinted at such a fine hostelry. Anna and an older woman stood at the oak counter, working through the tedious details of registration. "Where's the phone?" he asked.

"Don't have one," the graying woman answered. "No need. Not in Greystone Bay. Who'd want to call out?" She smiled in a way reminding him of his grandmother. "And who'd ever want to call in?"

"You got a point," Wexler said.

"He only wants to call his lawyer. I swear, Larry, you spend too much time with her." Anna straightened her shoulders even more until she looked like a toy soldier.

"The company's going broke. I want to save it and Hill's damned good at what she does."

"Larry," his wife said primly. "This is not the time or place to discuss such matters."

"You'll have the room, top of the stairs, second on the right. A nice view of the bay," the clerk said. She seemed oblivious to the currents flowing around her. "It's a special room, one just filled with history."

"Great," Wexler said sarcastically. "Let's hope it has a firm mattress, too."

He started up the stairs, and then paused. In the shadows above moved a form, an amorphous shape that fleetingly came into light and vanished. Wexler blinked. It looked the world like the bum out in the street.

"Is there a back way?" he asked, eyes fixed on the stairs.

"This is it. Not much in the way of fire regulations when the inn was built back in 1893."

Wexler hurried up the steep, narrow wood steps and stopped in the hallway littered with maple stands with marble tops and a dozen different varieties of artificial flowers. Of the bum he saw nothing. Wexler looked at the floor, thinking he'd find wet tracks. The only damp footprints he found were those behind him—his own.

He walked along the hall, listening intently. As far as Wexler could tell, he and Anna would be alone in the Bentnail Inn. For a second honeymoon, that would be nice. For a man on edge of business and life unraveling, it might be hell.

Wexler opened the door and peered into the small room dominated by a huge brass bed. He edged around the bed and dropped the suitcases by a head-tall wardrobe. A small sound attracted his attention. Wexler looked back into the hall and caught sight of the bum in a mirror mounted on one wall. He spun out of the room to face the man and found only empty, echoing hallway.

Puzzled, Wexler went back to the lobby where Anna still talked with the other woman.

"Where did that scroungy hobo vanish to?" he demanded.

"What are you talking about?" asked Anna.

"You must have seen him. About five foot seven, bent over, tattered rags for clothes. He was upstairs in the hall. He didn't have time to duck into any of the rooms—I'd have heard the door shutting. He had to come by you."

Wexler saw the expressions on the women's faces and fell silent. He had no desire to create a scene. Shaking his head, he said, "Must be too tired from driving through the fog."

"Nothing a night's rest won't cure," the clerk said. "And I'll see that you get a good breakfast." She smiled and touched Anna's hand. "In bed."

Anna returned the smile, but her face lost all warmth when she turned to her husband. She took him firmly by the arm and led him upstairs to their room. Once inside, she closed the door.

"What was all that about?" she demanded. "Are you trying to prove you're crazy? Is that what your lawyer told you to do to avoid bankruptcy?"

"Anna," Wexler said tiredly. "I saw this bum. Out in the street, then in the hall. Twice."

Anna sniffed derisively and poked about the room, getting her clothing from the suitcases and into the wardrobe, examining the spotless adjoining bath, pointedly ignoring Wexler.

He lay back watching her, his thoughts diffuse and disconnected. Wexler tried to sort through his troubles, both marital and business, and found himself slipping off to sleep, the soft lapping of Greystone Bay providing a soothing counterpoint to his breathing.

...the water, the water rising around him, buoying him, letting him drift, drift to...

Larry Wexler jerked upright, eyes wide and heart pounding. He looked around the room, not recognizing it at first.

"Larry, what's wrong?" asked Anna, returning from the bathroom. "You look a fright."

"I..." Wexler paused to get his thoughts into a semblance of order. "A dream, I guess. I was out on the bay, swimming or just floating. But it was different somehow and I went into a...a different place. Not this world."

Anna Wexler looked unimpressed. "It's the stress. You're letting it get to you." Her words stung like a whip, an accusation she had made in a dozen different ways during the past months. Wexler wanted to shout, to cry out that he hadn't created their problems, that Anna ought to accept some of the blame.

But he couldn't. A part of his mind refused to release the taunting memory of that other...place.

Wexler lay back down, eyes staring at the ornate patterns on the plastered ceiling. The patterns began to blur, to shift and move away. Wexler snuggled down in the softness of the comforter, tried to follow the infinite plaster curlicues and listen to the distant tide working its way to land. Again, he slipped into a dream-filled sleep.

...Wexler swam in the frothy surf, working his way to land, sighting the ancient buildings and—almost—recognizing them. This had to be Greystone Bay. A part of him said that it was while a more rational fraction of his mind worried over the dream state so obviously affecting him.

Wexler pulled himself onto the sandy beach and shook himself like a wet dog, sending water droplets flying in all directions. Bright sun caught the drops and turned them into miniature rainbows.

And Wexler instantly found the pot of gold at their ends. Strewn over the beach were thousands of gold coins. With a whoop of joy, he dropped to his knees and scooped up a handful. At first, his eyes refused to focus on the wealth he'd found.

The coins hardened as he held them and the edges sharpened.

"Kruggerands! Maple Leafs! Coronas! This is a fortune in gold!" he cried. On hands and knees Larry Wexler began pulling the riches in, stuffing the gold coins into his pockets until they weighed him down heavily.

"I can save my business. I can get out of hock and pay off the bank and the loan shark and—" He looked up when he came to the slim, tanned legs blocking his way. Slowly, he tipped his head back, taking in the full picture of the lovely blonde woman standing in front of him.

Legs too slim and tanned and perfect to be true blended smoothly into flaring hips sheathed in skin-tight red silk jogging shorts. A flat, bare midriff, also tanned to perfection, drew him ever upward. Breasts, full and firm and lush, hid behind a halter top which had been designed with him in mind. Wexler licked his lips unconsciously as he saw—almost—the woman's breasts through the peekaboo mesh fabric.

But it was her face that truly captivated him. Never had he seen a woman more beautiful. If an angel had descended from heaven, for all its divinity, it would have seemed ugly in comparison.

When she spoke, silver bells rang. "Please, Larry, let me help you."

"What?"

"The gold. You do want it taken back to the house, don't you?"

"House?" He tried to shake off the feeling that he ought to know who this gorgeous woman was, where the gold had come from, that he had been here all his life.

"Oh, silly," she said, picking up the nearest coins. As she bent, he stared at her. She turned dancing green eyes on him. "Unless you don't really want to go back. Unless you want to do something else here."

"On the beach?" He looked around. No one was in sight. He tried to push out of his mind the worry about such a warm sun beating down in the middle of February. Then Larry Wexler found more to think about.

She came to him, softness and strength, loving and urgent.

His arms pulled the woman close and...Wexler yelled as hard floor smashed against his legs and arm. He thrashed about and finally pulled himself upright.

Anna peered myopically at him. "You fell out," she accused. "Get back into bed and go to sleep."

Wexler shook himself, trying to regain a sense of place. It had seemed so real to him, the gold, the sunny beach, the lovely woman.

"What a dream," he said, standing. His foot batted against something hard, but he ignored it. Wexler dropped into bed beside his wife. This time he slept dreamlessly.

When Larry Wexler awoke, it was to the sound of eating. He pried open one eye and peered out. Anna worked her way through the large breakfast the clerk had promised. Wexler moaned and tried to pull the covers over his head. He only succeeded in getting himself tangled. With great reluctance, he sat up.

"Save some for me," he told her.

"Good," Anna said. "But almost all gone."

"To hell with it," Wexler said. He ate two pieces of thick toast smeared with the best homemade jam he'd tasted in years, then carried the remains to the hall and placed the try beside the door. He paused, hearing faint sounds. Trying not to appear obvious, he looked around but saw nothing.

Wexler closed the door, waited and listened. Again he heard small noises. He jerked open the door. Eating the scraps of food from the breakfast tray was the bum he'd seen too many times before.

"You!" cried Wexler. He grabbed for the man's collar. Greasy cloth ripped and let the bum escape. "Come back here, dammit!"

"What's wrong, Larry?" asked Anna, crowding past him and into the hall.

"The bum I told you about. He was eating our garbage."

Anna shot him a strange look. "I don't see anyone. And even if this bum of yours was finishing off our breakfast, so what? You aren't into collecting garbage, as you call it, are you?"

"Go on, be sarcastic. I'm going to find him. The landlady should at least know he's prowling around."

"Sometimes you worry me, Larry."

Wexler was torn between going back into the room with his wife and seeking out the bum. Being clad only in his underwear decided him. He went back in and dressed.

"I'll find him," he told Anna. "You wait and see."

"What is it with you, Larry? This isn't supposed to be a big game hunt. You're not the local police, though heaven knows this man doesn't seem to have done anything but take a few crumbs from a tray."

"You don't even believe he exists, do you?"

Anna looked at him, head tilted slightly. In a low voice she said, "No, I don't."

Wexler slammed out of the room and took the steep steps leading to the lobby two at a time. The gray-haired woman stood behind the counter. He didn't bother with her. Rushing into the street, he looked up and down Bentnail Lane. Tendrils of fog lingered, obscuring his view. Wexler started walking, as much to work off his frustration as to find the bum.

He slowed when he came to the piers. The dock area seemed familiar; it took several seconds for him to remember it from his dream. But the reality was so different. Oil spills stained the pilings and a heavy, catch-in-the-throat, fish odor pervaded the area. No pure golden sand dotted the beach. Only refuse strewn as far as he could in the fog met his eyes.

Wexler walked and thought. The pieces of gold on the beach? What of them? He saw only flotsam washed ashore during the night.

And the woman? Of her he saw no trace. But the buildings had the same aspect. The dream had revealed them as cleaner, more livable. Greystone Bay struck Wexler as virtually unlivable as it was. But the dream world had been perfect!

"Perfect," he muttered to himself, eyes misting with tears as he remembered what he'd had and then lost. "Only a dream, it was only a dream," Wexler told himself.

But it had seemed more than that. Much more. No dream had such texture, such reality.

A feeling of being watched turned Wexler cautious. Slowly, he turned and looked into every noisome shadow, every spot where someone might hide. From behind rusted oil drums he saw darkness moving in darkness. Quicker than a tiger, he pounced. He stumbled as he grabbed hold of a thin, sinewy arm but recovered in time to pull the man to the ground.

"Got you!" Wexler cried. He held the bum in a schoolboy pin, his knees on the man's shoulders. Eyes wide with fear stared up at him.

"You found the way!" the bum accused.

Wexler blinked in confusion. This wasn't what he'd expected the man to say when finally confronted.

"You found the way!"

"What the hell are you talking about?"

"I can see it in your face," said the bum. "I can. I know you've been there."

Wexler shifted his weight to one side, letting the man sit up. Something deep inside him told of extreme importance in finding out what this derelict meant.

"Tell me everything," Wexler ordered.

"You know it. You came here. You stayed in that room, at the Bentnail Inn. There's no other reason. You want to go there."

"We stayed in the room because it was available. My wife and I are on our second honeymoon." The words rang hollow and burned like acid on his tongue. Wexler saw that he hadn't convinced the bum.

"You went there and saw it all. You've tasted paradise and want more. I can tell." A stricken look came over the bum's face. "I went there once and I was fool enough to return. I shouldn't have. I should have stayed there."

"I had a dream," said Wexler. "Is that what you're talking about?" Then it struck him as ridiculous. "But you couldn't know what was in my dream."

"Paradise," the derelict said firmly. "You found everything you've ever wanted there. And it can be like that forever." The bum leaned forward and put his face in his hands. "I was there but I came back and now I've lost it! I've got to go back. I've got to!"

Crazy, thought Wexler. The man is a stark, staring crazy.

"Uh, what do you mean?" asked Wexler, trying to calm a man who might become violent.

"You saw the place. What did you find? Wealth? It's there for the taking. Beauty? I could paint the landscapes and people forever!"

"You're an artist?"

"Michel Dupree."

Wexler rocked back on his heels and sat heavily on the ground. He knew of Dupree's work—and how the artist had mysteriously vanished more than two years ago. No one had seen him since he left his loft in the TriBeCa in New York City. Wexler was no art connoisseur, but Anna had claimed that Dupree's work was among the finest being produced in America. Wexler had stopped her from paying an exorbitant sum at auction for a small watercolor the artist had done.

"You've been in Greystone Bay since you left New York?" Wexler asked.

Eyes sharp with cunning fixed on Wexler. "We're both looking for it. That bed has something to do with opening the way. Unfinished dreams. I don't know what or why, but it no longer works for me. But it does for you."

"You sneak in and sleep in that particular bed?" asked Wexler, perplexed.

"That's the only way. The only way there."

"Just sleeping in the bed opens the way?" asked Wexler. "Why didn't my wife mention it? Why didn't I see her there?" He shook himself. He was talking like Dupree.

"Your wife's not got much of an imagination, has she? That might be part of it. I can't say. All I know is that I must go back. It's every artist's dream."

"Being famous and rich?"

"Creating, damn you!" shouted Dupree. "That's all there is to life. There I can create art no one has ever before seen!"

"And riches? Like the gold I found along the beach?" Wexler had almost believed. The flare of insanity in Dupree convinced him that he had been pulled into a madman's fantasy.

"If that's what you want. Or beautiful women. Or men. Anything. Success? It can be yours. There."

"How have you been living? No one's seen your work in years."

Dupree shrugged. "Odds and ends about this miserable sinkhole."

"Stealing crumbs off breakfast trays?" suggested Wexler.

"Dammit, yes! To return, I'll do anything. But I dare not leave. If...if I do, I might lose my chance. Nothing can stand between me and there!"

Wexler stood and brushed the dirty sand from his pants. Dupree might have been committed and escaped. If not, he ought to be locked away where he wouldn't hurt anyone. Then Wexler laughed ruefully. Greystone Bay was as good a place for a social misfit like Dupree. Who could he hurt in this town that would matter?

"If you find the way, tell me, please!" pleaded the artist.

"Yes, yes, I will," said Wexler. Both knew he lied.

Larry Wexler wandered the narrow streets of the town, seeing little of the quaint shops and small plaques commemorating this and that from a time long past. He walked and considered and decided that Michel Dupree had deluded himself.

Paradise? Wexler shook his head as he turned back toward the Bentnail Inn. This world was more like hell. Only that could exist. Not paradise. Never.

He went up the steep, narrow staircase and entered the room.

"Anna?" he called. His wife had gone out. That might be just as well. He didn't feel like facing her again, hearing her accusations, her put-downs about their life together and how he had run the business into the ground.

Wexler threw himself on the bed, a pillow slipping out from under his head. He reached over to pick it up off the floor when a glint of gold caught his eye. Curious, Wexler fumbled under the bed and found a gold coin. His mind recoiled. When he had awakened from the dream, he remembered having kicked something under the bed.

It was an Austrian Corona, just like the one he had picked up off the beach before encountering the blonde.

Wexler's hand began to shake, and he went cold all over.

"Dupree's not crazy," he said. "This proves it."

Wexler sat on the edge of the bed, trying to control his shaking and order his rampaging thoughts.

"Sleep, if I go to sleep," he said aloud, the words echoing in the room. "I can get to sleep, find more gold, bring it back and save my business." He smiled wickedly. "Maybe divorce Anna. That's what she wants." Ideas of dalliance with the sun-tanned blonde on the beach floated across the surface of his mind.

"Why save the business? Why come back? Maybe Dupree was right. Stay there. Stay there!"

Wexler lay down and tried to sleep, to get caught up in the dream that would transport him back to the world of success and perfection and all the things he desired most. But the harder he tried, the more awake he became.

After almost an hour of tossing and turning futilely, Wexler rummaged through his suitcase and found the bottle of sleeping pills. He took two and quickly swallowed them without water. Stiff as a board he lay on the bed, waiting for sleep.

Slowly, he relaxed and felt the familiar lethargy of sleep overtaking him. Eagerly he sought it. The world faded into darkness for Larry Wexler then returned, brighter, better, perfect.

Smiling, he sat up on the beach strewn with the gold coins. The gorgeous blonde waved to him and started running to greet him. Wexler reached out for her, stumbled and fell—was pushed!

"At last, at last, I'm here!" cried Michel Dupree.

Wexler looked up to see the artist. Somehow, Dupree had crowded through with him.

Wexler started to complain, and then smiled. There was no need to be angry. Paradise could be shared. He need never see Dupree again, unless he wanted.

He shrieked as the perfection around him began to fade, to turn gray and amorphous and frightening.

"Goodbye," Dupree said, smiling, his arm around the blonde who had transformed into a slim-hipped, dark-haired Latin beauty. "There can be only one guiding genius here. Paradise cannot be shared."

The artist's mocking laughter brought Wexler upright in bed, cold sweat pouring down his face and body. In panic, he looked around—and saw only the tiny room at the Bentnail Inn.

He clutched the single gold coin so tightly in his hand that it drew blood around the milling.

"No," Wexler cried, "no, I won't give it up. Not like this."

He tried to go back to sleep, to again find the way into that other, better world. Larry Wexler tried and failed repeatedly.

On nights cloaked in fog, a solitary figure can be seen—barely—along the streets of Greystone Bay. He lives off refuse and never strays far from the Bentnail Inn as he seeks the single dream that will take him back to a world he possessed for a brief instant, then foolishly lost.

# The Black Mists of Hell

*This was an excursion into the style and format of the master of fantasy, Fritz Leiber. The genesis of the story is, well, lost in the black mists of Hell, and I am not even sure what market it was aimed at. The story is intriguing, however, and obviously a part of a grander tapestry of stories involving Breis and Tymon that have yet to be written.*

"What does it matter that they will die, if they do your bidding up until they reach that fine point in an otherwise futile existence?" Lsyss asked of Illyeso Three-fingers. The two wizards sat across a low table, forming a study in opposites. Illyeso's huge bulk more than filled an over-burdened chair, his suet-like body rippling as if fleshy tides ebbed and surged on his vast ocean. The corpulent wizard raised a hand and studied not the three fingers there but the missing ones. What a contest that had been! Would he ever see its like again?

Then his brightly glowing, piercing eyes darted across the table to paper-thin, dwarfish Lsyss. The other sorcerer accepted the full weight of the gaze and returned the stare with his own fathomless one. For his life, Illyeso could not tell the color of the other's eyes. Green? Gray? Changeable? But it was not the eyes that bothered Illyeso.

Lsyss cast no shadow. It had been cleft from him, leaving him trapped half in this world and half in the...other place. With a perverse curiosity, Illyeso raised his maimed hand and watched the shadows dance merrily on the inlaid wood table between them. This was one thing he could do that Lsyss could not. How might he turn it to his benefit?

"My minions are not expendable. I need them for other tasks," Illyeso said.

"Breis and Tymon," scoffed Lsyss. "I know them. I know of them, I should say. They are petty thieves and no more. But they are expert at their tawdry trade."

"They are the journeymen you need," Illyeso said, confidence growing as he came to a decision. The stories of Lsyss' wrath abounded, but he was only half the wizard he used to be. "How is it you are still of this world?"

"This can be yours, should you retrieve what I seek most," Lsyss said, drawing forth a small bag. The leather pouch cast a shadow; his hand did not. The wizard permitted only a glimpse of the contents, but it made Illyeso catch his breath.

"So that is how you have survived," he said in awe.

"If I were whole, a trifling crumb of this would make me a god."

"A godling, perhaps," Illyeso qualified, still entranced.

"If you should taste the manna superiorum..." Lsyss began, letting Illyeso's agile mind finish the equation. Illyeso could be a god—a godling, at least. His powers would soar, and every spell cast would be trebled in effectiveness. His vast bulk quivered at the notion of such puissance.

Knowing his interest in the manna was too intense to conceal, Illyeso dried his sweaty hand on his magenta robes of the finest Isle Royal silks and then reached out, his three fingers trembling. He hesitated, looking at the smallish wizard. Illyeso's eyes blazed like twin noonday suns.

"Touch it. Be assured it is true manna superiorum," Lsyss said as a sneer curled his thin upper lip.

Illyeso quivered with delectation at the feathery touch he was allowed.

* * *

"This is the life," Breis said, throwing back his arms and thrusting out his chest to accept the warm embrace of a new day's sun.

"Yes, it is," said his tall, one-eyed companion. Tymon checked to be certain his sword rested easy in its scabbard, tested the edge of his razor-sharp dagger, then began pacing like a caged animal so his bulk repeatedly cut off the sun's rays shining through the window.

"We have everything we could want," Breis went on. He looked around the store where they slept in exchange for guarding valuable brassware. A young fortune in goods was stacked floor to ceiling, on shelves, in every possible nook and cranny. Some caught the edge of the rising sun and reflected rainbows possible only from valuable gems inset into brass ornaments that would lend added beauty to any woman wearing them.

"Food in the belly, a merchant who cares little what we do if we keep his wares from being stolen, yes, we have it all."

The two squared off and stared at each other. Breis' sharp green eyes fixed on Tymon's single orb.

At the same instant both said, "I'm bored."

For a heartbeat, they said nothing more, and then both laughed.

"What horrid curse has fallen on our heads?" asked Breis. "We have all we could desire. What other job in Ostmarch is so lucrative? Doesn't Uwer pay twice what any other merchant does for guard duty? He feeds us well from viands shipped through his market—"

"Then the wine," went on Tymon. "Never have I tasted better. He doesn't even mind if we bring back women for the night. He is a prince among merchants."

"Among all employers," Breis added. He heaved a deep sigh. "But the work is boring. We know all the tricks of thievery and easily catch would-be light-fingered pilferers. That's why he hired us. Not one item has been filched from his shop since we went on duty a full month ago."

"Not so much as a bent copper coin has left this store without us noticing," Tymon agreed.

"It's too easy. We need a challenge." Breis looked around the store and realized their skills in stealage were eroding from lack of use. That craft required constant practice, careful and intense thought to develop new techniques, daring and every other trait they had traded for security.

"It would be far too simple to empty this store," Tymon said. "We would get enough, even fencing at a few coppers to the gold, to last the rest of our lives. What benefit is that?"

Breis' rabbit-like pink nose twitched. His hand went to his sword but he did not draw. A slow smile lit his face.

Tymon started to protest, then sagged a little.

"Yes, even his commission would break the monotony." Tymon rubbed his nose and sneezed. It was always thus when he caught the scent that Breis' keener sense already had detected. Illyeso Three-fingers reeked of sulfur from long residence underground and had somehow unlocked a crevice beneath the shop floor where they stood.

Both men stepped back as the boards creaked and smoldered, then popped open like an obscene door onto a nightmarish panorama of flowing, molten rock and a single, treacherously narrow white pathway leading into the bowels of the planet. Neither hesitated to jump into that fulminic pit to find what Illyeso wanted of them.

* * *

Breis held the small packet as if it might bite him. He had to grab fast to keep it from blowing away as a sudden gust ripped across the top of the mountain.

"Be careful," Illyeso said anxiously. "It is fragile. Tear it and you will never return. Never." Behind him boiled yellow clouds of brimstone from deep inside a crevice. Breis, Tymon and the wizard had climbed up the narrow opening to reach this lofty vantage point. To the north lay Ostmarch, and southward stretched the Sinking Lands, swamps so foul that neither Tymon nor Breis had ever ventured there.

"When we catch this shadow, we open the package and cover it with the magical cloth," Tymon said, repeating Illyeso's instructions. He sounded skeptical.

"Be sure you are both under the cloak when you spread it. I need to place the proper geas on it so you will return directly to this spot. But first, the shadow must be underneath. That is why you are being paid so handsomely."

"Not so handsomely," Breis said, still enjoying the barter of his and Tymon's service for some small trinket. True, he had never seen a diamond as large as his head before, nor one that shone with such intense inner light as Illyeso had proffered, but the prospect of adventure mattered more. They had rejected this prize in exchange for one favor each from the wizard.

Illyeso ignored the jibe. The wizard wiped his lips with a silken cloth and peered upward. Thick swirling clouds hid the sky. He took the packet from Tymon and began his incantation, then hastily handed it back.

"There, done," Illyeso said, stepping away. "Remember, this will work only once and will return you only to this exact location."

"I'm more interested in knowing why we have come to the top of a mountain," Breis said, looking around. As elevated as the view was, the bitter wind whipping past his small frame froze his bones and robbed him of any appreciation of the countryside.

"You go up. This requires a shorter journey," Illyeso said, clapping his hands. A hissing sounded and writhing in the air before them appeared a rope of snapping, dancing black smoke.

"A trifle insubstantial, don't you think?" asked Tymon. He reached out to touch the rope. His hand repelled it so that it fluttered just beyond his grasp.

"Here, lower, yes, not so above. To get you to the point where the rope becomes sturdier, observe!" With a grand flourish and wave of his arms, Illyeso conjured up a wicker basket held aloft by four flapping white doves. "Get in, ascend quickly, then do what you must to find and retrieve the shadow."

"Where do we look above?" asked Breis, climbing into the basket with more grace than his larger comrade. "What will we find?"

Illyeso's myriad chins quivered as he shook his head.

"I have no idea, nor do I want to know. It is neither fish nor fowl, neither alive nor dead. That is all I can tell you. Now go, hurry, hurry!"

The sorcerer clapped his hands, and the four doves strained mightily, lifting the basket higher in spite of the load.

Breis let out a yelp of delight as they shot upward, the black rope slipping through the center of the basket floor to guide them aloft. White pinions fluttered down about him as the doves strove ever harder to lift. Breis leaned against the basket and peered directly down at Illyeso, who waddled back to the crevice leading into the mountain.

"Such a view!" he chortled.

"I left Ostmarch and the brass store for this?" muttered Tymon. His single eye screwed shut tightly, and his knuckles turned white as he gripped the edge of the basket. "I have no liking for such heights."

"Then you won't mind that we're going into the clouds," Breis said, disappointed that his vista was stolen away by fog.

"That's better," Tymon said. Then he let out a great cry of anxiety as they burst through the clouds a few seconds later.

Breis swallowed hard when he saw how the doves fought to continue their upward flight. One by one the doves faltered. Then he saw a ray of hope above.

"There, the end of our trip! It's not too far," Breis said, pointing to what appeared to be a palace formed from eddies of black mist. "The birds might weaken but they have enough strength left to get us to our destination."

"I trust so," Tymon said. "Look below. The black rope is not only vanishing, it is as if someone set fire to it so it burns up to meet us."

Breis held back his own cry of fear. The black rope evaporated at an increasing rate, moving upward. The doves could never carry the basket—and them—higher without the guiding rope that soon would be gone.

"What?" yelped Tymon, batting at a bird falling past his face. "The doves! One died."

"No," Breis corrected. "Two." He licked dried lips. "Three."

The basket stopped ascending, and then began inching backward toward the hidden, far distant mountaintop. If they fell from this altitude, only death awaited them below.

"The black rope," Breis said, clutching it. "As Illyeso said, it has become more solid and isn't repulsed by our touch up here. Climb, Tymon, climb for your life." Breis jumped and took hold as the final dove's valiant efforts ended abruptly. The bird, dead from its herculean efforts, tumbled downward until it was swallowed whole by the cloud.

"You climb," Tymon said. "I can see the end of the rope not a sword's length beneath me. Climb as if your life depended on it. Climb as if mine does!"

Breis began scaling the rope, Tymon immediately under him. His muscles lacked the bulk of his friend's but he was wiry and strong and agile. Still, Breis felt the burning deep within his very bones after only a few minutes frantic effort.

"Faster, curse you," panted Tymon. "I'm hanging on only by my hands. There's no rope for my feet to entangle."

Breis gritted his teeth and envisioned himself following the last dove on its death plunge to the ground. He would not end up a jellied smear on some mountain that had no name. Hands cramping, sweat pouring down his face and body in spite of the growing cold and bitter wind flogging him, Breis climbed until he felt the magical black strands beginning to turn to vapor. To hesitate even an instant meant his death—and Tymon's. Breis gave forth a huge cry and mounted the disappearing rope with the last of his strength.

Then he could give no more. The black rope flowed like fog through his fingers and he fell.

He hit solid ground an instant later. Breis lay stunned for a moment, then rolled onto hands and knees and shouted for his friend.

"Tymon! I made it!" He peered over the edge of what seemed solid ground and saw nothing but emptiness stretching down to the top of the billowing cloud hiding the ground. "Tymon!"

"Stop yelling and give me a hand," growled his friend.

Breis shoved his head around the curve and saw Tymon clutching what appeared to be icicles of black ice just under the firmness he had gained. Without thinking, Breis stretched out his hand and grasped Tymon's, then heaved with all his might. For a moment, Breis thought his comrade's weight would pull them both from safety, then he found soft dirt to dig in his toes and applied the power of his legs to the rescue. Adding a second hand, he clutched both of Tymon's and flopped him around as if dropping a netted fish to the shore.

Tymon lay face down, shaking like a wet dog. Then he rolled over and sat up. His weathered face was pale and his hands trembled.

"I hate birds," he said. "You can never depend on them."

"Especially doves?" asked Breis.

"Yes, doves, especially doves." Tymon growled like a bear and got to his feet. Breis stood beside him as they stared at the wall of billowing black mist, and then looked at one another.

"That must be our destination," Tymon said. "I hope there aren't blackbirds inside," Tymon said. "I hate them worse than doves." He struck out, his distance-devouring stride forcing Breis to half-run to keep up.

"So what do we do? Knock on the door and see who answers?" asked Breis, panting a little when he came up beside his comrade. He stared up at the towering doors, seemingly formed of ebony. Breis reached out hesitantly and touched the door—or tried. His hand sank to the wrist in the door. Startled, Breis jerked back.

"You've opened the way for us," Tymon said, hand on his sword. The door swung away, revealing a hallway paved with the purest onyx. Dark columns rose on either side, vanishing into a cloudy ceiling above.

"It's brightly enough lit," Breis said uncertainly. He stepped forward and looked about. Halls radiated from the atrium, corridors stretching so far that they disappeared into the distance. "I had feared we would blunder about in the dark."

"Your brilliant wit would have cast light enough," Tymon said.

"Is that a joke?" Breis turned slowly, studying each of the spokes radiating from the entrance hall. One looked like another to him.

"How do you propose to find the shadow Illyeso wants stolen away?"

Breis started to suggest a systematic search, then paused. The corridor directly in front of the door seemed...right.

"This way," he said, strutting off with more confidence than he felt.

"I agree," Tymon said, surprising him. "It is right."

They walked side by side, senses straining. Breis heard nothing, not even the sound of their boots against the glistening onyx floor. The walls were less substantial, but he saw shadowy, unmoving forms inside them. Breis went to one and tentatively reached out. The mist danced away from his hand, whirled about like water down a drain and vanished tracelessly to leave behind a lovely young woman, frozen like a statue. But Breis knew she was not carved from any cold, lifeless stone. There was a vibrancy about her, flesh begging for a soft caress, all arrested in time.

"There is a golden arrow in her breast," Breis whispered. "She might live if I pulled it out." He reached out, but Tymon's hand clamped firmly on his wrist, stopping him. "What?" Breis demanded. "What's wrong?"

"I know her," Tymon said in a choked voice.

"Who is she?" Breis saw the shock on his friend's face. "Someone who mattered greatly to you, I suspect."

"Eivia, my first love," Tymon said. "I never knew what happened to her."

"Your first love?" Breis looked from Tymon to the woman and back. "She is young."

"It was twenty seasons ago, perhaps one or two more. I was very young, so very, very young, but she was radiant. Eivia came to my town with a traveling troupe. She was a chanteuse with the most beguiling voice I'd ever heard. But there was so much more. The scent of her hair, the lightness, the deftness of her touch. She—"

"She was your first love," Breis said. "And your first lover?" He saw that he had guessed rightly. "What do you think might happen if I pulled out the arrow?"

"She would decay and be damned to suffer forever. As she stands now, she feels no pain, no joy, nothing. She just is."

For a moment, Breis thought his friend had spoken. Then he realized another had joined them and mimicked Tymon perfectly. Breis blinked as he stared at the newcomer, who might have been a younger Tymon. He was almost as tall but had both eyes and no faint spiderweb of pink scars crisscrossing his face. But the girth, the hair, the way he stood and talked—all were echoes of Tymon.

"Who are you?" Tymon asked.

"A poor fool destined to wander these magical halls forever," the newcomer said bitterly. "I am Tryuro and doubly cursed. She and the others are frozen, with no sense of the passage of time, but I roam the halls eternally."

"What is this place?" asked Breis.

"The Palace of Black Mists," Tryuro said. "At least, that's what I call it for want of anyone telling me otherwise."

"Yes, yes, but what is it?" pressed Breis.

Tryuro laughed without any hint of humor.

"There is paradise and there is perdition. Then there is here, where those whose mortal flame has been snuffed out by vile magicks are doomed to remain. We hang dangling forever, unable to achieve either peace or damnation."

"Eivia?" Tymon stepped closer and reached out as Breis had. This time Tryuro stopped the gesture.

"Let her be. She is the most beautiful of any of the inmates of the Palace of Black Mists," Tryuro said. He looked sharply at Tymon and then stepped away. "What is she to you?"

Breis watched the two as Tymon poured forth both story and soul. Tymon finished with the question, "Do you know what happened to her? How did she come to this place?"

"She was murdered by a wizard named Lsyss," Tryuro said. "He sought her favors and she rejected him. He shot her with that arrow, dooming her to this timeless existence of non-existence."

"There's more to this story, young Tryuro," said Breis.

"In revenge, I tried to slay the wizard with his own dagger but was only partly successful. I cut away part of him." Tryuro sneered. "It is trapped here and I sometimes amuse myself prodding and tormenting it, but his corporeal body remains below."

Breis and Tymon exchanged glances.

"Were you her lover?" asked Tymon.

This startled Tryuro, who finally smiled and shook his head.

"Not that, but I loved her. And she loved me."

"This piece of the wizard you sliced off," Breis said, "what does it look like?"

"A shadow. It's as if I cut off his shadow."

"Could we see it?" asked Breis. He motioned Tymon to silence. The one-eyed giant had started to ask more of Tryuro, undoubtedly about his lost love. Breis glanced at Eivia and had to admit, even at a young age, Tymon had impeccable taste in women.

"Why not? There is time." Tryuro laughed at this, making Breis uneasy at the sardonic edge to it. The tall young man strode off, heading down the corridor. Breis and Tymon followed.

"Will it be this simple?" Breis whispered to Tymon.

"Is it right that Eivia remains in such a state of oblivion? She deserves more. She was so gentle and kind."

"She was killed by a wizard," Breis said. "We can return the shadow to Illyeso and find out where this Lsyss is and take revenge on him."

"Yes, yes," Tymon said. "Would you agree to accept that vengeance as our due from Illyeso?"

Breis nodded, not trusting himself to speak. Tryuro had stopped in front of an alabaster door set into a slightly convex wall. Something about the door robbed him of speech and confidence.

"Inside," Tryuro said, fixing them with his intense stare. "What I robbed from Lsyss." As an afterthought he added, "I hate Lsyss most of all but there is another I loathe. One day, I shall deal with him, too." Tryuro shook himself free of this fond dream and asked, "Would you enter and see?"

"I'll go in," Breis said.

Tryuro cautiously opened the convex door a crack, then swung it wide. The sheer whiteness of the room caused Breis to squint, but he stepped forward. Inside, the light came from everywhere. He reached out and saw that his hand cast no shadow. His body might have become transparent. Nothing he did produced a hint of darkness. But there was one element of darkness inside, flat against the wall of the circular room.

"It's like a man casting a shadow," Breis said in wonder. "But where is the man?"

"Go on, try to touch the shadow. It runs from me," Tryuro said. "I am certain it will from you, also. Tormenting it will amuse me so be sure to do your best to catch it."

Breis prided himself on his quick reflexes, but he found himself woefully lacking in speed and agility when it came to snaring the elusive shadow. As he ran forward, the shadow would duck and dodge and dart away with twice his speed. Frustrated, Breis let out a shout and sprinted to the wall, grasping for the shadow. The darkness slithered away, following the arc of the circular wall. No matter how fast Breis ran, the shadow remained enticingly close but stayed too distant to nab.

"Help me," Breis panted. He turned to his comrade in time to see Tryuro open his jerkin. A glowing golden dagger protruded from the man's chest. Tryuro seized it, yanked hard to free it and than drove it into Tymon's belly. With a quick step forward, Tryuro embraced his victim and spoke in his ear, then stepped away to spit on Tymon.

Tymon stared up from the floor, his face white with pain. Never looking back, Tryuro slammed the door.

For the life of him, Breis could not see the slightest crack in the wall. He rushed to his fallen comrade's side.

"Why did he stab you?" Breis touched the golden dagger handle and felt the magicks locked within.

"I feel my life slipping away," Tymon said. "You must capture the shadow. Let me rest against the wall. Chase it around and I'll block it."

"But your wound!"

"Do it!" Tymon sagged against the wall, hands on the dagger hilt.

Breis hesitated, and then saw his chance. The shadow had foolishly ventured closer, as is the wont of so many when they happen upon a bloody accident. With a prodigious leap Breis reached the wall behind the shadow, which found itself trapped between the two men. Breis whipped out the fragile cloak Illyeso had given him and swung it out like a fishing net to pull in his catch. The shadow struggled, but Breis held it firmly in the magical cloak.

"Let's get out of here. Illyeso can repair the damage that whoreson did," Breis said, getting ready to drape the cloak over himself and Tymon.

"Wh-what he said," Tymon grated out. "He—"

"The knife won't steal your life," Breis declared. He plucked the dagger from Tymon's belly but the man's usual vitality did not flow back. If anything Tymon sagged even more weakly.

"He told me, the two men he hated most. The wizard Lsyss and his father."

"Yes, yes," Breis said, working to keep the shadow trapped while pulling the cloak up over himself and Tymon.

"I'm his father," Tymon got out. "And Eivia is his mother."

Breis tried to speak, but the words were jammed back down his throat. He gagged and fought, but the sensation refused to release him. He thrashed about, then stumbled and fell to his knees. Wind whipping across the rocky summit lifted the cloak, forcing him to grab hold and prevent it flying off.

"You've returned quickly," Illyeso said. "That is good."

"He has it. He has it!" crowed a thin, short man next to the corpulent sorcerer. The man rushed over and grabbed before Breis could stop him.

A thunderclap sounded and an invisible hand pushed Breis flat to the mountaintop. He stared up to see the man grow in stature. The darkness of the shadow infiltrated his body and lent substance where none had been before.

"Whole! I am whole again!"

"Lsyss!" Breis murmured under his breath.

"The reward," Illyeso said eagerly.

"Yes, of course," sneered Lsyss. "I have no need for manna superiorum now." He tossed the wizard a small pouch.

"A moment," Breis said, scrambling to his feet. "Tymon was sorely wounded retrieving that patch of murk. I had to leave him. The cloak didn't bring him back."

"He was injured?" asked Illyeso uneasily. "By a magical device?"

"Yes," Breis said, his fingers curling around the handle of the golden dagger he held hidden from the two wizards.

"He must remain there," Illyeso said. He clutched the bag with the manna superiorum close to his fat bosom.

"Your powers are greater now, Three-fingered One," Lsyss said mockingly. "You might be of help."

"Not there. It is death for a wizard to go there."

"To the Palace of Black Mists?" asked Breis. The two sorcerers looked curiously at him.

"Is that the way it appears? Intriguing," said Lsyss.

"You have the ability to ensorcel the cloak so I can go back where I left Tymon, then return here?" asked Breis, mind racing. He clutched the dagger more firmly.

"Why, yes, I suppose."

"Do it. That is the reward I claim."

"I—"

"Go on, Illyeso. Humor him." Lsyss laughed, and the mocking sound echoed from far distant mountaintops.

"Very well," Illyeso said. He opened the leather pouch and pinched off a scruple of the contents and popped it into his mouth. For a moment, he grew taller, more muscular, radiating intense power. Illyeso passed his crippled hand over the now-exhausted cloak.

"There," the wizard said. "It is done. It will return you to the exact spot where you left, thence to here. But be quick. The spell will fade."

Breis gathered the cloak and turned to Lsyss.

"I met an acquaintance of yours," Breis said. "His name was Tryuro."

"Tryuro? I know no Tryuro. Wait, yes, I do! His mother was a whore. I killed her. And then I killed him, but later."

"With this?" Breis asked in a deceptively mild tone. He stepped forward and slashed furiously with the golden dagger. The impossibly sharp blade glided through Lsyss effortlessly, but the blade did not sever artery or sinew. It separated the wizard from his shadow once more.

Breis swung the cape about, covering the three: wizard; shadow; thief.

Again Breis experienced the soul tearing, gut wrenching transition. He fell to his knees in the same room where he had left Tymon.

"Are you alive, old friend?" demanded Breis. He knelt by Tymon and saw the faint flicker of eyelids. The giant lived, but barely.

"What is this place?" asked Lsyss, looking about. As his shadow danced past him, the wizard grabbed for it but missed by a hair's breadth. The ebony silhouette plastered itself once more against the featureless white wall of the circular room.

"The Palace of Black Mists," said Tryuro, coming through the door. "I never thought to see you again."

"You and that slut mother of yours dwell here? It is too good for you!"

"Because she resisted your foul advances?"

"You have no quarrel with your father," Breis said, looking up. "He never knew you had been born. Eivia and he separated before he knew she was even pregnant."

Tryuro hesitated.

"You lie to save him."

"Nothing can save him," Breis said. "Or is there a way?"

"If the dagger remained in his body, he would be trapped in this reality fugue forever, but you removed my dagger. Now you will be caught here, also, but you will be forced to watch him wither and die while you remain as you are for all eternity," said Lsyss.

"You parted his shadow from his body?" asked Tryuro.

"To rescue your father," Breis said. He tossed the golden dagger to Tryuro. "Use that as you will."

"I am slowly decaying, but with this..." Tryuro rammed it savagely into his own chest. He staggered, bracing himself against a wall. A smile crept to his trembling lips. "This returned to the fatal wound stanches the decay."

"Good," Lsyss said. "Then you will endure forever, which might be little enough time to appreciate the nature of my retribution."

"And you will forever chase your shadow," Breis said. "Go on, try to catch it. I did."

Tryuro and Breis had to laugh when the wizard made one frantic, futile grab after another to capture the elusive shadow.

"He did not abandon your mother. Truly, Tymon did not know," Breis said to Tryuro.

"Go. I would close the door to this room," Tryuro said.

"You'll doom him to forever chase his own shadow?"

"It is little enough torment for all he has inflicted on my mother and me," Tryuro said. He hesitated at the door, looked down at Tymon and said, "Perhaps I was wrong about you, you who have such a loyal friend. I wish we had known one another. Good-bye, Father." The door clicked shut.

"How do you catch it? I need it back! I can't leave without it. My powers are too weak without it!"

"Run faster," Breis suggested, spreading the cloak over Tymon and then hastening to join his friend. The last he heard of Lsyss was the wizard's anguished wail as he—almost—caught his shadow.

Once again deposited on the mountaintop after the gut-twisting transition, Breis flung back the cloak. This time a gust of wind ripped it from his hand, sending dark tatters fluttering away. He let it go, knelt beside Tymon and propped him up.

"He is alive," Illyeso said in amazement. "That you retrieved him is a tribute to your cunning."

"The manna superiorum," said Breis. "Give it to him. Let its magicks restore Tymon's life."

"No!" Illyeso clutched the leather pouch to his chest. "You already received your reward. The cloak! I ensorcelled it so you could return to the Palace of Black Mists and fetch him here. You can bury him yonder. That's a nice spot."

"I claim what is in the pouch," came Tymon's feeble words. "You paid Breis. You have not paid me. A boon from you was to be payment. I demand..."

"The manna superiorum," Breis finished for him.

Illyeso's full lips worked like a beached fish gasping for breath, then he thrust the pouch with the magical restorative into Tymon's weakened grasp. Breis helped his friend push the entire wad of chewy, sticky manna into his mouth.

For a few seconds nothing happened, then Breis grinned. Tymon's strength returned bit by bit, then at an accelerating rate.

"Will he be stronger than before?" Breis asked.

"No," Illyeso said. "He might be weaker, though I doubt it. I shall certainly be weaker."

"No less the wizard than you were," Breis said. Tymon got to his feet and stretched mightily. His hands shook, but strength flowed into him now.

"No more, either," Illyeso said glumly.

"You have done the honest, honorable thing by paying your debt," Breis said.

"You are no better off, either," Illyeso said, trying to find some solace in the misery of others.

"Not so," said Tymon, a touch of sadness in his voice. "I have discovered a lost love and an unknown son. Perhaps some day I shall find the magicks that will restore them."

"And I have relieved my boredom with a great adventure," Breis said.

Illyeso Three-fingers glared at them, lifted his arms, and opened a crevice in the mountain where he vanished. For a moment, the two adventurers remained on the mountaintop, Breis looking toward distant Ostmarch and

Tymon above, into impenetrable roiling clouds for any trace of the Palace of Black Mists.

Then both followed the wizard into the heart of the planet.

# Used Books

*The launch of Charlie Grant's Greystone Bay anthologies was, suitably, Greystone Bay, where this story happily appeared in 1985 alongside those of such luminaries as Robert Bloch, Robert McCammon, Chelsea Quinn Yarbro and Al Sarrantonio. The idea came to me as I considered the power of the written word and the worlds of imagination unleashed. The usual "What if?" question became: What if you could tap into another's life experience?*

"Boy, I'd love to get into her pants." Tommy Kidd's pale blue eyes followed the girl's trim form as she swayed down Port Boulevard, aware of the male attention she received.

"Michelle?" Tommy's best friend Alan Wolsky snorted derisively. "She's nothing but a prick teaser. Look at the way she flutters those eyelashes at anything wearing pants." He turned and studied Tommy critically. "Hell, if she gives you the hots that bad, go ask her for a date. Bet she'd put out at the drop of a hat."

"Shut up. You don't know what you're talking about."

"Hell I don't. But you wouldn't know about that, would you? You're too chicken to even talk to her, much less go all the way. You've been going with Patty and haven't even tried to cop a feel."

"That's not true." Tommy flushed hotly at the accusation.

"Patty's a professional virgin. Everybody knows it. That's why you go with her, so you won't have to do anything. You're scared shitless of getting laid, Tommy, aren't you, aren't you? Come on, admit it!"

"Get lost," Tommy shouted, turning down the street and wanting to run. Only through great willpower did he keep his stride short, but he clutched his schoolbooks so tightly his knuckles turned white. As he walked, the fifteen-year-old convinced himself this always happened to the superheroes he read about in the comics. Nobody appreciated them; nobody appreciated him.

He closed his eyes and leaned against a cool store building, took a deep breath of salt air, and imagined himself walking along the street with Michelle—lovely, tall, sultry Michelle. A gang of Hell's Angels would come riding down on her astride their dangerously roaring chopped hogs, threatening her, yelling obscenities. He would stand up to the greasy bastards and run them off. Yeah. And she'd flutter those long, black artificial eyelashes in his direction and throw herself into his arms and then they'd...

He looked around guiltily, moving his books so that he held them in front of him with both hands to cover up his embarrassment so anybody passing by wouldn't see.

Why couldn't it be like he imagined it could be? Why wasn't he less of a coward?

He walked on another block before turning a corner, relieved when his excitement finally passed. Five minutes later he stopped in front of a store window in bad need of washing. Lurid paperbacks proudly marched along a brick-and-board shelf in the window. He licked dried lips and looked up and down the street. No one knew he was in sight. He'd tried once to buy a copy of *Playboy* down at Krueller's Drugstore and God and everyone had seen him. Alan had told anyone who'd listen, and Tommy had been laughed at for weeks and weeks.

No one saw him now. Maybe he could buy a dirty book. Maybe the owner didn't care who he sold to. He started in, but fear grabbed his heart and squeezed. He wanted to run.

When the door opened and a brass bell tinkled, he jumped a foot.

"Didn't mean to scare you, son. Were you coming in?" The man in the doorway looked like he was a million years old, all wrinkled and tanned. The odd clothes he wore captured Tommy's attention, though, and kept him from bolting and running.

"Uh, yeah, guess so. What kind of, uh, bookstore is this?"

"If you can't read the sign, you won't get much out of the books." The old man in the billowy-sleeved shirt pointed to the sign. "Cesar's Used Books. Cesar, that's me. Don't get much business down this street. Too far away from the Boulevard."

Tommy looked nervously looked up and down the street and finally nodded.

"Come in and look around. Tell your friends, for all the good that will do. No one reads today. Watch the damn telly."

"Telly? You British?" Tommy began wondering about the baggy pants and the calf-high black leather boots that needed polishing. "You look like something out a Lon Chaney movie. The Wolf Man."

"I should," Cesar said. "I am Romany and I know the secrets of the universe. They are passed down from generation to generation." His voice lowered and he added, "My books contain all the knowledge of the Gypsy. Come in and see."

"Wow," Tommy said, his eyes wide. He moved as if drawn by a magnet and began looking over the dusty rows of books. The acrid tang of cheap paper turning yellow and brittle thrilled him, as it always did. Soon enough, he was sitting cross-legged on the floor going through a stack of books written by Sabatini and the Baroness d'Orczy and Fritz Leiber.

He didn't find any Gypsy lore in *Captain Blood* or *The Three Musketeers* or *The Winds of War,* but he did find cheap prices on the battered paperbacks. He had accumulated a stack marked "fifty cents each"—and would be eating candy bars for lunch for a week because of it—and was working up his courage to ask Mr. Cesar if he had any porno books, when a short man dressed in a three-piece suit came swinging into the store, a heavy attaché case in one hand.

"You have it, Cesar?" asked the short man.

"But of course. It will be yours. For one entire week."

Tommy sidled back along a spinner rack filled with old pulp magazines, imagination running wild. The short guy must be a gangster, Mr. Cesar a dope dealer. Or maybe he was arranging for a mob hit. Tommy's heart beat faster. Mr. Cesar was a contract killer and would snuff the star government witness on the stand just as he started to spill everything.

"Here. Count it," said the short man. He opened the attaché case. Tommy blinked twice. The case was crammed with twenty-dollar bills. Cesar closed it quickly and shook his head sadly.

"I trust you, my friend. If you ever shorted me, there would be no more of these..." Mr. Cesar smiled and drew forth a package the size of a hardcover book. Tommy couldn't see what it was, but the short man snatched it as if it meant his very life. He turned and left the store without another word. Mr. Cesar chuckled and placed the attaché case under the unpainted counter.

Tommy waited another ten minutes, heart ready to explode. Gone was all thought of asking Mr. Cesar about dirty books. He hadn't hallucinated all that money. There wasn't anything in this crappy secondhand bookstore to bring a price like that. There must have been a thousand dollars in the case. More.

He approached the counter with his trove of books, trying to keep from straining to look over the far side and see if the black leather case was actually there or if he had only imagined it.

"A good selection, son," said Mr. Cesar. "Four dollars and fifty cents."

"Uh-oh," said Tommy, suddenly realizing he had only three crumpled dollar bills. "I guess I'd better put back a couple."

"No money, eh? Never mind. I am an old man, and it cheers me to see a young man read. The books are yours for three dollars."

"I couldn't."

"Please, humor me. It is a whim on my part. Please."

Tommy eyed the books and guessed at the worlds hidden within them. He nodded, thanked Mr. Cesar, and almost fled the shop.

The street outside was empty. By the time he had walked the eight blocks home he knew he'd only imagined the money, just as he imagined himself taking Michelle in his arms and...

\* \* \*

After dinner Tommy curled up in a corner chair and started reading. His dad had come by, looked at the cover, and shook his head. The man sat down and unfolded his newspaper.

"Can't understand what you see in junk like that, Tom," he said. "You sit there reading like you were hypnotized or on drugs. You ought to show more interest in current events."

"Like you, Daniel?" said Tommy's mother. "All you read the paper for is the sports page and to see who got killed in the most gruesome way. I swear, you're like some sort of ghoul."

"It's the times we live in, dear," he said. "Look at this. One of those hotshot million-a-year basketball players was found dead this morning. Cops stopped him wandering the streets like he was some kind of zombie. Brain was burned out, on dope, probably. They're all junkies. Died an hour later."

"See? Gruesome."

Tommy ignored them and lost himself on the high seas, commanding a pirate ship. He ordered a broadside. Another, and then ordered the captured merchanteer boarded. He swung across the gap between the two heaving ships, his arm circling Michelle's waist. She melted against him, kissing him for rescuing her...

\* \* \*

Tommy Kidd awoke just after midnight. He lay on his back, staring at the shadows dancing slowly across his bedroom ceiling.

"I did see something," he said. The boy tried to put the picture of all those twenties out of his mind, but he couldn't. The more he fought to go back to sleep the more awake he became.

Finally he rose and silently dressed. He opened his door and listened for a moment, hearing the measured ticking of the grandfather clock in the hallway and the rattling snores of his father from the master bedroom. He swallowed hard and almost chickened out and returned to bed.

No, he thought, I get pushed around enough. This time I'm going to find out what's going on. Maybe get a reward when I turn them all in to the police. He had no clear idea of what crime had been committed or who he was going to call the police on, but that money meant something illegal was going on.

All the way to Mr. Cesar's used bookstore Tommy imagined himself as Dirty Harry kicking in the door and shouting, "Police! Freeze! Unless you want to make my day." Outside the dingy storefront he experienced a rush of confidence. Dirty Harry was never scared.

He peered through the duty window and saw nothing but the shelves of books and a yellow sliver of light coming from under the door leading to a back room. He jumped when the squeal of car tires on the pavement echoed down the street. The flashy sports car started braking. Tommy ran to an alleyway and hid.

The elegantly dressed woman climbing from the car made Tommy catch his breath and hold it. "Monique Dupree," he whispered, air leaking from him as if he'd sprung a leak. "She must be about the biggest star in Hollywood."

Monique Dupree didn't even knock on the door; she pushed through into the store, the brass bell tinkling lightly. Tommy started to go back to the front window, then stopped. High over his head was a small window, lit from within. Clambering up the piles of trash in the alley allowed him to peer into the back room of the bookstore.

"Mademoiselle Dupree," Mr. Cesar greeted her, bowing low. "It is so good of you to give your time for charity."

"My agent didn't tell me we'd be working in such a filthy place." Tommy cringed. Monique Dupree's voice sounded like a nail file on metal. It wasn't anything like the sexy, seductive voice in her movies. He knew. He'd sneaked into all of them, especially the R-rated ones.

"Just read from this book. I shall record it and do the transcription for the blind later."

"My fucking agent's got balls for setting me up with something like this. I got a hot date waiting for me at Luigi's."

"The famous nightclub?" asked Mr. Cesar. "Please, let us get on with it. Only a few minutes and then you can go and, how do they say, boogie till the cows come home."

"What? I never heard anything like that. But yeah, let's get on with it." Monique Dupree cleared her throat and out came the caressing voice that made Tommy uncomfortable with its immediate intimacy. She read from a romance novel as if it contained the most interesting and revealing words in the world.

Tommy moaned and tried to keep from embarrassing himself. He wiped sweat off his forehead and pressed his head against the wall, hoping it would help. It only made it worse. He craned his neck and got a good look down into the dimly lit room.

Two walls were lined with leather-bound volumes, obviously expensive and not like the cruddy paperbacks in the front room. But he didn't care about the books. His eyes fixed firmly on the blonde woman, the way her breasts almost spilled out of the sequined evening gown, the way her fingers slipped up and down the pages of the book. Tommy closed his eyes and imagined Monique running her slender fingers all over him, up and down.

His eyes shot open when the woman stopped reading. She lay with her head on the simple wooden table, asleep. Mr. Cesar turned off the cheap

Japanese tape recorder and stood. Tommy heard him chuckle and say, "Well worth fifty thousand to her agent."

Cesar took the book lying open on the table and carefully examined it. He smiled more broadly. He went to a small cabinet and unlocked the door, removing a tiny vial of green liquid. Tommy watched in rapt fascination as the Romany began placing one drop of the fluid on each page of the book. When he had done this for all the pages, he closed the book and shelved it.

The man hoisted the actress into a fireman's carry. Tommy nervously rubbed one dirty hand over his lips, wondering if Mr. Cesar had killed her. The roar of the sports car and the sight of Monique propped up in the passenger side, Mr. Cesar driving, further confused him.

"Maybe she had too much to drink or something and Mr. Cesar's taking her home." But even as he said it, Tommy knew that wasn't true.

"Come on, don't be chicken," he said, looking back into the room. He climbed down from the tottering tower of boxes, went to the front of the store, and tried the doorknob. Unlocked. The tinkle of the bell almost gave him a heart attack, but Tommy quickly ducked inside, afraid Mr. Cesar might return at any instant and find him.

The door leading to the back room stood ajar. Tommy advanced slowly, as if this were the gateway into hell. His hand shook as he grabbed the knob and opened the door.

The room was exactly as he had seen if from the high, narrow window. Two walls were lined with books, from floor to ceiling. On the third wall stood the tiny wooden cabinet from which Mr. Cesar had taken the bottle of green ink. And the fourth wall was a mass of peeling paint.

"Wow, biographies," he exclaimed, running his fingers over the soft leather bindings. In bright gold along the spines were names both recognized and unknown to him.

Adolph Hitler. Marilyn Monroe. Ambrose Bierce. Wiley Post.

He took down a volume marked "Jim Morrison."

"Wonder who he is?"

His eyes scanned the first sentence of the book. The very words burned in flame on the expensive parchment. Tommy stiffened as the crowd roared his name.

"Morrison, Morrison! We want the Lizard King!"

He strode out on stage, arrogant, aware of the power he exerted over the thirty-seven thousand screaming fans. Fingers locked in his silver conch belt, he thrust his leather-pants-clad hips far forward, wantonly far, and began a slow gyration as the band behind him swung into a driving, provocatively sensual song.

He held the dumb sonsabitches in the palm of his hand and the power excited him. Sexually excited him.

Tommy stared directly at the floor, and it took a few seconds for him to realize the book had fallen from his nerveless fingers. He bent down and closed the book, returning it to the shelf.

He walked on shaky legs and looked at the other books. Eva Peron. D.W. Griffith. Douglas Fairbanks. Manfred von Richtofen. William Thomas Turner.

Tommy took down this book and read the fiery words. He heaved a deep breath, sucking in a lungful of the salt air as he peered out across the bridge of his 32,000-ton liner. Galley Head lay before the *Lusitania*. The dawn turned deadly when he saw the tropyl-laden torpedo from the U-20 running toward his ship.

Tommy slammed the book shut, eyes stinging and feverish. He replaced the tome and ran his fingers along the spines of the others until he came to the new one.

Monique Dupree.

With hands barely able to grip the leather cover, he pulled it down and opened it. The words leaped from the page and etched with acid intensity into this brain. His lover came to him, one hand on the white satin sheet and the other on his tender, yielding thigh. His legs widened and he reached out to take the handsome, mustached man into his arms. Never had he wanted a man more than he did now.

"Oh, my God," Tommy muttered, forcing himself to close the cover. He put it back into its place and sat down at the wood table, shaking all over.

He looked at the shelves in wonder. No other books had been so alive for him. His imagination had been weak, pathetic, in comparison to the emotion, the violence, the lust he had experienced.

He knew he ought to leave. Mr. Cesar wouldn't want anyone even knowing he had all these books. But Tommy couldn't. He wiped more sweat from his forehead and picked up the book on the table, lying to himself that he'd just read this one and then go.

Tommy Kidd frowned. The pages were almost blank. Only a word here and there appeared and the story made little sense. He leafed through, glancing at the pages, trying to figure out what this one meant, why it didn't have the impact of the other volumes.

As he flipped through the pages, he yawned, and his eyelids grew heavier. Tommy rubbed his eyes and yawned again. Wait till he told Alan about this. And Patty.

No, he'd tell Michelle! That'd impress her. She'd have to go out with him then and he could...he could. Tommy forgot what he'd do with her.

"To, uh, to..." He tried to remember the name and failed. But it didn't matter. His head tipped forward. He jerked awake. "Got to tell my...my friend. His name. What's his name?" Tommy drifted off again. "Home to...where?"

He meant to rest for only a moment, to get the sleep from his eyes. Tommy Kidd's head rested on the open volume and he snored as loudly as his father.

\* \* \*

"That's all?" the wizened old man asked. "Only fifteen hundred? Why so cheap?"

"This," said Mr. Cesar, "might be looked upon as something of an experiment."

"You mean it's no good."

"Not at all, not at all," Cesar denied. "This book is crammed with youthful courage, adolescent lust." Mr. Cesar lewdly winked at the old man and nudged him with his elbow. "And that commodity we lose as we age—curiosity. It's all here, all as vibrant as any of my special editions. But it is short, very short."

The old man tried to straighten his age-hunched shoulders and said, "I'll take it." He reached for his wallet as Mr. Cesar smiled and began wrapping the book.

# Thief of Dreams

*Fantasy worlds are populated with thieves and various others living at the edge of the (usually feudal) laws. Estebar is a self-made millionaire, in fantasy terms, at least, from selling his unique brasswares. But he hears the Siren's song of the sea, and when his world is shattered at the end of "Thief of Dreams," he answers. The story originally appeared in the 1995 premier issue of* Adventures of Sword and Sorcery, *edited by Randy Dannensfelser.*

Screams of intense pain and fear woke Estebar an hour before dawn. He tried to ignore the second wave of screams, rolled over, pulling the fluffy pillow over his face, then realized he could never get back to sleep after hearing such agony echo through his bedchamber. Surrendering to the inevitable, he sat up in bed, stretched his long arms, and reached for an expensively embroidered robe nearby. Estebar pushed aside the keen-edged sword and dagger atop the robe. There would be no need for them.

There never was. Coralla was efficient. And merciless.

Estebar shivered against the chill coming up the stairs from his shop at the bottom of the steps spiraling down from his quarters, wondering how Coralla endured the low temperature. A beast from the tropics ought not to enjoy such freezing conditions. Estebar worked his way down narrow aisles between the cabinets crowded with fine brasses, the finest in all the lowlands of Freena it was often said, until he came to the front door of the shop. The heavy wood portal stood open, chilly spring wind whipping in from the market square. To his left stood a darkly disguised burglar, frozen in death, pain etched on his hatchet-thin face. Curled about the corpse-statue's legs was a small red-and-yellow banded larr snake.

Intelligence shone in the ebon orbs staring up at Estebar. A forked tongue shot forth, sampling the air, then vanished as signal all was well again. Estebar smiled, bowed low in acknowledgment of his reptilian watchman's expertise, then asked, "Was it necessary to kill him?"

A sardonic hiss was his only answer.

"You might have frightened him away rather than killing him." In reply, Coralla slithered from his perch, wiggled swiftly across the stone floor and curled intimately around Estebar's leg. The brass merchant allowed the snake to work up his leg until safely ensconced under the robe, next to warm skin. Estebar gently stroked the poisonous reptile's spade-shaped head as he studied the latest of the inept thieves who thought it a simpler task to rob a prosperous merchant than to toil for their daily fare.

He shook his head. A nothing, this one, with no talent—a man of no obvious cunning. Estebar swung around when footfalls approached and the night guard cautiously pushed open the door with the tip of his sword. Lieutenant Doon knew better than to set foot into Estebar's shop when Coralla stood watch.

"Disposal required?" asked the guard officer. "That is three in a year."

"When your wares are in demand..." Estebar let his words trail. Already his mind turned to other matters. Pink fingers of dawn worked their way into the heavy clouds so typical of spring in Freena. He was to have breakfast with Leonie of the golden tresses, Leonie his love, Leonie the one with whom he would share his wealth and his life.

"This work does not make you happy, Estebar," said the watch officer as he moved around the shop poking in dark corners, assuring himself of only the lone thief. "I see it in your eyes as you sell. You are a master craftsman, but you are not happy with your brasswork. You long to return to the sea. It is in your soul to roam, and do not deny it." Doon struggled to swing the stone-rigid thief around to the door.

"My seafaring days are long past," Estebar said, a note of yearning putting the lie to his words. Did Doon know he often went to the docks and watched the ships sailing for distant ports, watching so long their masts shortened and finally vanished over the distant horizon? Estebar shook off this small annoyance. He was content in Freena, and when with Leonie he forgot the sea. "I wish only to become the most prosperous merchant in the realm and—"

"And marry Leonie," Doon finished for him. The guardsman quickly searched the thief, finding a small pouch filled with copper coins. This vanished beneath his uniform tunic as his due for performing the next task required.

"Why do you not approve of her?" asked Estebar, stroking Coralla's head in the direction of the scales. "She is all any man could desire. Beauty, of great standing in the realm, from a fine family, charming."

"If those are the things you want, may you be happy for all your days." Doon grunted as he hefted the burglar and started for the guard station across the market square. With luck, he might get the thief from sight before the merchants opened their doors to the hordes of buyers that came to Freena in these days of prosperity and festival.

"What more can there be?" shouted Estebar after the struggling guard.

He did not hear the mumbled reply. Estebar pushed it from his mind. Doon saw much that the ordinary citizen did not, but this did not make him an expert in matters of the heart.

"Jealous," Estebar decided. "Or envious. And what man would not?" Coralla hissed, but Estebar ignored his friend. Humming a bawdy sea chantey, he went back to his quarters above the store, dressed in his finest clothing, strapped on the sword and dagger, fastening them with a resplendently jeweled buckle, and then returned to the shop in time to oversee his three clerks as they prepared for the day's business. Only when he assured himself all was in readiness did he place Coralla on a high wooden perch at the rear of the shop for a well-deserved sleep.

Life was good for Estebar. He hurried to Leonie's.

\* \* \*

"Leonie! Are you up yet?" Estebar frowned as he banged on the door to the woman's palatial house. Leonie was an early riser and expected him. Listening carefully at the thick door, he heard rapid footsteps inside and smiled. She came to let him in. But the sounds faded and filled Estebar with a confusing mixture of anger and anxiety. Something was not right, and he had spent half a lifetime on the sea trusting his instincts. Hand on jeweled sword hilt, Estebar went around the house in time to see a nimble, black-robed man hurrying down the street.

"Stop!" he yelled. This only lent speed to the retreating man, who clutched something small and shiny white to his chest. Estebar let out an aggrieved sigh. The town filled with petty thieves. Who knew what had been taken from Leonie's home, replete as it was with fine statuary, delicately bound tomes of vast lore, the boxes of gems she owned—or even the fine, personally crafted brasses Estebar had lavished upon her as evidence of his love.

Finding a side door open, Estebar stepped inside and turned wary immediately. The hair on the back of his neck rippled as his sense of wrongness grew. Thieves in the night did not harm their victims. The penalty for theft was severe, but only if the thief was caught in the act. None of the guard sought to recover stolen merchandise or find a long-gone thief. A death, however, brought down the wrath of the entire countryside. During the eight years Estebar had lived in Freena, he remembered only two murders. Both had been avenged quickly and savagely.

Still, he feared for Leonie. A thief might accidentally have injured her from fright at being discovered. On cat's feet, Estebar made his way through the house—one rivaling even the royal family's in richness—until he came to her sleeping chambers. Heart pounding, Estebar stood stock-still as he called to his love.

A muffled moan was his only answer.

Estebar rushed into the bedroom and saw Leonie, lovely Leonie, asprawl on her bed. Face unnaturally pale, her breast rose and fell under the sheerest of silks in a rhythmic, mechanical fashion. Estebar went to her side and stared into her open sea-green eyes. She lived, yes, but there was no recognition in those eyes. Only emptiness.

\*\*\*

The chirurgeon closed his book of spells and moved away from Leonie. He shook his head in sadness as he placed a hand on Estebar's shoulder to comfort him.

"There is nothing I can do," the chirurgeon said softly. "It is damnable, perfectly damnable since they have invaded us from the northlands."

"What are you saying? Her mind is gone for all time?"

The white-haired chirurgeon nodded solemnly. "I fear it is so. They steal our dreams as we sleep, but too often they take more. Leonie has lost all her memories along with her dreams. She is nothing more than a mewling babe in arms."

"But why!" Estebar raged. But he knew the reason. Dream parlors catered to a sickness that festered in this city he did not understand. Magicks only dimly perceived sucked away a sleeping man's—woman's—dreams and trapped them in a ceramic mask. When placed on another's face, the stolen dreams were relived with a vividness transcending ordinary experience. The more vital the person robbed, the more desirable the dream-laden mask.

Leonie was beautiful and filled with memory of adventures only immense wealth and passion could provide. As Estebar stared at her, he knew she was living but no longer alive. The part of her that transformed earthly flesh into a soul had vanished in the night, stolen away by magicks wrought by some interloping mage.

"What has happened?" came a gruff voice from behind Estebar. Turning, the brass merchant saw Leonie's majordomo, if the tall, muscular blond young man could ever be called that without a touch of contempt. Estebar saw no reason for Leonie to have the lazy lout around all day. He did not pursue his duties with any skill and often insulted those visiting his mistress. And if Estebar was any judge, Bolliban allowed the house to fall into disrepair without seeming to notice.

The chirurgeon took Bolliban aside to explain what had occurred. Estebar watched the majordomo's reaction with disgust. Bolliban showed no outrage at his mistress' attack or her condition. Rather, he seemed vexed.

"Does this mean the house is to be shuttered?" Bolliban finally asked. "Should I tend to the accounts?"

"There is no need," Estebar said quickly. "I am capable of handling Leonie's debts. You will receive your due." Even as he spoke, he wondered if he ought to insist on a scrutiny of Leonie's monies. A majordomo had access to more than the house and personal property, and Estebar did not trust this man to handle Leonie's accounts properly. Bolliban was too inexperienced to do a competent job—or too preoccupied with his own future. The obvious relief when Estebar had said he would receive his pay spoke more of greed than loyalty to his mistress.

"See that Leonie gets only the finest of care," Estebar said in a voice too loud. To Bolliban he said, "Will you contact her parents? They are at their country home." Bolliban shrugged, as if this meant nothing to him.

"I know where they reside. I will send a messenger to inform them right away," the chirurgeon assured Estebar. "You should rest. It has been a trying time for you."

"Rest!" flared Estebar, his hand tightening on his sword hilt. "My love lies abed like...like a warm corpse. I must recover the dream mask. With it in place, can you restore her to...to—"

"To her former condition?" The chirurgeon looked uneasy at this. "These are arcane magicks used. I am adroit in the healing arts but these, well, these damnable spells work in opposition to all I have learned."

"With the dream mask, can you restore her?"

The chirurgeon recoiled from the fire in Estebar's eyes, as if he might be burned.

"I can," he said after recovering his voice.

This was good enough for Estebar. He pushed past Bolliban and went in search of a black-clad thief of dreams.

* * *

"It's expensive, this sampling of another's dreams," the dog-faced man said. Estebar wanted to reach out and grab the man's throat under the dewlaps and squeeze until life fled, but to have done so would prevent the flow of information he needed about the thief who had robbed Leonie of her mind and memory. "But it's a pleasure unlikely to be surpassed," the corpulent man said in a conspiratorial whisper though they were alone in the dark alley.

Seldom did Estebar come to this mean section of Freena, but for Leonie he would walk through the flaming netherworld with its exploding mountains of liquid stone.

"I have money." Estebar touched his robe and tapped his fingers suggestively.

"More, I will need more than you carry." Seeing Estebar's flash of anger, the man rushed on, feigning sincerity. His greed shone forth like a watch fire in the night, though. "For security, for secrecy, so no one will ever know of your perfectly acceptable desires. The citizens of this backwater town do not easily accept sophisticated pleasures."

"Very well," Estebar said. He had spent days of agony finding this ugly man, as Leonie lay motionless in her bed, staring vacantly at the ceiling. Estebar held his anger in check. He was close to the sorcerer conjuring the spells, close to the thief who had committed this heinous act. The very secrecy mentioned by the jelly-jowled man also protected the purveyors of the dream masks. Those partaking of stolen dreams were not likely to boast of it—or where they had received the illicit, magick-racked dream mask. Estebar had left more than one whimpering after his inquiries.

What worried him more than the broken bones and severed ears he left behind as a trail was Lieutenant Doon and his devotion to duty. Estebar and Doon were friends, but Doon would never permit anyone, friend or other, to maim and kill indiscriminately. Estebar would hate to kill Doon, but kill him he would to recover Leonie's dream mask.

During his seafaring days, Estebar had done worse than slay a friend. In the hours to come, he might do far worse.

The dog-faced man held out his hand and wiggled his fingers suggestively. Estebar dropped a leather pouch of coins into it and blinked at the speed it vanished.

"This will do for now. You must have more, ten times more, to sample the delights of youth, the passion of the highborn, excitement and fear of killing, the thrill of forbidden lovers in the night." As he recited his litany, the man slowed and eyed Estebar more closely.

"What is it?" asked Estebar, touching his dagger hilt hidden under his robe.

"You are not the sort who usually indulges in such an adventure."

"What sort does?"

Mud-brown eyes turned shifty. "Those less muscular, those lacking in confidence, those with money and no daring." The man talked himself into denying Estebar what he needed.

"I seek something unique, special, that which I cannot get any other way," Estebar said to allay the man's suspicions. "I am a visitor to Freena, here for only a few more hours. I sail with the morning tide and wish to partake of all I can." Estebar smiled wickedly as he continued the lie: "It gets lonely on a ship away from land for months on end."

"A captain recently ported, eh?" The dog-faced man nodded in agreement that such a journey might account for Estebar's request. "And what pleases you most?"

Estebar told him, and the man laughed heartily.

"You have come to the right source for such diversion," the man said. "Be here in one hour. With the money. You will not be sorry." The dog-faced man hurried away. Estebar watched him vanish.

"I will not be sorry," Estebar promised quietly.

* * *

The smoky haze made it difficult for Estebar to see his guide clearly. The fleet-footed youth who had met him had brought him to the outskirts of Freena and this huge building with its magicks-driven mist inside. Estebar had traveled widely and knew when he was being blinded by spells. The vague shapes were only illusion, but what illusion!

Demons and lovely, naked nymphs and their sexual play together flowed all about him in a provocative manner. And none of it was real. Estebar reached out to touch a smoothly curving breast, only to have it melt away under his fingers. He shook himself free of the magically created enchantment. He was not here to enjoy but to avenge.

"Not so fast," he protested. "You vanish in this damnable mist."

"Hurry, if you would enter the dreams of a nubile young woman wrapped in the throes of passion with her lover," the young man said, his face indistinct through the fog.

Estebar almost stumbled as the full import of what the mist-cloaked stripling said struck him. He had purchased the right to don Leonie's dream mask and relive her experiences and wallow in her emotions. Estebar wondered what it would be like, seeing himself through her eyes, feeling the passion he ignited within her sleek body—feeling this passion and remembering how she lit his desires.

The youth laughed. "It is beguiling, wearing another's dreams, isn't it? What does a woman feel as you make love to her. Soon, you will know as no other of our sex can!"

Estebar shook himself, anger replacing the curiosity. The magical mist constantly altered his intentions in coming to this evil place. "How do I know this is not some sham?"

"The dream masks are fashioned by a powerful mage from Greystone. You have heard of Greystone?"

"To the north, where there is no check on magicks," Estebar answered.

"The finest magicks are used, and I personally placed the mask on this one's face. A lovely woman of high station," the youth said, to entice Estebar. "Long, blonde tresses, a face like a goddess. Think of the passions she has experienced—and they will be yours to share. Come, come along." The slender youth slipped into the magical fog, forcing Estebar to lengthen his stride to keep up. Through the mist he went, anger mounting. This slip of a youth was the black-clad thief who had stolen Leonie's soul. Estebar recognized this from his gait, the way he held himself, even the echo of his footsteps on the bare floor.

"Here," the youth said. "Lie back, enjoy fine wine from Orrewia, and let me fetch your prize." Appearing from nowhere came a sumptuous couch with the promised wine and viands on a small table alongside.

Estebar sank to the couch, alert for a trick. The youth left the room through a side door suddenly revealed by a chance parting in the mist. Estebar shot to his feet and caught the edge of the door before it closed and locked. Slipping through the opening, Estebar saw the youth vanish around a turn in a dimly lit, mist-free corridor. Running softly, Estebar followed and saw the dark-haired stripling press his hand against a blank wall. The youth lowered his head, muttered a few words of an unlocking spell to let a section of wall slid back.

Before the youth could enter, Estebar moved quickly behind him, shoving hard. They both stumbled into the small room. On shelves from floor to tall ceiling gleamed white ceramic masks, the dreams and memories of hundreds held captive and awaiting voyeuristic prurience.

"You cannot come in here," protested the youth. "Master Qunin does not permit it!"

"You steal souls for Qunin? As you stole away Leonie's?" Estebar saw the youth's eyes dart to a mask resting on a table to the side of the room and knew where in this multitude of trapped souls he would find Leonie's memories.

"Return to the viewing room or I shall never—" The words died as Estebar's fingers closed around a slender windpipe and squeezed powerfully. Qunin's minion died quickly. Only the master's death remained to Estebar.

He released his powerful grip on the broken throat, panting harshly from emotion rather than exertion. Long years at sea, shorter years fashioning brass, had given Estebar immensely powerful hands. The neck had been nothing more than a twig to snap. He stepped over the body and went to the table, steps slowing as doubt assailed him. With trembling fingers, he lifted Leonie's dream mask. Or was it truly Leonie's? He assumed much, perhaps too much, for he stood in a room filled with hundreds of pilfered souls.

Estebar held up the dream mask and studied it carefully. The smooth ceramic surface had been lovingly fashioned by a master craftsman. Appreciating the workmanship even as he loathed the very idea of what the mask held trapped within its cool ceramic, Estebar moved it so rainbows reflected from the surface, giving hints of the glory that was Leonie. On the inside he made out indentations where the gentle swell of cheeks and chin would fit. He ran the tip of one finger over the surface where Leonie's eyes would have opened and released her dreams and memories to the damnable magicks locked in the mask and imagined the electric tingle as her vitality drained.

"Leonie," he said in a choked voice. "Is it you I hold?"

Estebar knew he might have come to a hasty and erroneous conclusion. He could not take the mask without sampling Leonie's passions, however briefly. Just to be certain he truly held her soul, he told himself. Just to be sure.

Estebar lifted it to his face and found the mask surprisingly warm to the touch. Slowly at first, he insinuated himself into Leonie's mind and soul. Memories of another became reality for him. Leonie's memories became his. The touch of silk, the scent of perfume and another's body, movement of flesh against his—hers—the exhilaration of anticipated lovemaking. It was all his—all Leonie's.

She—he—propped himself up on one elbow in the darkness of the candle-lit bedchamber. A flush rose to her breasts—his—in anticipation of the man approaching. Estebar felt the swift rush of his love's passion, savored her last memories as a hand touched her here and there, moving intimately, thrusting, vying, surging. He knew her passion and hopes and dreams, but he was still a distinct and separate entity intruding.

As he grew accustomed to her, this changed. He meshed fully with his lover's mind and screamed, yanking the mask away. Shaken at the ordeal, Estebar stared at the mask in horror.

As if it might burn him, he placed the mask on the table. Shaken, he leaned against the wall and wiped sweat from his face. He had faced pirates and tentacled creatures in and on the high seas and never before experienced such... revulsion.

Reaching inside the heavy folds of his robes he felt cool smoothness gliding along his arm and down into his cupped hand. A small, weak smile came to his lips.

"A boon I ask of you, dear Coralla." The snake hissed, eyes fixed on Estebar. "Qunin is a northern mage and like all of his ilk, undoubtedly a cautious, fearful man. I can never approach him." Coralla hissed again and flipped agilely from the man's grip. Two silent, quick S-wiggles took the snake from sight.

Forcing himself, Estebar took Leonie's dream mask and carefully placed it in a padded pouch dangling at his belt. He left the room of masks, never looking back.

\* \* \*

97

Estebar held the dream mask, his strong fingers threatening to crush it to dust. He forced himself to relax and give the accursed magical device to the chirurgeon.

"How long will this take?" he asked.

"I cannot say. Perhaps only seconds, if I have properly unlocked the spell. It is far from my field of expertise."

"You are a healer," Estebar said in a monotone. "Heal her." He stared at the supine woman swaddled in her silks and comforters from faroff lands, bedclothes he had given her. The chirurgeon took the dream mask from his rock-steady hand and moved to sit beside Leonie.

Estebar was aware of Bolliban entering. He said nothing. His attention focused solely on Leonie's delicately boned face, the tiny roses blooming in her cheeks, the only sign of life remaining. Then even those disappeared as the chirurgeon placed the dream mask onto her face. The low chant was meaningless to Estebar. He felt the electric surges of magicks at play in the room and knew the chirurgeon did his best to restore the woman's dreams. Her memories. Her passions.

"What is he doing?" asked the majordomo.

Estebar did not answer. He continued to watch the woman for signs of animation. They came quickly. Leonie jerked on the bed, groaned and wrapped her arms about her body. She rolled to one side facing away from him, the mask falling from her face to fall softly to the carpeted floor. Light shone off the mask and made Estebar squint. He shifted his attention from the mask to the woman.

"My darling," she said in a husky voice. "I have dreamt of you. Come to me, come to my bed with your hardness and make love to me again!" Leonie sat up and held out her arms—to Bolliban.

The majordomo blanched, and Estebar thought he would bolt from the room, but Leonie's insistence pinned him to the spot.

"Quickly, Bolliban, come and enter me quickly. There is so little time before that boorish brass merchant arrives."

The chirurgeon gasped but Estebar said nothing. Inside him now dwelled a vast hollow wasteland, there since he had donned the dream mask in Qunin's chamber.

"Go to her," Estebar ordered Bolliban. "You deserve one another." The majordomo swallowed hard, still undecided. Only then did Leonie notice others in the room. She clutched at the bedclothes, holding them under her chin in false modesty. Her mouth opened and closed in confusion.

"Estebar! How did you get here so quickly? It is hardly past midnight." She blinked in bewilderment at the bright rays of sun angling across her bedchamber from the western windows. Leonie swung from Bolliban to Estebar and back.

"You knew, yet you allowed me to restore her memories," said the chirurgeon in a wondering voice. "You could have shattered the mask. Why did you not do that as any other man might have?"

"I love her," Estebar said simply.

"Bolliban means nothing to me, my dearest," cried Leonie, tangling herself in the bedclothes in her haste to reach Estebar. "You are my world. Come to me, come to me!"

Estebar left, ignoring her pleas to return.

\* \* \*

"I do not blame you, Estebar, no, I do not," Lieutenant Doon said, propped against a piling. A dozen yards distant heaved a ship at the dock, bound for Escollandia and other exotic ports along the western coast. "To sail freely once more, to see sights stay-at-homes such I only dream of." Doon sighed.

Estebar stared at the *Serpent's Breath* without really seeing the fine sailing ship. It was only a way out of Freena to him, nothing more.

"Yes, I understand your desire to leave," Doon rambled on. "Freena was once a safe place. Why, in the past week there have been so many deaths. A man who looked like a rabid dog with a knife in his fat gut, and a young man with his neck broken." Doon snapped his fingers. "Just like that. A powerful man, perhaps one driven by intense passion, committed the crime. And there is more. A crime of mysterious origin and cause."

"Oh?" Estebar turned the guardsman.

"A mage, some say, was found frozen in death at a dream parlor, the cause of death both mysterious and of some dispute. Did he die from another mage's curse or some other cause? It is a true puzzle."

"Fancy that."

Lieutenant Doon fixed Estebar with his sharp, appraising gaze. "All these are great and terrible crimes, ones I am sworn to avenge for the good of all citizens."

"You have always done your duty well," Estebar said. He no longer cared if Doon took him into custody for those murders. He did not board the *Serpent's Breath* running to something. He ran from Freena and memories, his own and Leonie's.

"These crimes are complex, perplexing, unlike the usual ones I am called upon to solve." Lieutenant Doon's bored into Estebar's soul, then the guardsman smiled crookedly and said, "You do me great honor, Estebar. Some might say too great a one, making me an equal partner in your flourishing shop."

"You have a mind for business and know all that occurs within the city. You might miss my craftsmanship fashioning the brass for a time, but there are others who are as good. Find them, buy their wares and sell at a healthy profit," Estebar said. "I shall be gone only for...a time."

"Yes, a time. And leaving behind so much."

Estebar said nothing.

"Yes, you leave so much, Leonie and her position in society, her obvious physical charms," Lieutenant Doon said, fingers drumming on his sword hilt. He seemed to come to a decision. "You also leave a friend who wishes you only the best. Here, take this. A small present to keep you amused on your journey, wherever the cresting waves take you." Doon held out a small green, enameled box.

Estebar took it. Doon saluted him smartly, smiled his lopsided grin and went off down the dock without a single glance back.

"All aboard!" bellowed the mate of the Serpent's Breath. "We sail in five minutes. All 'board!"

Estebar walked with great deliberation to the ship, going up the gangplank to lean against the railing and stare back into Freena. In less than the promised time, the ship creaked and sails strained to gather wind. It was hardly soon enough for him. The docks diminished in size and soon vanished entirely as the ship reached the high seas. Only then did Estebar examine the small box Doon had given him. Carefully, he opened the lid. Inside lay Coralla, the snake's black eyes gazing up in reptilian joy at being reunited with his friend.

For the first time in a week, Estebar laughed heartily and knew the future to be brighter than his past.

# Yesterday's Ghosts

*I wrote this short story back in 1976 to have something to read at Yuccacon, where I was GoH. Looking back now, I see the story combines a lot of themes I have used in other stories in other ways. There is even a hint of Wild West history tossed in, eight years before I wrote my first western novel. When Bruce Arthurs opened up the 1991 World Fantasy Convention anthology, asking for stories with Southwestern themes, I sent this in and it was accepted for* Copper Star.

The asthmatic coughing of a poorly tuned engine disturbed the silence along the treacherously narrow mountain road. Pebbles rattled down the side of the cliff, skittering off other, larger rocks as the jeep edged along the sheer drop, with inches to spare. Now and then a stone dropped into the Gila River with an echoing splash; other than this occasional disturbance, the distant river's flow was drowned out by Harry Norton cursing volubly, never repeating himself until he reached a widening in the rocky road. Then he lapsed into silence, his head resting on the cold plastic steering wheel.

"What's the matter, Harry?" Lefevre was as nervous as his friend but didn't want to show it. "I thought you knew how to drive a four-wheel."

"God, Lefevre, I'm terrified of heights. That had to be a good five hundred feet straight down back there."

"No," Lefevre said lightly, "couldn't have been more than two-fifty. Besides, the way this damned darkness swallows up the headlights, you couldn't possibly see half that far. It's the cold that's getting to me." He pulled his windbreaker closer to a body going to paunch and shivered. Not even when he was on assignment in Canada, doing the piece on those fools trying to reopen the Northwest Passage, had he felt this chilled to the bone. There was something insidious about the White Mountains and their freaky air currents he disliked intensely.

"If McIntire hadn't given us triple pay and golden time for this, I'd've told him to cram it. I'm getting too old for this. And all for what?" Norton straightened and got the jeep into gear again.

"I know what you mean. Do a crummy story on Indians, and all of a sudden we're the bureau's resident experts. We did parlay that Navajo killing into front-page stuff, though. My byline, your pictures."

"This story had better be damned good, Lefevre," Norton told him. "I hate heights, and if I so much as see a snake, that's it."

"Hell, the last person eaten alive by a rattler was a long time ago. Maybe last month."

Lefevre saw his cameraman's mouth thin to a line, the lips a frostbitten blue. He reached out and shook the man's shoulder enough to reassure him. "Hey, that was a joke. This John Blue Claw's waiting for us with a nice cup of hot coffee and a Pulitzer-Prize-winner of a story. McIntire wouldn't have shipped us all the way to Nowhere, New Mexico, if it wasn't good. The accounting department has been on his case since they found that trip of his to the Bahamas last year."

"I wish I were home."

"Me, too." Lefevre wanted to bitch about the cold and the lonesome drive into the mountains and his hemorrhoids and how he'd been cheated out of a date with the slinkiest honey-blonde he had seen in years, but he didn't. Harry Norton could be such a prima donna. He had to humor him, keep him happy and get some of his prize-winning photos of whatever malarkey this Indian with the Death Valley Days name planned. News first, comfort second. He wished they could have found a more modern four-wheeler to rent, but Silver City wasn't exactly the crossroads of America. The sputtering 1947 Willys barely made the climb up each successively steeper hill.

He pulled out a pencil-sized silver flashlight and peered at the map spread across his lap. He looked up at the dark mountains and tried to puzzle out their location. One pine-tree-studded ridge looked like another to him, and he wasn't at all sure the bitter, clear air was an improvement over New York smog. At this altitude there wasn't enough oxygen.

He wiped his nose, wondering if he was allergic to the cypress brushing like cobwebs against his face as they drove along.

"Harry, there it is! We finally got here."

"Wherever that is," grumbled Norton.

The jeep clattered to a halt a few yards from a fire blazing in the center of a sandy pit. The cheery fire should have lightened his mood. It didn't. Lefevre couldn't shake the feeling of walking into a library and having to whisper. He tried to rationalize it as an overactive imagination, or even the nagging claustrophobia from being cooped up in the stone-walled canyon.

Dim figures crouched near the fire for warmth, their silhouettes revealing only a vague claim to humanity. The presence of others normally excited Lefevre; they meant a story wasn't far off. The utter silence dampened his usual high spirits.

Norton clambered from the jeep to unlimber his Nikkon. He checked the settings, grumbled until he found a roll of high-speed black-and-white film, and then buttoned his knee-length brown trench coat to prevent elusive body heat from abandoning him totally, as a slight breeze kicked up from up the canyon.

"This," Norton said, "should be Blue Claw's sacred ground. Want me to get a couple establishing shots of it?"

"Yeah," said Lefevre. "I'll get the tape recorder ready. If we're really going to see anything important tonight, as McIntire promised, we'll want everything in the can."

The metallic click and hiss of the automatic film winder told Lefevre that Norton had already begun his work. He snapped on his recorder, tapped the mike until the VU meter jiggled, and then slung the unit over his shoulder. He was ready for bear—or Blue Claw.

As he approached the fire, a voice that came from behind said, "You are early."

Lefevre and Norton spun around, trying to locate the source. When Lefevre turned back, the figures he had seen crouching at the fire had vanished as surely as if they had turned to smoke and joined the lazy upward spiral from the pinon-fed fire. As he turned in a full circle, the wind kicked up even more and left a frosty sensation in his limbs.

Lefevre covered his nervousness by blurting, "I'm Lefevre, UPI. Are you Blue Claw?" He still didn't know where the damned Indian was and that made him nervous. Thoughts of massacres raced through his head. How did he know this Blue Claw wasn't some whacked out serial killer who had duped McIntire into sending them here?

"I am Blue Claw."

Even though Lefevre stared directly into the deep shadow, he never saw how the Apache managed to just appear. One instant there was nothing, the next a man stripped naked to the waist stood in front of him.

"Aren't you cold?" he asked, not knowing what else to say. Blue Claw wore only leather leggings and a few swipes of gaudy paint on his upper torso that couldn't possibly hold back the cold winds blowing through the Gila Wilderness.

"The Winds of Change chill only the soul, not the body," Blue Claw said. "Come closer, to the fire. The ceremony will begin soon."

Lefevre glanced down at his recorder. It picked up every word. He wasn't sure what kind of story he'd get out of this. Certainly nothing as memorable as Wounded Knee, but events like that happened only once or twice a decade.

"What ceremony is this? I've seen most of the dances. The Eagle Dance, the—"

"Tonight the flow of time will be dammed, and the river's bed will be altered to its proper course. Lives long past will be again, and those that are now will be as if they never were."

Lefevre snorted quicksilver plumes of kinetic art swirling into the night air. He sniffed and cursed his dripping nose, knowing every snort and sniffle was being picked up by his condenser microphone. "That sounds like New Age, channeling bullshit." He started to turn off his recorder. McIntire had sent him on a wild goose chase. His boss would owe him for this one—dearly.

"You want any more pictures?" asked Norton.

"Let's go. If we hurry we can be back at the motel in Silver City before the bars close at two."

"Mountain men," Blue Claw said unexpectedly. "Your great-grandfather was Clyde Carstairs."

"What?" Lefevre was fed up now. "My family came from France. Come on, Harry."

"Wait," said Norton. "My great-grandfather was a mountain man. Up around Taos. How did you know that?"

Lefevre snorted again. "He's like any other fraud psychic. He looked it up somewhere."

"Carstairs killed the Apache." Blue Claw's eyes burned in the night. Lefevre shook his head. It was a trick of the light, nothing more. But he felt unexpectedly giddy. He had to take a deep breath to steady himself.

"Lefevre..."

"Come on, Norton. He's running a scam. I'm surprised McIntire fell for it. We should let Gloria handle this. She's the expert in mediums and psychic bullshit."

"You forefathers were explorers, trappers, stealers from my people," Blue Claw said, pointing at Norton. "And your ancestor, Mr. Lefevre, was a conquistador, a haughty Spaniard. He stole from the Jicarilla Apache, he killed and enslaved." Lefevre wasn't sure but Blue Claw had dismissed Norton and focused on him without seeming to move a muscle.

"So sue me," Lefevre said, getting angry. "Even if that's true, I don't buy the notion that the crime of my father is also my crime. The damned courts might, but I don't." Lefevre started away but Norton hung back. Lefevre turned to order his cameraman to join him. What he saw in the dancing yellow and orange flames made him hesitate. Smoke stung his eyes—and the forms. The forms he had seen before were back. They leaped and twisted in pain in the fire.

In the fire.

And yet there was only the soft trilling of wind through the tall pines. How could there be such pain and no cry of agony accompanying it?

"I am Harvard educated, a psychologist," Blue Claw said. "I know your ways, but you do not know mine. There is a gestalt, a mass mind greater than the individual so cherished by your culture, that makes the Ceremony of Changes possible when forces come together at a nexus. This night, here, now, there is such a joining of forces."

"There's no one else here," Norton said, turning around. Lefevre looked from the tormented figures in the fire to his cameraman. How could he say that, when the men and women in the fire were just a few paces away?

"All Apache come together in me this night, just as the life-threads of your people come together in you. We begin." Blue Claw took two deliberate steps forward, allowing the reflected firelight to highlight his features. Prominent cheekbones rose on either side of a well-formed Roman nose. Ebony black eyes stared past—through—Lefevre, and coarse black hair cropped straight across his forehead made Blue Claw look more like a barbarian than an Ivy League scholar.

Lefevre cursed himself for not doing more research before coming to New Mexico and this god-forsaken place hidden in the Gila Wilderness. McIntire should have briefed him better, but he had gotten the feeling his boss hadn't understood the story. That happened often enough. A tip came from another department or higher up in UPI, and McIntire responded with his best team. He had instincts that counted for more than any research.

But Lefevre was unable to figure what McIntire had picked up on to actually dispatch them halfway across the country. Blue Claw was some sort of crazy. A story might come out of it, but it was more a National Enquirer story than anything the UPI would want.

"Punishment. Revenge. Retribution for years of crimes against the Apache. We will swim up the stream of time and shift it into the proper direction, the direction without the white man putting his foot on our necks!"

The words took Lefevre by storm. He inhaled deeply, coughed as he sucked in a lungful of the pungent smoke, and finally choked out, "What are you talking about? You were a bunch of savages before we came. You're parasites living off us now. We've given it all to you on a silver platter. Hell, look at you. You say you've got a Harvard education, when my own kid struggled along to pay tuition at a cheap state university."

Lefevre stopped, shaken. He never involved himself emotionally in a story, but something inside him had risen up like a leering beast and lashed out, unchecked and powerful.

Blue Claw smiled as if hearing a joke. Lefevre started to apologize, then became confused. The whirlwind around him robbed him of words, stole logic, stirred prejudices he denied having.

"Our language, Mr. Lefevre, is more complex than English or French. Athapaskan tongues combine much into a single word. I could utter such a word fully describing you, and all Apaches, be they Chiricahua, Jicarilla, Western, or Mescalero, would know instantly of your heredity and what you will become this night."

Lefevre found himself hypnotically captivated by Blue Claw. He didn't want to pour gasoline on an already explosive situation, but he heard someone speaking and knew it was his voice. "We were stronger. We took your land because you were constantly warring among yourselves."

"The time nears. Waves from the past break against the shores of your mind, bringing old thoughts to the surface. To achieve the fullest humiliation of knowing victory and then suffering defeat, you must know your fate."

"That metaphysical claptrap might impress Harvard academics or simple savages, but not me!" Lefevre wiped at sweat popping onto his forehead. The harder he tried to stanch the torrent or words, the more he insulted Blue Claw. And it felt good, it felt right.

Norton shook Lefevre's shoulder. "You wanted to go, man. Let's get out of here. There'll be lawsuits out the wazoo if you don't cool it."

"Mr. Lefevre finds it hard to leave," Blue Claw said softly. "He has been selected as the vessel of contempt that will be broken. He claims French ancestry but there is more of the Spanish in his blood." Blue Claw chanted, too low for either Lefevre or Norton to make out the words. He spun in a tight circle and raised his hands, imploring the diamond-edged stars above.

"Tonight time will slow and then stop. I will merge with the Great Spirit, and the Apaches will again dwell in harmony. We will again live honorable lives, killing our enemies with stealth and cunning!"

The flames danced in tightly constrained circles and became fuller-bodied figures. Lefevre swallowed hard, and his mouth turned to cotton. Women and children died in those flames. Rifles and knives slaughtered, and scalps were taken, and never did he see the assailants—but he knew. White men did it. Sand Creek. Lefevre knew. Lefevre remembered. Slowly, the bloody memories returned, and he wept even as hatred welled inside him.

Damned redskins! Red niggers! He hated them all.

Blue Claw reached into a pouch dangling at his waist and pulled out a gut string with a single bear's claw tied to the end. He held it, watching its slow circular motion.

Lefevre tried to back away, to run from the claw. He couldn't. He was transfixed. The claw began to spin faster and faster. A *deja vu* sensation warned him where it would stop. As if dodging a bullet, he weaved and wobbled and tried to fall to his knees to avoid it pointing at him. He tried. He failed. The claw unerringly trained on him as surely as a compass needle found north.

"It is decided," said Blue Claw. "You are the nexus of power for your people, as I am for mine." He clapped his hands twice. From within the fire came a world swirling of embers that arched into the air, touched the cold night sky, and slowly floated back, becoming a book that lightly touched Blue Claw's fingers.

Blue Claw stepped forward and thrust the book out. Lefevre took it and strained to see the title of the embers-born book. *The Spanish Conquest of the New World.*

"What am I supposed to do with this? It's written in Spanish. I don't understand..."

"When the time comes, you will know what to do," Blue Claw said. He stepped back and began heaping wood on the fire, nurturing it to a blaze that sent a cloying curtain of dense smoke into the air. Blue Claw vanished behind this veil.

"What's going on?" asked Norton.

"He's purifying himself in the smoke to avoid ghost sickness. He doesn't want to become infected with the spirits of the dead," Lefevre said, not knowing how he knew. Memories assaulted him from all directions, ugly ones, shameful ones. He tried to cry at the agony he remembered, but opposing emotions rose to blot out any compassion. He hated. Those women and children dying deserved their fate. They weren't human. Subhuman. Slaves and nothing more.

The baleful hooting of an owl in the distance fed his tension. He watched as Blue Claw emerged from the thick smoke and donned a buckskin shirt decorated with fragments of glass crazily reflecting light as he moved. A headdress appeared from the darkness and fitted itself to his head, not a single strand of his sacred hair being touched by human hands. When his clothing was settled properly, Blue Claw reached into his pouch and pulled out a tiny bag with three dangling rawhide strings.

"That," Lefevre said, his voice coming from another's lips, "is the medicine man's *hoddentin*. It's magic powder made from tule."

"How do you know?" Norton was puzzled by his friend's knowledge.

"I...I don't know," whispered Lefevre, hating himself for not being able to raise his voice. The hooting of the distant owl sounded again as the cold breeze died.

"Those are medicine cords," he said dully. Lefevre watched as Blue Claw swung them over his head. Lefevre stepped closer to the smoking fire, ignoring the surge of heat from tendril-fingers reaching for him. He thought he heard distant screams.

The fiery figures beckoned to him. Perversely, he tried to join them. Norton held him back and kept him from setting himself on fire. The tiny screams were drowned out by the slow booming of a drum, monotonous and in counter-tempo to the owl's hooting. Something elemental about the rhythm caused Lefevre's stomach to knot like a hangman's noose. His eyes were unable to stray from the human figures locked within the flames.

Blue Claw gyrated, twisting and dancing faster and faster around the fire, darting in and out, sprinkling his gray powder everywhere. Lefevre jumped back when he saw a brilliant vision of silver and gold in the flames, as a cascade of the *hoddentin* floated into the hungry vortex. The images had formed perfectly and showed a Spanish nobleman in full plate armor, arrogantly sneering as he examined a golden platter.

The Apache seemed satisfied with the sudden flare of color. He undid first one, then another, and finally the last of the medicine cords. Carefully placing them in a triangle around the fire pit, he chanted louder and louder. The drum reached a harmonic frequency that threatened to explode Lefevre's brain. He was being ripped apart by the sound. Thoughts of leaving drifted across his numbed mind, yet...yet he was held captive by the flames. He drowned in a new maelstrom of color and memory when Blue Claw sprinkled more *hoddentin*.

Casteñada sneered haughtily as he rode into Chicilticalli. The disdain on his patrician lips told of lands conquered, dreams of more people to be enslaved. An army marched beside his froth-covered steed, muskets at ready to fend off the emaciated *indios*.

The scene in the fire changed. Casteñada wavered, a figure caught in a desert's heat mirage. Growing indistinct, he vanished. The entire expedition searched frantically for their missing leader until one by one, they too rippled from sight and...nothing...was left.

The mountains jutted serene and lonely in the distance. Save for a single band of Apaches trudging on foot across barren lands, the burning country was undisturbed by human presence.

The flames exploded in a rainbow of color as Blue Claw tossed more *hoddentin* into the fire. For the first time, Lefevre was aware of the man's words. Not English, he decided, but Apache. And he understood the exhortations as if they were in his native tongue.

"Great Spirit, aid me! Great Spirit, become one with me! Drive them from our lands. Make your will known through me! Change the way it was. Give us a new today!"

The flames roared higher with the blinding suddenness of a lightning bolt, and Lefevre saw a frontiersman scalping Indians, claiming bounties. Squaws, warriors, children, it made no difference to the Scotsman. He indiscriminately slaughtered and scalped any human crossing his path. The man who looked so much like Lefevre's boss McIntire became transparent, clearer than a pane of glass. He vanished entirely when Blue Claw invoked the names of Cochise and Victorio and Mangas Coloradas.

"Great war chiefs! Fought our common enemy! Fight the Comanche! The white man is no longer among us! His presence fades as the Great Spirit sucks it up. Give battle to the Pima, steal their women, gain honor, great chiefs, as you return us to our rightful place!"

Lefevre understood it all. The Chiricahua dialect was second nature to him. The heat from the fire of lost souls warmed him, even as it threatened to consume him. Momentary fear at what was happening made him want to run, to escape from—what? He was held firmly in the grip of the chant, prisoner in the circle of Apache magic, Apache minds melding together. Yesterdays faded and were replaced with different ones. The Spanish were no longer preeminent in the New World.

Stomach churning and lungs burning from the *piñon*-fed blaze, he turned to Norton. As he watched, the cameraman faded like one of the visions in the fiery viewing screen of the bonfire. Lefevre tried to reach out, to grip his friend's sleeve, but lead-heavy arms refused to obey. His voice was caught and trapped deep in his throat. He couldn't even warn Norton to...to what?

Confused, he looked at the sandy spit. Blurred footprints in the sand reminded him of—who? Someone he knew. Harry Norton, his friend of twenty-three years. He'd known him back in Quebec. No, not Quebec. What made him think that? He'd meant to say New York, the British capital. But what did—the name eluded him. He knew no one in New York. He hated the British with Gallic fervor.

Lefevre's attention lifted from the empty sand to the cotillion of flame. General Crook melted like a snowman in a blast furnace to be replaced by General Nelson Miles. He lasted scarcely longer. Lefevre felt a thrill of menace as he saw Geronimo walking away from the arched doorway of a Dutch Reformed Church, moving backward from St. Augustine and racing home to Ojo Caliente. The reservations in the far-off land never existed.

There were no whites to put Nachez or Mangas or Geronimo there.

The chanting thundered in his ears. His hands shook with the victory of the moment, fingers clenching the parchment book he'd been given by Blue Claw. He stared at its fluttering pages and knew what he must do. The book had been born of fire. It must return.

Pages and embers mingled as he threw the book into the blaze. A clap of thunder split the night and staggered him, rolling on and on and on across the mountain range. Then there was nothing.

The sudden cessation of all sound released him from the grip of his trance. For a long minute, he thought he was deaf. Then, in the distance, he heard the mournful hooting of an owl, the harbinger of the spirits of the dead. Luckily it was receding, a good omen. And what was a good omen for the Apaches was sure to delight the governor-general.

He waited until Blue Claw came to him. Bowing deeply in his most courtly fashion, Lefevre said, "Chief Blue Claw has spoken with his gods?"

Blue Claw sneered. "You are ignorant, Lefevre, and a fool. The medicine man becomes one with the Great Spirit. I have done so this night. The proposed dealings between your people and mine are acceptable."

Lefevre experienced a momentary disorientation. What was this savage talking about? The sensation passed and he said smoothly, "You do King Philippe great honor. Our firearms are the finest in the world. You have heard of their efficiency against the Huns, how the Kaiser was crushed a second time using our new rapid-firing rifles."

A horse neighed loudly. Lefevre's attention strayed to the animal. Surprise at seeing it instead of a battered jeep washed over him. Giddiness caused him to weave about as if he were drunk on cognac. Jeep? What was that? Of course the Apache had horses. They had stolen then from the careless British.

Looking into Blue Claw's dark eyes snapped the negotiations into the proper perspective. The sudden gleam in the savage's eye told him the mission was successful. The rapid-firing rifles—machine-guns they were called by the Huns—were the inducement needed to crack the trade barrier to the Apache Nation. French intelligence told of increased depredations by the Comanches and even the Pimas. Since the Navajo had been forced to the far west by the Apache, only those two hereditary enemies remained between the Crow to the north and the Aztec to the south. Blue Claw needed the weapons if his people were to survive.

"You still prize the yellow metal? We have raided along the Great Sea and stolen much from the yellow skins. Their ships come from afar for this metal. It means so much to you that you will give us many rifles?"

"Many rifles, Blue Claw." Lefevre would do anything to annoy the Japanese, including incitement of the Apache against them. Their gold mines on the western shores were world-renowned. The King could do with a little of that wealth flowing into his royal coffers and away from the avaricious Shogun's.

"Many rifles to attack even the British outposts?"

Lefevre smiled wryly. The savage wasn't stupid. He knew how the French wished the British hold to be lessened in the east.

"Perhaps," Lefevre said, "we could spare even a few of the motor vehicles captured from the Huns."

"What does the Apache need of such smelly things? We have our horses and now the finest of rifles! Arrange it, Lefevre. Arrange it with your governor-general."

Blue Claw leaped to the back of a powerful white stallion, put heels to the animal's flanks and raced off, brother to the wind. As the dust cloud settled, Lefevre saw only empty mountains reaching to the starlit sky. The Apache medicine man and war chief had vanished completely.

He took a deep breath and let it out slowly, watching as the silvery plumes danced joyously before him. The next time it would be easier. It would continue growing easier until the Apache was dependent on Quebec. When that happened, the Sun King's old dream would be realized. All this vast wild land would be under direct French rule.

Adjusting his ceremonial saber, Lefevre swung into the saddle of his own mount. He winced as the muscles of his inner thighs protested. This was a barbaric method of travel. He much preferred the motorcar in his native Quebec, but for the prestige of this diplomatic coup a little discomfort was a minor price.

As he fell into the rhythm of the trotting horse, he had the sudden sensation of someone watching him. Glancing over his shoulder, he thought he saw a man dressed in a ridiculous knee length brown coat clutching a small box as he stood beside the embers of the dying fire. As Lefevre stared, the wraithlike figure faded and evaporated like mist. Ambassador Lefevre could not rid himself of the uneasy feeling that he had known a man like that before, somewhere else.

But that was ridiculous. He spurred his horse toward the North Star. It would be a hard ride to Acoma and then to the French outpost on the Mississippi, and he was eager to return home. Because of this night's success, the Indians would soon pay obeisance to the King. Soon. Soon.

# Dragon Debt

*Novellete lengths are difficult, being neither concise enough for a short story nor long enough for a novel, but Fred Saberhagen was kind enough to let me do this for his 1995 anthology* An Armory of Swords. *Playing in another author's universe again, this time Fred's Swords' world, was a distinct pleasure because I "had" to reread so many of the original stories. Don't throw me in that briar patch! Of all the swords, Dragonslicer has to be my favorite—and thus came about the story. Fred and his son Tom, as well as Walter Jon Williams, Mike Stackpole, and Pati Nagel, all have dazzling stories within the covers, too.*

The gleaming, impossibly sharp sword slashed through the air so close that Trav Gorman jumped back in panic. The blade swung around, and the fifteen-year-old couldn't take his eyes off its steely meter-long length. For a brief instant it refracted sunlight into a delicate fan of colors, then came whirring back at him. This time he forced himself to remain rigidly immobile, no matter the cost to his nerves.

The dragon-slaying blade lightly touched the young man's pendulous earlobe. Trav had thought it would be warm with its special Vulcan-forged magic. Instead, it was as cold as any ordinary metal blade.

"And that's how I slew the last of the great dragons preying on my village of Hues," loudly boasted Kennick Strongarm. The tall, muscular man twisted his wrist slightly and the god-forged Dragonslicer heavily dropped to Trav's shoulder, as if conferring knighthood on him.

But such was distant from Kennick's mind—and Trav's. Trav's face burned hotly with shame at showing any emotion, and he tasted salty blood from a tongue bitten in fear. Kennick did all he could to disgrace him to bolster his own image, and today was the worst yet, with half the village of Slake looking on. Worse than this, Trav's sister Juliana stood just behind Kennick, laughing at her brother's humiliation.

"You're so brave," Juliana said, hanging onto Kennick's sword arm. "Tell us again. How many dragons have you slain with this marvelous weapon?"

"Eight," Kennick said, puffing up and turning to slide the blade back into its gaudy sheath. Trav found it impossible to tear his eyes from the blade. Its length was encrusted with gems the size of his thumbnail, and the silver-wire-wrapped handle seemed made for Kennick's huge grip.

"I thought you said nine," spoke up Trav's father, Merrick Gorman. "I definitely counted nine in your tale."

"Eight, nine, I lose count in the heat of battle. There has never been such a weapon as Dragonslicer," Kennick said, again whipping out the blade and holding it high in the autumn sun. His dramatic gesture quelled more questions, but Trav saw only reflected light in the blade and nothing in the wielder. "And the gods have granted its power to me!"

"Juliana," Trav said around his bitten tongue, trying not to let any of the blood in his mouth trickle forth and further humble himself. "Juliana! We were on our way to gather berries."

"You go," Merrick Gorman told his son. The man was slightly stooped from too many years of desperately hard work in fields that produced too little. His lined face, more leather than skin after the long sweltering summer, beamed with approbation for the newcomer. "Let Juliana have some time with the champion of Slake."

"Champion!" cried Trav. He spat, as much to show his disgust for Kennick as to clear his mouth of blood. "He's no champion. He's only—"

Merrick Gorman slapped his son and sent him reeling. "Don't speak of Kennick that way. He is a hero. You can tell from his demeanor—and don't forget that he carries one of the twelve swords forged by Vulcan. For that alone, he deserves your respect."

Trav saw the fear in his father's muddy eyes—and hope, hope that was seldom there of late. To marry his only daughter to a hero, a slayer of dragons, commanded his ambition and imagination. The opinion of a fifteen-year-old boy with no particular skill nor hope for apprenticeship mattered far less to him at the moment. And Trav had to admit the glow in Juliana's tanned face was more than adulation.

It might be love. That rankled more than any prolonged emptiness in his belly. He was the only one who saw Kennick for what he was.

"Why can't you see what a liar he is?" Trav backed away. His father didn't hear his mumbled retort, nor did any of the others in the small crowd. The village of Slake was as short on dreams as Merrick Gorman, the dreams Kennick offered with his wild tales. Trav turned and ran through the muddy village, passing no great houses, no fine stores brimming with merchandise such as in Westering and other big towns, and worst of all, he passed many miserable sod huts left empty by the withering sickness that had held Slake hostage for three long months.

A tear welled in the corner of Trav's eye as he thought of his lost mother and three brothers. He brushed the wetness away. There was work to do, and standing about lionizing a stranger who had come to Slake only a week before accomplished nothing. Trav didn't resent his sister not being sent with him to gather berries, but he wished she saw with clearer vision. He didn't want her hurt. She and his father were the only family he had left.

"A braggart, that's all he is. Well fed because foolish people listen to his stories and believe them and give him food to be lied to again!" Trav spat more blood and tried to calm himself. Why was he the only one who heard the hollowness of Kennick's tales?

Trav knew the answer, and it burned inside him like a festering wound. The people needed a hero to take their minds off their dreary, dangerous lives. The withering fever and poor crops, and the demon that had ravaged Slake a year earlier, all broke spirits and made any diversion welcome. And Trav knew his father wanted Juliana to marry well. No man under the age of forty remaining in Slake qualified, most being dim or dirt poor or crippled. A wandering paladin expertly swinging one of the Twelve Swords—the Sword of Heroes!—might be Juliana's only chance to marry away.

"But he lies," moaned Trav, going over the conflicting tales Kennick had spun. Each repetition grew like a tumor, and always so that the teller fought greater battles and triumphed more heroically.

Trav slowed his run and turned toward the chain of S-shaped lakes that gave the village its name. Half a hundred streams fed the lakes, and he had found his special place along a small streamlet ignored by others in the village. The day was warm for autumn, but the leaves had turned into a rainbow of shimmering colors, and the sharpness in the air from dying summer and birthing winter was second to none for Trav. The winter would be cruel because the summer had been so brutally hot, but now the days were warm and enveloping like a cherished blanket if he stayed in the afternoon sun.

Walking along his special stream, he found the black-and-red-striped berries that would supplement their meals for months after the snows came. Trav gathered slowly, picking with care, trying to forget his father and sister and Kennick and the entire village. Surrounded by the forest, he could imagine life being better.

Movement at the edge of his vision caused him to stop his work and whir about. The gnarled, black-barked limbs of a walnut tree weaved, and a few dead leaves fluttered softly to the ground.

"Who's there?" he called. "Who are you?" Trav put down his berries and ran as hard as he could for the tree. He saw the sharp snap of a limb rebounding into its wonted position, now that it was deprived of a man's weight. Someone had been spying on him—and not for the first time.

Trav searched in vain and returned to his berry picking, when a voice cracked with age echoed across the forest. "Come see what happens, but take care, Trav Gorman!"

Trav heard a distant crashing sound, as if something heavy had fallen through the leafless tree limbs. Heart pounding, he ran as hard as he could in that direction. He twisted and turned through brambles and got turned around, but these were his woods, this was his private place, and no one intruded without him knowing the reason. The young man burst into a small clearing, a streamlet wandering through to form a glade of unparalleled beauty.

And amid the beauty came death. Two huge white birds swooped down, talons raking and beaks pecking. On the ground, its long barbed tail snapping nervously, reared a dragon of such immense size that Trav turned white with fear. The dragon roared and snorted fitful flames at the Great Birds, fangs slashing, and short, talon-tipped hands raking.

One bird, more daring or less agile, came too close. The dragon's breath singed it, and huge jaws snapped shut, sending a curtain of blood and white feathers high into the air. A drop of the spilled blood spattered on Trav's face and burned like molten metal. He backed away, then turned and ran. How long he ran, Trav couldn't say, but he eventually stumbled onto the Slake-Westering road and knew where help lay. Legs rubbery from fear and long exertion, he finally stumbled into the village and found Kennick with Juliana beside the public watering trough.

"Dragon!" he blurted. Kennick turned, gave him a sour look and continued his witty discussion with Juliana.

Trav's sister turned and gestured angrily at him. "Go away, Trav. You're bothering us. I must tell Kennick of available lodging. He intends staying in Slake!"

Trav looked at Dragonslicer leaning against the trough in its hand-tooled leather sheath and started to reach for it. Kennick snatched up the magical sword and laid the long blade across his lap.

"Don't go telling stories, now, boy," Kennick said. "There aren't any dragons in these woods. I've already killed them all." He laughed and returned to romancing Juliana.

Trav backed off, not knowing what to do, where to go. He ran hard back into the woods, daring the gathering darkness and rising wind with its chilled steel edge. He found the streamlet and worked his way up it, not knowing a more direct route. The closer he got to the battleground, the slower he crept and the harder his heart pounded.

At last he saw the glade. The Great Birds' white feathers were strewn everywhere, and one carcass lay across the stream. Trav approached warily, hardly daring to touch it. He remembered the drop of blood on his cheek; the burned spot still stung. The Great Bird was dead, its neck snapped and rent by powerful dragon fangs, but of its killer Trav saw nothing.

But he saw a milky whiteness in the sluggishly flowing stream that was unusual. Trav dropped to his knees and cupped his hands, scooping at the surface and coming away with dozens of small, slick-coated spheres. In the darkness they shone with an inner opalescence that Trav had never seen before.

Holding one up, he fancied he could see shadows moving within. Opening his palm, he let one egg rest there, only to have it dance and roll about.

Trav scooped more from the streamlet and broke open a few of the tiny globes. A pungent yellow and white fluid gushed forth.

"Dragon eggs," he whispered. He had never seen one before, but he had heard the tales, the whispered, fearful warnings. "The she-dragon was laying eggs in the stream, and the Great Birds attacked to stop it."

He looked at the slick of millions of dragon eggs and saw not untold misery and destruction but opportunity. Trav carefully gathered as many of the eggs as he could and went looking for a cool, wet, hidden nest.

* * *

Winter wind whined past the tumble of rocks Trav had pulled into the mouth of the cave. The small sweeps of crystalline white snow blown past the rock stopped a few feet from the nest Trav had built. Keeping the eggs damp had been easy for the first few weeks. Small drips running down the cave walls formed puddles enough to cover the eggs, but Trav had worried when the eggs began drying out after a month in spite of his care and amount of water around the pearly orbs. The shells had turned a mottled brown and hardened—and a few weeks earlier, just before the first heavy storm brought blankets of clinging wet snow, the shells began cracking.

Trav sat tailor-fashion on the cold floor and poked at the four dragons weakly tumbling over each other, looking more like bugs than the land behemoth Trav knew had laid the eggs. He picked up the smallest of the clutch, a dragon smaller than the end of his thumb.

Holding it aloft, he peered into the unfocused yellow-slit eyes. Trav stroked over the dragon's head, marveling at the brown scales softer than any fleece covering the miniature body. A tiny black tongue flicked out of a mouth too small for Trav to insert even his little finger.

"You're so tiny, you're a nothing," he said, cradling the dragonlet. With more bitterness, he added, "You're just like me. Piddling. Nothing more. The runt of the clutch." Trav smiled slowly and said, "That's your name. Piddling." He laughed with delight when the yellow eyes seemed to fix on him, clear, and appraise him with childlike adoration.

Trav put Piddling back into the tiny puddle and watched the dragon stumble and fall, splashing water everywhere in its uncoordinated attempts to stay upright on feet more mouselike than reptilian. Picking up another dragon, Trav recoiled when the beast made a savage snap at his finger. The small mouth failed to circle his finger, but he felt bony ridges scraping his skin. He dropped the green-and-gray dragon back into the puddle. The dragon glared at him, then turned and snapped at Piddling, frightening the smaller dragon.

"You are the biggest," Trav said, "and will grow up larger than Yilgarn." He heaved a deep sigh as he pushed Piddling away from the more combative dragon. "I'll call you Yilg. And you," he said, poking another dragon, "You are ferocious and the stuff of legends. You will be the one to challenge Kennick Strongarm." Trav spat the name. "I'll call you Grendl."

The fourth dragon curled its long, thin tail around itself and went to sleep, oblivious to the struggles between Grendl and Yilg. Piddling stood to one side, watching its brothers fight, with more than a trace of anticipation and anxiety on its expressive face.

"And you, sleepy one, I will name Drowsy." The sleeping dragon snorted and rolled over, never waking.

Trav rocked back and got his feet under him, rubbing his cold hindquarters. He worried that the cave was too cold for his small charges, yet they seemed to thrive. A small dark form scuttled along the cave floor. Trav grabbed quickly, cupping the insect. He felt the pig-bug struggling in its fleshy prison—and then the scavenger bug went berserk when he dropped it between Yilg and Grendl. The two newborns snapped at both the pig-bug and each other. The larger Yilg won after a brief but fierce skirmish, gulping the bug down whole and looking for more.

Trav had already caught several more torpid pig-bugs and dumped them where the young dragons could feed. "Enjoy your dinner," Trav said, his own belly growling. He sat back and watched, marveling at how different the four dragons were. When they had finished their feast, Yilg and Grendl turned on the smaller Piddling.

"Hey, stop that," Trav said, scooping up the small dragon and holding it close. Piddling hissed slightly, and Trav jerked in surprise. The dragon had burned him with a tiny spark from its nostrils.

"So, you're growing," Trav said, knowing a full-sized dragon could burn down a house with a single flare. "Let's see if this puts out your fire." He carried Piddling to the cave opening and dropped the young dragon into a snow bank. The dragon floundered about, legs thrashing. Then Piddling snorted real flames.

Trav grinned and finally applauded his small ward. A plume of steam rose from the superheated snow. Piddling lapped at the puddle he had created, backing off when it froze against his tongue. A second gust of flame was larger, stronger, and created a veiling curtain of steam.

Trav watched in silence as the tiny dragon's intensity increased. It would be some time before Piddling—or even Yilg or Grendl—grew to a size capable of battling Kennick, but the day would come soon, since dragons grew quickly, and Trav would enjoy watching the swaggering dragon-killer face a real opponent.

\* \* \*

Trav shivered hard, trying to keep his teeth from clacking. Juliana lay on the far side of the room, a blanket thrown over her quaking body. The way she shook gave the only sign that his sister still lived. The unnatural quiet after the storm had settled both inside and out preventing them from getting outside for more than a day.

"Where is he?" muttered Merrick Gorman, walking painfully back and forth across the small room in a vain attempt to keep himself warm. "Kennick should have been here by now."

Trav tried to speak but his teeth began chattering. He wanted to tell his father that Kennick wasn't likely to return from Westering if it meant any discomfort. He might have promised to bring wood and much-needed food, but Trav would believe the dragon-killing paladin when he saw tangible proof. Warm proof. Food proof.

"We need wood for the stove," Trav got out. "We cannot last another night. It is still now, and cold, colder than I ever remember."

"So get the wood," snapped his father. "There is no way to get to the woods and chop enough to last more than a few hours, not in this damned cold." He looked at their pot-bellied metal stove, long since cold from lack of fuel. "Why your mother wanted that monstrosity is a mystery to me. A good stone fireplace would serve us better."

Trav wanted to point out that any source of heat would be appreciated, but he lacked the strength to argue. He saw from the way his father's left leg increasingly dragged that he would be unable to gather firewood, even if a new storm wasn't threatening. And Juliana was in no condition to move. All she could do was lie under her inadequate blanket and mutter Kennick's name from between gray-blue lips.

Trav pushed to his feet and went to the door. Snow drifted high, leaving only a small, wan rectangle at the top to escape through. He burrowed a few minutes, ignoring his father's orders to shut the door. Scrambling onto the crusted snow, he looked out over a land that had been totally altered. Slake had vanished, save for a few lucky souls whose chimneys sputtered fitful puffs of white smoke. Gone was the poverty and the horror of the past months, and replacing it was a blinding whiteness, a snowy renewal that brought both beauty and death.

Trav pulled his thin coat tighter around him and began trudging toward the distant woods. It was far to go, too far. The easy wood had been collected long since, and he had scant notion what he might do once he found decent forest. His father had traded their axe for two bushels of grain, on Kennick's advice. The grain had proven of poor quality and hadn't lasted nearly as long as Merrick Gorman had anticipated when making such an extravagant exchange.

Razor-edged wind began blowing, and white ice crystals whipped against Trav's exposed face. He turned up his collar and pulled a scarf woven by his mother over his mouth and nose. The cold still insinuated itself and slowly paralyzed both body and brain.

Hardly knowing where he walked, Trav realized he had blundered across the ice-encrusted "S" lakes and up the streamlet toward the cave where his baby dragons must have frozen by now. It had been weeks since he had been able to tend them. Tears freezing on his cheeks, Trav broke through the tough rind of snow over the cave mouth and was met by a blast of hot air.

Trav rocked back, the sudden heat painful against his frozen cheeks. For a moment, he thought some strange volcanic activity had warmed the cave. Then he realized the heat came from the dragons' own internal fire. The dragons huddled together, their considerable fiery breaths splashing against rocks glowing with red heat. The dragons then settled down and basked in the radiated warmth.

Trav wasted no time in scrambling into the warmth of the once-cold cave. He hunkered down and just stared at the beasts. It had been a month since he had tended them, but they had thrived. Trav reached out and waited for the cat-sized Piddling to waddle over to him and nuzzle his frozen hand.

"You've done well for yourselves," Trav said, picking up the dragon and stroking its head. The dragon snorted and made growly noises, and Trav no longer felt softness in the nut-brown scales, but Piddling made no move to wiggle free of his grip. The dragon turned its head up, as if begging to have its chin scratched. Trav started to run his fingers along the neck and belly but Piddling snapped, yellow eyes glaring.

"So, you've developed a personality," Trav marveled. He looked around and saw Yilg and Grendl sitting near their heated rock, but nowhere did he see Drowsy. He stood and walked around the small cave, hunting for the fourth hatchling. He paused when he saw the skeleton at the rear of the cave.

"The winter has been cruel," he told Piddling. The dragon growled and snorted again, this time snuggling closer to Trav's chest. The youth jumped when an unexpected spot of heat burned into his coat. Trav rubbed at the cindered area Piddling's fire-breathing had sparked. The dragon peered up at him again, this time with more than a little affection in his expression. Like a dog marking territory, Piddling had marked his with fire.

An idea began to form in Trav's cold-numbed brain. Of the dragons, Piddling was the smallest and most amenable to handling. Trav wasted no time

119

stuffing Piddling under his coat. He winced as sharp scales cut into his flesh, but he didn't want the dragon exposed to the bitter cold outside—it would do more than kill the hatchling.

Darkness had settled over the still fall of snow, and the wind had died, leaving behind a glacial temperature that was as bad as the snow and wind. Head down, Trav made his way back to his home, trying not to get turned around in the dark. Everything looked different with more than three feet of snow covering familiar landmarks. Hours later, feet turned into numb lumps of frozen flesh, Trav found the cold chimney of his family's hut.

He found the small tunnel he had pushed away from the top of the door and scooted down on his rear to keep from crushing Piddling. The dragon stirred peevishly for the first time during the long hike home but did not ignite his flame in ire.

"In," called Trav, "let me in." He banged on the closed door but got no answer. Again and again he banged, to no avail. Frantic, Trav burrowed down farther until he reached the latch. The door opened with a suddenness that sent him tumbling into the still, cold interior.

For a ghastly moment, Trav thought both Juliana and his father were dead, but their slow, tortured breaths left faint, feathery trails in the air. Not wasting a moment, Trav went to the iron stove and opened the door. He carefully drew Piddling from under his coat. The dragon shivered with the exposure and crouched inside the stove, eyes wide and questioning.

"Here, Piddling, try this," Trav said, giving the dragon a small amount of the grain Kennick had urged his father to get in trade for their axe. The dragon sniffed at it and turned away. Trav shivered with the cold and realized dragons did not eat grain.

But what could he feed the carnivorous dragon?

There was only one source for the needed meat. Trav slumped to the floor and began pulling off his boots. His toes had turned blue from frostbite, too numb for any feeling. Trav placed a small knife against his smallest toe, closed his eyes and shoved down hard. For a moment, he dared not look—it hardly seemed anything had happened. Then Trav looked and saw he had severed not one but two of his toes and had never felt the pain.

"Here," he said, placing his severed toes inside the stove next to Piddling. The dragon sniffed at them, then stared balefully at Trav, as if asking permission. Trav felt a giddiness resulting from shock at what he had done. He waved a hand, hoping Piddling interpreted the gesture properly.

The dragon sniffed some more, then began daintily nibbling, using its rudimentary claws as hands to hold the frozen meal. Trav tried to turn away but watched in rapt horror and fascination as Piddling cleaned the toe of all meat. Then the dragon belched a powerful flame that spread inside the stove. Not content with a single short blast, Piddling kept up the flame until the iron glowed cherry red. Then the small dragon settled down to eating the second digit Trav had given him.

Sitting next to the hot stove, Trav did his best to bind his foot. Then he pulled his father and sister closer to the stove. They stirred, and then turned toward the heat generated by Piddling's flame. The hut would never be hot, but it would be warm enough.

Especially after Trav fed Piddling four more frozen toes.

\* \* \*

"A great day, it is," said Merrick Gorman, briskly rubbing his hands together. "It is a truly great day for an engagement."

"Father, please," said Juliana, blushing. "Kennick doesn't want any fuss over our betrothal."

"I'm telling the entire town!" Merrick Gorman danced about the small room, now lit with warm spring sun pouring through the door.

Trav stood painfully and hobbled outside. He couldn't bear the notion he had saved his sister from freezing—Piddling had saved her—just to marry Kennick Strongarm. The small dragon had continued warming the iron stove for a week until the cold broke. Not once in that time had either Merrick Gorman or Juliana questioned how Trav had kept them warm, nor had they asked where Kennick had spent the winter.

Trav had returned Piddling to the small cave, sure his three remaining dragons were well-fed with insects and a small rabbit that might have gone into his own stew pot. Those dragons would be Kennick's undoing. When they grew larger, Trav would use them to show the paladin's true colors. Dragonslicer was a fierce, magical blade, but the wielder was weak. Why couldn't Juliana see that? Why couldn't his father?

Trav hobbled outside into the sun, then paused. From behind the sod hut not twenty meters away, Trav saw a hunched-over figure watching him. The village smith and his family had all perished during the winter, no one knew when.

"Wait, who are you?" Trav called. The man jumped as if stuck with a firebrand and bolted across the muddy plains surrounding Slake. Trav started after him, but he couldn't maintain the pace. The man kept glancing back over his shoulder, but he continued to put more and more distance between himself and Trav.

Feet hurting, Trav grimly kept moving. The watcher had dogged his steps for two seasons now, and Trav worried that the unknown man might think to harm the dragons flourishing in their cave and ruin Trav's plans for discrediting

Kennick. If the man belonged to the White Temple and called down Ardneh's wrath, Trav might even find himself damned by the gods for nurturing the dragons as he had done.

What he intended to do with the dragons was dangerous and even sacrilegious, but he did it for a good reason. Nothing else but Kennick's total exposure as the hoodwinker he was would do. Trav was sure that if Kennick was faced with a dragon of any real size, he would turn and run.

It took longer than the previous autumn for Trav to make his way to the cave where his brood hid. Along the way he picked up a few choice bugs and put them in his pocket. The pig-bugs were special treats for the dragons, Trav knew. He approached the cave with some trepidation, looking around for the man he had chased and lost.

Only when he was sure no one spied on him did Trav duck into the cave. The dim light filtering into the cave wasn't sufficient for him to see at first. Only slowly did his vision adjust. The musky smell of nesting reptiles came to him—and more, something he could not place.

Trav jumped when he felt something hard and sharp rub against his leg. He yelped and grabbed at the long, deep scratches before seeing that Piddling rubbed against him, the dog-sized dragon's scales slashing like razors.

"Piddling!" he cried in genuine glee. "You have grown so!" Trav knelt and held the dragon's head in his hands, not moving to stroke or pet as he had once done. "I have a treat for you. And Grendl and Yilg." He pulled the pig-bugs from his pocket and held them out.

Trav jerked back when Piddling snapped ferociously, fangs impaling the pig-bug before it hit the floor. The dragon ate noisily, and then turned yellow eyes to him begging for more.

"I want you to share," Trav said, but he gave the hungry dragon another bug. As Piddling ate, Trav hunted for the other dragons. He found one, small and huddled at the rear of the cave. Trav frowned and tried to identify the dragon. It might have been Grendl, but he thought it was Yilg. Of the third dragon, he saw no trace.

Trav dropped a few squeaking pig-bugs and the dragon—he finally identified it as Yilg—avidly devoured them, but something was wrong.

"You are so small compared to Piddling," Trav said in wonder. The runt had grown twice as fast as his egg mates, leaving the once large Yilg far behind. Yilg was hardly bigger than he had been in the midst of the winter storms.

Trav winced as Piddling rubbed against him once more, begging for more bugs. Trav pulled the last one from his pocket, looked from Yilg to Piddling and back. He dropped the bug between them. Piddling snorted once and sent a gust of flame in Yilg's direction. The smaller dragon backed away and let Piddling eat uncontested.

Trav left and looked around, for the first time his gaze lowered from the possible hiding places a spy might use. White bones, well-chewed, were scattered around the mouth of the cave. Most had sunk in deep mud, partially hiding the remains, but it was obvious the dragons inside had begun foraging on their own.

A moment of fear surged through Trav. He had known how dangerous the dragons were when he had rescued their eggs from the stream. If they hadn't been, Kennick would never be shown for the coward Trav knew he was. The dragons were not as deadly as those allowed to grow up in the wild, away from human contact. These were more pets than predators. But had he really done the right thing nurturing Yilg and Piddling?

Trav didn't know.

\* \* \*

Plans for the late-spring wedding proceeded too quickly for Trav's taste. The entire village, or what was left of Slake, wanted to take part in the festivity of the year. Thinking it possible to discredit Kennick in some way other than risking his dragon pets, Trav had followed Kennick on his self-appointed rounds from village to village. After leaving Slake, Kennick had hurried along the road to the larger town of Westering. Trav had feared he wouldn't keep pace, unable to walk as he once had before frostbite had taken his toes.

He need not have worried about finding Kennick. A large crowd had gathered in Westering's town square when he arrived hours after Kennick. And, as in Slake, the paladin boasted publicly of his fierce fights and punctuated his claims with wild swings of Dragonslicer. The magical sword whished through the air, and gems flashed in the bright sunlight, but Trav felt only emptiness. Kennick talked a good battle, but where was the iron resolve a true hero showed? Trav had seen nothing of it.

The young man worried that he might be wrong, that his father and sister saw with clearer vision than he did. Kennick might be the great champion he bragged of being.

And then Trav's uncertainty turned into seething anger. Hanging on Kennick's arm was a young woman, blonde and beautiful and laughing. She kissed Kennick at the end of his story—and the hero returned the kiss with even more fervor. The crowd cheered and roared even louder when Kennick swept the girl off her feet and carried her away.

Trav shuffled closer and nudged one of the townsmen, asking, "Who's that?"

"Kennick Strongarm? Why, he's the most famous dragon-fighter in the land. Killed a full dozen of them, he has." The man stared at Trav as if he had fallen from the moon.

"No, not him. I know of him. The lady."

"That's Beryl, Kennick's wife-to-be."

"What?" Trav was sure he had heard a'right, but had to be sure.

"Beryl, she's his betrothed. They're to be married in a fortnight."

"She's a lovely woman," Trav said, keeping his anger in check. "She has the look of wealth about her, too."

"Well that she should. She's the daughter of the town's grain broker." The man called and waved to a friend, leaving Trav standing in the center of Westering, alone in the crowd still milling about. Most joked about Kennick and Beryl, making lewd comments about the man's prowess. From all Trav could tell, Kennick was well known and had cut quite a swathe through the womanly segment of Westering's population.

"And through Slake's," he said to himself.

All worry over raising the dragons to challenge Kennick burned away in his rage. He had been right about Kennick Strongarm. Too right for his own satisfaction. He began the long trip back down the road for Slake, knowing Juliana would never believe what he had to say—but she would believe when Kennick showed his true colors when he faced a real dragon and fled.

\* \* \*

Trav's feet ached horribly, but he kept moving, not returning to Slake with his news of Kennick. He knew he couldn't convince either his father or sister of Kennick's treachery. If they followed their paladin, they would see that he had a woman—a wife!—in every town. But simply telling them would accomplish nothing. They knew he disliked Kennick and wanted to discredit him.

The dragons were Trav's only chance to prevent his sister's tragic wedding.

Twilight slipped like soft velvet over the forest and the chain of "S" lakes a dozen kilometers from his home. Following his special stream and turning for the dragons' cave, Trav had the feeling of being watched.

"Who are you?" he called, stopping to peer into the murky forest. Heavy limbs dangled and hid any spy from sight, but Trav felt another's presence. "Why are you snooping about like you do?"

"You tend dragons," came a voice creaking with age. "They will kill you. Even now they are abroad, killing and eating human prey."

Trav hobbled a few meters and yanked at a low-growing shrub. The man he had almost seen so many times before crouched, staring up at him with rheumy eyes gone glassy with cataracts. Trav stepped back, the odor from the old man overpowering.

"What is it to you?" Trav spoke with more assurance than he felt, even when confronted with the pathetic reality of his watcher.

"They kill. They are creatures of evil. I spent my life killing them, but they have killed me. Look at me, look!"

"I see an old fool with nothing better to do than creep about."

"I killed dragons with Dragonslicer," the old man said in his quavering voice. "The burden was too great, so I put aside the sword."

"And Kennick Strongarm picked it up."

The old man coughed loudly and shook his head. Trav was repelled when he saw the lice jumping from the long, unkempt greasy gray hair. He and his family might be poor, but they knew the value of bathing.

"He lies."

"On that score, we can find common ground for agreement," Trav said, anxious to see how his wards fared. After the excursion to Westering, he wanted Piddling and Yilg to grow as big as houses to frighten off Kennick.

"I placed the sword in a cairn not twenty kilometers distant," the man said. "Call me Wyatt. I am Wyatt the Magnificent, Dragonslayer and champion of the oppressed." He coughed and spat a black gob. Where the phlegm touched new growth, the grass died. More established grass fared little better under the poisoned onslaught.

"Of course, of course," Trav said.

"Young, I am. As young as you. Well, not quite. A few years older, but I carried Dragonslicer. It wore down on me, wore me down like water dripping on a stone, year after—"

"Enough," Trav said, tired of Wyatt's senile meandering. "You are old. Ancient. And you have no business following me."

Wyatt cocked his head to one side and said, "They're gone. Not in the cave. Both are out killing."

Trav tensed. How much did this crazy hermit know of his scheme?

"They range farther now, out to slay humans. I have watched them growing this past week. Quick, very quick. Out on the road this morn, the bigger one killed a riding-beast—and its rider."

"None will believe you."

"Why do you nurture them? Why do you loose them on the country? Can't you see their evil? Feel it?" Wyatt wiped his nose on his tattered arm and straightened, surprising Trav with his height. The two were on a par in both height and girth. For the first time, Trav feared the hermit.

"Never mind. You are the one who must undo the evil you have created. The sword." Wyatt coughed and pointed, his finger gnarled as an old tree root.

"There, to the north. You are the one who must bear the burden now. Follow the pointer stars twenty kilometers north. The stone cairn glows blue in the night."

"A demon watches over it?" Trav couldn't decide what to believe or think.

"No demon, just the legacy of that which birthed them. You must fetch the sword and kill the dragons before—" Wyatt started coughing so hard he couldn't stop.

Trav backed off, turned and hobbled away as fast as he could. The hermit might destroy all he had worked for. Trav knew the dangers of raising the dragons, but Piddling and Yilg weren't killers. Not like Wyatt claimed. He had raised them, and they were gentled to humans. That didn't stop the pair from looking intimidating to anyone lacking a backbone. Kennick would never stand and fight a pair of dragons, even ones hardly larger than a dog.

It took until midmorning for Trav to return to Slake, and his resolve hardened when he saw Kennick riding into the village on a fine new riding-beast and a tooled saddle chased with silver under him. Kennick jumped to the ground and embraced Juliana.

As he hobbled up, Trav heard the paladin say, "Juliana, my love! I am glad you are safe! There is a dragon marauding along the roadway. I feared for you."

"With you here, there can be no danger," Juliana said, adoration glowing in her eyes. She clung tightly to him.

Trav wanted to spit, as the old hermit had done. Instead he hurried forward and said in a loud voice, "I've seen the dragon. I know where it lairs."

"What? What's that you say?" Kennick spun, his face suddenly pale. He touched the hilt of Dragonslicer, fingers drumming nervously. The discomfort in the champion's face was all Trav might have hoped for, but Juliana still did not see it.

"A day's walk from here," said Trav. He amended this to, "An hour's ride on that fine steed. Did you come by it in Westering? From an admirer?"

"You do not joke with me?" Kennick tried to recover his composure. To Trav's critical eye, he failed. Trav dared not let the paladin escape now that he had secured the hook. One look at a real dragon and only Kennick's dust would be seen in Slake.

"You must face the dragon or Juliana will be in jeopardy. You spoke of depredation yourself."

"But it was far from here. That way. The reports—" Kennick swallowed hard, and Trav revelled even more in the man's discomfort. Revenge was sweet, but the danger of Kennick not being exposed for the scoundrel he was worried Trav.

"Only Dragonslicer can slay this dragon," Trav pushed. "I can show you the cave they—it—lives in."

"No, Kennick, don't go," cried Juliana, true fear in her voice for the man she mistakenly loved.

"He must. Otherwise, who can tell what the dragon might do to Slake? To Westering?" Trav enjoyed Kennick's uneasiness every time he mentioned Westering.

"Come with me, youngling. Show me this dragon and I shall slay it." Kennick turned to Juliana and said, "I dedicate this creature's death to you, my love." They kissed, and Trav wanted to snatch Dragonslicer from Kennick's sheath and end the farce. But he didn't want to kill the man as much as humiliate him and show his sister her mistake. They were family, and a brother's duty was to look after his sister's best interests. That was especially true now that their father had taken leave of his senses and been bedazzled by Kennick's flash and thunder.

Kennick grabbed Trav's arm and hoisted the youth behind him in the high-backed saddle. They charged off, Trav doing his best to hang on, but he had to admit riding was superior to hobbling along on his mutilated feet. Before he realized it, Kennick was reining back and demanding to know where the dragon was.

"There," Trav said, pointing to the dragons' cave. He knew the pair of reptilian beasts weren't full-grown, but that might not matter. Piddling could snort some fire and that would send Kennick running. He might never return to Slake, and, Trav hoped, the would-be champion would never even slow down when he raced through Westering. Faced with two dragons ensured an exit for Kennick Strongarm from Slake, Juliana's life, and Trav's emotions.

"It hasn't the look of a dragon's lair about it. I know. I've seen dozens." The man struggled to keep the quaver from his voice. He dismounted and fingered Dragonslicer again, then drew the sword and advanced on the cave. Kennick stopped outside and called, "Come meet your death, vile beast!"

"You'll have to go in after the dragon," Trav said, enjoying the paladin's fright. "I'm not sure a dragon understands our language."

"They are clever monsters," Kennick said, but he didn't argue. He edged forward, both hands on the sword's handle. Kennick looked back at Trav, and then plunged into the low cave, swinging and slashing. Trav saw fat blue sparks explode from the steel blade as Kennick swung wildly.

Then there was only silence.

Trav frowned. Yilg ought to be growling or Piddling snorting fire—or Kennick screaming in abject fright. There was nothing. Trav shuffled toward the cave mouth and peered inside. It took a few seconds for him to understand what he saw.

Kennick stood over a dragon's skeleton, but the champion had not killed the creature. The flesh had been stripped from the bones. Looking closer, Trav saw that Yilg had died and been eaten. The gnaw marks on the gleaming white bones were unmistakable. Something had happened to Yilg, and scavengers had picked the bones clean.

"What did this?" Trav asked, confused.

"It matters little. The dragon is dead. Once more I have triumphed!"

"You've done nothing!" cried Trav, outraged that Kennick would take credit for a tragic accident. "You can't claim any honor in finding a dead dragon." He tried to stop Kennick from taking the skull as proof of death and failed. The man was too strong for him.

"Walk back, youngling," Kennick said, hurrying from the cave and mounting his riding-beast. He never looked back as he held his trophy in his lap. Trav grumbled and started walking as fast as his feet would take him. Anger burned out pain, and he returned to Slake almost as quickly as if he had possessed a full set of toes.

But he did not return to the celebration he thought sure to be in progress. The village was more deserted than before. Even during the withering fever, some people had been outside, wandering the muddy trails between the pitiful dwellings. Not now.

Frowning, Trav made his way to his home and stopped outside. The roof had been burned off, leaving only a charred shell.

"Father!" he called. "Juliana! Where are you? What's happened?" Trav rushed to the door and peered into the charred husk of building. He blinked in surprise when he saw Kennick huddled in the far corner, arms curled around his knees and mewling pitifully. Taking a single step, Trav stopped and then vomited.

He saw his father's body, burned and ripped apart—and partially eaten by huge jaws.

"It was a dragon, a big dragon," moaned Kennick. "When they eat human flesh they grow huge quickly."

"Where is Juliana?"

"I don't know, I don't know," moaned Kennick.

Trav spun when he heard feet pounding behind him. His relief was boundless when he saw Juliana. Her dark hair flew in all directions, and she was flushed but otherwise unharmed. It was up to him to tell her of their father's death.

"Juliana, wait," Trav said, trying to keep her out of their house.

"I know he's dead, Trav, I know. I saw it and I ran and hid. The dragon! It's half the size of this house and it's coming back." Juliana pushed Trav out of the way and dropped to her knees in front of Kennick.

She grabbed him and shook hard. "Kennick, you've got to fight the dragon. It's vicious! Terrible! And it's coming back!"

"No, no!" Kennick threw the sword from him.

"Kennick, you must. You're our only hope. The dragon feeds constantly on us. It...it's out there!"

Trav looked from Juliana to Kennick to the dragon lumbering outside, heading toward them. It shocked him to see that the marauding dragon was Piddling, the puny hatchling he had nurtured to humiliate Kennick. From the look on Juliana's face, he had succeeded.

He glanced at his father's half-eaten body and knew he had done more, too much more. He scooped up Kennick's fallen sword and ran outside, screaming. Trav swung Dragonslicer as hard as he could, counting on the sword's magic to pierce the thick brown scales on Piddling's chest.

The blade glanced off, not even scratching the beast. The recoil staggered him, and for a moment he stared up into the dragon's yellow eyes. Trav wasn't sure what he read there. Not anger. Not malevolence. It was more like surprise or even delight.

Piddling roared and let out a long belch of flame that surged above Trav's head. He ducked low and swung again. The blade bounced off the dragon's tough, scaled hide again. This time Piddling spun with startling speed and caught the blade between imposing jaws. The dragon's neck muscles tensed slightly, and the sword shattered like glass.

Trav stared at the sundered blade shining on the ground, and then backed off from the dragon. He stopped and stood his ground.

"Piddling, here," Trav said, reaching into his pocket and pulling out a crushed pig-bug and holding it in a surprisingly steady hand. The dragon bent over, and its darting black tongue flicked across Trav's palm. The pig-bug vanished.

Trav didn't know what to feel. This was his pet, and it had killed his father and ravaged the village. Worse, all Trav could focus on was Piddling being responsible for Yilg's death. Trav took a deep breath and shuddered. The smallest dragon might have also killed Grendl and Drowsy, carnivorously feeding on its own kind to grow this large.

"Trav, get back," called Juliana.

"No, wait, I—" Trav screamed when Piddling moved with dazzling quickness and caught Juliana in heavy jaws. The girl screamed once before being broken in half.

Trav snapped, not knowing what he was doing. Dragonslicer had failed against Piddling; he beat at the dragon's haunches with his bare hands. Somehow, this attack was enough to make Piddling break off his feasting and stare at him with wide, questioning yellow eyes. Piddling snorted flame and moved off, walking slowly until he vanished into the gathering twilight.

Trav sobbed and wanted to kill himself. He couldn't bear to look at Juliana or his village. He was responsible, and all because he had wanted to shame Kennick.

"Kennick!" he cried, knowing who he could vent his towering wrath on. He hobbled to his burned out house and looked around wildly, trying to find the object of his hatred.

"He's gone. Saw him running away toward Westering. Might be there by now, the way he was running."

"What?" Trav whipped around, fists balled and ready to fight. He saw the hunched figure of the old hermit, Wyatt.

"That wasn't Dragonslicer. I carried the magical sword and know. He was a liar about everything." Wyatt spat a gray-green gob that hissed on the ground. He grimaced and showed blackened, broken teeth, then coughed. The rattle sounded deep in chest.

"What are you saying?" Trav wanted to strike out and there was nothing to hit.

"Kennick was a fool and a liar, a blowhard who never saw the Dragonslicer. That's not even a good copy. Too long, not sharp enough—and lacking in any god-forged magic. Vulcan would never do such sloppy work. And those gems. Fake. Fake, just like Kennick."

"You are as big a liar. You never held Dragonslicer."

"Told you where it was. Sorry now I put it under that cairn. As ancient as I am, I could have killed that monster you raised."

Before Trav could reply, he heard Kennick's loud shout. "That's him. He's the one. He's a demon! He commanded the dragon to do his bidding!" Kennick stumbled at the head of a dozen people, most from Slake but a few Trav had never seen before. He jerked around to face Wyatt.

"You? You're a demon?"

Wyatt coughed again and spat. "Would a demon assume such a sorry form? No, my young fool, he means you. He's damning you. You might not be a demon, but you're responsible." Wyatt sank down, amid a loud crackling of joints. He shivered though the air was still warm and stared at Trav.

"You'd best run, my boy. They want someone to blame—and you know you are responsible."

"No, I didn't mean all this." But Trav darted away as fast as his feet would take him. He felt the stumps of his toes turn bloody with the relentlessness of his flight, but he never stopped or looked behind him. Slake was a world carried to the far side of the moon and beyond. His life was gone, his family, his friends, everything gone. And he ran without knowing where his feet took him until he fell to the ground, exhausted.

It might have been the next morning or the next or even the next when he came to know where his destiny lay. The nights were better for travelling, there being less risk of discovery. The people of Slake had not pursued with any tenacity, his pet dragon still loose on the land, but he felt their presence as surely as if they grabbed at his collar and tugged on his sleeve.

Their anger and fear and hatred burned at him like an unbanked fire.

"North," he grated between clenched teeth, turning the journey into an endurance contest. He feet hurt worse each day, but he never slowed his relentless pace. Time came to mean nothing, and finally Trav sat atop a small rise, looking over a thickly forested area. The sun sank slowly, leaving behind bloody smears in the sky. The few clouds above him quickly vanished, and into the satiny dome popped star after star, but his eyes were fixed on the horizon.

"It glows," Trav muttered. The old hermit had said Dragonslicer lay under a stone cairn that shone with a blue haze in the darkness. He continued his single-minded journey, across river and through forest and finally to the pyramid.

For a long time he stood and stared, warming himself in the heat radiating from the pile of rock. Then he stepped forward and began to dig, hardly believing old Wyatt had spoken the truth. But he had. Twenty minutes of hard work displaced enough rock to reveal the hilt of a sword. The instant Trav grabbed the sword and pulled, he knew Kennick's blade had not been Dragonslicer.

On this hilt rose in relief a golden dragon, and the keen steel blade gleamed even in the darkness, catching the smallest ray of starlight and magnifying it until the weapon shone brightly. Trav swung the sword through the air and listened to the shrill whine, a keening that tore at his senses and made him want to cry with pain. But he did not stop swinging the blade. Power flowed through him and grew until he knew he could stand against any beast, dragon or demon.

"Revenge," Trav said, then fell silent. He shook his head and amended this to, "Justice. It will be nothing more than justice."

He whipped the blade, feather light, in a broad arc and created a new shrilling, a higher pitched wail that rose in frequency and intensity until he no longer heard it. But in the distance came a trumpeting reply he knew well.

"Piddling," he said. Trav continued to whirl Dragonslicer about, the shrilling an allurement the dragon could not resist. When his arms began to tire, a deep rumbling came to him, and Trav saw his one-time pet.

Piddling stood even taller, the diet of human flesh augmenting both bulk and height. Half again as large as before, Piddling had grown into a formidable killer. The dragon moved with a litheness that astounded Trav, but he found himself not appreciating the movement but remembering the deaths caused by the dragon.

Juliana. Their father.

"Come here, Piddling, come to me," Trav urged. He swung Dragonslicer about his head and moved forward, his legs rubbery and feet bloody from the hard journey.

The dragon's head bobbed about, its long black tongue snaking forth as it sampled the air. Tiny sparks ignited in its nostrils and flames leaped out, only to die a few meters short of Trav. He paid no heed to the dragon's warning and surged forward, Dragonslicer driving out with magic-driven power.

The blade touched Piddling's chest scales and did not bounce off. The blade cut deeply, sinking far into the dragon's body. Trav shoved as hard as he could, Dragonslicer gouging a deep chunk of flesh from the reptile's body. Piddling snorted more in surprise than pain and lowered its head, as if to butt Trav.

The youth gripped Dragonslicer with both hands and sent the keening blade into an arc that ended behind the dragon's head. The sword cut deeply, even as Piddling twisted and tried to escape. The huge beast dropped to the ground, mortally wounded. It twitched and kicked, and its fires extinguished into dull-burning embers.

Panting, Trav stared at Piddling. He felt years older and remembered what Wyatt had told him. The blade's magic exacted its toll on the wielder. He had paid untold years of his life to slay one dragon.

"Worth it," he panted. "It was worth it. You killed my father and sister and—"

Trav's voice trailed off. An eyelid twitched and opened; one large yellow eye fixed on him. Piddling tried to reach out a taloned claw but lacked the strength. The dragon said in a growling voice "Papa" and died.

For a long time Trav could not move. He stood and stared at the large corpse now drawing insects, including the pig-bugs Piddling had loved so well as a hatchling. Trav fought back tears and turned away, Dragonslicer weighing him down terribly. He hurled the blade from him. It spun through the air and landed point-down in the soft dirt a dozen paces away.

For a long time, he stood and cried openly. But Trav Gorman could not leave. Not yet. He hobbled to Dragonslicer and pulled it from the ground, for the first time realizing the real burden he had assumed.

# Me and Mr. Jones

*I lurk on the WolfPak, a newsgroup of extraordinarily talented CGI artists and animators. Their credits include scores (yeah, scores) of Emmy, Oscar and Telly nominations—and wins. They've done work on various* Star Trek *TV shows and movies,* CSI, *book covers (Fred Gambino did the cover on my* MechWarrior: Ruins of Power, *as well as most of the other titles in the series), music videos, and government stuff they can't talk about. Now and then they post something done for their own amusement. In January of 2002 Terry Halladay posted one of a guy in a lawn chair holding a beer. In the chair next to him is a green alien reaching a tentacle to curl about a beer, too. "Jack's Reptile Ranch" stretches across a sign in the background. My mind went all whimsical when I saw this, and this story came rocketing out. This collection marks its first appearance in print.*

He ate my two-headed rattlesnake. I know he did, even if I can't prove it.

That rattler was about my top attraction after the Tic-Tac-Toe-playing chicken. The trouble with the chicken is the way the computer chip rigs the game. Tourists drop in a quarter to against play the chicken, which pecks at a button. They make their move, the chicken plays and gets a kernel of corn and so on until it comes down to crunch time. The birdbrain actually beats most of the tourists, but when it's going to lose, the computer chip in the mechanism cheats so the chicken always wins. It takes most folks a dollar or two to figure out they can never beat the increasingly plump refugee from KFC.

But the two-headed rattler wasn't a fraud, and that drew the marks like flies to fresh cow flop. And Jonesy ate him. I found the picked-clean, gnawed skeleton out back, down past the arroyo where I let the kids hunt for real arrowheads and dinosaur bones for a dollar. The son of a bitch probably didn't even cook the meat, unless he brought a can of Sterno with him, because I didn't find a firepit or ashes from a fire. Just the bones, which I mounted and put in the back of the Cosmic Mystery Museum.

The Cosmic Mystery is my place along the freeway out in the middle of Arizona between Flagstaff and the New Mexico border, and Jones owns the Desert Way Station ten miles closer to Meteor Crater down the road, or has for the past three months. Before that, Claude Garrison ran the place more as a motel than a tourist attraction, and he went belly-up since he never modernized. Jonesy, at least, has tried to put in some attractions more interesting than yet another bogus mummified hand belonging to Geronimo, or water that seems to flow uphill but is really nothing more than an optical illusion.

Truth is, I wish he hadn't bothered trying to improve his place. Jones began drawing away my trade with his fancy electronic gizmos he advertised as genuine alien artifacts, and that's when our war started. But he didn't have to eat my two-headed rattler, in spite of what I did last week. That was mostly an accident anyway, since I really didn't intend blowing up his concrete tepee and still don't know what happened. All I wanted to do was knock out the air-conditioner on the back of the tepee—Jonesy has motel rooms in concrete tepees, a real draw for the Easterners. Ever been in a concrete tepee in Arizona desert during July? I figured stopping the flow of chilly air would chase off a few tourists, nothing more. Would it have been my fault if they moseyed on down to the Cosmic Mystery and cooled off with my beer, soda, and guaranteed arctic-temperature air-conditioning?

That's business, nothing more.

But the little business I did to the concrete surprised me. I short-circuited the power line going in, and the next thing I know the concrete is burning. Damnedest thing I ever saw. After it burned for a few minutes, it kinda melted and then the real fireworks started. I figure Jonesy had some illegal firecrackers and stuff like that inside, from the size of the explosion. Filled the sky with sparks for close to twenty minutes, and even woke up the state cops. By then I was back at the museum, but Sgt. Larson stopped by later and told me about it while he sucked down the Sierra Mist I gave him gratis, like I always do. I pretended it was all news to me, but I felt bad about it, until I remembered why I had wanted to sabotage Jonesy in the first place.

I really loved that rattlesnake.

The familiar noise of a car door slamming made me look up from the magazine I was pretending to read and see a family coming inside the Cosmic Mystery to get out of the noonday heat.

"Howdy, folks," I said in my most winning manner. "What can I get you? Something nice and cool to drink?"

"Yeah, whatever," the man said, looking both tired and irritated. That wasn't so unusual. If you're not used to the desert, the summer heat can wear on you in a hurry. Especially if you have two small kids in the car along with a wife who's even more frazzled.

As the kids pointed, I put the goodies on the counter. "You want to take in the museum, too? Got some great items in the back, if you've got the nerve to see real cosmic mysteries."

The man recoiled, then shook his head vigorously.

"What's wrong?" I asked.

"The guy down the road at the Desert Way Station says you're a killer and have people in pickle jars," the little girl said. "Can I see 'em, Daddy?"

"Jones said that?" My face must have turned red. "The same fellow who ate my rattlesnake?"

This crossed the line. The man dropped a five on the counter, herded his kids ahead of him and lit out, the woman muttering to him as they went. He didn't even wait for his change, though there wasn't much. I listened to them roar off in a cloud of dust and sat and fumed. Jonesy didn't have to lie. All I've got in pickle jars are desert critters and a couple small dolls made up to look like the gray aliens that were supposed to have crashed in Roswell. As I was making up the display, I thought of putting in a human look-alike doll for one of the cast from that television show, but reception's terrible out here without a satellite dish, I've never seen the show, and besides, there might be some kind of copyright violation involved. In spite of the publicity I might get if the show's producers sued, it wasn't worth the money hiring some shyster to defend my ass over in LA.

I walked around the Cosmic Mystery to get rid of my mad, my mind circling around to what I had to do to get even. This was a pretty good place and had been for years. I stopped in front of the wildlife display and stared at the snakes, lizards, and other critters put up in formaldehyde, like some berserk high-school science lab. These were the real creatures. The ones I cobbled together to look like aliens out of some sci-fi horror movie looked better, if you asked me. Scarier and more believable than the horny toad and the skink and that blue-tailed lizard I caught a couple months back trying to eat black ants from a hill north of here.

Picking up a jar, I sloshed the yellowish, smelly fluid around and watched the eyes of the fake alien roll.

"Damned good work," I declared, admiring my own artistry, maybe a bit too much. But these alien embryo sell. Not many kids look at the aliens in a jar and don't want a key ring or the Alien Brain Candy—this is really cool stuff, the Alien Brain Candy. Kids lick the hard candy top of the skull until it vanishes, and then they can suck out the gooier grayish blob from the brainpan. Drives their parents over the edge and doesn't taste too bad, as long as you're not too squeamish. But then, there aren't many twelve-year-old boys who are.

Pacing up and down the aisles lined with display cases put me at ease and let me think.

A fitting revenge came to me, and by midnight, after shutting down for the night, I was ready. A piece of scrap sheet metal, some paint, a stencil for the lettering, and a few minutes of expert work were all I needed before tossing it all into the back of my truck. Finding my portable drill and some metal screws took a while longer, but I wasn't in any hurry. I wanted it to get good and late before I drove out onto the highway.

Jonesy's sign was a real pretty one. I don't know what he's done to it, but the letters glowed all on their own. Luminescent paint needs light on it to shine, but this didn't. Maybe it was radioactive, like the old watch dials painted with tritium. I'd heard he had taken a trip to Vegas right after he bought the place, so maybe he went out into Yucca Flats or Area 51 or somewhere to get the stuff. The letters shone a neon orange, visible for a mile down the road—until I fastened my CLOSED—QUARANTINED sign over it. I climbed into the bed of my truck, hoisted my sign and awkwardly held it into place for a moment. Then my drill whined and drove the metal screws through my sign into his, holding everything together like a meatless metallic sandwich. Even if someone knew the Desert Way Station was down this particular off-ramp, they'd figure it had gone out of business and keep on driving until they reached my place.

I stood back and admired my handiwork. In the dark it was hard to see the lettering I'd put on, since I hadn't bothered with fancy reflective paint, but as an occasional car sped by fast, I watched the headlights play across the lettering. Good. Damned good, even if I said so myself.

Jonesy would have a cow when he found out, but it might not be for a few days. I got into my truck, but instead of going back to my place I took the road leading to his. Don't ask why, but I would have missed everything if I hadn't gone snooping. A few hundred yards away from the Desert Way Station, I pulled off the road and stared.

Lancing into the sky was the brightest searchlight I'd ever seen, including that monster laser they have on top of the Luxor in Vegas. I shielded my eyes as it turned in my direction, and then it blinked out, only to come back on a few seconds later. On and off it flashed, as if the power supply was going to blow. Or maybe it was like Morse code, though I heard on the news nobody uses that anymore because of all the digital communications equipment.

I wondered how Jonesy thought this would pull in people. It might work for used car dealers, but we were fifty miles from nowhere out in the middle of the Arizona desert. Who'd see it and come in? People flying to LA at 35,000 feet?

The hum drew me like an insect to one of those electronic bug zappers. I got out of my truck and edged closer, staring at the flashing beam piercing the heavens. One reason I like it out in the desert is the clear night sky scrubbed clean of light pollution that oozes from cities. Jonesy's lights blotted out most of the stars. It struck me that this was defiling Nature's beauty. It also struck me he might not need his sign out on the freeway to pull in tourists, if this aerial advertising did whatever it was supposed to do.

Another of the concrete tepees was the source of both the hum and the light. Looking around, I saw that Jonesy didn't have any overnight guests. All the guest tepees were empty, and no cars in the parking lot told of a bad week for him. I took no satisfaction in that, especially after I saw the hole in the ground where the other tepee had melted down due to my tinkering.

My resolve hardened when I remembered the two-headed rattler and its sorry demise.

I ducked down when Jonesy came out of the tepee, his stride long, smooth, and almost boneless. He hurried to the back of the Desert Way Station and went inside, giving me a chance to see what was going on in the tepee. I stepped to the door and shielded my eyes from the dazzling light. I fumbled out my sunglasses and put them on and still had to squint. In spite of myself, I stepped into the motel room that had been stripped bare of all furnishings. The bed and dressers and usual crappy chairs were gone, leaving only a small panel of electronics at the rear, controlling what looked to be a half dozen lasers focusing on a small metallic disk.

The disk rotated slowly—in midair. It might have been held up by black thread, but I didn't think so. Jonesy had himself a first-rate display here, one that would wow the tourists. They were always suckers for bright lights, low humming, and stuff that moved. Levitation can be done in a lot of ways. Magnets work and so does a small updraft against an object that's lighter than it looks. But this was something new.

I walked around, staring at the disk. As it caught the light and reflected it straight up through the hole in the top of the tepee, it spun faster and faster and then began tumbling until it looked like a blurred sphere. Whatever it was intrigued me. I whipped off my gimme cap I'd got over at the Chevy dealer in Flagstaff and used it like a fishnet to scoop the disk from the lighted column. No way was I going to reach into that beam. Burning ants with a magnifying glass is bad. Having your hand punctured by a laser is a lot worse.

The disk weighed more than I'd thought from the way it spun and twisted on its axis. I staggered back and looked at it glowing a lovely pearl white in my hat. It sounds crazy but it touched something deep inside me. I'm not sure if I'd ever seen anything more appealing in all my life. I put my hat back on and went to the tepee door in time to see Jonesy coming back, lugging a long, thick metal pole.

"What're you doing?" he shouted, dropping the pole. "Get out of here!"

"Don't get bent out of shape over it," I said, as I edged around the concrete tepee and got ready to make a run for it. The panic in his tone told me he was going to crack. Anybody who'd eat a guy's star attraction was living on the edge anyway.

"Shape! What of my shape? What're you doing?" he repeated.

I blinked. For a moment I thought he had lost his right hand, but in the dark it was impossible to say what I'd really seen. He might have been waving around a gun with a long barrel.

I ran for my truck, in case the dark cylindrical shape was a gun barrel.

"Stop!" Jonesy shouted. "You cannot have that...that thing you stole!"

I felt the disk banging around under my hat, burrowing down like a dog on a soft flannel blanket into my hair. It made me feel good, wanted. There was no explanation for that, but it did. If Jonesy had made one of the disks, he could make a second. I wasn't going to give him back this one.

Skidding to a halt by my truck, I grabbed for the door handle, wrenched at it, jumped inside, and roared off. I saw Jonesy in my rearview mirror, madder than a wet hen. I sobered a little, thinking he might use his gun, but from what I could see, he had put it away and only waved his arms like long stalks of wheat blowing in the wind.

I got back to the Cosmic Mystery and didn't bother turning on any lights. It was almost four in the morning, and I never catered to tourists at this time of night. Besides, I wanted to be alone when I held the disk I'd filched from Jonesy. Gingerly removing my cap, I fumbled around in my long hair and finally pulled the disk out. It felt warm and trembly like a little kitten in my grip.

It made me feel good like a purring kitten does, too.

The front door of the Cosmic Mystery exploded inward. I spun, staring at Jonesy.

"Give it back. I need it!" He came forward with his easy stride, but I saw the fire in his eyes, in spite of the darkness. They glowed like the letters on his sign that I had covered up with my quarantine warning.

"You ate my snake," I said.

"I...was hungry," he said, somewhat lamely I thought. "The communication...thing. I must have it if I am to leave."

"What?" I didn't have a clue what he was talking about.

"The device in your palm. I must have it. There is no time to lose. Please." He changed from belligerent to pleading. "I have been stranded here too long."

"What're you saying?" The disk warmed my hand and buoyed my soul. This was what Jonesy wanted, but I didn't understand what he meant about being stranded.

"My scout ship crashed in the desert. I was entrusted to hunt for a renegade but my engine..."

I tried to figure out what he said, but the words blurred and refused to penetrate. It was as if he lisped, and I struggled along, almost understanding foreign words. Or heavily accented English spoken by a foreigner. It was crazy, and I wasn't going to take the time to puzzle it out.

I started to let him know what he could do with his demand. Instead, I gaped when Jonesy reached up and tugged off his face. It came off just like that, leaving behind a reptilian snout, greenish yellow eyes with bright blue dancing spots in them. He held his face in his hand. Or had he pulled off a mask to show another mask?

"That's pretty cool," I said uneasily, "but sideshow tricks don't make it. Not out here where the marks stop to be mystified, not scared. I'm not giving it back. Consider the disk payment for the snake."

"I need the..."

The word vanished in a sibilant whisper I didn't, maybe couldn't, understand. He pointed to my hand clutching the disk. The metal began to burn me now.

"Stop it," I said. "However you're doing it, stop! The damned thing's heating up."

"I am saved!" he cried, rushing me.

I didn't stick around for the lizard-masked maniac to grab me. I lit out through the museum, out the back way and into the desert, past some displays of dinosaur bones and petrified wood. As I ran, the radiant disk warmed from pleasant to painful. I had to juggle it from hand to hand as I ran.

And then I felt ropes lash around my legs, sending me crashing facedown into the sand. The shock of landing caused me to drop the disk. It went rolling, and Jonesy swarmed over me. I saw his arms extend to unnatural lengths. Those had been the ropes—his arms, I mean. They snapped and twitched like a whip. His hands vanished to be replaced by thready tentacles grasping for the disk.

I rolled over and got my feet under me. Glancing up, I froze. My heart threatened to explode in my chest as the massive circular shape descended like a falling elevator and blotted out the stars. Tiny ports opened on its silvery metallic belly and revealed green lights in a dozen spots, before the entire circular ship was swallowed by a shimmering white nimbus like the Northern Lights.

A million thoughts flashed through my mind. Aliens. UFOs. Roswell. Jones.

My toes dug into the sand, and I shot forward, grabbed his ropy arm, and slid my fingers down to the tentacles so I could wrest the disk from him.

"I need it to contact my rescuers," Jonesy cried, held facedown by my weight. "Please. I do not want to stay here."

I wrenched the disk free, shoved him back down and sprinted back for the back door of the Cosmic Mystery. A sudden heat from above made me look up and see how the once-roaming rays were now focusing. I let out a yelp of pain as the disk began burning my hand. Without realizing what I was doing, I threw the disk as hard as I could into the opened rear door of the museum.

Then all hell broke loose.

I remember turning and throwing my arms around Jonesy, holding him tight and wondering at the sinuous body under his clothes. Then I wasn't wondering about anything. A huge fist crushed down on me, lifted me, and threw me a mile. Well, not a mile. A hundred feet. Or maybe just a few yards. But I landed hard, my body a shield over his as green rays swept the entire area.

Then there was nothing. And I mean nothing. Silence so complete I thought I'd lost my hearing until, in the distance, I heard sizzling, crackling sounds and sniffed a burning smell that made my nose wrinkle. I pushed to my feet, and Jonesy followed so nimbly you'd never know he had been through what I had. Then I saw the museum. The Cosmic Mystery was nothing more than smoking crater.

"You saved me," Jonesy said.

"My museum," I moaned. I'd thought losing the two-headed rattler was bad. Everything was gone in the wink of—what? The wink of an alien death ray.

"Those were the renegades, not my rescue. They tried to kill me so I could not report. How did you know they meant me harm?"

"The disk?" I was still a bit on the shaken side. The last thing in the world I'd intended doing was to save him. I'd wanted the gadget I had thrown into the museum a few seconds before the UFO nuked it.

"I activated the device and thought I had sent out a rescue signal, a homing signal, but they came instead."

"Nasty sons of bitches," I said, looking aloft. The stars were blotted out sporadically by thick smoke from the Cosmic Mystery Museum, but other than that, all trace of the UFO was gone.

"Yes," Jonesy said. I turned and looked at him and swallowed hard. If anyone else had told me what he just had, I'd've copied it down and used it in an exhibit. But I saw the truth standing in front of me. He looked like some kind of a lizard without his mask and makeup. That made me shiver even more.

He'd eaten one of his kind. Sort of, since rattlesnakes are pretty much like lizards.

\* \* \*

I leaned back in the lawn chair and studied my day's work.

"Not too shabby," I said. "I got the air-conditioner working in Unit Twelve." The hum from the electric unit hanging on the back of the concrete tepee satisfied me. Even more satisfying, there was a full house tonight. Every last one of those rooms had a tired but content tourist family inside, and this wasn't the first time this week, either. Since Jonesy had offered me a partnership in the Desert Way Station in return for saving his life, and as payment because his enemies had destroyed my place, things had been going real good. He didn't have much of a sense for what appealed to tourists. I did. But he had that alien know-how for gadgets. It was like balm for my soul watching the marks gawk at his humming, flashing hypnotic "alien" equipment in the new museum, sometimes staring so long they needed a second bottle of soda pop or beer. After I took down the quarantine sign and apologized a while about trying to run off his business, we'd set to work and turned Claude Garrison's old dump into a mighty fine place.

Nothing like it between Flagstaff and Gallup. His knowledge and my marketing.

"There's where the new reptile garden'll be," I said, pointing to the vacant spot bulldozed out of the desert a couple days ago. "Jack's Reptile Garden, I'm going to call it."

"You have a new chicken?" Jonesy asked, pulling up a chair. What I liked about him was how he anticipated what I might like. He'd brought a cooler with a couple six-packs of beer from of the store and put it between our chairs.

"I can always get another one later, though I do miss that pecking son of a gun. It could bring in a hundred dollars a week, easy. Even better than a chicken, I've got a line on an albino rattler. A snake wrangler in Albuquerque's willing to sell for a decent price, since he's already got a couple others." I looked at him hard. His latex mask had slipped a little, and I could see the scaly alien skin poking around the edges, but I didn't say anything. None of the tourists ever noticed, and it didn't bother me.

"I know, I know," he said in his soft, sibilant voice. "I am not to eat this one."

"You're not to do up another one of those communication disks, either, not unless you can be sure who's on the other end of the phone."

"I have shut down that equipment."

"Good," I said, meaning it. I lounged back, pulled a bottle from the cooler, and twisted off the cap. "I've got big plans for this place. We can do better than The Thing and the Desert Mystery Spot combined. We'll be famous. Me and you'll make great partners."

A sinuous tentacle curled around a Long Neck and deftly popped the cap.

"Yes," Jonesy hissed, and then sucked back the entire bottle of beer. I finally had a partner who could match me beer for beer and hold his liquor.

# Passion Isle

*The character of Estebar in "Thief of Dreams" proved beguiling to me with endless possibilities. A rich, seafaring adventurer who could be anything he wanted in any story. This was written as a follow-up in May 2000 to "Thief of Dreams," but as happens all too often in publishing, the magazine slipped beneath the surface of profitability and was never seen again. RIP,* Adventures of Sword & Sorcery. *It was a fine magazine, and I miss the S&S stories.*

"Ye have a taste for gettin' yerself killed, do ye, now?" asked Captain Norron. "It was a sorry day when I traded for that accursed book."

"Traded?" Estebar laughed as he held *Fordor's Magical Guide to the World against* the railing of the good ship *Serpent's Breath.* "Traded? You killed the mage and stole it!"

"I traded him his life for it, I did," Norron said gruffly. The man peered at the ship's owner through his cataract-milky left eye, choosing to close the sharper right one for effect. Strong hands gripped the railing as the old sailor edged closer. His bowed legs would have looked more at home on a steppe rider who lived astride his horse. For all Estebar knew, Norron had been a steppe rider. And a dozen other things before finding his calling on the sea.

"Look," Estebar said, holding the book open so the pages leaped into three-dimensional splendor. "Have you ever seen such a lovely island?"

"A mage's island, it is. See how the warning shimmers in that damned book?" Norron peered closer at the image rising off the page. "Avoid it, Estebar. Keep yer distance. Have nothing to do with mages. Mark me words—"

"Why not, since you mark your cards?" Estebar laughed again as salt spray stung his face. He had been a landlubber until chance brought him aboard this ship. His partner in a brasswares business in Freena was an honest enough crook, not stealing more than he should. Every time the *Serpent's Breath* put into Freena, Doon delivered a dozen bags bulging with gold coin from the profits. This steady income allowed Estebar to sail as he saw fit, little worrying about earnings from trading.

"Do not mock me," Norron said sternly. "Adventure all ye want. The crew likes it, and if ye press me, so do I. But avoid this...this Delcentro. There lies danger." His stubby finger sliced like a knife blade through the floating image to emphasize his point.

"Of course it does," Estebar said cheerfully. "And adventure, as well. The guidebook tells of Heodisi and his potions, a potion for any occasion. Surely, you would not turn down a mixture clearing your eye?"

"What do ye seek from this mage, Estebar? Forgetfulness?

Ye'll never forget Leonia."

"I don't want to forget her," Estebar said, lying. "She is a part of my life, a part now long passed. Set sail for the isle of Delcentro. I would see what this mage has to offer."

"Ye'll regret it, ye will," grumbled Norron, but the captain shouted orders to First Mate Garmendian and got the crew into the rigging. With a decent wind they could reach Delcentro in five days, and then be off to some decent port for liberty.

\* \* \*

"Not a sociable one, is he?" observed Norron.

"The guidebook says nothing about that rocky flyspeck being as close to Delcentro as we can sail," Estebar said, irritated at the mage and his private ways. Delcentro loomed a lovely emerald of an island, showing great promise for trade goods, but Heodisi had cast ward spells to hold the *Serpent's Breath* back. If they wanted to deal with the mage, they had to row to a nothing of a rock well away from Delcentro and meet Heodisi there.

"Now don't that beat all?" muttered Garmendian. The first mate pointed. "I want a boat like that. He's makin' it go faster than the wind, and there's no one a' rowin'!"

"Into the tender," Estebar ordered. "I'd see what Heodisi has to say for himself." The tall, dark man lithely vaulted the rail and landed lightly in the dinghy as it was lowered on its davit. Garmendian and a sailor named Pugg rowed Estebar to the rocky spire, where he scrambled ashore to meet the mage.

Estebar sized up the sorcerer quickly enough. Short, razor thin, a face not even a mother could gaze at without cringing, he was an outcast and, as a result, erected magical—and other—barriers around himself. More than this, he smelled of stale beer and potent onions.

"What potions are you wanting?" Heodisi asked in a shrill voice.

"I've heard you have many, but it is trade I seek," Estebar said. "Yon island of yours must produce fine fruits and—"

"You buy what I offer. Anyone trying to go to the island dies!"

Estebar remembered the notation in Fordor's. As with all description of spells, it couched its admonitions in flowery, cryptic phrases. What Estebar could make of the ward spell Heodisi had cast, logic rather than magic provided the way to Delcentro. However, even logic went only so far. The guidebook warned that only one of five attempting to reach the island survived. Estebar counted himself as both quick enough and lucky enough to be in that number.

"My captain needs a potion to clear his eye."

"No, nothing for any of you. I know why you are here, and you won't steal her from me!" With that, Heodisi spun, hopped like a frightened rabbit, and headed his magical boat back to Delcentro.

"Rude bloke," Pugg observed. "Let's get on. The captain's promised us a decent shore leave the next time we port."

"Wait," Estebar said. He watched Heodisi's boat cut back and forth in the water, avoiding certain darker colored patches of water. Did the mage sail over only the shallower sections? It appeared so. Estebar hefted his spyglass and scanned the distant shoreline. A smile crept to his lips. He passed the 'glass to Garmendian.

"Well, as I live 'n breathe," the first mate muttered. "He leaves his gold out on the shore for all to see."

"Not exactly. It has washed out of that cave, and Heodisi failed to notice. The storm last night might have done it."

"A dinghy could make off with a king's ransom," Garmendian said.

"Signal Norron. Use the semaphore flags to let the captain know to drop anchor and that we'll be back later." Estebar rubbed his clean-shaven chin thoughtfully, dark eyes fixed on the distant treasure.

Lucky enough? Smart enough? Yes!

"I dunno," Pugg said uneasily. "Them mages are a treacherous bunch."

"Owner's share for each of you," Estebar said. "One-quarter each for us, with the remaining quarter divvied among the crew."

He handed Pugg the spyglass, knowing the crewman's greed would decide the matter quickly. It did.

\* \* \*

"There's no shallows under us," warned Garmendian, peering over the side. "Nothin' but deep water here."

"Row, then, row for all you're worth!" cried Estebar. His heart hammered as he grabbed one oar and pulled hard. They had penetrated almost to the lush, green island with its tantalizing spill of gold and jewels along the shore. To die now would be an affront!

"My back's a' breakin'," complained Pugg, pulling on the other oar.

"Let it snap," growled Garmendian. "You were always the worst of a layabout crew. I—" The first mate's mouth gaped, and he sat hard on the bench at the prow. Estebar glanced over his shoulder and went white with fear.

"Row!" he cried. "Our lives depend on it!"

He rowed. Pugg screamed. The scaled horror rising from the deep jerked about and roared loudly. Tiny black hateful eyes spied the straining sailor, and a long green tongue the texture of sandpaper lashed out, curling about Pugg's head. The sea monster twisted using flippers, and Pugg sailed helplessly through the air. Where he landed in the water boiled with smaller monsters intent on devouring him.

He screeched once then died.

"Mercy," Garmendian said, taking the sailor's place at the oar.

"We'll find none here. Row, Garmendian, row!" Estebar guided them toward a shallow area not far away, where the huge sea creature could not swim. When the bottom of the boat scraped rocky beach, Estebar let out a sigh of relief.

"We made it, we made it," Garmendian shouted over and over in glee. He jumped to the beach and dragged the dinghy ashore, allowing Estebar to get out without soaking his hand-tooled leather boots.

"We certainly did," Estebar said, eyes on the cave and the stretch of beach leading to it. Everywhere he looked glinted bright gold. Coins, jeweled daggers, boxes laden with precious gems, it all lead into the cave like a royal highway.

"Estebar, a question," Garmendian asked, licking his lips and rubbing his hands on his pants as he stared at the incredible wealth strewn so carelessly before them. "Owner's share. How much, now that Pugg got hisself et by the monster?"

"Each of us gets one-third and the crew divvies the other third," Estebar said. Even with the crew's portion being split twenty ways, every sailor would be richer than a king if they fetched back only a portion of this treasure.

Estebar looked around. No mage protected his island so jealousy, only to imprudently leave such a powerful lure out where any might see and covet it.

"Start loading what you can," Estebar ordered the first mate. "Choose well because one trip is all we get."

"Aye, and we got to row past them monsters, too," Garmendian said, but his mind was not on the dangerous trip back to the *Serpent's Breath*. He hurried off to fling open treasure chests and toss out the minor baubles. Estebar watched him at his rapacious pursuit, and then set off along the beach to see more of the island.

A small trail wound up the cliff toward the summit looking out over the ocean. From there Estebar knew he could see the *Serpent's Breath* and suspected Heodisi of watching from there. What the reclusive mage's purpose was in luring them to his island in this manner, Estebar could not say, but he intended to find out. Trudging up the arduous trail tired him rapidly. Estebar got little enough exercise aboard his ship, and it told on him now. By the time he reached the crest, he was out of breath.

"You found me," came anxious words from inside a silken tent pitched atop the cliff. "I knew you would. You are my savior!"

"Milady?" Estebar stepped around to peer into the tent. A luxurious mattress had been spread, and lying on it was the homeliest woman Estebar had seen in many a year. Not ugly, he reflected, but plain. Very ordinary yet surrounded by sumptuous wealth that would make many a noble queen envious.

"You are the captain of yon ship?" She lifted a scrawny arm and pointed toward the *Serpent's Breath* bobbing on the waves just beyond the rocky isle where Heodisi had rejected Estebar's offer of trade.

"The owner," Estebar said, seeing no reason to lie. "The name is Estebar. And you are...?"

"A prisoner," the woman said, with such bile that Estebar recoiled. "Heodisi holds me prisoner here. I hate him!"

"Then leave him," Estebar said.

"I can't," the woman sobbed, burying her face in her hands. "I love him."

"I don't understand. You just said—" Estebar's eyes went wide when he realized the depth of the woman's dilemma.

"Yes, you understand," she said, looking at him with tear-filled eyes. "I see it in your face. Heodisi has cast a potent spell on me, a spell I can never break."

"A love spell," Estebar said.

"Yes, and I hate him for it. But I cannot leave because I love him. It is tearing me apart. Please, Estebar, save me. Take me from this terrible island. I cannot stand another moment on Delcentro!"

"You cannot stand being with Heodisi," Estebar corrected. Looking inland revealed fabulous fruit groves, grassy swards with delicate horned beasts lightly grazing. Delcentro was truly a fabulous garden of plenty. And across the meadow rose a palace unlike any Estebar had seen in his life. Gentle arches of parti-colored glass supported walls of shining alabaster. The sunlight caught stained-glass windows and lent an air of a cathedral to the palace, yet he knew it was no church.

It looked like the sort of mansion he would build, if he had limitless funds at his disposal.

"Your home?"

"Yes." The woman's bitterness increased. "For eight long years I have been held captive here. Heodisi stole me away from my family and binds me in servitude through my love for him." She swallowed hard. "I would kill him, but I can't."

"The spell," Estebar suggested.

"Yes."

"How can you accompany me if this love spell is so potent?" He wondered if the drab woman might leap over the rail of the *Serpent's Breath* in a vain attempt to swim back to the island, should they reach his vessel and succeed in sailing away.

"Chain me in the hold. Tie me to the mast and whip me with a cat-o'-nine-tails! The spell cannot hold me everywhere in the world. I...I would die before I spend another day in his foul embrace!"

Estebar walked to the edge of the cliff and looked down. Garmendian had packed the dinghy with treasure. The bulk of it worried Estebar. They had to row back through the bevy of monsters. Now was the time they could have used Pugg's strong back. More than the effort required to row, Estebar worried about the dinghy's seaworthiness. Riding so low in the water, it might be swamped by the smallest of waves.

"Heodisi refused to deal with me," Estebar said, growing uneasier by the moment. He looked back toward the palace, wondering if the sorcerer spied on his beloved. "He is an unpleasant person."

"Please, I beseech you. Take me with you. My name is Consuela and I will do anything!"

At the mention of her name, leaden storm clouds swirled above the cliff and a bolt of lightning rent the sky. The thunderclap was so powerful its force knocked Estebar to his knees.

"What's happening?" he demanded of Consuela.

"Heodisi! He has activated the ultimate ward spell. He thinks to close off the island and keep me here."

The intensity of the storm built until the wind almost took Estebar off his feet again as he made his way to the edge of the cliff. Peering down through the swirling gale building, he saw Garmendian pushing the dinghy out into the water.

"No, you can't go!" cried Estebar. "Don't leave me, you son of a squid!"

The first mate struggled to push the heavily laden boat into the tossing waves now assaulting the beach. Estebar started back down the trail to the beach, hoping to catch Garmendian before he got too far.

"Stop, wait, you can't go without me." Consuela staggered from the tent, now snapping like a whip in the strong wind. "I won't allow it!"

"If you can keep up with me, I'll take you," Estebar said, never intending to take her. Norron had been right. Dealing with a mage—and his loved ones—was a fool's errand.

"Stop!" Consuela took a step forward. She reached into the folds of her silken skirts and drew forth a small blue ball. Estebar hesitated at the top of the trail, and this proved his undoing. With a force and accuracy he had not believed possible in the gusty wind, the globe thrown by the woman smashed into his chest.

Estebar gasped, straightened and then felt...transformed. Transformed by his undying love for this ravishing creature.

"My love, my heart and soul," he cried out. Staggering to her, he took the woman in his arms and smothered her with kisses. His passion knew no bounds. He had to possess her, no matter the risk to life and possession.

"No, no, you fool," Consuela grated out, pushing him from her. "Take me—"

"Yes!"

"Take me to your ship. Get me off this island!"

"If it pleases you, it thrills me!" declared Estebar. Even as the words exploded from his lips, he knew what Consuela had done. The spell binding her to Heodisi now bound him to Consuela. More than this, Estebar understood the hatred she felt for the mage.

He shared it—and directed his toward the woman responsible for so amorously binding him.

"Too late, it's too late," moaned Consuela. "That fool with you is lost!"

Estebar saw it was true. Garmendian got the boat into the turbulent water, only to be swamped by a powerful wave and capsized. The frothy rush all around the first mate told Estebar the story. Heodisi's monsters dined messily once more on human flesh.

"I'm trapped," moaned Consuela, "trapped on this damnable island!"

"I will not share you!" Estebar cried. "I will kill him!"

"Yes, yes, do that," Consuela said, as if she did not care. Estebar knew she discarded him like an old boot now that he could not help her escape Delcentro, but knowing and feeling were different for him now. He had to kill Heodisi because it would please his lover, the love of his life. Whipping out his dagger and holding it high above his head, Estebar shrieked in rage and dashed off in the direction of the translucent palace, gleaming damply in the eye of the hurricane whipping all around the island.

Even as he ran toward the palace and his destiny with the mage, Estebar knew how foolish this was. He knew but could not stop himself. Against a powerful mage he had only a dagger—and his love for Consuela.

Gasping by the time he reached the front doors to the fabulous manor, Estebar wanted to stop and rest. But love drove him on. How Consuela had gained possession of the same spell Heodisi had used on her, he did not know. But she had, to his everlasting regret.

Bursting into the entry hall, Estebar cried, "Come here so I may kill you, you foul monster!" All around him lay the wealth of nations, gold and diamond mixed with silver with emerald. Furniture of the finest, most exotic polished woods, a floor inlaid with pearls the size of his fists, tapestries woven by masters, and paintings done by artists long dead. All these riches, and Estebar thought only of death and killing.

"So, she bewitched you, eh?" At the head of the stairs stood the smallish, skeleton of a mage. He wobbled down the stairs, a thick book under his arm. "There is no counter-spell I can cast, no potion strong enough to erase it. I was too clever by half when I formulated the spell of binding, but I can help. A little, I can help."

"I don't want you to lift the spell," shouted Estebar. "I want to kill you!"

He rushed forward, taking the mage by surprise. Heodisi stepped back, hit his heel and stumbled. Trying to catch himself only caused the sorcerer to plunge head over heels down the stairs. Every riser he struck caused a new grunt of pain from the tumbling mage. Heodisi crashed into the floor at the bottom of the staircase, lying bent and broken from his perilous descent.

"I...I know you want my help," the mage said.

"Why would you help me?" demanded Estebar.

"I want her for myself, all for myself," Heodisi grated out, his pain mounting. His trembling hand slipped into his robe and drew out a small bottle. "Drink this, just a drop and no more. It will...free you."

"It will kill me!"

"You will wish for death eventually if you don't drink," Heodisi said. "I love Consuela more than you can understand. Never have I loved another so much. I had to spell-bind her to me. She is so lovely, so caring."

Estebar rocked back, shaken. Consuela lovely? She was homely! No, no, she was pretty. She was his one true love. Never would he find another to cherish like her.

Estebar fought the tides of loving and loathing washing across his heart and soul. He believed Heodisi truly loved her and wanted to hold that love at any price, even if it meant having Consuela hate him. And the mage had to know how desperate Consuela must be to use the same spell on Estebar.

"Release?" Estebar choked out. Sweat beaded his forehead, and he felt torn by indecision. He loved Consuela. He loved her. He reached for the potion.

"Only a drop, only a drop," whispered Heodisi.

Estebar forced himself to uncork the potion. The pungent odor made his head swim. Barely did he wet his lips with a drop when he felt a new overpowering sensation seize him. Estebar had been punched in the belly now and again in fights, but this was a giant's blow that doubled him over.

"The ward spell on the island," Heodisi said. "You feel its full power now that you are free of Consuela's spell."

"I must leave," Estebar gasped.

"The potion, the potion, take it. The spell is forever. You must use the potion when it begins to wear off and..." Heodisi's voice trailed off. Then, stronger, he called out, "Consuela, my love! Come to me!"

Bursting through the front doors came Consuela, wild-eyed and bedraggled from the storm. She looked at Estebar, hatred in her eyes. Then she rushed to Heodisi and knelt beside him, cradling his head.

"My poor love, you are injured. What can I do?"

"Stay with me. My back. I think it's broken. Care for me, love me, love me."

Consuela turned her muddy eyes to Estebar, beseeching him. He backed away, then stopped. With the speed of a striking snake, he snared the potion bottle beside the mage and jumped away before Consuela could knock it from his hands. Thanks to the liqueur, he slipped free of her enchantment. But freedom from that spell left him duly exposed to the ward spell Heodisi had cast.

Estebar had to leave. He had to.

As he backed away, Consuela pleaded with him to stay. He ignored her and kept moving, letting the force of the ward spell hurry him along. Consuela tried to follow but Heodisi held her. She sagged down and cried openly—but she stayed with the paralyzed mage.

Estebar got to the doors, turned and ran. Through the storm he ran, stumbling and falling often, until he reached Heodisi's private dock where the magic-powered boat bobbed on the stormy waters.

Jumping in, Estebar wondered how to get the boat moving. He finally cast off the line and pointed toward the distant *Serpent's Breath,* now hidden in swirling dark clouds. The boat lurched and started away. With every fathom it moved away from the island, the gut-ripping sensation in Estebar's middle eased.

More than this, he saw how the boat sought only the shallows to avoid rampaging sea monsters. Heodisi's enchantment protected the boat as well as propelling it. As the boat lurched through the water, a provocative thought came to him. Estebar knew it was dangerous, but he had come to Delcentro for adventure. What he had found so far was only danger.

"There," he ordered the boat, changing his destination. "Go there!"

The boat slued and headed for the rocky beach where he had first landed. Of Garmendian he saw no trace, but the treasure that had drawn them to the island—bait planted by Consuela, Estebar guessed—still beckoned.

"Stay, stay until I command you," Estebar sternly ordered the boat. He climbed over the gunwale and dropped to the beach. He staggered as the power of Heodisi's ward spell hit him fully. Estebar forced himself to pick up the baubles Garmendian had discarded. He dared not go deep into the cave and sort through the better treasures. The spell tortured him every instant he remained on Delcentro.

When he had the magical boat half-filled, Estebar could stand no more. He tumbled into the bottom and weakly ordered the boat back to sea, toward the *Serpent's Breath*. Red curtains of pain caused his vision to fade as the boat cut through the storm, oblivious to the high waves and snapping monsters on all sides.

Estebar cried out when the boat crashed into something and came to a sudden halt.

"No, no, to the *Serpent's Breath*," he cried out.

From above came an angel's voice. "Ahoy, Estebar, that ye a' wantin' to come aboard?"

"Norron! Norron! Get me out of this damnable boat. And the treasure. Unload it, too."

Estebar tried to stand, but his legs turned to water. Strong hands pulled him erect and rough hemp rope circled his body, hoisting him into the air. He fell heavily to the deck of his beloved ship.

"Safe, safe at last," Estebar gasped out. He sat up, noting how the razor-edged pain in his gut faded away now that he was aboard.

"Ye brought back a fortune, ye did," Norron said, "but the boat's a goner. No sooner 'n we got it empty 'n it went to the bottom."

Estebar struggled to his feet and went to the railing. He stared through the storm clouds whipping about Delcentro and felt a longing unlike anything he had ever felt before. No pain from the ward spell seized him. No. Love held him in an increasingly powerful grip. Consuela, his lovely Consuela, waited for him on the island. He threw his leg up over the rail, ready to dive into the water and swim to her open arms.

"Stop 'im. Estebar's out of his mind!"

Strong hands pulled him back, again rescuing him. Estebar struggled, having to get to the island because Consuela waited for him there.

"Set sail! Get this godsforsaken ship under sail!"

"I need her, I need her so," Estebar whimpered. He fell to the deck, sobbing for his lover. His hand touched the bottle in his pocket. Estebar pulled it out and saw it was the potion Heodisi had given him on Delcentro. Estebar wetted his finger and ran the droplet over his lips. The overwhelming need to be with Consuela faded, replaced with the gut-tearing pain delivered by Heodisi's ward spell.

Estebar waved off Norron's anxious need to help.

"I am better," he said. Estebar stared at the receding green of Delcentro, then at the potion in his hand. Heodisi had said the love spell was permanent, forevermore. Only the potion he held robbed it of its power.

Temporarily.

"You thinkin' on returnin' any time soon, Estebar?" asked Norron, turning his good eye in Estebar's direction.

"Not unless I use all this," Estebar said, putting the bottle away safely. He worried that he would run out of the potion, but perhaps he could find another mage to blunt the spell or even remove it. Heodisi could not have been the most powerful sorcerer in all the world.

"Where to?" asked the captain of the *Serpent's Breath*.

"To port, to liberty for the crew," Estebar said. He laughed and pointed to the pile of treasure on the deck. "We must find someplace where we can spend such bounty!"

Estebar spoke of new ports and exotic entertainments, but he could not stop himself from looking back at Delcentro with just a pang of longing. For Consuela.

# Dance into the Fire

*This was not the published title. Al Sarrantonio bought this in 2001 for* Red Shift, *his SF follow-up volume to the blockbuster horror anthology* 999: Tales of Horror and Suspense, *but insisted on changing the title to "Feedback." Not a bad title, all things considered, but I liked my original better, so I'm resurrecting it for this collection. Your call. Which title do you like best?*

Visions of half-eaten junk food danced in Greer's head. He closed his eyes tightly and concentrated on only a few of the murky, indistinct fried tofu chips shaped into faux pork rinds. Too many extraneous images intruded for him to block, like a cannon fired in his ears, a laser shone into his eyes. As he focused the best he could on the ever-shifting, tormentingly shouted words and mind-searing images, a migraine headache started, far back in the vast reaches of his mind and spreading until it was a dark web sticking like glue to his every thought, dragging down every synapse, making his life a living hell.

*What shit,* blasted into his mind, causing Greer to reel. His thin-fingered hand clung to the desk as new waves of pain built in intensity to punish him for keeping this job. He sensed the tsunami approaching and tried to break off and get out of the man's mind. All he ever did was take abuse, and he hated it.

"Don't," came the cold words. "Don't you dare. We have to find out why the test group doesn't approve of Tofu Tasties."

Greer's watery eyes blinked open. Tears welled and ran down his cheeks. He did not wipe them away. The pain surged now and threatened to tear away his sanity.

"They taste like shit," he grated out.

"Did you receive that, or are you trying to weasel out of work again?"

"Th-that's what he's thinking." Greer swallowed hard and finally wiped away the tears with a crisp linen handkerchief taken from his coat pocket. He dragged it across his nose. For such a thin, small-nostriled nose, it produced an incredible among of gunk, as it always did when he delved too deeply into another human's mind. Into a non-telepath's squalid, unfocused mind.

*Why couldn't I get a telepath for a damned taste test? They wouldn't torture me like this with so much unmanageable fury. They focus themselves,* he screamed mentally. The echoes of his own thoughts rebounded from distant unknown corners in his own mind and produced even more pain.

*Are you all right, Greer?* came a faint, distant thought as soothing as the other was grating. Controlled, soft, like a cool drink on a sweltering day.

"Kathee," he gulped out, not sure if he sent it telepathically or spoke aloud. Greer cursed under his breath when he heard Lawrence Macmillan snort in disgust. The head of research marketing considered any telepathic contact other than with his precious test human "resource elements" to be a waste of valuable assets. Find those markets. Get them to buy. Dig into the consumers' deepest hidden thoughts and find out what they really think so they can be coerced into buying Tofu Tasties shit chips.

"You are on company time," Macmillan said coldly. "No personal communication."

"My head hurts," Greer said.

*Greer?*

He took a deep, calming breath, but the migraine refused to fade. He absorbed not only the vile taste of fried-in-pork-grease tofu but also the pent-up anger of the test subject. The man felt intense guilt because he was being paid to sample a product he hated. He wanted to speak out negatively but felt it would be a betrayal of taking money to try what he was told was a fine, tasty, healthful new comfort food. It was worse for Greer because he worked so hard to insinuate himself into the man's mind and had finally found what he thought of as a mental resonance. He meshed with the non-telepath through extreme effort and then paid the price for it by absorbing the undisciplined output.

It was like struggling furiously to get a funnel into his mouth and then choking when a fifty-five gallon drum was emptied into it. He hated the feeling, he hated commoners, he hated Macmillan most of all for forcing him to do this. Still, this was a better gig than most telepaths got, no matter how awful it might be.

*I'm hurting, Kathee, but I can make it through. Meet after work?*

*Don't know, too many arrested today. I still have to interrogate witnesses. Sergeant Fatass might make me work overtime.*

Greer sniffed, wiped again at his nose, and then tried to relax, using some of those silly mantras Kathee recommended. It was hell being a telepath, or even a half one like he was. What must it be like for Kathee, able to send and receive? She had to worry about everyone near who could pick up her telepathic transmissions, especially if she became angry. All he had to worry about was receiving. He was sensitive enough to pry into non-telepathic minds through great effort but could shut out the dull roar from those commoners if he got far enough away from their thronging crowds. It helped even more if he got drunk or distracted himself.

When would Macmillan get trained subjects?

Greer moaned again and pressed his hands to the temples. He knew that would never happen. Most people thought telepaths were something imaginary like Sasquatch and the yeti, no matter how the tabloids tried to cover the story.

"Greer, Greer!"

"Yes, sir."

"He verbally said he liked the snack all the way up the likability scale to a nine out of ten, but you claim he was thinking that Tofu Tasties were less than, uh, palatable?"

"Shit, sir, he said it was shit."

"Very well. Mr. Nakamuri will not be happy. This makes it unanimous on all test subjects this week."

"Can I go? I don't feel too good." Greer could not care less what their district manager thought of the survey results.

"I am sure you will feel much better the instant you are out of the office," Macmillan said with a nasty twist in his voice, as if he had found an oral knife and turned it savagely in a wound.

"Whatever you say, sir," Greer said. The lacy webs of migraine now thickened and burned, as if a rope net had been set on fire in his head. But Macmillan was right about one thing. Once he got away from the commoners, he would feel better.

* * *

*Haven't seen her tonight,* the man behind the bar thought.

Greer looked around but did not see Kathee. The usual crowd had drifted in, the ones too bored or too damaged by their work to tolerate the outside world much longer. He settled on the high stool and mentally ordered his usual.

*Hey, Greer,* called Erickson. Greer thought of him as "numb nuts" after he realized Erickson was his opposite, a transmitter and not a receiver. If there was a more worthless talent, Greer could not think of it. At least non-telepaths hired him to spy on each other. What did Erickson do? Implant thoughts? No amount of mental coercion could make anyone like Tofu Tasties.

"What do you want?" Greer asked nastily. His mind raced over all kinds of lewd possibilities for Erickson and reveled in knowing the man could not pick up a single one.

*I'm going to a screamer. Want to come?*

"What's that?"

*Something special, something you'll really like.*

Pictures leaked around what little control Erickson had in transmission, enticing Greer in spite of himself. He preferred solitary pleasures, but Erickson was excited and broadcast emotions along with the flood of kinky images. Greer knew he ought to keep his distance, but it had been a hard day, Kathee wasn't here, and he was perversely intrigued by what he received in Erickson's thoughts.

All telepaths were freaks to be exploited, but valuable ones to the police and corporations and to the government. Greer did not want to think what some of his colleagues were made to do for the black ops groups. The genetic tinkering had come from that segment of the government and to a large extent had remained the province of the spook, the spy, the saboteur...and assassin. It was about time he stopped being used and enjoyed himself.

His head began throbbing again. He needed some R&R. Why wasn't Kathee here? She was ugly as mud, but she was a two-way. When they fucked, Greer had no words for it. Feedback. Ecstasy. His passion fed hers and he picked up hers until they could not stand it any more. What difference did looks make when they could rock the heavens with their lovemaking?

"I want to wait a while longer," Greer said.

"She's got to work late," Erickson said aloud. "I heard. Besides, you might not want a nice girl like Kathee seeing this."

"A screamer?" Greer was intrigued against his own better judgment. Nothing Erickson had anything to do with could be good. The man was a loser. Then Greer reeled as a flood of new, more intense images hit him. Erickson was so excited he could not control himself.

"You can wait, but I want to get there for the special...show."

"You're part of it," Greer said in astonishment. "They tie you up and then—"

*Shut up!* came Erickson's frantic thought. *I don't want everyone to know. You're a friend. Special.*

Greer nodded, marveling at his bad luck to have a man like this consider him a friend. Hating himself for it but not able—unwilling?—to resist, Greer left with Erickson, headed down back alleys and past more than one alert telepathic sentry until they reached an abandoned warehouse near the old airport at the edge of town.

From inside Greer *heard* the excitement.

"This is it," Erickson said, licking his lips. Then he rubbed his hands together. "You and me, we got a special bond, don't we? You can really get off when I—"

Greer stared in wide-eyed fascination at Erickson. "I never thought you were like this."

*So they tie me up and beat me,* Erickson thought. *It's more exciting than anything else.*

"You want everyone in the warehouse to pick up everything you're thinking and feeling? Even humiliation?" Greer felt his heart pound a little faster. Telepaths were all potential voyeurs but generally avoided it among commoners since it was so difficult and distasteful, not to mention most of them were ordered to snoop as part of their jobs. At the end of a long day, getting out of a commoner's head was more important than diving back to eavesdrop. Among themselves, it was considered impolite in their mostly male society where offenses were settled more violently than in the commoner world. When you knew the depths of another man's thoughts, it provided a potent rationale for using force to decide an argument. After all, it was never impersonal.

"I wanted to be an actor. My company wouldn't let me. They wanted me to beam out motivational thoughts to their workers, for all the good that does. Like fucking Muzak stuffed into the head. That doesn't matter any more. This...this is better," said Erickson. "It's what I want to do."

They opened the heavy metal door and slipped inside. Guards stood on either side of the door. Both were receivers like Greer, checking to be sure they belonged. Erickson obviously did. Greer wasn't so sure about himself, but the guards let him pass. He heard their acknowledgment of his telepathic abilities.

The warehouse was dusty and dark, with only a few spotlights shining on a man-high thick metal post equipped with shackles. Greer scanned the crowd quickly. Perhaps a dozen, all men, which wasn't too unusual. The XY chromosome combination produced ninety-nine male telepaths for every female. While men were mostly receivers, a few were only transmitters like Erickson. Greer had never found both talents in one man. That combination seemed reserved for women.

Too bad Kathee wasn't here. Greer would have enjoyed *feeling* what she did as she took in the anticipation of the crowd, their enthusiasm, their perverse excitement and rebroadcast it with her own slant. He felt dirty and discovered he liked it. Even worse, he thought Kathee would, too.

Greer was suddenly pushed out of the way as two men, stripped to the waist and sweating, grabbed Erickson and dragged him off. Greer recoiled at Erickson's response. Fear. Anticipation that became something more than sexual as the shackles locked around his wrists. They ripped away Erickson's shirt and the slow, methodical lashing began.

Every crack of the whip caused Erickson to send out agonizing waves of mental pain. Agonizing for him but also curiously enjoyable for the baker's dozen of spectators. Greer found himself transfixed, hypnotized by the sweet-and-sour mixture of emotions flooding from Erickson's mind. He loved the pain and degradation.

He loved the pain and degradation of others receiving his deepest, darkest thoughts as much as Greer loved sharing it.

\* \* \*

*That's disgusting,* Kathee thought.

Greer caught small hints of possible betrayal in the woman's thought. As light as a feather falling or a butterfly wing brushing his cheek, she considered telling the vice squad about the screamer. Kathee worked for robbery division but was often loaned to other departments for interrogation of difficult or important witnesses. When the courts decided if using a telepath to squeeze information out of a defendant was legal, she would be even more in demand.

Greer hated his job, but sinking into the minds of people who might be rapists and murderers was worse. How did she tolerate it?

*Is it worse than letting that fool Erickson degrade himself like that?*

Greer focused. Kathee could pick up his thoughts as easily as he did hers.

*It was something he wanted to do,* Greer thought. *Even commoners for blocks around got off on it. I saw some of them reeling as we left the warehouse. They didn't know what had happened, but they had gotten enough from Erickson's transmission to experience his thrill.*

*It shouldn't be something you want to eavesdrop on,* she shot back.

*But Kathee, this isn't eavesdropping. Erickson knew I was there. He knew everyone wanted to...share.* It sounded feeble, but Greer laced it with some of the excitement he had experienced. He felt her wavering. Kathee knew what was moral, but this transcended the ordinary. This was uniquely telepathic. Was it wrong to share that which is freely given?

*Erickson is going to get into trouble.*

"How?" Greer asked aloud. He stared into her myopic eyes and wondered what it might be like if she had been there, to take in Erickson's pain and stark emotional response and then filter and magnify it through her own mind. That might be the experience of a lifetime.

*Are you so bored?*

*Bored, tired, disgusted, all of that,* he agreed. Greer caught her fleeting agreement. Kathee was all that—and more. Life had become too ordinary for them. A screamer gave a new, if outlandish, diversion.

*What happens if he is seriously injured? Erickson is a powerful sender. You know how dangerous it can be for a telepath to be close when someone is hurt.*

*No, no, I don't,* Greer said. This was one of the questions that had never been answered to his satisfaction. While he had not pursued the query too aggressively, he had never found a telepath who had been with anyone who had died, who had been mentally linked to the dying person. There were so few telepaths—and those who might have been in a position to tell had died with everyone around them in a variety of accidents.

Commoners had their distinctive urban myths. Telepaths had their own.

*There are so few of us, you should be careful. Erickson is a dangerous man because he's not quite right in the head.*

"You're right in one respect. It was disgusting, but it was also, I don't know, intriguing. I couldn't force myself away."

*Erickson might have died.*

Greer sucked in a deep breath and let it out slowly. That had occurred to him, and it excited him as much as the flood of pain and desire from the shackled Erickson as the men took turns whipping him.

"Yeah," he said, looking at her. She was worse than plain. She was downright ugly. Greer made no effort to hide the thought. Kathee knew her appeal lay in other directions. Greer had heard of only three other telepaths who could both send and receive thoughts, and they might be part of the myth structure because no one he knew had ever met them.

He was lucky Kathee had chosen him among all the other telepaths.

*Damn right you're lucky,* came her thought. *That's why this is so out of character for you. Why?*

"I can't explain it," Greer admitted. "I was repelled and attracted at the same time."

*More attracted than repelled or you would have left.*

He had no answer to that. She was right.

"Have you heard about such things going on? This was the first anyone had mentioned it to me."

*Rumors. Always rumors.*

"Screamers might be fairly new," Greer said. "There have been so few of us, but there are more all the time."

*Receivers,* Kathee thought bitterly. "And men," she said aloud. Her muddy brown eyes blinked myopically as she stared at him from inches away. They were naked and lying alongside one another in bed and yet felt a thousand miles apart.

"And men," he said, grinning. He moved closer and began making love to her. Somehow, as he climaxed, his thoughts were not on her passion being fed telepathically into his brain but of Erickson.

Erickson could have died.

What would that have felt like?

\* \* \*

He tried everything in the next two weeks. Nothing matched the thrill Greer had felt at the screamer. It began taking on an almost mythic proportion

159

in his thoughts, even pushing aside sex with Kathee. Greer became fascinated—or obsessed. He wanted more.

He hunted for Erickson, but the man had vanished. No one had seen him or even caught a vagrant thought from him. Greer was positive Erickson did this on purpose to annoy him, because nothing else about the man was pleasant. They weren't friends, but Greer found a bond between them after the screamer that he could not deny.

Erickson enjoyed sending out waves of pain. Greer liked sharing.

*It's because you don't have to worry about scars,* Kathee said, sitting down beside him at the bar.

"It's more than that," Greer said, eager to discuss the matter. The more he talked about it, the more he remembered. Or so it seemed.

Too much of the screamer was like a will'o-the-wisp, there but not there when he looked too hard. Fairy gold. Reach out and try to touch it and it evaporated. A handful of ocean. Wet remaining but more the memory of the salty water.

*For all you know, he might have died,* Kathee thought.

*I checked the hospitals. And no one has seen or heard about him. You know how we gossip. Someone would have heard.*

"Honey," Kathee said in her unpleasantly shrill voice as she moved closer. "Don't you see anything wrong?"

"No, of course not," Greer said huffily. "If you'd been there, you would have felt the same way." He paused when he looked into the woman's face. A smile crept onto his lips. "You would have enjoyed it, wouldn't you? That's what is bothering you."

*It's so good when we make love.*

*What would it be like if dozens of people magnified those feelings and returned them to you?* he asked.

Kathee shivered and tried to push the thought away. Greer caught snippets, no matter how she tried to deny it. She was as intrigued as he had been—and as repelled. It was a powerful combination.

*Let's find him,* Greer suggested. "Or another screamer. There were enough people there that it can't be a one-shot occurrence."

She looked at him, disapproval on her face. But he saw into her mind. Hand in hand, they left to find a screamer.

\* \* \*

*I recognize most of them here,* Kathee said, surprised. *I don't know why that strikes me as unusual since I have contact with so many officially.*

Greer realized how insular his job was. Kathee knew the other telepaths. Hundreds and hundreds of them, all flocking here for the same reason he and Kathee were. Some of the crowd he had seen before, in the bar and at social gatherings. Most were complete strangers, but not strangers, either. He caught some of their arousal at the idea of sharing the sadomasochist exhibition. Finding this screamer had been easier than he thought, and no one had tried to hide it.

Greer licked his lips. Three posts were erected in the middle of the clearing in the junkyard. No spotlights, just crowding close, mingling, moving around as the three men were shackled. The entire assemblage crushed in close so they were almost shoulder to shoulder. Kathee squeezed his hand as if he might try to flee.

Greer wouldn't go. Not now. He felt the excitement mounting and shared it in much the way he did with Kathee when they were having sex. But this was different, had different layers and emotions and was infinitely more varied and complex.

*Philosophical emotions?* Kathee asked.

*Don't analyze it. Just enjoy it.*

*I don't know that I can. It is so...so unnatural.*

*That's what makes it exciting,* Greer said. Look! *The man chained at the far post. That's Erickson!*

He held her in his arms as the first whip rose and lashed against Erickson's bare flesh. Both he and Kathee moved to only a few feet away and received Erickson's full mental anguish and ecstasy.

The woman tensed in his arms and then snaked her arm around his waist and held him closer.

*I've never felt anything like this,* she admitted.

*You like it.* He did not accuse. He only said what was obvious.

*Yes.*

The crowd grew in size, and the intensity of the emotion flowing from the three men being lashed grew. Erickson did not see them. He was too deep in relishing the pain he received. The emotions were pure and laser-sharp and shared by everyone in the junkyard. This was illicit and wrong and forbidden and ever so much more exciting because of the shared weakness.

The shared transgression.

The shared sexual excitement.

*Closer,* Kathee thought. *If we get closer, it will be more intense.*

They moved to Erickson's side. So did the others in the crowd. They touched now, shoulders rubbed and bodies jerking in response to every lash. It wasn't planned, but the three men using the whips began striking their blows in unison on their victims' backs. This caused the flood of emotion to magnify itself a hundredfold, in synch like a laser beam powering up. Greer and Kathee moved even closer until they could almost touch Erickson. He looked at them, his eyes wild and bright with transcendence. They both felt his rapture.

Greer felt weak in the knees. He knew he should leave. This was wrong. Kathee had said so, and he was too impotent to listen. He moved closer, as eager as a boy at his first peep show.

*More, more, more!*

Greer wasn't sure if the crowd thought this or if Kathee sent it. The men chained to the posts sobbed and moaned and took every lash. Only Erickson could speak—or project his thoughts clearly. He wanted more, too.

A feedback began that drew Greer even closer. Kathee was beside him. Her face was pale and strained. He realized she was accepting the telepathic outpouring and then retransmitting it, filtered of extraneous thoughts so the emotion became stronger and more stimulating. Pure pain. Pure pleasure.

Greer's body began to respond. Around him he heard other men crying out, but he could not move. He turned to the heat, the telepathic heat that drew him like a moth to a flame.

*I want more,* he got from Kathee. She directed and shaped and magnified the emotional outpouring of the crowd. He saw how pale she had become, how indistinct and ghostlike. Her hands shook as she edged closer. He liked the feel of her body against his, the way her thoughts surged and beat against his like ocean waves rising at the start of a storm.

More, Greer wanted more. He held her and knew the others in the group crowded toward them, too. Before, when Erickson had been the sacrificial lamb, it had been thrilling but not like this. Greer had been a virgin then and unable to accept all that was sent his way. Not now. He shared his expertise with Kathee.

*Kathee,* he thought. *You are the difference tonight.*

Greer felt the hundreds in the crowd suck in their collective breaths as the feedback built in intensity. From the three being whipped to the receivers and Kathee, through Kathee and back, filtered and magnified for everyone to relish, even those shackled to the posts. Their excitement mounted and fed the crowd and Kathee and him. A link formed between Erickson and Kathee, stronger and more potent than anything Greer had ever felt before.

Spinning dizzily, Greer felt the migraine at the back of his head begin. He ignored it. The feelings cascading into his body and soul were too intense for mere pain now.

*Greer,* Kathee thought. *I...I—*

Words were no longer enough as the pressures within grew, pressures of guilt and lust and illicit sharing.

Greer screamed and felt as if he had been launched on a rocket. His mental echoes quivered forth and resonated with the others that fed Kathee.

Feedback. Growing intensity. Tidal wave. Out of control. Deliciously out of control!

Greer experienced a freaky second where he knew they would all die from ecstasy. He had discovered what it meant to be a telepath. He liked it.

Over and up and around and ever increasing their exhilaration grew until they were consumed in a huge flame of stark rapture that destroyed them and then began snuffing out the lesser lights of non-telepaths across the world.

The world did not end in fire or ice. It ended in orgasm

.

# Jug of Evil

*Ruminations on good and evil abound in fiction. "Jug of Evil" fits nicely into that niche, with a fantasy twist, of course. Writing it back in mid 1998, I used a common thief sent to steal something decidedly uncommon. The protagonist, Netissen, learns a hard lesson and inflicts the result on all humanity.*

"Get out of my way, you piece of filthy offal!" the merchant shouted, kicking at the mendicant. The one-legged beggar curled into a ball against a crumbling mud wall as the merchant stumbled and fell over him when a poorly delivered kick missed. This enraged the merchant even more. He began beating the beggar with a silver-tipped walking stick. The beggar whimpered and moaned with each blow, thin arms up to protect his head.

Only Netissen blundering into the merchant stopped the rain of powerful blows.

"Sh-sorry," Netissen slurred, clutching at the merchant for support. "You wanna j-join me for a drink? Th-that place back there. The Wounded Boar is t-terrible. Must be some place around this miserable t-town th-that doesn't water its wine."

"I own the Boar!" the merchant shouted, his wrath turning from the beggar to Netissen. The wine merchant scowled into the handsome face, marred by a long thin white scar from the upper right forehead, across the nose and cheek, ending in a gouged-out cavity on the left jaw. Netissen's bright green eyes were half-closed but never left the merchant's bloodshot ones.

"Then you are a public n-nuisance," declared Netissen, stumbling forward again. His arm caught the other man's and made the merchant drop his walking stick. It clattered on the cobblestones. "Sh-sorry, let me." Netissen bent to pick up the fallen stick. He managed to bump the merchant and knock him down.

The man grabbed his stick and swung awkwardly at Netissen from the ground. The blow missed by inches.

"Get out of my sight!" raged the merchant.

Netissen fell to the street beside the beggar and hiccupped loudly, his head sagging. The merchant gasped and struggled and finally got to his feet, grumbling to himself about finding a constable.

Only when the merchant had gone did Netissen brighten, reach into the folds of his cape and pull out a leather bag heavy with coin. He tossed it to the beggar.

"Have a good day, sir," he said, lithely getting to his feet.

"There must be a hundred silvers in here!" cried the beggar.

"Little enough payment for enduring such churlish behavior. And he does water his wine," Netissen said cheerfully, walking off. He was inordinately pleased with himself, both stealing the merchant's receipts for the day so adroitly and applying the wealth in a more equitable fashion. No one was a better thief than Netissen, no one.

A heavy hand crashed to his shoulder, stopping him in his tracks.

"I saw you steal Blekko's money," came the accusation.

Netissen turned, ready to fight the constable for his freedom, although he carried only a short knife. Unlike many thieves in the fair city of Thoda, he preferred not to carry a sword. It only got him into trouble he never sought. Stealth and a quick wit worked better than a long sword and powerful thrust.

Netissen smiled. There were some powerful thrusts of a more intimate sword he far preferred.

Netissen pushed such thoughts away when he saw his accuser. He bowed deeply.

"Seldom do I come across a priest of the Holy Pentangle with such a sharp eye. I applaud your acuity."

"You stole. That is a sin," the stocky, tonsured priest said firmly.

"Which is the worse crime, to beat a defenseless beggar or to steal from the fiend and give the money to one who sorely needs it?"

"Perhaps the money might be considered settlement of valid claim," the priest mused, rubbing his chin. Netissen saw the man had missed few meals. His robes were clean and new and his hair was waxed back in the elaborate Predorian style favored by both high-born lady and holy man.

"Yes, so it might," Netissen said. "If you do not mind, I have business across town." He bowed again and again a strong hand held him in place.

"You are a thief." The priest did not indict as much as he stated a simple fact. Netissen saw no reason to deny it. The priest seemed taken aback by the honesty in his confession.

"I have no reason to lie. By my lights, I am an honest man. A thief, yes, but one also who aids society where court and king often fail." Netissen saw how this caused the priest to stiffen slightly and stare more attentively at him, if this were possible. Netissen felt like some specimen brought to an academic for study.

"I have need of an honest...thief," the priest said.

"You intrigue me with such a requirement," Netissen said. "Come, let us find a quiet place to discuss this matter. Is your rectory near?" Netissen suggested this to see if the priest meant to discuss something legal or if he intended to circumvent the moral teachings of his church. It surprised Netissen when the priest led the way to the Cathedral of All Souls, the holiest sanctuary in Thoda. Whatever the priest intended, it would not be immoral.

165

Or so Netissen thought as he entered, bowed reverently in the five directions, then settled into a pew to the left in the nave. The priest made his lengthy absolutions, which gave Netissen time to consider why he had accompanied the holy man. Life had been dull of late. He had plenty in his belly, a good roof over his head, and a lovely companion—he sighed just thinking of honey-haired Fionella. So exquisitely talented, that fair young lady.

The priest sat beside Netissen, robes hissing slightly as he moved. The scent of burned candle mingled with that of the priest's pomade. The holy man's uneasiness mounted; Netissen did nothing to break the tension. He would find out more by remaining silent rather than filling the vacuum with meaningless chatter.

The priest almost blurted, "I can no longer stand the impiety that abounds in the kingdom!"

"Combating such iniquity is a life's work for a priest of the Holy Pentangle," Netissen said cautiously.

"But it runs rampant. Evil overflows and threatens to drown even the pious! It must be stopped, even if it means I must do something immoral. Is not a sin justified if a larger wickedness is eradicated?"

"Do you wish my pledge never to steal again?" Netissen asked, wondering at the penalty to his soul for lying to a priest in such a holy place.

"No!" The fervor of the priest's denial caused Netissen to sit up straighter. He studied the man and saw the fire of righteousness burning in his deep-set eyes. "This is a complex moral issue for me. Is a lesser sin justified to remove a greater one?"

"Such philosophical disputation is beyond my limited powers," Netissen said, still not sure of the priest's intentions. "What do you want of me?"

"I want you to remove the source of all this debauchery, all this crime, all the boundless impiety that blackens the very soul of our great society!"

"You are better suited to this pursuit than I," Netissen said, shrugging and making an elaborate gesture with his long-fingered hands. "Aren't you?"

"Here," the priest said, thrusting a scrap of paper into Netissen's grasp. "That spot marks the Vale of Tunhiti. You must go there and stopper the jug you find there and return it to this cathedral. Steal the jug and you shall win accolades eternal."

"What is the nature of this jug you, a holy man, engage me to steal?" asked Netissen.

His heart beat faster when the priest told him.

\* \* \*

166

The journey to the foothills of the Marse Mountains had been arduous, but Netissen had enjoyed his traveling companions in the commerce wagon, at least to the point where two tried to rob him. He carried precious little of worth with him, save for the curious silver-chased stopper the priest had given him. It had been blessed and might have been beatified and canonized for all Netissen knew, but it was the stopper he needed for the jug in the Vale of Tunhiti. As such, he could not allow it to be stolen, especially by such inept thieves.

He ended up with their scrawny purses and a bumpkin of a constable chasing after him. Eluding the lawman had taken the better part of a day, then Netissen had entered the mountain pass leading to the vale. Often checking the map given him by the priest slowed his advance, but he knew a mistake now might mean long hours following a false trail. So many small footpaths branched off like strands in a drunken spider's web from the pass, forcing him to study his map several times an hour.

He felt the rightness of his path as he trudged along a narrow, rocky, uphill trail that emerged into a narrow, verdant valley that stretched unnaturally halfway up the sheer rocky slopes.

"Ah, priest, how did you happen upon this tasty tidbit of knowledge? That is a question I ought to have asked." Netissen fingered the stopper, wondering at the intelligence gathering that had preceded his trip to Tunhiti. He had heard of this place, but always in hushed tones as if the speaker feared for his life should the very name be overheard by the wrong people.

Not for the first time, Netissen wondered if he was the only one the priest had sent on this dubious quest. The road to the foothills had been packed with pilgrims—and thieves—but had someone else walked this way previously on the identical mission? The priest had given no hint as to the wards and traps protecting the jug.

Netissen laughed as he considered it. The Jug of All Evil, the priest had named it. The holy man thought the jug created a counterbalance to good and caused the weak, worldly wanderer along life's byway to go astray. Such a cosmic device would not rest in this lovely valley, thought Netissen, though treasure of some worth might be unearthed. That alone would be reward for the trip away from rich Thoda and Fionella's warmth and bed.

"This is where he traveled, I tell you. I am an expert tracker."

"You are expert only at playin' with yourself, you—" The second voice cut off in a gurgle.

"Hush. He will overhear," came the first speaker's loud voice. If Netissen had not overheard their dialog, he would have noticed the rock tumbling down the path as they carelessly walked or even the stench drifting on the wind from their direction. Not only were they meat eaters, they chose never to bathe.

Netissen's nose wrinkled at the olfactory insult as he squeezed into a rock crevice to allow the argumentative pair to pass.

He nodded to himself when he caught sight of them. They were the two who had tried to rob him, only to have their own purses emptied for his financial advancement. Pin and Volphi they called themselves, Volphi the leader. He was a bulky brute with a prominent brow and piglike eyes and reminded Netissen of a bull pawing constantly at the dirt and absentmindedly wondering what had irritated him. Pin was shorter but no less sturdy of build. If anything, he seemed even less bright than his companion in thievery.

Neither dressed well, both stank, and either might have overheard the priest in Thoda giving Netissen his final instructions before departure.

"How'd he get so far ahead of us?" whined Pin. "We been damned near runnin', we have."

"He might be behind us," Volphi said. "If he is, we can lay a trap for him. I tell you, I'm a good tracker."

"So good you can get in front of him on this narrow trail without ever seein' him?" asked Pin.

Netissen smiled. Volphi had to be a decent trailsman to follow this far, but he was not bright enough to realize he could not follow a trail Netissen had not yet made. The two went on into the valley, arguing and making enough noise to raise the dead. Netissen slipped from his hiding place and followed cautiously, knowing Volphi might decide to lay his trap at any time.

He need not have worried. The pair of thieves hurried on, sure of themselves and their skills. Netissen, however, grew increasingly uneasy as he descended into the valley, a curious blend of euphoria and dread twisting his senses. This combination changed when he reached the floor of the valley. He did not need to be told the jug lay ahead.

He felt it in his bones.

And it was evil.

Netissen stopped in front of a low, locked gate and laughed aloud. This could never stop a determined man. He went to vault the low stone fence, only to find himself thrown back, as if caught by a giant invisible hand. Shaking his head, Netissen returned to the gate and reached out.

He jerked back as if stung. Some spell protected against entry. Netissen dropped to his knees and studied the lock on the gate. It took almost twenty minutes for him to use picklocks and skill to pop open the hasp. A slow smile crossed his face, causing his scar to wiggle a little.

"Who's the best thief in all the land?" he asked himself. Netissen slid past the gate and waited for the next challenge to his skill. The lack of planning that went into the deadfalls and spring traps amused him. There was no challenge to his talents.

As he walked along the narrow path into a deserted, destroyed city, a clutching horror grew within him. Netissen might circumvent any lock or trap but this feeling might drive him away unless he screwed up his courage. The priest depended on him to accomplish this mission. He became turned around following the corkscrewing paths, then closed his eyes and let his natural talents dictate his course. Every step filled him with dread, but he continued.

Netissen swallowed hard, wondering if the priest had not stumbled onto a secret of the universe hidden from all others. Believing this peaceful appearing valley was the core of evil came easily as Netissen penetrated further. He heard Volphi and Pin ahead of him, but the winding trail kept them hidden from his direct view. They argued with increasing rancor until he left the trail and cut diagonally across the valley to avoid them.

"I should kill them," Netissen said to himself. "Avoiding them is cowardly, however." He found himself torn between stabbing them as they slept and running away, neither solution to his problem likely to have occurred to him before entering the Vale of Tunhiti.

He sank down and settled his mind, piecing together the thoughts of the old Netissen and those of the new—the Netissen who had entered this place. Sorting out the two and comparing them left him cold and shaken. He wanted to steal—that could be either of the facets he discovered within himself now. But he wanted to steal from anyone having more.

A beggar with a rotted apple? A cruel prince with a gold hoard seized through unjust taxation? Both were equal to him now.

Now.

Netissen wiped his lips and knew the changes in his values blew fitfully like the very wind. One second he fought a mindless killing frenzy and the next he experienced only the cold certainty of an executioner willing to slay one he knew to be innocent. Evil. And it ebbed and flowed like the very ocean's tide through him.

"I must hurry and find the jug," Netissen said softly. "To linger in Tunhiti will mean my death—or sanity."

He was a thief and proud of his skills, but he felt the nudging and twisting and even bludgeoning of his ability to choose whom he robbed. Thievery for its own sake grew as a reason within him.

Netissen hurried on, following the sensation of growing iniquity. He went deeper into the ruins of the city—Tunhiti?—and made his way through debris-strewn streets. Skeletons long since picked clean and bleached in the hot sun littered the streets. Some had daggers thrust between ribs—often from the back. Others had been savagely dismembered before death. And everywhere hung the choking miasma of heartless, inhuman killing.

Netissen crouched by a tumbled down wall and peered into the central plaza. On a pedestal of the purest black granite stood a simple clay urn, hardly a foot high. If Netissen had seen this on a shelf in a store he burgled, he would never have given it a second look. He could not take his eyes from this jug. Tiny wisps of blue and yellow vapors curled over the lip of the jug and ran down the sides of the pedestal, carried into oblivion by the gentle wind caressing the plaza.

Or were those vapors truly digested by the wind? A slight hint of a purplish gas touched Netissen, and he experienced an insane urge to rape. As quickly as the sensation smashed into him like a hammer blow, it vanished, leaving him terrified and exhausted. Never had he felt such potent, wicked emotion before.

Hands trembling, he took out the silver stopper the priest had given him. But how was he to reach the jug and stuff the blessed plug in? The faintest whiff of evil from the jug had left him weak in reaction. More mist from within the jug whipped out and into the wind turned brisk and blowing from his back. But Netissen dared not rush forward under cover of this favorable wind because it was so capricious. Even as the thought came to him, the breeze shifted.

Every color of the shimmering rainbow was represented in the gases pouring forth. Netissen knew every hue matched a sin, a venal urge, an uncontrollable need to perform the vilest of acts. This jug might send forth its vapors across the entire world, causing untold immorality to be perpetrated, but here it was most powerful. Too powerful. And too dangerous to approach.

Netissen considered holding his breath, but the distance to the jug on its pedestal was great. And then he saw another problem. From across the plaza came the grating voices of Pin and Volphi, still arguing, still not sure what they had blundered into.

"Lookit that," declared Pin. "A vase. Might be worth something, you think?"

"Why'd they leave anything worth a bent copper in the center of a ruined city where any fool could see it?" demanded Volphi. "It can't be worth the trouble of carrying it off."

As the two thieves approached the jug, their argument turned more violent—and Netissen saw how the jug of evil responded to their presence. The vapors creeping over the lip now curved and writhed like misty snakes in the direction of the pair, leaving one side free of influence.

Netissen hoped this side was entirely innocent of the evil vapors. He sucked in his breath, clutched the stopper and ran as hard as he could for the black granite pedestal and the jug perched on it.

Lungs at the point of exploding from his exertion and the distance he had run, Netissen stumbled closer to the jug. The mists still flowed toward Pin and Volphi. The two had drawn their swords and faced one another, their curses increasingly vile and personal. All this Netissen saw from the corner of his eye as he struggled toward the jug and its blast of colored, airy evil. Fingers of red and yellow and green and purple sneaked from the mouth of the jug now, mostly wending toward the dueling thieves.

Head spinning, pulse hammering, hand shaking, Netissen saw the jug sense his presence and begin to spew forth clouds of ebon steam in his direction. The lightest touch of this black miasma triggered every evil impulse he had ever considered in the dead of night, with no one to accuse him.

The vileness staggered him. Netissen fell to his knees, arms still raised above his head as if he worshipped the evil coming from this fountain of the profane. Volphi screamed as Pin's blade pierced his gut. Pin grunted when Volphi's fist crushed his face.

Netissen jerked erect again and fell forward, the silver stopper in his hands. The instant the plug filled the jug's mouth, the hideous impulses vanished. Netissen crashed to the rubble-strewn plaza and gasped. What foolish mage had loosed this on the world?

"What god?" he asked in awe, staring at the jug. It seemed so innocent, yet he knew. He knew too well.

Netissen picked up the jug and walked to where Volphi and Pin lay. One had cut the other's throat in his death throes. So much blood pooled around them Netissen could not tell which had died the messier death. He skirted the area and walked away, feeling nothing, not triumph and not sorrow.

Nothing. He had triumphed over the ultimate evil and he felt nothing.

\* \* \*

The blind beggar held out a cup. It was empty. Netissen felt no urge to give from his own considerable purse. He walked about the central market of Thoda, noting the lack of eagerness among its merchants for their dickering, the deadness of spirit in the customers, the utter neutrality of it all.

He accidentally bumped into a burly man, who spun away, saying nothing. Not a curse, not an apology. The collision had simply...happened.

Netissen walked on to the Cathedral of All Souls. No one had attended vespers, normally the most crowded service of the day. Only the priest knelt at the altar. Netissen entered, considered genuflecting in the five directions and then decided not to. No evil could come to him if he failed morally. There was no protection now that he had brought the Jug of All Evil to the priest—and no need of it. There was no evil. There was no way to fail morally.

Simple to the point of being nondescript, the jug sat on the altar, protected by the holy five points, at each burning a scented candle.

"Your service is poorly attended," Netissen observed.

"So it is," the priest said. "Little need of my assistance in spiritual matters is required now that evil has been contained." He glanced at the jug. "Thank you for doing what I and so many other prelates have failed to do over the centuries. Evil need not walk among us any more."

Netissen took no pleasure in his accomplishment. He took no thrill in anything. The urge to steal had left him. So had the urge to do good. He could look at the starving faces of the beggars in the streets of Thoda and feel no outrage. They starved; he felt...nothing.

"How are the church's collections for good works?" Netissen asked.

"What? Why, I have not checked. There seems to be little of late."

None, guessed Netissen. He sank to his knees and tried to pray and found he could not. The priest continued to ramble on inconsequentially about this and that. Netissen hardly heard.

"Thank you again," the priest said, patting Netissen on the shoulder. There was no real emotion behind the acknowledgement of what he had truly done. Netissen said nothing as the priest left to do who knows what. No parishioner required absolution for venal or mortal sin now. None was committed. In all Thoda no crime had occurred since Netissen had stoppered the jug.

And no act of charity, heroism, or loving benevolence had occurred, either.

Netissen knew what had to be done, even if it cost him his soul. When the priest vanished into his cloister, Netissen forced himself to action, sprang forward before he changed his mind, his quick hands finding the smooth, cool sides of the jug. In a minute he had left the Cathedral of All Souls. In an hour Thoda lay far behind him. In a week he entered the Vale of Tunhiti.

And in a week and a second, standing by a black granite pedestal, Netissen popped free the silver plug from the jug.

Without evil there could be no good.

# Enduring Art

*Robert Bloch was not only a master of horror, he was also an accomplished editor. Most authors with a name so indelibly etched in your mind would banner that name and let someone else do the actual work on an anthology. Not Bob Bloch. He selected the stories and he edited the stories, ensuring that a Robert Bloch anthology was, I swear by Norman Bates' mother, his sweat and blood. The* Psycho Paths *anthology was released in 1991. (No word yet when I'll be released from the psycho ward...)*

"It's a masterpiece. A goddamn masterpiece, isn't it?" Marvin Arthurs looked expectantly at his girlfriend. Anita Kovel stepped back, nervously pushed a vagrant strand of dishwater blonde hair from her eyes and then licked her lips. Arthurs read her like a book. The bitch didn't like it. She hated it. And it was good. It was better than good. She never liked anything he did, not any more.

"Art, it's...so strange," she said. She licked her lips again and her sea-green eyes darted around. She was looking for some way to escape confronting his genius. Work of such magnitude frightened her, and it should, he thought. This was better than anything the other environmental artists did. Even Jean Verame's painted stones near Amarillo couldn't compare when he finished. The maquette would be translated from the bare rock of a mountain in ways not seen since Gutzon Borglum chiseled away at Mt. Rushmore. He would make an even more notable contribution to environmental art than the current master, James Turrell and the Roden Crater!

"It's the best work I've ever done." Arthurs turned from the chubby woman and smiled. It was good. Damned good.

"It's a piece of shit, Art," Anita said in a quavering voice. "And it's messed up the entire apartment. The place looks more like a pigpen than ever before."

It took him a second to shift from his appreciation of the six-hundred-pound welded iron bar and concrete maquette of a fornicating Cerberus to his surroundings. The welding torch had singed a few of the frilly things Anita had scattered around, and the cement he had used so freely lay like a gray shroud on the furniture. It hardly mattered what he had done to the wood floor. The place was rented. What did she want from him? He had to create. The maquette was his blueprint for the finished piece, an entire mountain carved into the dog's likeness.

"What—" he began.

"Art, I can't go on like this. You rob garbage cans and landfills and hang it all together and call it a...masterpiece. You live like a slob. And you haven't paid your share of the rent in six months."

"You've got a grant."

"It's hardly enough for me to live on. I can't keep supporting both of us, Art. I can't!" Anita's voice rose an octave and grated shrilly on Arthurs' ears. He wanted to flip down his welder's mask, turn on the torch and cut out her vocal cords.

"You haven't lost the grant?" His voice was accusing. She was dumb enough to do something like that. They needed that money to keep going. Arthurs wasn't quite sure why the University of Colorado gave her a red cent for studying pre-Raphaelite poetry, whatever that was, but he needed the money. After finishing with the three-headed Cerberus maquette, he could sell it for thousands and put them on easy street. Who wouldn't buy the miniature of an entire mountain of sculpture known around the world?

"I haven't," she said angrily, "and that's not the point. You're the point." Anita turned and pointed in the direction of the bedroom. "That's the point, too. And so are they." She puffed out her chest and Arthurs knew she was really mad at him. Tears leaked from the corners of her eyes.

"They're my friends. They need a place to stay." Arthurs faced Jamil and the two men with him. They had returned at a bad time. Why did Anita always have to make a scene in front of his friends?

"Of all the places in Boulder, why do they have to crash here?"

"Please," spoke up Jamil, seeing the problem. "You are upset. My friends do not speak the good English. Art has been kind enough to allow us to reside here. It is not for long." The silent communication passing among the three Iranians was undecipherable. Anita was past caring.

"You stay, I'll go. I'll have my things out of here in an hour—if you haven't welded them into some hideous sculpture weighing a million pounds." She jerked free when Arthurs tried to take her arm. Storming into the bedroom, she slammed the door hard enough to send a shock wave through the apartment.

"Mr. Arthurs—" began one of Jamil's friends, but Arthurs wasn't in the mood to listen. He threw off the welder's mask and dropped the torch. He didn't bother checking the tanks to be sure they were tightly valved down. Let the whole place burn—and Anita with it! She deserved it. She couldn't treat him like this. He was an artist. A great one!

Marvin Arthurs stormed into the hallway, saw Jamil's van keys on the table and scooped them up. He heard Jamil and the other two yammering away in Farsi. They were upset. Arthurs thought they had every right to be. Anita could be such a shrew.

He slid into Jamil's battered maroon van parked at the curb. The key was the only thing about the van that worked well. The engine sputtered and sounded as if it were ready to throw a rod. When Arthurs got the van moving, he thought he was driving through molasses. There wasn't any acceleration. He wanted to jam his foot down and roar off. Maybe he could find a pedestrian over by the university. He hunched over the wheel, thoughts of running down someone giving him a moment of savage satisfaction.

Driving aimlessly, he turned onto Baseline Road.

The sheer rock face of the Flatirons rose on his right. He wheeled the protesting van up the road to the Flagstaff Mountain lookout. He needed to be above the pettiness, the small minds, the people who refused to believe he was a great sculptor. The van gave out before he had gone a quarter of the way up the steep road. Cursing, he pulled over and got out, slamming the door as hard as he could.

Arthurs walked the entire way to the lookout. The cold wind whipping through the Rockies helped take away some of the anger, and he did enjoy looking down on Boulder and the mental midgets there. What the hell did they teach in that red-tile-roofed madhouse they called a university? No one in the art department would even talk to him. They had even poisoned Anita against him. They must have told her she'd never get her damned degree if she didn't dump him.

His watery blue eyes lifted from the city, and focused on distant Denver. They were no better out there. Almost two million people and they all conspired to keep him unknown. He'd show them, he'd show them all. His sculpture would bring adoring critics from around the world!

Marvin Arthurs, known to the world as Art. He would be art!

Heart beating faster, he started back down the road. He got to Jamil's van and couldn't start it. He pushed it out into the center of the road, then jumped in and let it roll. He got back to Baseline Road before the momentum died. The van refused to turn over. Earlier, this would have infuriated him. Not now. He had a mission. He knew his destiny.

Fame. Greatness. Those were his.

He pushed the van into a deserted lot and left it. Let Jamil fix it. He started walking. It took almost an hour to reach the tree-lined street where he lived.

Arthurs frowned when he neared his apartment. Police cars with lights flashing and military vehicles of all descriptions blocked the street. Arthurs started down the sidewalk but was barred by two soldiers carrying M-16s.

"Secured area. No admittance," one said.

"But I—" Arthurs clamped his mouth shut tightly. He had started to say he lived here and for them to get the hell out of his way. He saw the gurneys coming out of his apartment. Bright orange bags filled with bodies loaded down the wheeled carts. "What's happening?" he asked.

"That's classified information," one said.

The other soldier sneered at the idea of anything being secret and said, "Iranian terrorists. Wasted three of the bastards."

Frightened, Arthurs backed away. He didn't break out in a dead run until he reached the end of the street. Dead. Terrorists. Jamil? Arthurs had known him at Brown University before he had flunked out. He figured Jamil had gone on to graduate. He hadn't seen or heard from him until a week ago when he showed up with his two friends begging for someplace to stay.

He sank down, his back to a tree. He started tracing patterns on the street, using his finger to cast a shadow. Faster and faster he sketched, inspiration on him. The police hadn't thought Jamil was a terrorist. Not really. They wanted him. They wanted to stop him from creating his masterwork. Anita might have called them. They'd all move in unison to keep his genius in check. Poor Jamil and his two yammering friends had only gotten in the way.

He'd have to hurry. Without the Cerberus maquette as a guide, he'd have to create something else that would be too great for a mere police department, even one in league with the federal government, to ignore. Arthurs' mind raced. What could he do? His finger worked harder, building shadow on shadow until a name rose to taunt him.

Christo. The Hungarian Christ man. The one who always commanded attention with his artistry.

He could do better than the Running Fence or pinkly diapering entire islands in the Bay of Biscayne or the nylon curtain across Rifle Gap. Christo's work was transient, but it was of the proper scale. Big. Magnificent. Arthurs could do better. He would do better.

Arthurs walked aimlessly, turning over one scheme after another in his mind. Walking along Pearl Street, he stopped suddenly, grabbed a pencil stub lying on the sidewalk and began scribbling on a wall. He quit only when the owner of the store came out and shouted at him. Arthurs walked on, more excited than ever.

"Art by Art," he muttered. He stopped in front of an appliance store. Fourteen televisions blinked and flashed at him. The opening fragment of the news anchor's lead story caught his attention.

"Three members of the Iranian Freedom Jihad were killed in a shootout at an apartment on 32nd Street this afternoon. Authorities refuse to reveal details about the shooting, but KVKK news sources have uncovered that the three entered the country illegally two weeks ago, crossing the Canadian border near Banff. Being sought for questioning is the apartment's occupant, Marvin Arthurs."

Arthurs cringed. He hated the name Marvin. He was an artist. Artists didn't have pansy names like Marvin.

"If you have information about this man, contact the Boulder Police immediately or phone the district office of the FBI." Numbers marched across the bottom of the fourteen screens, but Arthurs had moved on.

They wanted him. They wanted him. He had to create! He wouldn't allow the so-called authorities prevent him from producing the greatest art the world had ever seen. How dare they try to stop him?

He roamed for hours until the streetlights winked on. Arthurs dodged frequent police patrols on the city's main streets. It was as easy to avoid the unmarked cars loaded with men in plain suits and grim expressions. He didn't even have to see the white and blue government plates to know they were federal agents. And they wanted to keep his genius from the world. All of them.

Arthurs returned to Jamil's abandoned van and crawled into it to sleep. He pushed against the curtain separating the front seats from the rear and, to his surprise, found the van filled with a large crate. Squeezing past, he slithered to the back where Jamil had made a small nest.

A rumpled blanket showed how Jamil had curled up and slept. Empty cereal boxes, bags and a few beer bottles marked what his friend had eaten here. Under a pile of potato chip sacks Arthurs saw the edge of a small spiral notebook. He pulled it free. He couldn't understand the curlicue script on most of the pages. It might as well have been written in code, but the parts in English in Jamil's precise hand made him read faster.

A map of Colorado Springs clearly marked NORAD and Cheyenne Mountain. But these had been crossed off with heavy black Xs. A smaller section carried the caption "The Second Big Blue Cube." Odd footnotes about a spy satellite control center meant nothing to Arthurs.

Details to detonate the 30-kiloton nuclear device in the van did, though. Any fool could have followed them because Jamil was a meticulous planner.

Arthurs licked the grease from inside several discarded potato chip bags. His stomach growled, but a fire burned in his belly and brain. He knew what to do. He knew how to make all the damned critics—including that bitch Anita—sit up and notice him. Marvin Arthurs curled up in the tight space on the dirty blanket, his head resting against the bomb crate, thoughts of creating irresistible art fluttering across his tortured dreams.

\* \* \*

Arthurs awoke, feverish and afraid. He thrashed around, smashing his hand against the bomb. He recoiled, then calmed. His eyes fixed on the simple wooden crate. Reaching out, he placed a trembling hand on it, caressing it like a lover's hair. Then he pulled back.

"I must work. Work. I cannot make any mistakes." He found Jamil's notebook and went through it page by page. The light shining in the van's dirty back window fell on the pages like a laser. Only one line at a time was illuminated. That was fine with Arthurs. He didn't want to miss a single detail.

As he read, he realized some of the Arabic snake tracks were done to keep prying English-reading eyes from secrets. The English parts were intended to keep Jamil's two assistants from discovering that they were to be sacrificed in a funeral of fire, dying for the glory of the Iranian Freedom Jihad. These pages Arthurs hurried past. He lingered on those describing the blast range, the radiation release, the radioactive filth to be kicked up into the atmosphere. Jamil had intended not only for the spy satellite control complex to be destroyed, he wanted fallout to blanket Denver for years to come. With any luck, the entire Rockies might be overlaid with deadly dust, forcing the Air Force to abandon NORAD and Cheyenne Mountain.

Arthurs knew nothing of politics, except as it applied to his art. He had been denied NEA grants repeatedly. The thought crossed his mind that he might have been refused because of Jamil. How had they known he was friends with an Iranian terrorist? He hadn't known that himself.

Arthurs shook off such a notion. They wanted to keep him in the ghetto. They didn't want the world to see the splendor of his work. He let out a deep sigh. It was a pity to lose the Cerberus sculpture, but he dared not go back to his apartment. He might drive by and not see anyone, but they were watching. The authorities were everywhere, all searching for him.

Again he patted the side of the atomic weapon. He had no idea where Jamil had gotten it. He'd mentioned something about touring India. Maybe he had stolen it there—or been given it by the Indians. They never cared for the US, after all, cozying up to the Commies every chance they got. Arthurs felt a rage building. The Indians might have sent the bomb over to prevent his public from viewing his work.

The 30-kiloton explosion Jamil envisioned in Colorado Springs would take all the attention away from Marvin Arthurs' work, where it belonged.

A stub of a pencil wedged between the van's floor and wall popped free. Arthurs began scribbling on the back of a blank sheet from Jamil's spiral notebook. Radiation. X-rays. Set up a functional, if expendable, sculpture that focused attention on a bigger arena.

He chuckled to himself, rubbing his finger across the now-clean potato chip bag. Who needed to eat? He had his art to sustain him!

Arthurs went to work in earnest looking for the right place for the van—and his tour de force, his masterpiece, the sculpture that would bring him the celebrity his genius deserved.

\* \* \*

Flagstaff Mountain was less than 7,000 feet high, but the Flatirons were prominent enough for his work. Marvin Arthurs eyed them critically, estimating height and width. They must be a full three thousand feet high. Rock climbers scaled their treachery throughout the year, several dying in the attempt each year. The mountains rose majestically, inclined just slightly away from true perpendicular, flat, bare, barren rock.

Christo's work was forgotten in a few weeks. It was nothing but gaudy nylon and rope and fencing. Arthurs knew how to create permanent sculpture, a work so vital that tourists and art lovers the world over would flock to Boulder to see it.

And it would be his work. No one else's. They'd never be able to forget him after he unveiled it.

He wiped away the sweat on his upper lip and studied his stony easel. Then he set to work accumulating the material he would need.

\* \* \*

Arthurs grew increasingly nervous. The police had been hunting him for three days. Jamil's van was too conspicuous. But he had made progress. He had wood struts. He had damned near a square mile of thin sheet aluminum, or so it seemed as he lugged it out of the construction site where he had stolen it.

"Don't need that much," he told himself. "Just enough for Proud Aphrodite." Arthurs glowed when he thought of the sculpture. His name for it sang lyrically in his ears. He wheeled through the steep streets of Boulder, going past the university, searching for just the right spot to build.

"She'll be worshipped by millions," he muttered, swerving and cutting off a young woman in a battered blue VW. She honked. He paid no attention. His eyes were on the Flatirons. He wouldn't need the entire expanse. Just fifteen hundred feet. That would be enough to burn in his artistry.

Arthurs slammed on the brakes when he saw the rundown flophouse. His mouth went dry and his heart clenched like a tight fist in his chest. The brick building dated from the turn of the century; it was sturdily built. And it was the four stories high he needed.

He fumbled for Jamil's notebook and his calculations. Proportions and triangles and lines ran everywhere. He found the part about being 320 feet away to give the proper angle for the radiation from the blast.

"Here, here it is," he whispered, as if touching a holy relic. His grimy finger traced across the page, smearing it. He lifted his finger slightly, letting the shadow delineate the angles and heights. "I need to park 320 feet from a four story tall building. And then Proud Aphrodite goes onto the roof!"

Arthurs fell forward, face down over the passenger's bucket seat when he spotted a prowl car cruising down the street. They were everywhere. And if he avoided the police, the FBI and CIA picked up the trail. Having to cut the CIA spy's throat yesterday with the jagged piece of glass had bothered him. She had been so pretty. But she would have kept him from creating his art. She'd had to die.

Cautiously looking up over the dashboard, he saw that the cruiser had moved on. Arthurs jumped from the van and ran to the side of the building. He had thought about this for hours. He knew how to do it right. Finding the Flatirons was easy. They stretched up the mountain five miles behind the hotel. He started pacing, each step a precise one yard.

"One hundred six, one hundred seven," he finished. He swallowed hard and wiped more sweat from his face, in spite of the increasingly brisk, chill wind blowing down off the Rockies. His stomach growled in protest from not having eaten in days, but when he turned and sighted along the line the blast would follow, Marvin Arthurs knew the fast was worth it.

He parked the van as close to the spot he had marked as possible, and then went to take a room in the hotel.

\* \* \*

"Mister, I don't care jackshit what you're doin' in there, just be quiet, will ya? It's past midnight and people are trying to sleep."

Arthurs hunkered down, his body protecting the frame for Proud Aphrodite. The hotel room was cramped. He had to move to the roof soon now that it was dark, but when he did there would be no turning back. Everything had to be precisely in place.

The irate clerk left, mumbling all the way down the hall. Arthurs heard the elevator clank in protest as it lowered the fat clerk to the lobby where he belonged. Arthurs smiled crookedly. Soon enough the clerk would become part of history. He would die in a fiery blast that both destroyed filth and created marvelous art. Arthurs wished he could tell him of his noble role, but he didn't. Too many cops came and went. And the man across the hall might look like a derelict, but he had to be a spy for the military. There was a glint in his eye that didn't go along with the vast quantities of cheap wine he guzzled.

They were everywhere and they wanted to stop him. But they were too late!

Arthurs peered into the hall. The only sounds he heard were the settling of the building and the soft gusting of night wind off the mountain. Dragging the wooden frame behind him, he got to the emergency door leading to the roof. He cursed at the time it took to file off the padlock. They'd put it here to slow him down. He knew it. It wouldn't do them any good. It wouldn't!

The sweat matting his T-shirt to his body dried as a sudden frigid blast of the ever-present wind tugged at him. Arthurs pulled the frame onto the roof and closed the door.

"That side of the roof. Over there. I can anchor it with wire. There's time. There's plenty of time." He dropped the frame and went back to his room. The sheets of thin aluminum would be perfect for his shadow creation. He didn't remember where he had read it, but radiation would cause neutrons to explode from the aluminum as it vaporized in the onslaught of X-rays. This would darken the shadow left on the Flatirons even more.

Proud Aphrodite would be etched into stone for all time. His conception would endure longer than Mt. Rushmore!

Arthurs wrestled the aluminum sheets onto the roof and began working. Over the past two days, he had cut the pieces, preparing them for assembly. His vision would be magnified from the ten feet on the roof of the hotel to fifteen hundred feet on the Flatirons. Fired directly into stone, Proud Aphrodite would combine classical artwork with the modern technology of the atomic bomb.

His hammer rose and fell in just the right amounts. Nails held the sheeting to the wooden frame, but only in the exact spots art demanded. Always art. It spoke to him. It commanded him to create. And Marvin Arthurs obeyed.

When he began walking the ten-foot-high sculpture up to the side of the roof, it was perfect. He used thick wire to anchor Proud Aphrodite upright, taking several turns around vent pipes and other convenient protuberances. Arthurs stepped back and stared at it.

"They'll know now. They'll know. Anita laughed. The bitch didn't think I had it in me, but I do."

He looked down from his four-story perch through the faint dawn and saw Jamil's van. Arthurs turned and stared up at the Flatirons five miles away. More than half their expanse would be branded with true art by noon.

High noon. Gunfighters. Daring men living and dying for their convictions. Sun directly overhead. A new sun, a creating sun on the ground. Jamil had figured that this small a device would only kill everyone within a half-mile radius. Arthurs regretted that they had to die for his art, but it was worth it. Most were spies and police trying to stop him, anyway. Let them die for the glory of Proud Aphrodite!

Arthurs hurried to his hotel room, shucked off his sweaty clothing and put on another set he had taken from an undercover policeman who had almost caught him the evening before. The plaid shirt was bloodstained and too small, and the pants almost cut him in two, but Arthurs barely noticed such discomfort. To be so close to completion was all that mattered.

He took the clanking elevator to the lobby and ignored the clerk at the desk. The man looked at him curiously, but Arthurs refused to catch his eye. To do so might create alarm. He radiated victory. They must not know until it was too late.

The back of the van seemed even more crowded than it had before. Arthurs gently worked off the side of the wood crate. With Jamil's notes spread on the bomb casing, he began the tedious work of setting the timer. It was entirely electronic, and he wasn't sure he had set it properly. He went over the instructions left by his dead friend and patron of the arts. When Arthurs had finished, he ran through the directions a third time.

All was ready. At noon, the searing nuclear blast would produce art unlike any ever seen in the United States. Why go to Hiroshima when real artwork could be viewed at home?

Marvin Arthurs stood next to the van and stretched mightily. It was a lovely day, the first fingers of false dawn stroking the far horizon. This was one thing he liked about Boulder. When the sun rose, it cast its rays across plains and city and foothills in a panorama unmatched anywhere else in the world.

Tomorrow, the rising sun would shine for the first time on the dark likeness of Aphrodite—his masterpiece.

Wind whipped along the street, kicking up dust and debris. Arthurs started walking toward the bus depot. He had almost six hours to get to Denver. That ought to be far enough away for him to view the result of his artistic innovation.

He had gone only a half block when a sudden gust of wind, stronger than the others, blew against his face. A grinding sound startled him. Arthurs' eyes widened in horror when he saw Proud Aphrodite wobbling.

"No! No! You can't! Don't do this to me!" He turned back to the hotel and ran through the lobby.

"Hey, buddy, you stayin' another night? You got to pay in advance. And no more of that bangin' noise."

"Proud Aphrodite," he muttered.

"What's that? You have a broad up there?"

Arthurs ignored the ignorant clerk and punched repeatedly at the elevator button. The cage was stuck on the third floor. Frantic, he turned for the stairs.

"Mister, wait—"

He left the complaining clerk behind. The man might have crept to the roof after he'd left and cut the wires. Just one or two undone guy wires would bring the entire sculpture down. Arthurs cursed himself for not having dealt with all his enemies. The clerk was a guilty party, he knew. And what about the man in the room across the hall? That had to be a spy hunting him down. The clerk and the derelict must be in a partnership of evil to keep him from completing his life's work.

Out of breath, sweating from every pore, Arthurs burst onto the roof. The sheet-aluminum Aphrodite swayed precariously in the high wind coming down the mountainside. He rushed forward, hands trying to steady the ten- foot-high sculpture.

The aluminum bent. Two support wires whipped about from a new gust. Arthurs caught at the sculpture, trying to support it. He failed. The heavy outline of the Greek goddess of love slipped flat onto the roof.

"There's time," he muttered. He set to work with a feverish intensity unlike anything possessing him before. He hammered and strengthened, he pulled and shaped and formed until Proud Aphrodite whole was once more.

The sun crept up in the sky as he struggled to finish his repairs. Everything had to be perfect. Nothing less would do. Hours later, he pushed the heavy sculpture back erect. A period of relative calm allowed Arthurs to cinch down the guy wires. He stepped back and stared up at his noble work.

He went to the edge of the roof and checked the van. He almost puked when he saw the police car. Relief better than any sex swept through him when the cruiser didn't even slow.

"Proud Aphrodite, my sweet goddess. You'll give loving testimony to the world of my genius."

The wind from the mountain blew the sculpture over the edge of the roof. It broke part before it hit the ground.

Arthurs stared at the ruined work four stories below him. Then he looked at his watch.

A few seconds before noon.

His eyes darted from the van with the armed nuclear weapon in it to the Flatirons, all pristine and barren of true art. He had to change that. His hands rose.

The forty-seven thousand people who died or were blinded by the blast never saw the product of Marvin Arthurs' genius. Burned into the Flatirons was his seven-hundred-foot silhouette and a one-hundred-foot-high finger-play shadow dog barking forever at the world.

183

# The Platinum Spike

*Combining SF and western styles is not something I'm prone to do, though I write extensively in the western field (check out www.KarlLassiter.com for a look at some of my western fiction). A while back, 1994, I saw a market listing for such a blending of genres. Sure, why not? This story didn't sell, but it morphed into "The Celestial Railroad," which did sell to* Trails: Intriguing Stories of the Wild West, *edited by David B. Riley in 2006. But "Platinum Spike" has qualities of its own I like. Enjoy my recounting of the Wild West's least-mentioned event.*

"Looks like a cadaver," John Malloy observed as he sipped the whiskey his friend Kelly had ordered. Malloy touched his sweat-stained shirt and pressed a hard hand into the pocket. Empty. He hadn't seen a greenback—or a nickel—in too long. Taking charity from the likes of Kelly galled him, but Malloy wasn't so proud he would refuse a spot of whiskey.

"Sickly. Coughs all the time," Kelly agreed, glancing over his shoulder at the man across the room, "not that I'm one to be talkin'." The burly Irishman used both hands to drag his left leg from under the table. "Crushed, it was. Shoulda knowed better than to let a greenhorn do my blastin'. Brought the whole danged cliff down on me. But Mr. Benck stood by me, he did. He's salt of the Earth, a good man."

"If he lives longer 'n midnight," Malloy said, eyeing Benck critically. "Don't like workin' for a man who might up and die on me. I'm the best there is at layin' track but don't much cotton to bein' in the middle of the Rockies when the boss goes the way of all flesh."

"Don't know where he came from. Back East, I'd say, from that pale white skin," Kelly said, as if he hadn't heard Malloy's complaint. "A good man to work for. And what do you mean you're the best at layin' track? If it wasn't for my gimp leg, I'd show you a decent day's work. You ain't never—"

Malloy finished the liquor, letting it slide down his gullet. It pooled warmly in his belly and decided him. He hadn't worked since the Denver & Rio Grande had gone into bankruptcy for the third or fourth time. Rumors had it General Palmer dickered with the Kansas Pacific, and the Union Pacific wanted the route down from Cheyenne to Denver. Waiting on the railroad executives to get off their asses and get men working again wore something fierce on John Malloy.

"Make the introductions. I'll show you how to do a job right."

Kelly smiled and slapped his friend on the shoulder. "I told Mr. Benck you'd come through for him."

"I hope you told him he's gettin' the best."

184

"Second best," Kelly said, enjoying the joshing. "Even with my bad leg, second best." He got to his feet painfully, grabbed a crude crutch and hobbled across the room. Malloy followed, studying the pale-skinned, hatchet-faced man who was going to put money back into his empty pockets.

\* \* \*

"Never seen an engine like this one," Malloy said, standing behind Mr. Benck in the cab. The gangling man coughed and reached out a bony hand to clutch the brake lever. Malloy had never seen a road owner insist on driving his own engine, either, but nothing about Benck was usual. Taller than Malloy, even wearing his battered old bowler hat, the man always dressed in a long brown canvas duster buttoned tightly at the throat. In the four days during their stay in Denver and the trip west into the Rockies, heading along narrow-gauge Denver & Rio Grande track to the Georgetown loop, Malloy had never seen him open the duster. The man's pale eyes looked more like melting ice chips, and the thin, sandy hair might have belonged to a man in his seventies.

Malloy had tried to reckon how old his new boss was and had failed. Benck might be thirty or a hundred. However old he was, he wasn't long for this world. His sickly yellow complexion and constant cough spelled bad consumption, though Malloy had never seen Benck hawk up anything from his tortured lungs.

"I've constructed warehouses at the junction," Benck said, his voice reedy and thin as a desert grasshopper. "Trade goods are stored there."

"Goods? You ready to ship along your road?" The fancy engine stood on its own section of track, away from the D&RG narrow gauge. Malloy's experienced eye saw this track was slightly wider than the D&RG's, making the engine special-built for only this one segment of track in Colorado.

"Right away. I have a schedule to meet." He pushed back the sleeve of the duster and peered at a complicated timepiece clamped to his thin wrist by a silver metal band. Malloy had never seen one with three faces and five hands. Each seemed to mean something to Benck, though, and whatever kept the man happy also pleased Malloy. His hand touched the thick wad of greenbacks in his shirt pocket.

He had never met such a liberal man. Even with Kelly's glowing praise, Benck had no idea how good a worker John Malloy really was. The Irishman grinned crookedly. Might be a shenanigan on Benck's part, Malloy knew. He would get more than a day's work for this generosity.

"The rails stored there, too?" Malloy asked.

"Everything we need to get into Broken Back Pass."

Malloy shivered as a blast of cold air blew down off the Rockies. It was August, but winter came from those imposing heaps of rock. Getting the last three miles of track laid before snows made it impossible would be a challenge.

"The crew already up in the mountains?" Malloy looked around and saw only Georgetown. The town had filled with hundreds of miners intent on digging into the sides of the high hills around them when Cripple Creek played out. California Gulch at Leadville promised more than it delivered—again— and too many men hunted for jobs. Malloy thanked his lucky stars for Kelly and Mr. Benck.

"We will take a few up with us." Benck pointed his bony finger in the direction of a tight knot of burly, red-haired Cornish miners. Malloy had seen their like before. They were not his kind.

"They workin' the crew?" Malloy glared as the Cornishmen swung up onto the coal car behind the engine.

"Mr. Malloy, meet Mr. Gwynneth and his hard-rock miners."

"All from Cripple Creek, are you now?" Malloy did not try to hide his contempt. Still, Malloy knew the Cornishmen's reputation for blasting skills. From all Mr. Benck had told him, they would be needed. It remained to be seen if they could do an honest day's work. Malloy doubted they could keep up with any Irishman, even Kelly with his gimpy leg. They had a laziness about them that caused him to fret.

"All aboard!" cried Mr. Benck in his shrill voice. He worked the levers, got up a head of steam, and started up new track belonging to the Georgetown and Broken Back Pass Railroad. Malloy marveled at the ease the engine took the six-percent grade. He commented on it.

"My own design," Mr. Benck said proudly. "No engine this side of the Mississippi matches its power."

"Don't put much coal into the boiler," Malloy observed.

"It uses very little water, also." Mr. Benck loosed a long blast on the steam whistle, plowed through the congestion of the mining town, and quickly left behind Georgetown. Malloy turned to the men who would be working for him.

"How long you been in Colorado?" he asked Gwynneth.

The Cornish miner lounged back on the wood, picking his teeth. "Long enough to know there's no reason to have left home. Coal's poor in these parts, and there's no gold."

"Worse," piped up another of the Cornishmen, "the women are ugly and the ale's watered!"

Malloy had to laugh. "Aye, there's few lassies in this country who can match those of County Kerry."

"Kerry? Ha! Loose women, the lot of 'em," declared Gwynneth. "Now ye take those from—"

186

The argument between Malloy and the miners raged all the way to the camp eight thousand feet into the mountains. He found himself warming to the genial miners, in spite of them being from Cornwall and not having the sense God gave a goose. Malloy jumped down and took a deep breath of the thin, cold air, wondering how Mr. Benck stood it.

"There's hardly enough to breathe up here," grumbled a miner.

"Makes a man tire out real quick," Malloy said. "We're not goin' to let a thing like that hold us back, eh?"

"Glad to hear it, Mr. Malloy. I admire your spirit. There are the rest of your workers. Acquaint yourself with them and their language. I expect considerable progress tomorrow. I shall be in my tent." Benck shut down the engine, painfully lowered himself to the rocky flats, and walked to a large tent at the far side of the camp.

Malloy stared at him, mouth gaping. He started to call after his skeletal boss, then bit back the words.

"My crew? They're Chinese!" Malloy heard Gwynneth laughing at his predicament. He had thought, from Kelly's glowing words of laying a mile of track a day uphill, that he would crew Irishmen, good hardworking lads from Dublin and Ulster.

"Chinee," taunted Gwynneth. "Make do with 'em, Mick!" Guffawing, the Cornish miners went to set up their own tents, taking them from the freight Benck had brought uphill to the camp.

Malloy almost sought out his new boss to resign. Chinese!

Instead, he went to where the Celestials lay around guttering fires, working avidly at small bowls of rice. He stared at the heathens, wondering how he was going to get any work from the lazy bastards.

"Are you the new foreman?" A short, stocky Chinese came over, head bobbing. He bowed deeply three times. "Welcome to Broken Back Pass." The Celestial spoke with only a trace of accent.

"You speak good for a Chinee," Malloy said. "Somebody took a whale of a lot of time teachin' you, I'd say."

"You can say that," the man said, bowing deeply. "I am called Wu."

"John Malloy."

"Mr. Malloy, we are honored at your presence. It is a pity Mr. Kelly's fate was such that he became unable to complete our project."

Malloy snorted. Long plumes of hot breath condensed instantly, forming silvery cobwebs in front of his mouth. "We get to work at dawn. No malingerin'. I won't tolerate it."

"We are not shirkers, Mr. Malloy," Wu said.

"Nothin' to eat 'less you do your work. That's the new rule. My rule."

Wu said nothing, but bowed deeply, then backed off. He spoke in a singsong voice to the others huddled around the poor fire. Malloy knew the miners in Georgetown had raped the hills hunting for wood to shore up their mines and to keep them warm through the bitter winters. Getting enough wood for railroad ties would be a problem, and he didn't want these Chinese burning wood that could be put to better use. Malloy stalked off to pitch his own tent, muttering at his pitiful fate.

Chinese!

\* \* \*

"Go find some, you lazy oaf!" Malloy roared at the miner. The Cornishman muttered something Malloy didn't hear, but it was none too complimentary. "There's wood to be had, if you put your mind to it. And your back! Get your strong back and weak mind into the chore!" He growled deep in his throat. For a solid week the Cornishmen had not done a blessed speck of work, other than one simple blasting job.

Malloy turned and watched as Wu presided over the two-dozen Chinese. They worked quietly, only occasionally breaking into their singsong speech as they hefted a heavy steel rail or broke rock to level the bed.

"Keep 'em workin', Wu! No slackers allowed." Malloy wanted to say more but anger tangled his tongue. He stormed over to Mr. Benck's tent and hesitated. He never felt comfortable inside, though the boss never said anything cross to him.

"Come in, Mr. Malloy," came the invitation. "What is it I can do to speed the laying of the rails?"

Malloy entered and took off his bowler. He held it in his hands, running nervous fingers around the brim.

"It's like this, Mr. Benck. We're not finding solid wood for the ties. The whole area's been stripped bare. There's hardly enough to keep the Celestials warm at night." Malloy said nothing of the Cornish miners. They always seemed to have enough for their bonfires, though Malloy never saw them bringing timber any into camp. He suspected them of hoarding it for their own use while their comrades went cold, if the Chinese could be considered cronies.

"I understand. Perhaps I can be of some assistance. Wood is so inefficient." Benck went to his worktable and pushed aside the strange machines there. He held up a small tube, hardly longer than Malloy's calloused hand. Touching the base caused it to glow softly. "Take this. Let Wu and the others use it to keep themselves warm. Repeated touching will produce considerable heat."

"Never seen its like before," Malloy admitted. He gingerly accepted the rod. It was smooth ceramic like a thunder mug but warm. He rubbed his hand over it. The tingling that passed through his wind-chilled body made him reluctant to part with it. This was too good for the Chinese.

"You have spoken with them about this? The Chinese?"

"Can't speak their lingo. Everything passes through Wu. I'm never sure he's doin' much more than heapin' scorn on my head."

"You have been here a week and have not learned their speech?" Benck heaved a sigh that rattled his skeleton. "I forget. Others are not as adept at learning languages."

"You speak their lingo?"

"It is quite interesting how it differs from Athabaskan, though the roots are similar. Never mind."

Malloy stared at the equipment Benck had accumulated. Most of it had funny little windows and candles inside, glowing warmly. Why the boss wanted so many lanterns was a question Malloy couldn't answer. Too much about Mr. Benck begged explanation.

"We're reachin' a spot where we need to do some heavy blastin' to get a wide enough ledge, even for baby road."

"Baby—oh, the narrow gauge."

"You ain't usin' even the regular size narrow," Malloy pointed out. "Yours is a tad more than three foot."

"And according to the Pacific Act of 1862, regular gauge is set at four-feet-eight-and-one-half inches," Benck said tiredly. He coughed. "I have my reasons. And time is pressing. We must be at the summit of Broken Back Pass in seven days."

"That'll take an act of God, sir, if you don't mind me sayin' so," Malloy said. His eyes came to rest on a polished oak case, almost three feet long and narrow, very narrow, resting on the table. Seeing his interest, Benck picked up the case.

"This is the reason. At Promontory Summit they drove a golden spike. Here, Mr. Malloy. What do you see in the case?"

Malloy opened the latch, and well-oiled hinges on the lid yielded to show a burnished metal spike unlike anything he had ever seen. He shook his head, not certain what he held.

"Platinum, Mr. Malloy. That is a platinum spike, far more valuable than mere gold. When we reach the summit, this spike will be driven marking the connection of the roads, as was done by the Union Pacific and Central Pacific."

"We can't lay a mile a day in these mountains. Charles Crocker was hardly able to lay two miles a month gettin' through the Sierra Nevadas."

"Blast, sir, blast and build my road!" Something in the way Benck spoke told Malloy of the urgency. He started to ask if his boss was feeling poorly, if this was the reason. Maybe Benck wanted to see his railroad built before he died. But Malloy held his tongue.

"Here's your spike, Mr. Benck." He handed it back. "I'll get those lazy chinks to workin' harder. We'll get to the summit in a week, if it kills every last man of 'em!"

Malloy tried to read the expression on Benck's face and could not. The eyes turned to polar pools with specks of gold floating in them. He was being drawn into a vortex. Malloy forced himself to look away.

"Get to work right away," he mumbled, leaving quickly. Malloy shivered when a blast of air hit him. He had not realized how warm it was inside Benck's tent. All those lanterns put off quite a warmth. Malloy fumbled out the ceramic rod given him. Its soft heat sank to the bone and let him bend his fingers for the first time all day. Malloy slipped it into his pocket and hurried off, yelling at the Celestials to stop malingering and get to work.

\* \* \*

"Swing those picks," Malloy bellowed. Wu stared at him with his unreadable coal-dark eyes. Malloy glowered and pointed. "They're not workin' as hard as they should. There's no excuse."

"The altitude slows them, but they work," Wu said in his slow manner. "We need help clearing the rock. We are unused to moving such large boulders. It would help if they were blown into smaller pieces."

Malloy blew. "You callin' the Cornish blasters incompetent? You people do your work. I'll see to them!" Malloy stormed off. They were making only a few yards a day, laying only one segment of track every other day. It would take forever to get the final curve around the mountainside and into Broken Back Pass proper. Once around this section, the track laying would speed up. The area he scouted for the rails was relatively level, requiring only a few days of pick and shovel work to get the bed into condition for the rails.

"Gwynneth! Get on down here." Malloy motioned the big Cornish miner from his perch atop a large rock where he and the others sat watching the Chinese toil while making villainous comments.

"What kin I do for ye, me good man?"

"Blast the rocks into smaller hunks. The Celestials can't—"

"The Celestials can't do nothin'!" exclaimed Gwynneth. "Look at them lazy louts. They move so slow, molasses runnin' uphill would beat them every last time."

"Don't see you and your men movin' any faster. Might be good if you took a hand at gettin' the rock free. That's what you do best."

"Do their work? We're not likely to do that, now are we?"

190

"You're not likely to do much of any job, if you don't get off your asses and—" Malloy stepped back and let the miner's sledge-heavy fist pass harmlessly. But the Irishman couldn't let any of his crew take a poke at him without proving it a mistake. He stepped up and unloaded a hard punch to Gwynneth's rock-hard belly. Malloy didn't stop there. He landed a second blow on the side of the man's head.

Gwynneth staggered and then let out a roar. He charged, head low and arms reaching to encircle Malloy. The two went down in a heap, swinging, kicking and striving for supremacy. The fight was cheered on by the Cornishmen on their rock. Malloy could not tell if Wu and the other Chinese stopped to watch the excitement. He was too busy trying to keep from getting his face stove in.

The fight began to slow as both men tired. Malloy ended up supporting Gwynneth as much as the Cornish miner held him up. They sank to their knees.

"Give up?" Gwynneth asked.

"You gonna work?" Malloy managed to grate out past his split lip. He spat blood and wiped away a thin trickle running from his nose. He had given as good as he had received. That he felt like a mule had kicked him didn't get any work done, even if the fight had let him vent some anger.

"We'll work," Gwynneth said, "but no faster than the chinks."

"Do it, do it," Malloy said, spitting again. He pushed Gwynneth away and got to his feet. Turning, Malloy saw Mr. Benck watching silently. The man swayed in the strong breeze. Malloy wondered if his boss was more a willow than an oak, then the thought vanished. Yelling at Wu, Malloy shouted, "Rest time's over. Get back to work. There's track to lay!"

He walked off, a warm glow inside. He had settled matters with Gwynneth as he should have when he came to this crew. Malloy wondered how to settle matters with Wu and the Chinese when they never fought and kept to themselves. He would have to think on it and see.

* * *

John Malloy grumbled. The Chinese workers labored silently, stoically, never hurrying but never slowing. The same could not be said of Gwynneth and his miners. They grew increasingly slothful when Malloy needed their strong backs the most. The fall of rocks barring the way had to be cleared, and it required all of them working together.

The fight with Gwynneth had settled nothing, and Malloy found this hard to accept. Every other crew he had led settled easily when it was obvious their foreman could whomp the lot of them. Not so with the Cornishmen.

Malloy didn't know what to make of them—nor did he fathom Benck's obsession with bringing his trade goods to the end of the tracks when they were a mile from the middle of Broken Back Pass.

"Need help securin' those cars?" Malloy called to his boss. The skeletal Benck shook his head. He had hauled ten heavily laden freight cars up the tracks from Georgetown warehouses. As far as Malloy could see, Benck intended to leave the freight cars here. Backing down the steep grade with such a weight spelled nothing but disaster on a narrow gauge—or any gauge track. He left the slowly working Celestials and peered into one freight car, hoping it might have something useful inside.

"Coffee, tobacco, chocolate, the very things that will give the most return for my investment," Benck said from behind Malloy. The foreman jumped. He hadn't heard his decrepit boss come up.

"Mind if I parcel out some of the chocolate to the crew? The Chinese don't drink coffee. They prefer their danged tea. That stuff's nothin' but boiled tree bark. Take the hide off your tongue, but the chocolate might keep 'em workin' a spell longer."

Benck looked thoughtful, and then nodded slowly. "Very well. It is imperative that I reach the middle of the pass in exactly one week. If this will achieve that, so be it."

"We'll get them tracks laid to the middle of the pass. The folks on the other side, will they be ready? I scouted the area yesterday and didn't see any sign of another crew workin' toward us."

"They will be ready." Benck peered at his complicated timepiece, fiddled a moment, and then nodded absently. He went to his tent and curious equipment. Malloy had seen him taking sightings, just as a surveyor would, to keep them aligned. It hardly mattered since the road clung to the blasted side of a mountain, but it kept Benck content. Malloy had learned that a long time ago. Keep the boss happy.

He wished the Chinese would learn the same lesson. "Get yer backs into it, men. I want to see you movin' tons of rock!" Malloy barked, returning to the crew lifting their picks and lethargically dropping them.

"Would you show us your fine methods?" Wu asked, bowing and scrapping. "We are humble workers without your vast knowledge."

Malloy never knew when the Celestial was mocking him. The voice always carried a tone of derision but never enough for him to call the man on. Besides, Wu wasn't likely to swing at him the way Gwynneth had. If he couldn't keep them in line by his quick fists, Malloy knew only one other way.

"Gimme that pick. I'll show you what an Irishman can do." He began work, the cool breeze and burning sun tearing at him. It had been years since he had swung a pick or lifted a shovel, and he found his muscles aching even as he enjoyed the return to simpler days before he had to ride herd on so many indolent workmen. Altitude? It meant nothing. His lungs filled and emptied like a bellows. His strong back put real power into every stroke and soon Malloy saw Wu and the other Celestials matching his movement.

It felt damned good getting them moving. He might deliver the last rail next week, as he had promised Mr. Benck.

* * *

"You've been settin' on your behinds too long," Malloy said to Gwynneth. "I want to see that rock blown to gravel so we don't have to move it by hand. And leave a decent ledge for the rails."

"I know my job," Gwynneth said, more surly than usual. Malloy had carefully doled out the chocolate given him by Benck and had not seen fit to give any to the Cornishmen. The Chinese had earned it; Gwynneth and his boys had not.

"Then, by damn, do it!" Malloy stood with arms crossed as Gwynneth and two others stuffed dynamite into holes they had double jacked earlier. Malloy had kept after them to get the work done, telling them even the Chinese could do it faster and better. After spending four days with Wu and his men, Malloy knew that wasn't far wrong. What the Chinese lacked in knowledge of blasting they made up for with willingness to work.

"Does he truly know what he does?" Wu asked. Malloy frowned. He didn't like the Celestial questioning Gwynneth's skill. If that was to be done, he'd be the one doing it.

"They're hard-rock men. Miners. They know," Malloy said gruffly.

"The placement of the drill holes," Wu said softly. "It is wrong for such a large charge. The blast will go along the face of the mountain, not into it. I have worked on many railroads."

"Not as a blaster. You don't know. Gwynneth does." Malloy's temper, never far below the surface, began to boil. "Let them do their job. You do yours."

Wu bowed silently and turned to go when Gwynneth shouted, "Fire in the hole!"

The ground shook under their feet—and then vanished. Malloy let out a yelp that was drowned in an avalanche. He clawed for any security he could find. His fingernails tore out but he got his feet under him. Dirt and small stones cut his face, temporarily blinding him.

"The whole danged mountain's gone!" he cried. Then he calmed a mite and saw Gwynneth had blown away the rocky shelf—and carried half his crew with it. Worse, the blast had destroyed the ground beneath Wu's feet. The Chinaman clung precariously to a rock handhold a dozen yards away.

"Help me," Malloy bellowed. He had to work fast. Inching along the jagged face of the new cliff, he reached for Wu. The Celestial strained but failed to take the hand.

Malloy glanced over his shoulder to the relative safety of the top of the fall. Gwynneth stood there, staring at him.

"He'll go over if you don't help. Come down and—"

"I'm not dyin' for any chink. Or for any damned Irishman. Burn in hell, mate." Gwynneth vanished.

"Please, Mr. Malloy, your position is perilous. Save yourself." Wu swung and tried to draw himself to safety but only slipped further.

"Hush up," Malloy ordered. He dropped to his belly on a shelf above Wu and caught the thin yellow wrist in a viselike grip. Heaving mightily, he pulled Wu up as the rock gave way. For a moment, he held the miner's entire weight. Then he slowly drew him back to safety. Wu lay beside Malloy for a moment, then inclined his head.

"My humble life has been spared through your bravery."

"None of that now. Get on up with ye!" Malloy got the Chinaman climbing the rubble-strewn slope. Wu moved slowly but finally disappeared over the top. Malloy started after him, only to lose his grip. He slid a few feet and got his feet back onto the narrow shelf. "I—"

Malloy cried out in horror as the ledge gave way, sending him plunging down the cliff again. He barely caught a razor-sharp outjut of rock. He hung over a five-hundred-foot drop, not daring to look down. Malloy knew real fear. He closed his eyes, gritted his teeth and forced away the tide of panic washing over him. His fingers turned bloody from the effort of holding on, and he began slipping. He looked down. Five hundred feet. A thousand. It didn't matter. He had to grow wings or die.

His fingers slid from their grip and he plunged downward...a few inches. A steely band circled his wrist and lifted him easily. Startled, he stared into Benck's bottomless eyes. With a single hand, the cadaverous man supported Malloy's bulk with no apparent effort.

"You fell," Benck said softly. "I need you, sir." He turned and scuttled up the hazardous rocky slope with the grace of a gazelle, though still burdened by Malloy's weight. Only when they reached the safety of the top did Malloy find his voice.

"You saved me. How?"

"I cannot afford to lose any more crew," was all Benck said. "Some went over the cliff. I fear Mr. Gwynneth has left camp with his surviving friends."

Good riddance, John Malloy thought. He had a road to build and those Cornish cowards only got in the way of real men doing the job.

"No standin' around," Malloy told Wu. "We got rock to clear!"

They did.

* * *

"This the spot?" Malloy scratched his chin, trying to figure Benck's reasoning. "There's no crew to meet us."

"I have laid out the geodesic lines. The final rails will go where I piled the small cairn of rocks. Use the special rails."

"Been layin' track for well nigh fifteen years and never seen their like," Malloy said as four of Wu's men struggled under the long rail taken from a freight car. The dull, silvery luster looked nothing like good steel—and the way the four staggered, Malloy knew the rail had to be powerful heavy.

"Titanium," Benck said offhandedly. Seeing his foreman had no inkling what he meant, Benck added, "A very special metal. There is a second rail. Lay one on both sides. Then we drive the spike."

"The platinum one in the oak case," Malloy said, understanding this even less. In '69 the ceremony at Promontory Summit celebrated the joining of two railroads. He had driven Wu and his men to the middle of Broken Back Pass and...nothing else. No other crew laid rail to meet them. Their segment of track would simply terminate in the center of the pass. Malloy had always considered Benck strange. Now he worried he worked for a lunatic.

He touched the wad of greenbacks in his pocket. The boss paid, lunatic or not.

"Sir, I'm a railroad man. I love the sound of engines, and nothin' thrills me more than the clang of a hammer driving spikes. But we didn't go nowhere."

Benck paid him no attention. He studied the timepiece banded on his wrist. He went to a stack of equipment he'd spent the morning lugging from his tent. Malloy had offered to help or have one of Wu's men aid him, but Benck had refused. He continued to surprise Malloy with his strength, especially at altitudes where even strong men fared poorly.

"Get the rails in place, Mr. Wu," Malloy called. "We're in for a ceremony when they're done."

Coal eyes fixed on Malloy. Wu shared his confusion. He shrugged, then began bellowing commands at the other Chinese. Malloy wasn't sure he had made himself understood. He had tried to learn a few words of their lingo but Wu always added something, something smiling and then hiding it behind his hand.

Malloy oversaw the final laying of the titanium rails. He rolled the name over and over, then shook his head. He didn't understand. There was so much he did not understand. Wu kept his men working, letting Malloy stare at Benck. The man's equipment had been strewn along the roadbed, and various windows burned with the lanterns inside. Yet, unlike kerosene or coal oil, the light was bright enough to show in broad daylight. Benck went from box to box, turning knobs and adjusting equipment. And when the tall, thin man finished, he hurried back to the engine.

Malloy shook his head in wonder. Benck brought the engine up within a few yards of the newly laid titanium rails, as if he intended on going somewhere.

"All ready, Mr. Malloy?"

"Yes, sir. Last tie is down, last spike is in place—save for the special one."

Benck opened the oak case. With reverence, he took the spike out and held it in place.

"Mr. Malloy. Drive it in. As foreman, you have earned the honor."

Malloy picked up a sledge, measured the distance, and then hesitated. He saw Wu standing nearby.

"Grab a hammer, Wu. We'll both get this platinum spike in place in jig time." Malloy saw Wu smile and accept a sledge from another Chinese. In four strokes, Malloy and Wu had the spike driven in.

"Stand back," Benck said. "I will make the final connection."

"There's no track to connect to," Malloy began. He saw Benck drawing wire from his boxes. He attached a thick cable to the platinum spike and then retreated. He studied his timepiece again, reset it, and moved a lever on one box.

Malloy gasped. Blue lightning blasted into the rails, and a crackling sound filled the air, but what startled him most was the golden mist forming at the end of the titanium rails. It swirled and thickened—and things moved inside the fog. Things vaguely human in shape, but silvery and shaped wrong.

He rubbed his eyes, worrying the altitude had taken its toll. Then Malloy saw Wu's expression. The Chinaman prided himself on remaining stoic. A mixture of curiosity and fear worked its way onto his sallow features, a combination Malloy shared.

"Stand away, far away," Benck called. He hurried to his engine and began building up a head of steam.

"He can't drive that locomotive off the end of the rails," Malloy protested. "He'll kill himself. There's nothing but bare rock..." His voice trailed off. Insubstantial forms came through the golden swirls of mist carrying rail matching that already laid.

"They work well," observed Wu. "No wasted movement, such grace and ease." In the time it took him to speak, a joining had occurred, the juncture at the edge of the whirlpool of golden brume.

"Thank you, one and all," called Benck. He waved a bony hand as the engine built up speed and chugged past his workmen. "I will return in a few weeks with trade goods. Thank you." The engine plunged into the mist and was swallowed completely, both sight and sound.

Malloy took a few hesitant steps and peered past the end of the railroad. The engine vanished into the mist as if it had never existed.

"What do you make of that?" he asked Wu as the last of the Benck's freight cars rattled past to disappear in the fog.

"They lay track well but have much to learn." Wu squatted down and nudged the rail placed by the silvery ghosts who had drifted from the fog. "See how it is not quite in place? A few passages and it will jar loose."

"Maybe Mr. Benck doesn't intend for there to be more than a few," Malloy said, straining hard to see into the mist. He saw nothing but faint lines of titanium track fading into the thickness of the golden haze. "And then again, he said he would be back. Should we wait for him? We got food to last a few more weeks. It's gettin' cold but—"

"Their techniques are poor," Wu continued, still studying the way the rails from the other side had been placed.

"Maybe we ought to go show 'em a thing or two," Malloy said. Fear rose and then died in him as curiosity worked its fingers into his mind and Irish soul. Four of Wu's workmen heaved a handcar onto the tracks. Malloy jumped up and put his hands on the handle. He wasn't surprised when Wu climbed up opposite him.

"There's always track to be put down if you're a good worker. And you and me, Wu, we're the best danged track men in the world," Malloy said with passion. He started pumping. Wu joined the effort, sending the small handcar racing for the curtain of gold fog.

# Torero

*I so enjoyed the excursion into e-publishing and netzines that I did another story for Tre Chipman, which he also bought in 1996. When I was younger, growing up in El Paso, Texas, I'd watch Mexican TV for the old Republic serials they showed (I love Gene Autrey's* Phantom Empire *and have since seen it a dozen times). After the dubbed serials came the Sunday bullfights. Yup, televised. I liked tales of Murania and the Radio Ranch more, but the experience stuck with me. There is something about a torero that commands attention far more than a rock star. To me, at least. ¡Ay, torero!*

Francisco Guerrero y Campos tightened his grip on the cape, waggled it slightly to get the red canvas draped properly for the best dramatic effect, then drew the shining sword from its hidden scabbard. Sweat ran down inside his suit of light, tickling and arousing his flesh in an almost sexual fashion. His knuckles turned white on the sword hilt as he prepared for the moment of truth.

The blade was slightly curved, designed to enter above the head and then drive past the thick knot of shoulder muscle on the bull before slipping tenderly into the heart. A single thrust and a massive creature died instantly. A small miscalculation and horns would hook into Guerrero's body, spilling stomach and intestines and lifeblood onto the thirsty white sand crunching under his brilliantly polished boots.

Or worse, Guerrero, thought, there was something worse than dying in the hot sun. There was the chance he would not make a clean kill. Better to die than to endure the disgrace of being obliged to make a second pass at this magnificent creature. Better to stuff his own innards back into his abdomen than to show the wildly cheering crowd a moment of incompetence. Better to starve in the gutter outside the *corrida* with mud from passing carts splashing on his priceless suit than to miss a clean kill!

The crowd stood and roared in anticipation. The bull pawed, lowered his head, and waved his massive arms in futile anger. The minotaur clenched his fists, caught sight of the cape, and rushed forward, maddened by the crowd, barbed banderillas weakening his arms, and the clever motion as Guerrero danced about.

Guerrero became something more than a simple *torero* in that moment.

The world turned to crystal clarity before Francisco Guerrero y Campos' eyes. He moved with deliberation and precision. Every frenzied beat of his heart caused a vein in his temple to pulse, and the air turned to wine in his nostrils. His thin lips drew back in a smile as he raised his cape, the sword blade hidden behind gentle rippling canvas.

Eyes fixed on only the minotaur, Guerrero waited. And waited and waited. The bull charged at full speed, but it was slow for the fighter. He had ample time to decoy with the cape, raise the sword and thrust home, there, precisely there, the spot on the humped neck where the blade would deliver its swift death.

As if struck by a magic spell, the minotaur crashed forward to his knees, remained upright for the precise time to drive the crowd to even higher levels of riotous cheering, then fell facedown in the sand.

The smile widened on Guerrero's face. He threw the cape to the ground, lifted both arms high, and made a slow, strutting circuit of the arena to bask in the adulation of the crowd.

"Guerrero! Guerrero! Our hero! The greatest!" came their cries, and Francisco Guerrero y Campos believed them, for he was the greatest fighter who ever lived. No creature escaped death in the ring. Minotaur or medusa, hydra or harpy, sileni or gorgon, it did not matter. He was their master, he was their slayer!

"Guerrero! Guerrero!"

Their acclaim ringing in his ears, Guerrero made a final sally to the center of the ring and put his foot on the back of the slain minotaur. Apprentices rushed out with their handsaws. Sweating from the pressure of doing a satisfactory job in the hot sun, they quickly sawed off both horns and presented them reverently to their master.

The crowd's applause had been deafening before. As he held the horns above his head and turned slowly in a full circle so all could see him, the volume doubled, trebled. Guerrero stopped as he faced the dignitaries' box just above the ring.

Guerrero identified Jaime, Lord Jalisco, not by his visage but by the rather plain young woman seated beside him. Next to her, golden horn shining, sat her constant companion, an Andalusian giant unicorn. Long white hair had been washed and combed so it fell in soft waves down the powerful body. The unicorn shifted uneasily, nervous at the proximity of so many unruly fans, and pressed closer to its mistress. Merianna stroked the creature as if it were nothing more than a pet.

Guerrero held the horns above his head and swaggered toward the box. The cheers reached an earsplitting crescendo, then died to allow him to speak.

"Lord Jalisco, I dedicate this day to...your lovely daughter, Merianna!"

Lord Jalisco's eyes widened slightly, then he inclined his head and turned slightly in his daughter's direction, signifying acceptance of this singular honor. Guerrero stepped forward and, on tiptoe, handed the minotaur horns to

Merianna. She gentled the unicorn, which snorted and pawed, then rose and took the horns.

"I am deeply honored, sire," she said, staring at the minotaur horns as if they were the most precious thing in the world. She smiled shyly, then placed them on the ledge in front of her. The crowd cheered again, but the show was over for the day and already spectators made their way from the arena.

"Sire, you would do us great honor to take dinner with us this evening." The woman brushed back a strand of dull brown hair and licked her lips nervously, as if she had overstepped the bounds of propriety.

"The honor is all mine," Guerrero said, bowing deeply, first in Merianna's direction, then to her father. He backed away and straightened. Already Jaime, Lord Jalisco, and his daughter with her unicorn companion were making their way out the private tunnel, away from the press of the throng.

Guerrero paused, saw the cheering for his triumph was past, then made his way through the underground maze to the drab dressing room where his dressers awaited him. An hour later, after making certain his suit of light was properly stored, Guerrero left the arena.

Only a few diehard fans awaited him at the gates, none of them women of enough beauty to interest him. Not on this day, not on the day he had been invited to break bread with Lord Jalisco.

By his daughter.

* * *

Guerrero stood stiffly, back ramrod straight as he turned slowly. He might have still been in the arena, reveling in the worship of the crowd. But he was alone, and this bothered him. He was not a man used to his own company, not when he had so much to share with a world filled by adoring fans.

To make it worse, he had been escorted to Lord Jalisco's trophy room. Guerrero had little interest in the trophies of others. His were more important, having been taken by his hand. Still, a warmth grew in his breast when he saw the minotaur horns he had presented Merianna were already mounted on the wall. He strode over and stood before them, noting a small brass plate with the date engraved on it.

"You are a hunter, Sr. Guerrero?" came Lord Jalisco's soft voice.

"No, certainly not in your class," Guerrero said, bowing deeply as the robed lord shuffled into the room. "You have specimens of surpassing power and viciousness mounted all around, testifying to your prowess." Guerrero had a chance to see how truly savage these creatures were. In his salad days, Jaime must have been among the bravest, greatest hunters of all time.

"Not all are mine," Lord Jalisco said, smiling. "However, in my day, and those of my father and grandfather, there were certain predators deserving of death after a decent hunt. Take this one, for instance." Jaime, Lord Jalisco stopped in front of a Calydonian boar, one of the least of the creatures on display. "This tusker killed every hunter for a decade, including the King of Ojai and his squire. I brought it down with a single arrow at fifty paces."

"Your skills are great," Guerrero said, hiding his contempt. The boar would have presented no challenge to him in the arena. It was too small, and its narrow brainpan allowed no hint of intelligence. A single thrust and it would be at his feet, his apprentices hurrying out to claim its tusks.

"Were great. My palsy grows daily." Lord Jalisco looked around the room and finally settled on the minotaur horns. "Your gift to my daughter was most generous. Of all her trophies, those horns are the ones she cherishes most."

"It was a great victory. The minotaur had been bred for speed and strength by the Vargas farms."

"Antonio Vargas raised it? A good man, a good man," Lord Jalisco said, almost to himself. Louder, "It was generous of you to dedicate the kill to my daughter. Merianna spends too little time among those of her station."

"That's because you need constant attention, Papa," came the woman's sharp comment. It cut through Guerrero's consciousness like sharp-edged glass shards. He turned and bowed even more deeply in her direction.

The brief glimpse he had of her before confirmed all he suspected. She was no courtly flower, basking in radiance from the royal throne and partaking of the give and take of court intrigue. Merianna showed no interest in dress, not with her subtle mismatching of color and antiquated styles. Her coiffure was askew, badly in need of tending by expert hairdressers.

"I am not so infirm, don't you agree, Sr. Guerrero?"

"Please, Lord, call me Francisco." He adroitly avoided answering, not interested in soothing an old man's vanity.

"Then I must insist you call me Jaime. Come, my dear, is our meal ready?"

Merianna nodded and held out her arm for her father to lean heavily on, but her pale eyes fixed on Guerrero and remained there. He smiled broadly as reward. She shyly averted her eyes and exited the trophy room. Guerrero took one last look at the minotaur horns he had earned that day and sighed. They would have been a noble addition to his trophies, but here they might prove even more powerful.

The table creaked under the sumptuous feast. Guerrero sat at Lord Jalisco's right hand, Merianna at his left. Behind her the unicorn nudged aside a chair and moved to eat from the table.

"My lady, your pet eats with us?" Guerrero was shocked. "Is it not, uh, too wild for such a domestic setting?"

"Arian, wild?" Merianna laughed, and it was almost musical. She stroked the soft fur and scratched between the unicorn's ears until it tossed the long golden horn in the air, head rocking. "He is far more than a pet."

"Merianna feels Arian is as intelligent as any human," Lord Jalisco said, directing the servants in their food service.

"With such a fine horn, it would seem the unicorn is a ferocious hunter," Guerrero said.

"Gentle, Arian is gentle because of my touch. With others, he is more aggressive."

"The matter of the centaur is not suitable for dinner conversation, my dear," chided Lord Jalisco.

"But Sr. Guerrero—"

"Please, milady, do me the great honor and call me Francisco," Guerrero said in his most urbane manner.

"Francisco is a *torero* of great skill. He would be interested in how Arian killed the centaur with a single thrust."

"A female centaur?"

"A male in rut," Merianna said, her cheeks blossoming with red from the embarrassment this caused, yet she rushed on in an effort to impress him. "The centaur had run amok, killing three of Papa's most capable *vaqueros*. Arian charged and, using his horn, killed the beast with an eviscerating stroke."

"But the unicorn is allowed in your home, at your table!"

"As I said, with my daughter he is most gentle."

"Her protector?" asked Guerrero. He ate mechanically, not tasting the paella he shoved into his mouth. He stared at the unicorn, which ignored him completely. "Is he gentle with others if you are absent?"

"You know the reason he prefers my company," Merianna said, again averting her eyes, and the blush rising delightfully from her shoulders and to her neck and face.

Guerrero changed the subject, making light conversation in the witty fashion of the king's court, utterly charming Lord Jalisco—and his daughter.

\* \* \*

"Oh, Francisco, no, you should never have done this. It is so lovely!" Merianna held up the expensive gold chain with the locket so it gleamed in the sunlight. She sank back against the tree trunk and looked past the slowly turning locket and chain to Guerrero.

"It is not half as lovely as you, Merianna," he said, reaching out to touch her cheek. He pulled back when Arian snorted and came trotting up. Over the past weeks Guerrero had never seen the gentle beast far from its mistress' side.

And the few times he had caught it alone, no amount of torment provoked it. In spite of its powerful body and fierce horn, Arian was as gentle as Merianna claimed.

"Arian will not harm you, will you, Arian?" Merianna motioned the unicorn closer and he nuzzled her hand, then rubbed against Guerrero.

"He knows contentment with me. He might run away, but he would never hurt anyone, would you, Arian?"

"He is such a powerful beast." Guerrero closed his eyes for a moment, imagining himself facing Arian in the corrida, the crowd cheering as he fearlessly faced the ferocious unicorn as it began its attack.

Guerrero jerked away as the unicorn's wet tongue licked at his face and a soft cheek pressed to his. If he had not known better, he would have thought the unicorn purred like a kitten.

"You think in those patterns, Francisco. Do you ever contemplate more gentle ways?" She closed her eyes. Guerrero moved closer, cast a glance at the watching Arian and wondered if this might anger the beast, but it only watched with its wide eyes.

Guerrero kissed Merianna, then pulled away slightly to see if he angered the unicorn. Arian sank to the ground with a heavy thump, resting his head on crossed legs. The gold horn traced small circles in the air, but Arian made no movement to impale Guerrero for his impetuosity.

"Francisco, I—" Merianna shifted uncomfortably under him. He returned to shower more kisses on her. She forced him away.

"But, my love, what is wrong?" he asked.

"I can't, Francisco, no more, please. We are such good friends." Merianna looked like a caged animal, her eyes darting about. She looked from him to the unicorn and back.

"I had hoped to be more than friends," he said.

"Impossible, no, I must consider so many things. I am heiress to all of my father's property, since my brother Miguel died."

"Do you think I care for wealth or land? I am rich." Guerrero snorted so loud the unicorn jumped to his feet in surprise. "I do not know how rich your father is, but I suspect I am at least as wealthy."

"You have no title," Merianna said, her defensiveness growing. She struggled to find reasons for not allowing him to court her. Guerrero saw she argued with herself and lost.

"How many of your suitors do?" he asked, knowing the answer before she spoke.

"None. I...I have had no suitors. No serious ones," she added hastily.

"The landed gentry are fools. They ought to have their sons lined up begging for your favor. I am no indolent patron. For every *peseta*, I have fought.

Does my lack of lineage bother you? I had thought you a wiser person, one less snobbish." He judged her response and fought to keep a smile from his lips when he saw it forming.

"No, Francisco, I do not care if you are a lord or a pauper! I love you!" She threw her arms around his neck and burrowed her face into his strong shoulder.

"Not here, my love," he said, looking at the unicorn. Arian grew restive as he sensed what was happening to his mistress. He snorted and pawed at the ground. Guerrero ignored the unicorn as he swept up Merianna and carried her to the nearby barn. He set her down gently once they were inside.

"What are you doing?" Merianna asked, her eyes wide. She looked more like a frightened fawn than a woman.

"Closing the door so we will not be disturbed." Guerrero slammed and barred the barn door as Arian crashed into the wood. Before Merianna could protest, Guerrero swept her up again and carried her to a pile of clean, sweet smelling straw.

It was not the finest lovemaking for the torero, but it was adequate.

* * *

"He will not let me pet him!" Merianna reached out for the unicorn, but Arian backed away, nostrils flaring. She turned to her father, eyes wide in shock. "It...it is true, then?"

"I fear it must be," Jaime said to his daughter. He hobbled to her side, watching Arian dash off into the woods. It was the first time the unicorn had left Merianna's side since she was a young girl. "I am sorry you have discovered this truth of unicorns, but Francisco is a great man. If only you had waited for your marriage bed, perhaps it might have been different with Arian, but you are still gaining a fine husband."

"Husband?" Guerrero strutted up, leading his horse. "Who speaks of marriage?"

"My love!" Merianna ran to him, but he held her at arm's length. "What is wrong?" she demanded. "You are so different now. This afternoon, you pledged your love to me, and now—" She went white and stepped back as realization struck her.

"Nothing is wrong," Guerrero said brusquely. "It is just that I must go."

"A moment!" Lord Jalisco's voice carried the edge of steel in it. "You tell me you are simply leaving? When do you plan to marry my daughter?"

"Why, never," Guerrero said. "She is a lovely person and one whose company pleases me, but marriage? Whatever gave you this silly notion?"

"You cur!" Lord Jalisco lunged for the fighter, but his palsy prevented him from moving fast enough. As if making a grand veronica with his cape,

Guerrero stepped smoothly to one side and let Jaime stumble past, to crash into a wall.

"Get out!" shrieked Merianna. "How dare you! Get out, get out! Leave before I kill you!"

Guerrero bowed mockingly, spun and jumped easily into the saddle. He touched the big floppy brim of his plumed hat, smiled, and wheeled about to gallop off. He felt the woman's hot eyes burning into his back until he rounded the bend in the road leading into town. Only then did Guerrero slow his headlong pace. He rode easily for another few minutes until he caught sight of movement in the woods alongside the road. He reined back and sat impatiently, waiting.

Finally, anxious to return to the delights of the city, Guerrero called, "Enough of this nonsense! Show yourselves!"

"Sr. Guerrero!" From the bushes came a scarred, slovenly man, dragging his left leg slightly as he came to the verge of the road. "It is I, Dimitrios!"

"Yes, yes," Guerrero said, not wanting to even acknowledge this failed apprentice toreador. Dimitrios had not moved swiftly enough in a practice session and had been hooked by a pancusi's horn. The leg had become infected. Guerrero sniffed delicately and took a perfumed handkerchief from his sleeve. It was obvious why infection had claimed so much of the man's flesh. He was filthy then and remained so to this day.

If he had not been so useful, Guerrero would have removed him from his employ long ago.

"I've been waiting, just as you asked."

"I wanted you to do more than play with yourself in these fine woods. Is the task accomplished?"

"Yes, of course, of course. All that remains is to—"

"If you have done as you were told thus far, then you will continue to follow my explicit orders." For the first time, a smile curled Guerrero's lips. He was the finest torero in the world.

Soon, he would become legendary!

With this thought stirring his passion, he rode for the city and his destiny.

* * *

Guerrero had ordered his agents to summon the largest crowd possible, even if they sold tickets at a discount. He wanted a full arena this day of his greatest triumph. And how could he become a legend if only a few thousand avid fans saw him? He needed tens of thousands to whisper of his conquest, his mastery, his soaring victory!

Mariachis played loudly, then the trumpet player began the long, soulful solo to prepare the crowd for the entry of their *torero primero*. Resplendent in his suit of light, Guerrero stepped into the arena. For a moment, silence fell. He relished the quiet, then strode to the middle of the ring. Every footstep echoed, sand grating under his boots. Every eye fixed on him, anticipating his announcement. He had never been known to tease an audience, and he would not now.

He cleared his throat and called in a loud voice, "I have fought minotaurs and centaurs. They fell to my sword!" Turning slowly, cape draped over his arm, he studied the crowd. They were nervous, anxious for what would happen this day.

"I have fought exotic animals from far-off lands; I have fought bulls and sirens and fierce creatures with no name. But others have done this, also."

A whisper passed through the audience, a whisper like a hurricane through a thick grove of oak trees. It rose as all murmured to their companions what must be coming.

"Never has anyone fought the ultimate of all animals. Some call it a gentle beast, a shy creature of the woods. I have found a way to incite it to its full potential of fury, of cunning and speed and stark murderous ability. And this afternoon, I, Francisco Guerrero y Campos, the greatest torero ever, will fight the unicorn!"

From the far side of the ring, Dimitrios and two other apprentices struggled to open the door of the cage they had fashioned in the woods on Lord Jalisco's estate. After Guerrero had deflowered Merianna, the unicorn had run off—and into the clever trap specifically set for the frightened, confused creature.

Arian pawed at the ground, kicked up sand, and let out a bloodcurdling trumpet that caused Guerrero to take a step back in surprise. Never had he heard such outrage in a beast nor seen such fury in the eyes. Some creatures were poked and prodded into frenzy by his apprentices to provide a better fight.

Arian whipped himself into a rage without needing those barbed sticks. And more than the rage, Guerrero saw intelligence in those eyes peering at him around the shiny golden horn. Triumph surged within his breast. Then he prepared for the fight of his career. To vanquish such an opponent would put his name on every woman's lips as she drifted off to sleep to dream of him, on every child's lips as they spoke reverently of how they wanted to be another Francisco Guerrero y Campos, on every man's lips as they cursed his skill and bravery.

The unicorn charged.

The gold horn ripped a long gash in the tough canvas cape and almost opened Guerrero's gut. He sucked in his breath as he let the unicorn rush past.

Blood trickled down inside his suit of light instead of sweat. That would come later, to burn the wound he sustained on the very first pass.

Then he was buoyed by the knowledge no other fighter had ever faced a unicorn. Guerrero had chosen the proper bait, followed the exact course required to bring the unicorn to the arena in a grand fury. No longer would Arian follow his mistress, and the man responsible stood before him, waving the cape and making ritualistic battle between man and beast.

Twice more Arian opened bloody gouges on Guerrero's chest and belly before the expert sword flashed in the afternoon sun and the gold-horned unicorn lay vanquished in the sand.

Guerrero dropped his cape, crossed his arms over his front. The suit of light was traditional and lovely, but it served a purpose transcending mere beauty. It held in his viscera even as it had protected his belly from other slashes and penetrating wounds, but he felt no pain. He felt only triumph and the adulation of the crowd.

Guerrero saluted and waved with a free hand as he made his slow victory circuit around the arena. His steps faltered when he came to the dignitaries' box. Not only were seven of the royal family here to celebrate his expertise, but also in the box stood Merianna. He sucked in more air, endured pain, and then continued on the path toward everlasting glory.

He stopped in front of the box and bowed as much as his injuries would permit.

"This day, I dedicate my victory to—" Guerrero's fine words were cut off by Merianna. The woman shoved her way to the front and shouted at him.

"You defiled me, and you killed a fine, noble beast. There will be justice for you, Francisco Guerrero y Campos! Justice but no mercy!"

Guerrero considered presenting the gold horn to the woman, then changed his mind. That was his trophy, the symbol of the greatest corrida in all history!

"Should there be any contention," he said in a measured tone, "commend me to your father. From his trophy room, he is an accomplished hunter."

"My father is in no condition to defend my honor," Merianna called. Her anger faded and was replaced by something worse. "He died from the disgrace you brought to our house. And you are mistaken, Sr. Guerrero. The trophies are not his—they are mine."

Francisco Guerrero y Campos looked into the woman's eyes and knew she spoke the truth.

For the first time, the greatest torero in all history knew real fear.

# All the Colors of Life

*Heineken Beer ran a contest in the summer of 1996 for a new ad concept. Send in your vision of a Heineken ad and win. I don't even remember how much the winner was to receive. A lot. All for a 1,200-word story. I did not win, but elements of this short, short fiction have been woven through numerous stories of mine since then. (And this was a lot better than the tepid winner. If I do say so myself.)*

A flash. A flash of skin. Seductive, colorful, forever changing. You long to reach out and touch the woman's delicate skin, but you know better. The emoto-dyes, the emotion-activated dyes injected beneath her skin, would alter the eddying dyestuff design you find so beguiling.

Is it merely the shift of her emotions that cause the red and blue and green and yellow dyes to swirl, like an old 1970's mood ring, or is it something more? Can that gleam in her eye be for you and you alone? Such vivid sapphire pigmentation cannot be natural. And why should it be, in an era where colors are as transient as the sunset? A slow wink suggests so much, but when the eyelid rises again, the blue of a summer sky has changed to the delicate green depths of rare Chinese jade. She is a sophisticated, lushly responsive work of art, decorated in the latest bio-dye style, displaying the subcutaneous expertise of a master surgical beautician.

It is hard to believe permanent, static designs such as tattoos and body piercing jewelry were ever the rage at the close of the last century. You find current techno-dye fashion so much more appealing—and revealing. Holding out your hand, you watch the slow motion of the dye form distinct figures. An entire scene from the latest holomovie is reenacted, with the two actors you find most stimulating emotionally. You make a note to have the scene changed, although you still find the effect fascinating; everyone has copied you. Trend-following is not for you. Trend-setting is.

The invention of implanted color plates early in the twenty-first century allowed advertising to be flashed about ever so indecorously under the skin of those who thought it urbane to be seen with the expensive devices, no matter how gauche it truly was. Glancing around the room, you see a few revelers who do not understand how passé this mechanical technology is. The computer nanochip for the plates require small batteries and cause unsightly lumps for those who bother to notice. You notice. The plate displays—meat platter displays, you sarcastically call them—allow more involved scenes and can be changed more quickly, but they are so unrefined and never respond to the inner person like biologically active emoto-dyes.

You look across the room to the woman again and feel stronger desire build within you. The dyes on your cheeks and neck alter subtly, driven by new emotions. *What is happening with her fractal pattern dye scheme?* you wonder, seeking a hint to her intentions. Can she feel something for you, or is the change in her coloration due to annoyance with the others in her party?

They seem distant, their emoto-dyes dark and subdued. They are not in the spirit of the party. Not like the woman with the intricate dye job that dances about so charmingly across arm and cheek and deliciously exposed breast.

Your burgeoning peacock colors flash for her and her alone.

She plays coy, batting her long lashes, changing the color of her eyes with every blink. Such eye-dye requires total devotion to fashion. Injection is a delicate process, yet she underwent it for this party. For you?

Standing, you move through the press of the crowd toward her. Another woman brushes against you. You recoil. Her skin is the texture of parched leather. You mutter an apology and move on, although the collision was no accident on her part. Some fashion statements are not for you. Her skin has been turned completely dark with photo-dye. Indoors, under the dim lights at the party, she appears exotically Nubian. In the sun, the dye will turn nut-brown. Under artificial UV, she might appear radiantly olive or the dull red of a dust-streaked sunset.

But the price for such total coloration is too high. Her skin has lost its flexibility, and you enjoy stroking across bare flesh, letting satin skin ripple under your fingertips, and watching the dyes chase each other in increasingly awakened kaleidoscopic patterns.

You tug at your shirt and open the front, exposing your chest. Your heart races at the sight of the attentive woman, a vibrant oasis in the middle of her increasingly dull friends. The surge of your emotion and the catalyzing chemicals released bring into play new dyes, ones selected solely for this party. Not for you a larger version of the deliberate motion of the holomovie scene still playing across your hand. This new effect was created by an exceptional artist.

Mondrian? Dali? Rembrandt? Those were not the masters you sought. They worked in oils on canvas. A different artistry was required, one using the human body as medium for the emoto-dyes. Liberty was both your artist's name and his promise to you. The scene he created is unique, even at a gala filled with fashion seekers. The careful layering of the emoto-dyes produces a disturbing, flowing panorama that might be stolen from the room around you.

A slow smile crosses your lips as you glance down. The scene might have been imprinted by camera recording everything happening around you. Clever use of dark and light dyes blur detail and make it seem as if the party's revelers

*Robert E. Vardeman*

are somehow projected onto the canvas of your flesh. You are not only moving among the revelers, you reflect them and become transparent to their gaiety.

Your smile broadens when you realize she has understood the message of this art. You do not seek anonymity with a camouflage of shapes. You seek to make a statement. You are one—and one above.

Gazing into her eyes sparks new swirls of color, starbursts you have never seen before. She is outwardly cool, but the eyes betray her. You reach out. She hesitates, looks at her companions, then the aloofness vanishes. Even if you did not accurately read the ebb and flow of emotion-activated emoto-dye under her silky skin, her body language tells you everything you need to know.

Your hand rests on hers. Colors flow and seem to mingle. Then the two of you slip away into the night to invent new patterns and hues in private.

# Under Triple Moons

*The last story of mine published in* Adventures of Sword & Sorcery *came out in the fall of 1996. Not quite a masked avenger story, its hero is an improbable one—a stone statue. He has eons to ruminate and ponder his fate and eventually act. I don't remember the spark that brought this one to life, but it might have been some Greek myth. Or a Thorne Smith book, though my story is not as ribald as* Nightlife of the Gods.

Forty thousand sunrises he had seen, always staring directly east without squinting, no matter how the light hurt his eyes. Try as he might, Haymon, Lord Cyl, found it impossible to turn away or even to blink. After the first few months of his involuntary sentry duty, he had resolutely accepted this as he had other aspects of his curse laid upon him. Years of anger and hatred slipped into despair, and finally scores of years brought grim recognition, if not real acceptance of his plight. For all the daily annoyance, the garden where he stood was well kept and, save for the flocks of pigeons bedeviling and defiling him over the years, he had little else to trouble him.

Haymon reflected how the curse had given him the final triumph over the sorcerer laying the curse. The youthful, dashing, impetuously ambitious Algario's bones had turned to dust sixty years back—or longer. The sorcerer's worst enemy continued on, stolidly watching the sunrise and the passing of new seasons and the rise and fall of empires.

Haymon wished the vainglorious popinjay of a sorcerer had turned him to stone facing the west, though. The one-time ruler of Cyl had always preferred the splendor of dust-filled skies reflecting fabulous red rays to the more sedate sunrise. Even the century and more of introspection and appreciation of sunrises did not change this. Haymon wondered if that might have been part of Algario's true curse. Being cast into immobile statuary in the palace garden was bad, but always longing for what he could not get gnawed away at his soul.

If he could have done so, Haymon would have sighed deeply. His empire had crumbled quickly after Algario's death. Cyl was no more, nor was the following Empire of Solnme overrun by barbarians, nor the kingdom of King Vervon's offspring, nor Queen Bismie's ill-fated seven days on the throne nor the succeeding rule of the club-footed King Jocci. It had been almost a breath of fresh air through his unmoving marble lungs when Queen Elliorna had ascended the throne of an empire Haymon barely recognized.

Elliorna had been wise and long-lived, and her son Seatavio also proved a boon for his kingdom, being wise and compassionate when needed, and iron-fisted in defense when the barbarians returned. Haymon, the foremost tactician of his time, had tried to decide how he would have mounted a better campaign against the barbarous hordes looking only to destroy all that was civilized and could not. But the young Seatavio turned older with the ceaseless daily journey of the sun and now sought to pass his crown to another.

Had Haymon a pulse, it would have raced as the lovely woman passed through his field of vision. Never in all the days of his rule or after had Haymon seen a woman so stunningly gorgeous. If beauty had been all that Lenolla brought to the meticulously kept garden, Haymon might have been content, but she had a wit, intelligence, and liveliness that filled his static days with joy.

"When will he arrive, Anne?" Lenolla asked of her young handmaiden. "Soon?"

"You know this better than I, Mistress," Anne said. She averted her eyes, but they danced with merriment as she teased Lenolla.

Haymon enjoyed the joke, even as he felt some sadness, for Lenolla awaited her betrothed, Jiam, of the adjoining Duchy of Woldetta. He had never seen the young man to pass judgment on him, but from all Lenolla said—and more important, the private conversations of Anne and other servants—all thought highly of him. Still, Jiam could never provide a more loving or caring match than Haymon, Lord Cyl. Haymon was not certain when it had happened, but he had come to love Lenolla with all his stony heart and frozen soul.

The young princess with midnight hair flowing gracefully like a raven's wing spun about, causing her peach-colored, silken dress to press intimately to her perfect form. She laughed in delight and cried, "Jiam will be here in two days. Under the triple moons we will sit and talk, then we shall be married!"

"Sit? Talk under the light of the demon moons?" chided Anne. "Is that all you intend to do?"

"They are not 'demon moons,'" Lenolla said sharply. "Not this time, or so says Tymel. They are a good omen, and they shine on our marriage."

"What does Tymel know?" Anne turned somber. "He is old, and his sorceries are suspect. Many talk of his spells going awry and causing you great harm."

"Lies, all lies. Tymel's divination shows nothing but happiness in my future," Lenolla said, dismissing such concerns. "Come along. It is time for the morning court. You know how Father gets when I am late."

Lenolla, lovely Lenolla, and her handmaiden hurried out of Haymon's sight, leaving him to stand and stare into the rising sun. Soon the blinding light passed and permitted him some small comfort. From the movement of leaves on the well-tended bushes, a gentle breeze wafted through the garden. Flowers blossomed in well-ordered, aesthetically pleasing arrays of subtle color, hinting at fragrances Haymon only vaguely remembered.

He wondered if the wedding would take place in the garden where he might see the young lord and give his silent benediction. It was little enough, but Haymon felt protective toward Lenolla after watching her take her first steps, then toddle about the garden, and finally bloom into the great beauty she now was.

But triple moons? This caused him a small knot of worry. It had been under the triple moons Algario had cursed him and forever trapped him in stone. Anne was right to call them demon moons. Their irregular conjunction heightened the power of any spell cast under them. The old sorcerer Tymel had seldom acquitted himself well in matters dealing with magic, or so Haymon thought. The three moons coming together and merging into one in the night sky foretold dangerous times, perilous times that ought to alert everyone to treachery.

Haymon had lost kingdom and freedom under their light.

All day he pondered this and memories of blood being spilled and peculiar chants uttered as the shadows moved inexorably, lengthening in front of him to show how sunset neared. But more than this, he heard movement. The one person in Seatavio's court that most aggravated Haymon crept like a thief into the garden, choosing to remain hidden in the shadows. But Haymon always knew when Voz neared. The air turned colder, and he wanted to reach down to be sure the king's closest advisor did not steal sword and purse at his waist, in spite of them being stone.

Voz stood silently for several minutes, then made a beckoning motion. From under a shrub on the far side of the garden path rose a dark-clothed weasel of a man.

"You have the poison?" Voz demanded. The small, dusky man produced a pouch from the folds of his clothing. He snatched it away from the advisor's grip as Voz reached for it.

"First, the payment."

"You do not trust me?" Voz's voice poured forth like honey—deadly honey. Haymon strained to turn and get a better view of what vile transaction the advisor conducted.

"I am no fool. Anyone who thinks to kill the princess is likely to remove witnesses to his scheme. That might include the one supplying the means to your murderous end."

"I honor my debts," Voz said angrily. He grabbed away the pouch and hid it from Haymon's sight. "Your pay awaits, in the usual fashion at the same place. You know you will always have a secure position...when I ascend the throne."

Haymon's anger mounted until he thought, for the first time in more than a century, he might cast off the stony bonds holding him.

213

"What of Jiam?" asked the small poisoner. "Will you deal with him and his new wife on their wedding night?"

"That would be cruel," Voz said offhandedly. "The princess dies before the marriage. Jiam will have no claim to the throne."

"And our poor king, brokenhearted, will turn to you for solace. How long will Seatavio live after his daughter is no longer counted among the breathing?"

Haymon strained and struggled and fought, to no avail. The curse held him firmly. He could listen and seethe in anger, but he could not act. The sun died behind him, no longer giving warmth to his marble back, and the moons began their scatterbrained race into the evening sky. This night they would not merge into one, but soon. In two nights. And Lenolla would be dead by then.

"What's that?" snapped Voz. "I heard something."

He spoke to emptiness. The purveyor of traceless poisons had vanished into the garden as surely as if he had never existed. Haymon knew the weasel-faced man would be wise to leave the kingdom immediately, for Voz was not the sort to honor pledges of immunity.

Haymon saw Voz draw a sharp, slender-bladed dagger and step forward.

"Who is there?" called the king's advisor. "Must I summon the guard?"

"No, my lord," stammered Anne, coming into the range of Haymon's vision. "I am seeking my mistress. She—"

"How long have you been here?" Voz asked. Haymon tried to shout to Anne to turn and run, to scream, to fetch the guard. His cold marble throat refused to shape the words. He saw the dagger flash in the light of the racing moons. Anne cried out, gripped her breast and staggered away from Voz. The advisor used his dagger repeatedly, savagely, and then left the bloody blade protruding from Anne's back as she lay on the garden path.

Voz smoothed the wrinkles in his clothing, spun on his heel, and strode off, whistling tunelessly as Haymon watched in helpless rage.

"Anne," Haymon called. "Do not die. Tell your mistress." Over and over he screamed the words that never emerged from his throat. But the handmaiden stirred nonetheless. She moaned and reached vainly for the blade buried to the hilt in her back.

"Anne!"

It seemed to Haymon she heard him at last. The mortally wounded young girl raised her eyes to his. She gathered her feet under her and staggered forward, arms outstretched. Anne grabbed him around his ankles, her blood turning the marble slippery.

"Stop him, I beseech you. Stop him from harming my mistress," she said as she died.

Moonlight gleamed darkly on the blood staining the statue's marble legs. Phosphorescent fire began to dance wildly and wend its way upward until the entire statue was consumed in lambent flame.

\* \* \*

Forty thousand sunrises he had seen, always staring directly east without squinting, no matter how the light hurt his eyes. Haymon, Lord Cyl, screamed. For the first time in more than a century he heard his own hoarse voice. He coughed and rolled to one side, then sat bolt upright. He no longer stared into the rising sun. And he could blink his eyelids!

"I live!" he cried, the import of this discovery staggering. Then he saw the body of Lenolla's handmaiden sprawled gracelessly over the empty pedestal where he had stood accursed for so long. Haymon went to her and slid the blade from her back.

"Your blood brought me to life. I pledge on my soul that your death will not go unavenged." Haymon wiped off the dagger on grass sprouting at the marble base and tucked it into his broad, elaborately hand-tooled belt. Then he stretched. Every bit of agony was like a magical elixir to him.

On unsteady feet, Haymon walked from the garden. Only after a few minutes did it occur to him he had no idea where to go. The garden was recent, constructed in the last fifty years, but the palace was entirely renovated after its many sackings, uprising, and coups. Gentle arches soared where once ponderous beams of timber and stone had held together the walls. Stained glass decorated windows originally left open so archers could fire at approaching enemy soldiers. He walked along, hand on his sword hilt and simply gawked.

"May I help you, good sir?" came the question. Haymon turned to see a guard decked out in finery at the side door leading into the palace.

Haymon almost asked to see Lenolla, then bit back this request. He dared not reveal too much. This guard's allegiance might be to Voz rather than to his king—and his king's lovely daughter. More than this, he had questions that desperately required answers.

"I seek Tymel."

"Your name and business with the court sorcerer?" The guard made no overt move but four others joined him, all armed and dangerous looking. Haymon had watched many soldiers drill just beyond the garden and knew King Seatavio entertained no weaklings in his service. But were they loyal?

"I am Haymon, Lord Cyl, and my business is private with Tymel."

"Lord Cyl?" laughed the first guard. "Cyl's a name not heard for scores of years."

"Another Cyl, it is," Haymon said, groping for an explanation he did not quite have, "one far distant from here. Am I to stand exchanging pleasantries all night or do I see Tymel?"

"This way, sire," said the guard, after receiving the high sign from within the palace. "Tymel grants you an immediate audience."

"Pleased, no doubt, to entertain one from Cyl," Haymon said as haughtily as he could. His muscles still ached, but every step sent new energy into his body. He followed the guard through winding corridors that had grown in complexity since he had been cursed so long ago. The wall hangings, the statuary, the furnishings all bespoke of prosperity unlike anything in his time.

"Go on in. Tymel seldom has anyone visiting him these days," the guard said, sarcasm dripping from his words. Haymon did not reprove the man. Instead, his mission drove him forward. He entered Tymel's chambers and was immediately assaulted by foul odors and a dense yellow cloud billowing from an open beaker on a stained worktable. Hunched over it was the ancient sorcerer.

"Close the door. The draft affects the scrying spell."

Haymon closed the heavy wood door and stood to one side, where the yellow fumes would not sting his eyes. He continued to marvel at his ability to move, to experience, to actually have his nose wrinkle and cause a sneeze to build.

"No one comes here these days. No need for a court sorcerer. All the enemies are gone from the kingdom."

"Are they now?" asked Haymon. This caused the sorcerer to jerk upright and fix Lord Cyl with a steely gaze.

"Lenolla's impending marriage will unite the two most powerful nations."

"What do you think of Jiam?"

"A fine lad. Green in many ways, but he has a good heart and a strong arm. But there is another, more vexing question."

"That is?" asked Haymon, making a slow circuit of the sorcerer's chambers. In the slowly twisting yellow cloud appeared a distant figure, barely seen but dark and foreboding. Above it blazed a single sun. Or was it a sun? Haymon could not decide.

"Who are you? You have the look of someone I should know."

"You have seen me every day for all your life," Haymon said, glancing out the sorcerer's window into the garden where the empty pedestal stood. From this angle Anne's body could not be seen. In truth, had Tymel been watching, he could not have seen Voz kill the handmaiden. But the drifting yellow vapors made Haymon uneasy. Within their noisome folds was reenacted the crime.

"Triple moons," Haymon said suddenly. "You scry the future, you see what happens under the triple moons!"

"My earlier forecast of nothing but a beneficent future for Lenolla seems to have been amiss," Tymel said. "My powers have dwindled over the years." The sorcerer moved on arthritic joints and perched on a high stool. "Some of my powers remain, and I am sure I know you. There is a certain...power about you. You dress strangely, in the manner of the olden empires, and you have a regal bearing. No peasant are you."

"I am Haymon, Lord Cyl, and for one hundred and ten years have I stood in the garden below your window watching the empire I carved fall and rise from ash, only to be reformed and destroyed anew."

"Haymon?" Tymel laughed. "What a conceit you have. He was the greatest of our kings. That is why yon statue was erected." Tymel hobbled to the window and stared for a moment, then turned and cast his penetrating gaze on Haymon again.

"Algario cursed me under the triple moons to an eternity of vigilance as a statue," Haymon said with more bitterness than he intended. "I have stood guard, watching kings and fools, queens and harlots on my throne. And I have watched Lenolla grow into the fine lady she is."

"How have you thrown off Algario's curse? From all I have learned, he was a methodical mage, not one prone to mistake."

"Lenolla's handmaiden died at my feet. Her blood brought me to life."

"Anne? Lenolla was hunting her earlier. You say she has died?" Tymel hobbled back to his stool and folded his gnarled hands on his lap. "Do I detect Voz's influence here?" Tymel gestured in the direction of the floating yellow cloud, now almost dissipated. But within showed clearly the face of the king's advisor.

"He would poison Lenolla, then seize power for himself."

"Jiam would never permit that. Nor would Seatavio, as old as he is." Tymel cackled. "Seatavio might be older than dirt, but he is a doughty ruler. He would cut out Voz's heart and force him to eat it while it still throbbed."

"The poison is a subtle one," Haymon said. "I know nothing more than this. Voz must be exposed."

"He is a man of great power and is trusted widely," Tymel said carefully. "It was not until recently I came to question his motives. He has shielded his hunger for power well these years."

"Stop him. Help me stop him," Haymon begged.

Tymel shook his head. "My powers are on the wane. You saw how even the guards make fun of me. Even under the triple moons, I would have no real chance to defeat one as strong as Voz."

"Under the demon moons I was cursed," Haymon said. "You told Lenolla the moons are not evil. Why?" Haymon began to consider the treachery possible if Tymel joined forces with Voz.

"I have read the grimoires and I know such things. The moons will converge before midnight, not after. Their power will be for good."

"It was after midnight when Algario ensorcelled me," Haymon said. "Why was I released from such a potent spell?"

"A life to imprison you, a life given to free you," Tymel said, shrugging. "Who can say? I know nothing of such magic." He cocked his head to one side. "Was a plea made?"

"Anne bade me stop her murderer, as if I would do otherwise," Haymon said hotly. "Voz will never harm Lenolla."

"I detect more in your words. How did this love for our darling Lenolla come about?"

"I watched her from infancy," Haymon said, casting back through a score and more of years. "She laughed so prettily at her christening day, and I think I saw her first real kiss."

"That young scamp Deuparrian?"

"A lieutenant of the guard, blondish and with a scar on his cheek," Haymon said.

"Ah, yes, so it was Deuparrian. Lenolla has never mentioned him, not since he was lost in the Woldettan Campaigns some six years ago."

"I did not know," Haymon said, feeling the loss for Lenolla. "I do know I have shared so much of her life and her confidences that I have come to love her."

Haymon waited for the sorcerer to laugh at this. Tymel did not. He rubbed his hands together slowly and sucked at his teeth as he thought. Finally, he stirred from his stool and approached Haymon.

"You must prevent Voz from administering the poison. I have no power to counter the effect, once given. Even given the augmentation of the triple moons, I cannot reverse the kind of poison he would purchase from a bane broker."

"Will you see me to Lenolla's chambers?" Haymon asked. "Together, we can convince her of Voz's planned treachery."

"I know secret ways in the palace," said the old sorcerer. "Perhaps one passage goes close enough, but we must wait until just before dawn. Now tell me, Haymon, Lord Cyl, how came it about that you defeated the Haan armies with so few soldiers? Was it sorcery you used?"

For the time being, Haymon was willing to swap reminiscence for food, delightful food, intoxicating wine, and even the sheer pleasure of having someone to talk with after so many years.

\* \* \*

Haymon pressed his eye against the peephole, watching Lenolla move about her chambers. She seemed not to walk but to float, to move with such grace that it took away his breath. But Haymon knew he dared not tarry overlong. Reaching up, he found the spring catch and opened the panel.

"Who are you?" she called upon seeing him. Lenolla's hand went to a dagger on a nearby table. From the way she held it, Haymon knew she could use it expertly. More than this, had he not seen her practicing with the captain of the guard day after day in the gardens when she was but thirteen?

"Someone who means you only good," Haymon said.

"You are dressed strangely," she said, more curious than afraid. "I have seen you before, have I not?"

"The story is long and boring, Lenolla," he said. His heart raced at her nearness. The miasma of her perfume caused his nostrils to flare, and the impact of her beauty was a thousandfold greater this close than when seen from across the garden. "I must hurry with my warning."

"No! A thousand times no! I am going to marry Jiam!"

"I don't understand," Haymon stuttered, taken off guard by her change of topic.

"Voz sent you, I know he did. I love Jiam and he loves me. We will marry two days hence and no amount of argument will sway me!"

"You mistake my warning, Lenolla," he said. "I warn you of Voz! He plans to poison you and seize the throne from your father."

Lenolla's anger changed mercurially. She laughed. "That is absurd. Voz thinks he has my best interest at heart. That is why he counsels against marriage to Jiam. I don't care if Woldetta is a fraction the size of our kingdom. If Jiam were a pauper begging door to door, I would not love him less!"

Her passion brought roses to her cheeks. The way she tossed her head like a spirited animal and sent flying the dark banner of hair quickened Haymon's pulse. He loved her the more in that instant.

"Your trust in your father's advisor is misplaced. I witnessed him buy poison from a furtive man in the garden—before he murdered your handmaiden."

"Anne? She has been missing since yesterday, but—no! I do not know you, you who dress in ancient clothing and spout all this nonsense about a good and fair man my father has trusted for years. Get out or I shall call the guard."

"Loyalty misplaced can be fatal, Lenolla," Haymon said. "I have your best interest at heart—"

"You don't know me," she snapped. "Oh, I will be glad when the wedding is over and I can call upon Jiam whenever I want! Get out!"

"Lenolla," Haymon said, struggling to frame his argument in a better way. He froze, as if Algario's spell again seized him, when she reached for a goblet filled with wine. "Stop, wait!"

She drank. For a moment, nothing happened, then Lenolla simply collapsed. Haymon rushed to her side. She still lived, but her heartbeat was thready and her breathing shallow. He lifted her to the bed and gently covered her, knowing Voz had struck his vile blow.

Hand on sword, Haymon returned through the hidden passage to inform Tymel of the crime. Perhaps, with the help of the court chirurgeon, the old sorcerer might pry Lenolla free of Voz's poison. No matter the result of their enterprise, Haymon knew he had a duty to execute.

\* \* \*

Voz looked up in surprise when Haymon kicked in the doors to his quarters. Across a long table from the king's advisor sat the dark purveyor of the poison used to rob Lenolla of her senses.

"What is the meaning of this!" cried Voz, kicking his chair back as he stood.

Haymon's sword flashed out. The tip traced a line along the weasel-faced man's throat. He gasped and clutched his severed throat, falling away. Haymon strode forward, intent on Voz.

"The antidote to the poison you gave Lenolla," he bellowed. "What is it?"

"I know nothing of what you say," Voz said, backing away. "Who are you? You look familiar, but—" The advisor spoke only to gain time. He hurled a candlestick at Haymon, who batted it away with his sword. This still knocked his blade off-line and gave Voz the chance to draw his own weapon.

"Now you will die," Voz said, moving forward with the easy, graceful step of a skillful fencer.

"There is no antidote, is there?" asked Haymon, dropping into an *en garde* position and waiting. He had fought the best there were and had no fear of Voz or his skill with a sword.

"There is none. But for you, you dolt, there will be the antidote of death for stupidity!" Voz lunged. Haymon easily parried, then began the fight in earnest. For a few seconds, it seemed the two were evenly matched. Voz even bragged of his own skill, then slowly began to realize Haymon had only been taking his measure.

"A pink, nothing more," Haymon said as he drew a bloody line down Voz's arm. "There is more to come." He riposted as Voz attacked wildly and sent an inch of steel into the advisor's shoulder.

Haymon fell into the coldly calculating style of swordplay he had used to such devastating effect a century and more earlier. Each thrust hit the precise target. Every parry deflected Voz's blade the smallest amount necessary. But as he fought, Haymon's thoughts returned to Anne's murder and how Voz had poisoned Lenolla.

"Lenolla," he said, ire mounting. Haymon began to fight with more passion, using heavier thrusts, his strokes and slashes and lunges longer than necessary.

Voz fought for his life, no longer doing anything but defensive sword work.

Haymon became more reckless as he sought to end the vile poisoner's life. His heel came down on a patch of Voz's blood and he slipped, sword tip going wildly out of line. As he hit the ground, Haymon felt a moment of utter fear surged through him. His elbow cracked and sent his sword flying from his grip. Voz stood above him, hand trembling with his blade ready for the killing thrust.

"You fought well, but now you die." Voz lunged as Haymon rolled to the side. The steel tip scrapped along the stone and sent a shower of blue sparks flying. Haymon kept moving and rolled to his feet, hands at his sides.

"You only prolong your death," Voz said. "I know not who you are, but your meddling is at an end!" The king's advisor lunged.

Haymon waited and waited and waited, the world moving in slow motion around him. He watched the jagged tip of Voz's sword approach—and slide harmlessly past as he twisted and reached for the dagger in his belt.

The slender blade that had robbed Anne of her life now drank deeply of her murderer's blood. Haymon felt the sharp tip bounce off a rib and then slide into the firm, beating muscle of Voz's heart. He stepped away and let the treacherous man fall to the floor, the deadly dagger sheathed in his chest.

Haymon, Lord Cyl, felt no thrill of victory. Lenolla lay in her poisoned trance beyond the reach of even knowledgeable Tymel's magic. Voz's death could not reverse her slow descent into death.

* * *

"The king has taken to his bed. Seatavio is not well, not at all. His heart," muttered the court chirurgeon, as he bustled about Lenolla's bed. The lovely woman lay pale and slipping into death's icy embrace moment by moment.

"Jiam will arrive soon," Tymel said softly to Haymon. "His presence will do nothing to bring her back, but he deserves to be here since she was his betrothed."

"What of the kingdom?" asked Haymon. "If Lenolla dies unmarried and Seatavio is unable to rule, what then?"

Tymel shook his head. "Jiam is popular. Perhaps he can rally support among the nobles. More likely, there will be civil war the like of which has never been seen."

"I've seen it before," Haymon said grimly. He stared at Lenolla and wished he could cure her with the pass of a hand. An uproar from the corridor told of Jiam's arrival. He pushed through the gathered attendants and dropped onto the bed beside Lenolla.

"My darling," he moaned. "How could anyone do this to you? I'll kill the man responsible!"

"Haymon already has. He killed Voz for this treachery," said Tymel.

"For that, you have my undying gratitude," Jiam said. Haymon bowed slightly as he took this young man's measure. The sword at his side showed sign of wear from long usage. A few pale scars on his arm and face hinted at many battles, but Haymon did not want to jump to conclusions. He knew nothing of Jiam's mettle, in spite of all he had heard.

"I can lay claim to the realm," Haymon whispered to Tymel. "If necessary to avoid war, I shall do it."

"You, who has watched it change over the years, would do that? Surely, you understand what would happen if you pranced about claiming to be Lord of Cyl!" The sorcerer shook his shaggy head in amazement at such audacity.

"He is too young to rule," Haymon said, coming to a decision. "He—"

"Sorcerer!" cried Jiam. "What would it take to bring her from this horrible trance? If necessary, I will lay down my life to bring her back!"

"If she required a quart of your blood, would you give it?" asked Haymon, motioning Tymel to silence. He was surprised when Jiam drew back his sleeve and whipped out his knife, ready to sever an artery for his dying fiancée.

"Not now, not yet," Haymon said. "Go, Jiam, rest. Tymel will call you if there is any change."

"I will stay with my beloved," Jiam said doggedly.

Haymon would have done likewise—he wanted to do nothing more than that. He nodded and drew the sorcerer to one side of Lenolla's bedchamber. "The triple moons appear tonight."

"Before midnight," the sorcerer said. "For good they will come this time, but what good can there be when our dear Lenolla is slipping from us by slow degrees?"

Haymon spoke, slowly at first and then with greater certainty. At first Tymel doubted him, and then he reluctantly agreed. There was nothing to lose.

\* \* \*

"Jiam will not awaken until morning," Tymel said. "The sleeping potion I gave him is a potent one."

Haymon carried Lenolla in his arms, savoring the warmth of her body pressed into his, the perfume of her long hair, the sound of her breathing, and the soft rise and fall of her perfectly shaped breasts. How he loved her, how he had come to love her over the years as he watched her grow from gawky youngling to beauteous woman.

"The triple moons near congruence," Haymon said.

"This might not work. I am unskilled in such magic," declared Tymel.

"Are you afraid?"

"Yes," the sorcerer said, "but for Lenolla I will do anything."

"As will I," Haymon said so softly only Lenolla could hear. He carried her to the marble base where he had stood for so many years and propped her up so the light of the moons would fall on her exquisite face.

"These spells are so complex. I am not sure," moaned Tymel. "They might require more than is written. Some tidbits of a spell are only passed down from master to apprentice in secret ceremony. My master had no truck with such diabolical spells."

"Cast the spells," Haymon said coldly. "Cast them or be damned! My life for hers!"

Haymon glanced at the three moons racing toward each other from vertices of an equilateral triangle. He felt heat against his face as the moons melted into one. The power filled his body as if he were an empty vessel. And then he heard Tymel's chant. Low and intricate, it built in power fed by the magic of the moons.

"My life for yours, dear Lenolla," Haymon said softly.

"I feel no change. This is not working," protested Tymel. "There must be something more, and I do know not what it is!"

"Make it work, damn your eyes!" Then Haymon knew the element missing from the spell. He remembered the blood and the sacrifice needed to power a spell under the moons. With a rush, he drew his sword and slashed at the sorcerer. Black blood exploded from Tymel's torso and poured over Lenolla, the blood turning instantly to liquid silver. Haymon felt his joints stiffening as his life force flowed away from his body to Lenolla's, and Algario's damnable spell reasserted itself. This time, he felt exultant.

Haymon stood on the marble base, turning inexorably to marble. At the last possible moment, he pivoted so he could see Lenolla slumped against the eastern side of the pedestal, bathed in eye-searing light from the triple moons.

\* \* \*

More than forty thousand sunrises he had seen, always staring directly east without squinting, no matter how the light hurt his eyes. But Haymon did not mind. His last sight before returning to stone had been Lenolla stirring and sitting up, Voz's poison dissipated by blood and spell and the magical radiance of the three moons.

While he would have enjoyed the sight of a sunset now and again, facing east had a special benefit this day. Lenolla and Jiam's oldest daughter, Loreen, was being christened at the site of Tymel's grave in the garden. The ceremony proceeded with solemn dignity, Haymon looking on approvingly. At its end, the young girl came over with her mother and father and stood at the base of the statue, looking up with her wide-spaced, clear blue eyes. Hair as dark as her mother's rippled slightly in the soft spring breeze.

"Is it true, Mama?" Loreen asked.

"Every word of it is true, my dear," Lenolla said solemnly. "Haymon, Lord Cyl, is our sworn protector. As long as he watches over us, nothing evil can happen."

Jiam snorted at such fanciful story weaving. He and Lenolla went off, arm-in-arm, leaving Loreen to stare at the statue. Blue eyes met cold stone, and in that instant Haymon knew he had made the proper decision twelve years earlier, under the triple moons.

The daughter that might have been his smiled knowingly, then hurried off to join her parents.

# Blood Lilies

*A few years ago, Scott Phillips (screen writing credits include* Drive, Horrorvision, *and CW's* Kamen Rider Dragon Knight*) asked me to play a bit role in a zombie slasher movie he was shooting. I've been disemboweled and had my throat slit and turned into a green-arterial-blood-pumping alien monster and even been a mad scientist in his movies. I love movies! But the only one of all my short stories to ever spark any interest by filmmakers was this one, "Blood Lilies." An indie filmmaker (not Scott—he is completing his* Gimme Skelter *and has oodles of his own scripts to shoot afterward) is going to do this as a short film, aimed at indie festivals. Charlie Grant bought the story in 1990 for another of his Greystone Bay anthologies,* SeaHarp Hotel. *My story was chosen for the cover illustration, which made me inordinately proud since others in the anthology included Hugo-, Nebula- and Bram Stoker-Award winners.*

Alan Mitchell had come to the SeaHarp Hotel to die.

He leaned back in the sleek, comfortable, white Lincoln Towncar the hotel had sent for him, too tired to even look out the smoked-glass window. The driver opened the door. Mitchell heaved himself out and smiled wanly.

"I'll see to your bags, sir," the driver said. Mitchell thanked him with a vague wave of his hand. He found it increasingly difficult to concentrate. The doctors said it was his imagination, that the real ordeal lay ahead.

Mitchell refused to linger for months or even years. He had chosen the SeaHarp Hotel as the most luxurious spot he could find for his last week. Then he would take his life. Mitchell was nothing if not thorough. He had researched poisons to find the best, and had rejected it as an alternative. All involved risk and the possibility of lingering or outright failure. He shuddered at the notion of the pain when some virulent poison ate away at his stomach. The slightest gastric upset put him into such a state.

Asphyxiation. That was his researched choice. He would put a clear plastic bag over his head and securely fasten it. To keep the carbon dioxide level from rising in his blood and giving him even a moment's distress, he would pump helium into the bag. His lungs would be tricked into thinking all was well.

He had brought a small green-painted cylinder of the inert gas, with appropriate valves and regulator, in his larger suitcase.

Mitchell closed his eyes and imagined the event. The plastic bag fastened with a length of duct tape around his neck. Inelegant, undignified, but necessary. The rubber hose. The hissing tank of helium. A few barbiturates to prevent him from backing out when the moment came, but not so many that it would nauseate him. A soft and gentle death, slipping off into eternal peace without pain.

He winced as he moved. Something pulled loose inside him. Again, Mitchell pushed it out of his mind. The doctors said it was nothing. Kaposi's sarcoma didn't have symptoms like this. At least, he didn't believe so. He would have to look it up in his medical encyclopedia when he got to his room. Or perhaps in the most recent issue of *Morbidity and Mortality Weekly* he had sent to him from the CDC in Atlanta.

The driver fussed behind him, getting the luggage from the trunk. Mitchell stretched and looked out over Greystone Bay. The sunlight fought a heavy fog and won by slow inches. Here and there whitecaps danced on the bay, but it seemed too sullen to interest Mitchell. He had never enjoyed water or water sports.

He turned his attention to the six-foot-high field-stone wall that ran along Harbor Road. He smiled. The top of the fence had been adorned with more varieties of flowers than he could identify. Dying in the spring had advantages. The beauty of the flower-and-hedge-topped wall pleased him.

He stopped along the stone walk leading to the hotel's porch and drank in the beauty of the grounds. The SeaHarp's grounds keeper had not littered the fine lawn with the usual icons. Mitchell saw only neatly kept grass, not swing sets and chairs and boccie ball courts or even the ridiculous bent wire wicks of a croquet field. Just green, lush, well-tended grass. Mitchell liked the hotel more and more.

"I'll have the bags sent up to your room, if you want to look around first," the driver said.

"Um, yes, thank you." Mitchell hadn't realized it. He did want to explore. The SeaHarp's four stories of gingerbread front needed paint. The sea air tore away at the wood constantly. Mitchell wondered what riding out a storm inside the grand old hotel would be like. He wished he would live long enough to discover the mysteries of creaking boards and howling wind and hard-driving water against bulging windowpanes. He had lived too long in the dirty hustle of the big city.

"Don't go walking there," came an irritated voice. "You'll disturb the plants. They don't like it."

"Sorry," Mitchell said, stepping back. In his reverie he had walked across the lawn and blundered into a flowerbed. The gardener pushed back thick glasses with a dirty, calloused finger. He stared up in what Mitchell considered a belligerent manner unbecoming to the hired help of a resort hotel.

"Didn't mean to sound so brusque," the gardener apologized. "I take care of the flowers and hate to see them bothered." Almost as an afterthought, the small, sun-browned man added, "You wouldn't want to get your shoes dirty."

"You aren't from this area, are you?" asked Mitchell. He had always prided himself on identifying accents. Even if the gardener had spoken with the same clipped tones the others in the Greystone Bay area did, the suntan set this man apart. The heavy fog and winter storms didn't permit any native to get this tanned.

"From down South," the man said. His eyes looked like giant, brown fried eggs behind the thick lenses. Pushing back and getting off his knees, he struggled to his feet. Mitchell saw his first impression was right. The man stood a head shorter than he.

The accent didn't match any Mitchell had heard. Wherever the man did come from, it wasn't the South. Yet the tan suggested as much. And the gardener had no reason to lie.

"What kind of flowers are these? They look familiar but..."

"All kinds," the gardener said hurriedly. "These are a strain of marigolds. And those, the ones with the light red centers, are daisies."

"I've never seen daisies with such pale pink petals and red middles."

"My hybrid. I developed them myself."

"And those?" asked Mitchell, curious in spite of himself. He had the city dweller's love-hate relationship with flowers. They were pretty to look at but too much trouble to bother with.

"Those are Byzantine Roses."

Mitchell bent over and examined the delicate, involuted petals. They had fine red etching like veins inside pure white.

"They're lovely. You must be very proud of your garden."

The man nodded and smiled almost shyly. "They aren't the best I have to offer. The lilies are better. Want to see?"

Mitchell followed silently as the gardener led him to the rear of the hotel. He had thought the other flowers were gorgeous. These defied description.

"These are prize winners. I don't know much about horticulture, but from an artistic standpoint, they're unparalleled." Mitchell heaved a deep sigh. The world had so much to offer. He would miss it after he killed himself.

The lilies thrust up bold yellow trumpets. Tiny crimson spots decorated their interior. He blinked. They seemed to follow him heliotropically as if he were the sun. He reached out. The trumpet flared, and the bloom dipped toward his hand. The image of jaws opening flashed across his mind. He jerked back, embarrassed at his reaction. It was only a flower, after all.

"The insects like them," the gardener said.

"How do you grow them?"

"That's a secret." The gardener turned furtive and scuttled away. Mitchell shrugged. The flowers were as spectacular as the SeaHarp Hotel itself. Following a small path around the side of the building, Mitchell returned to the front stone steps. He passed between two large stone vases with more of the gardener's handiwork inside.

Mitchell opened the French doors leading into the hotel lobby, wondering why they didn't leave them open to catch the cooling, fresh breeze off the bay. He stopped and stared. If he had entered another world, the feeling couldn't have been much different.

Quiet fell over him like a blanket. He couldn't imagine what would shake the sense of serenity inherent in the room. A tear came to Alan Mitchell's eyes. This hotel would provide a fitting final week for him. He went to the registration desk to his left.

"Welcome to the SeaHarp, Mr. Mitchell," the clerk greeted.

He started to ask how the man knew his name, then remembered the driver had already brought his luggage in. A good hotel—a first class one— hired a friendly, intelligent staff. Of course the clerk knew his name. How many others would be arriving in the span of a few minutes?

"Thank you. I'd like a room on the second floor, please."

"That's been arranged. Your luggage is in suite 207."

"How did you know I'd want a room on the second floor?" Mitchell disliked the notion of being trapped in a burning building higher than he could safely jump out. It had been difficult living and working in New York with such a phobia, but he had managed.

"The lady told me." The clerk lifted a pen and pointed discreetly toward a writing desk with a Tiffany lamp. Mitchell tried to penetrate the darkness caused by the light.

"Hello, Alan."

He knew the voice instantly.

"It's been six years, Elizabeth." His heart almost exploded when she rose and moved around the writing desk and came fully into the cone of light from the lamp. Elizabeth Morgenthal hadn't aged a day, an hour, even a second, in the years since he had seen her.

She took both his hands in hers and pulled him close. The fragrance of her perfume was as he remembered. He closed his eyes and inhaled deeply, savoring the moment, transported back to happier times. The spell was broken when she kissed him. He recoiled slightly, unable to stop himself.

"What's wrong, Alan? Still angry with me?" Eyes so green they made emeralds envious stared up at him. He sought the tiny gold speck in her left eye and found it. The cute upturn of her nose and the pixy smile that quivered on her lips, threatening to break out into a laugh at any instant—he remembered them all.

"You have forgiven me?"

"I…" He had no answer. He had seldom thought of her in the intervening years. Seeing her, feeling the heat from her nearness, he wondered why he hadn't. "How did you know I'd be here?" he asked, trying to change the subject.

"You haven't forgiven me." She let out a deep sigh of mock regret. "Let me buy you dinner. You always did enjoy a good meal. The SeaHarp has the finest chef, not only in Greystone Bay but anywhere within a hundred-mile radius."

"No, no," he said, "the meal is on me. I insist. And you didn't answer the question. Did you peek at the reservations?"

"Nothing so elaborate. I saw you coming up the walk. I wondered what happened to you when you didn't come in."

"The gardener…"

"I saw. I decided to play a little prank on you." She stared at him with those fabulous green eyes. "You still don't like upper stories?"

"You remember my foibles. I hope you remember my better points, too."

She hesitated. Then Elizabeth's face broke out in a sunshiny smile. "I do, Alan. Thoughts of you have never been too far from my mind."

He swallowed, suddenly uncomfortable. "What brings you to this particular hotel?"

"My best friend got married last year and came here on her honeymoon. She made it sound so pleasant I decided to take my vacation here. I've been here a week."

"Are you staying on?" he heard himself asking. Mitchell fought down the memories—and Elizabeth's presence. He had a mission. He had decided. He would kill himself in one week. He would!

"For another week. It is expensive but restful. I've found it has restored my faith in the world. I was getting a little burned out, and other things weren't going well."

"Personal?" he asked.

"Naturally. The agency grossed two million dollars last year and will double that this year."

"You always were a fine businessman."

"Businesswoman," she said. "You always were such a fine, sexist man." Elizabeth gave another of the deep, almost shuddering sighs. "Business is fine. Personally, I'm a wreck."

"What was his name?"

"You always saw through to my soul, Alan. I hated that and loved it at the same time." Elizabeth took a step back and swayed.

"Are you all right?" Mitchell's arm went around her waist. He was still strong enough to support her. He got a chair and guided her into it. A ray of light slanted through a beveled glass window, sending gentle rainbows across her pale cheek. For the first time he noticed how peaked she was.

"It's why I came here. I work twenty-hour days. The doctor said I was killing myself and needed a vacation."

"After a week you're still faint?"

"Always the hypochondriac. When you can't fuss over yourself, you fussed over me," she said. In a low voice, she added, "I always enjoyed the attention."

"I have something in my suitcase..."

"I'm fine, Alan. Please. And the fainting spells only started a day or two ago. Stress. Or the relief of stress. Have you seen the porch? It stretches completely around the hotel. I enjoy sitting and watching the sunset."

"Do they serve a decent drink?"

"The SeaHarp? You've got to be kidding," she said, looking stronger. The paleness in her face remained. "The best, just like everything else in the hotel."

"Let me get settled, and I'll join you in an hour," he said.

"Not one second later," Elizabeth warned with mock severity.

"I'm always prompt."

"It's nice seeing you again, Alan. Really. And don't be mad at me."

"I'm not," he said, meaning it. What had drawn them together seven years ago was gone. Those days could never be recaptured. Mitchell felt a bleakness inside when he realized he would never see Elizabeth again after the end of the week. She would leave, return to the city and her job, find a new lover, and repeat endlessly the same drama she had written for herself.

And he would be dead.

Mitchell considered using the elevators to one side of the lobby, then decided to take the stairs. The sweep of the stairway reminded him of old movies about grander times, more elegant times. When he reached the head of the stairs, he was out of breath and had to rest.

He leaned against the highly polished mahogany railing and stared out over the lobby. Elizabeth still sat in the chair. The clerk had brought her a glass of water. From this distance, he wasn't hypnotized by her personal energy. She seemed frail, as if wasting away.

Mitchell pushed such nonsense from his mind. He was the one who was dying, not Elizabeth Morgenthal. She had always been the health fanatic, working at exercise the way she worked at her job. That had been part of her problem, he remembered. She met muscle-bound jocks in the health spas who invariably loved themselves more than they ever could her.

Rested, he sought out Room 207. The key given him by the clerk turned quietly in the well-oiled lock. The suite on the other side was everything he had hoped for. He could die peacefully in such a room.

Mitchell heaved his suitcases onto the bed and worked at the intricate locks he had put on them. Minutes later, he opened one and decided what needed hanging and what could be put in the wardrobe's single bottom drawer.

Only then did he open the larger suitcase. Fastened inside was the bottle of helium, a thick plastic bag, the roll of sticky gray duct tape, the brass fittings he needed, and a long, single-spaced, typewritten letter explaining his suicide. He leafed through the document, his eyes dancing over the will he had appended.

"How times change," he muttered to himself. He considered finding a lawyer in Greystone Bay and changing the will to include Elizabeth. She would share his last days, just as she had already shared fourteen months of his life. She deserved more than his company. "No," he told himself firmly. He had carefully weighed what to do. Altering his plans now would only introduce error.

He took a long, hot bath that relaxed the tension knotting his shoulders and upper back. Dressing carefully, wanting to impress Elizabeth, he studied himself in the full-length mirror. The light wool jacket and shirt collar hung loose. The weight loss would continue, but only this small hint betrayed his secret. He pressed out nonexistent wrinkles in his chocolate-colored slacks and studied himself even more critically. He decided he would pass all but the most penetrating of inspections.

He took the elevator to the lobby, saying nothing to the elevator starter. Mitchell tried to remember when he had last seen a human operator. The elevators in the Port Authority had men who sat on their stools in make-work projects, but he had no need to go to the rooftop parking garages.

The sun was dipping down over the high wall with its foliage when he walked onto the porch. Elizabeth had staked out a spot with a small table and two comfortable chairs. She waved to him. He couldn't restrain the smile that came to his lips. He had missed her and hadn't known it.

"You are right on time. You're a constant in the universe, Alan. Never a second late."

"Some people call that a compulsion. Or is it properly an obsession?"

"You haven't changed in other ways, either," she said in exasperation. "Don't try to be so precise. It doesn't matter if you're not in complete control. Really."

"Is this the New Age philosophy? Let previous lives intrude on the here-and-now?" He ordered a dry Gibson when the waiter came and silently stood beside his chair. "Never mind," he went on. "Let's just enjoy the sunset."

"Such beauty," Elizabeth said, sighing. "I've come out here every night for a week and it still awes me."

They sat and chatted about old times, the people they knew together and apart, the threads that had bound them. After awhile, they fell silent, content to watch the stars turning into hard diamond points in the velvet black sky.

Mitchell turned slightly in his chair and stared down the length of the long porch. Twin lights flared. He cocked his head to one side and got a better look. The gardener stood at the end of the porch. His thick glasses reflected pale yellow light coming from inside the SeaHarp's lobby. The man studied them. When he saw Mitchell returning the stare, he stepped back and vanished into the shadows.

"Let me buy you dinner. Anything you want."

"No, Alan. I'm the one with the successful business." Elizabeth's thin hand shot to her lips. "I'm sorry. I don't know what's happened in the past six years."

"The bookstore isn't grossing four million this year," he said, with a laugh. "But I'm comfortable. I can afford a brief vacation here."

"This is so nice running into you here," Elizabeth said. "And you may buy me dinner."

"Only if you have a steak. You need the protein." He reached out and touched her cheek. The flesh was porcelain-cold.

She laughed and held his hand close, giving the palm a quick kiss. "Whatever you say, Alan."

After dinner, they had another drink in the bar. They entered their own private world when they sat in the high-backed booths.

"It's nice finding a bar without loud music. I hate shouting to make myself heard," she said. Elizabeth giggled, then belched. "Sorry, Alan. Too much to drink."

"You've only had two glasses of wine, unless you had more before we watched the sunset."

"I just had a Perrier. I can't hold my liquor like I used to. I hate to break it off. This has been so nice seeing you again, but I'm too tired."

"I'm a bit sleepy myself. It was a long trip down on the train. May I see you to your door?"

"Always the gentleman. Of course you may." Arm in arm they left the bar and took the elevator to the top floor.

Mitchell's heart raced when Elizabeth stopped outside the door and handed him her key. He opened the door.

"Thank you," she said. She stood, head slightly tilted and eyes closed. The kiss he gave her was hardly more than a quick peck. She hid her disappointment well.

"Good night," Mitchell said.

"Breakfast?"

"Not too early," he said. "Let's say nine?"

She nodded. He saw the sadness in her eyes—and a curious haunted expression. Elizabeth spun around and closed the door behind her. The click of the deadbolt sliding home started Mitchell on his way back to his room.

He was drowsy, but he couldn't sleep. Rather than returning to his room, he went back outside onto the porch. A few other guests sat about in twos and threes, quietly talking. He didn't want their company, even if they had desired his. He walked across the dark, dew-damp lawn until he found the high wall. From here he started pacing slowly, intending to circumnavigate the SeaHarp's grounds.

Mitchell stopped and found Elizabeth's room on the fourth floor. He watched until the light went out. Six years ago there might have been more between them. Now, it was impossible. He started on his lonely walk again when the light in Elizabeth's room came on again.

He frowned when he saw that it wasn't the room light. A beam bounced and bobbed against the windowpane, as if someone with a flashlight had entered. Mitchell considered alerting the room clerk to the possibility of a sneak thief in the hotel. The light snapped off. Mitchell found himself unsure if he had seen anything important or if his active imagination played tricks on him.

Starting for the lobby, he paused when he heard a door at the rear of the SeaHarp open and close. Mitchell walked on cat-quiet feet until he saw the circular yellow disk of a flashlight moving on the ground. He stood beside a tree, indistinguishable from a distance.

The gardener hurried toward his flowerbed. In one hand he held the flashlight. In the other he carried a small, capped jar. He dropped to his knees beside the bed of lilies and carefully unscrewed the lid. Mumbling to himself, he poured the liquid onto the flowers, being sure each got a measured amount. A lewd sucking noise echoed through the stillness of the night.

Finished, he stood and tucked the jar under his arm. The gardener left, whistling off-key.

Mitchell waited several minutes after the man had gone before approaching to the flowerbed. The lilies tracked him like radar. Kneeling, he avoided their questing stalks and ran his finger along the damp soil, then lifted and sniffed what he had found.

"Blood," he said, startled. In the past few months he had come to loathe the sharp, coppery smell. Involuntarily he rubbed his left arm where so much had been removed for tests. Oh, yes, he knew blood. And he knew why the gardener's lilies and other flowers grew so lushly.

The Egyptians had used slave's blood to fertilize their crops. Mitchell wondered how many other guests beside Elizabeth Morgenthal contributed their lifeblood to the SeaHarp's thirsty flowers.

He returned to his room, but sleep wouldn't come. He sat in an overstuffed chair, staring at his opened suitcase holding the paraphernalia of his death.

At breakfast he watched Elizabeth eat double portions. "You're hungry," he said, knowing the reason. Blood loss would do it. His real questions were how the gardener entered her room when she had thrown the deadbolt and how he drew the blood without waking her.

"The past few days I've been famished." Her cheeks burned with a fever. The paleness was greater this morning than it had been. Mitchell wondered how much blood the gardener had sucked from his victim.

"Did you sleep well?"

"I have since I got here," Elizabeth said, smearing homemade preserves on her fifth piece of toast. "That's odd, really. I have insomnia. That's one reason I work such long hours," she said between bites.

"It might be the other way around," pointed out Mitchell.

"The doctor said that, too. It doesn't matter. Not at the moment, Alan. I'm sleeping like a log." Her green eyes locked on his. She didn't have to add that she wished he had been with her.

They spent the day walking along the shore of the bay, skipping stones like small children, examining seashells and discarding them, finding a peacefulness that hadn't existed for either in many years. They returned to the SeaHarp Hotel at sunset.

"It's been a wonderful day, Alan," Elizabeth said almost wistfully. She reached across the small table in the bar and touched his hand. His fingers twined with hers.

"It doesn't have to end," he said. Her eyes glowed with an inner light.

"I hoped you'd say that." She smiled almost shyly. "Your room or mine?"

"Yours," he said without hesitation, remembering the suitcase he had so carefully stored in his wardrobe. Even being in the same room with the implements of his destruction seemed wrong now.

They took the elevator to the fourth floor and entered her room, arms around each other. She flipped on the light switch. Mitchell noticed her room was much smaller than his, but still larger than the standard hotel room. He studied the room as she fussed about, dropping purse and kicking off shoes. He saw nothing to indicate how the gardener had entered.

"Aren't they thoughtful, Alan?" she asked. "They leave a fresh flower for me each night." She lifted the bud vase from the dresser top and sniffed at the delicate blossom. He watched as she weaved slightly. Her eyelids drooped the barest amount. She took another deep whiff. "I so love fresh flowers."

"You're giving your life for them," he said in a low voice, understanding one part of the riddle.

"What?" She sank to the bed and tried to unfasten her blouse. She fell to one side, sleeping deeply. The combined exertion of the daylong walk and the potent effect of the flower's narcotic perfume had caused her to fall into a light coma.

Mitchell struggled to get her off the bed and into the bathroom. He put a blanket down in the tub and rolled her onto it, hoping she would be comfortable. He didn't want her to awaken in the morning with a kink in her neck. It took longer than he'd thought it would. His strength had been taxed, too. That was the progressive nature of his disease. The T-cells in his blood turned traitor. Infections took hold more easily and conquered with little struggle.

His entire autoimmune system had betrayed him. AIDS. Tears formed at the corners of his eyes at the outrageous fortune that had visited him. He pushed the knowledge of a lingering, painful, ugly death from his mind and concentrated.

Mitchell went to Elizabeth's wardrobe and opened the door. At one end of the fragrant, redwood-lined cabinet hung a frilly nightgown. He stripped off his clothing and donned the gown. It was too tight across the shoulders but should pass in the dark. It hid the different flow of his muscles—what remained of them—and gave him a hope of stopping the gardener.

Before he lay down in the bed, Mitchell returned to the bathroom to check Elizabeth. Her deep, regular breathing showed she was all right. He took a few minutes to shave the hair from his left arm. Even in the dark the gardener might notice the hirsute difference. No longer. Mitchell thrust out his thin arm and knew it might pass for a woman's.

He returned to the bedroom and turned out the light. Crawling under the covers, his needle-marked left arm dangling over the edge of the bed, he waited.

The light going out gave the gardener his cue. From the ceiling came scurrying sounds, as if rats had infested the century-old hotel. From half-closed eyes Mitchell watched as a piece of the intricate plasterwork turned into utter blackness. The gardener dropped down to a chair from the exposed crawlspace. The flashlight's beam darted around, checking. The gardener hummed to himself as he came over and gripped Mitchell's arm.

A thin rubber hose circled Mitchell's upper arm. The needle sank into veins almost collapsed from too much blood being drawn. The gardener didn't notice. He had been milking Elizabeth heavily. Mitchell almost protested the amount of his blood taken. Even lying down and feigning sleep, he felt dizzy from the loss. To have taken this much from Elizabeth would have killed her.

Only when the jar was filled to the brim did the gardener remove the rubber constrictor hose and retreat. Mitchell watched openly as the gardener jumped from the chair and into the dark square overhead. Like a monkey, the man vanished. Seconds later, the ceiling was again whole.

Mitchell had to fight to sit up. The bloodletting had taken too much from him. An hour later he had wrestled Elizabeth into bed and left quietly. In two he had made his calls. In four his phone jangled for long minutes. He didn't answer it. He knew he would eat breakfast alone.

He slept fitfully, nightmares of grotesquely twisted blood cells chasing him. The sound effects accompanying the nightmares were worse. The sucking noise, the awful obscene sucking.

As Mitchell went into the dining room, a bellman stopped him. "Sir, the lady left this for you."

"Thank you," Mitchell said, knowing what Elizabeth had put in the note. He opened it and read anyway.

"Darling Alan," it began. "I'm so embarrassed about last night. I remember nothing—but do know it had to be as wonderful as you. I wish we could have spent more time together, but it's not possible. I received a call last night. There was a fire in my office and my manager was severely burned and is in critical condition. The quickest way back to New York was the 5:10 train. I tried to call your room but you didn't answer. Please, Alan, call me when you get back to the city. With all love, Elizabeth."

He tucked the note in his pocket. She would be angry and confused when she learned there hadn't been a fire and that none of her staff had been hurt.

Mitchell sat in the main dining room and stared out at the blooming flowers.

As he sipped his tea, white-uniformed men rushed past the window. Mitchell turned in his chair and craned his neck. They went to the bed of lilies the gardener had tended so carefully. In a few minutes, they returned, pushing a gurney laden with a black plastic bag large enough to hold a body. A body the size of the gardener.

Mitchell felt no triumph. What the lilies had become, he didn't care to know. He shuddered, thinking of them propagating. But that was no worry of his. He finished his Earl Grey, put the cup down with a steady hand and returned to his room.

The suitcase opened and Alan Mitchell began his journey to the undiscovered land, from whom no traveler returns.

# About the Author

In thirty years as a professional writer, Robert E. Vardeman has authored two *Star Trek™* books and, in a different Gene Roddenberry universe, wrote *Xander in Lost Universe™: The Cosmic Lens,* a tie-in with the Xander comic book and graphic novels.

Several works have been published in gaming and game tie-in universes. *The Ruins of Power* in the best-selling *BattleTech/MechWarrior™* series joined another set in the *Magic: The Gathering™* universe. A short story based on this card-game fantasy world also appeared in the anthology *Magic: The Gathering™ Distant Planes.* Another gaming tie-in novel, *Hell Heart,* was published in the *Vor: The Maelstrom™* series, and a novella, *The Great Helium War,* for the *Crimson Skies™* role-playing game, was serialized on-line before print publication

Vardeman has also published a high-tech thriller, three mysteries, and numerous series westerns for Berkley/Jove and Signet, with nine other western historicals published under his Karl Lassiter pen name.

Fantasy work in his 37 published novels ranges from the humorous to the starkness of sword & sorcery. "Road of Dreams and Death," set in Andre Norton's Witch World, was published in *Tales of the Witch World.* More recent short story sales include "The Power and the Glory" in the alternate history anthology, *Time Twisters,* edited by Jean Rabe, and three stories in the *Blue Kingdoms* anthologies, edited by Jean Rabe and Stephen D. Sullivan, and "Purification," a sword & sorcery fantasy set in the *Warhammer™* universe anthology *Invasion!* Other short work includes stories in anthologies edited by Robert Bloch, Charles Grant, Edward Bryant, Fred Saberhagen, Martin Greenberg, James Lowder, and Thomas Monteleone, covering the spectrum from hard SF to fantasy and horror.

Published science-fiction novels total 21. The body of work includes the adventure of space opera as well as scientifically accurate SF. His *Star Frontier* trilogy is scheduled for reprint in November, 2007.

Vardeman authored the novelization of *The Stink of Flesh,* a 2005 indie zombie movie. His horror short story "Blood Lilies" has been adapted for another indie movie scheduled to begin filming in late 2008.

A member of the International Association for Media Tie-in Writers, he was a judge for the association's 2007 Scribe Award and is a former vice-president for SFWA. Vardeman holds a B.S. degree in physics, an M.S. in materials engineering and worked in solid-state physics research at Sandia National Laboratories.

# WALKABOUT PUBLISHING
### Great stories by great authors.

Robert E. Vardeman—Marc Tassin—James M. Ward
Lorelei Shannon—Dean Leggett—Kathleen Watness—Paul Genesse
E. Readicker-Henderson—Jason Mical—Kelly Swails—Brandie Tarvin
Stephen D. Sullivan—Jean Rabe—And More!

Pirates of the Blue Kingdoms
Blue Kingdoms: Buxom Buccaneers
Blue Kingdoms: Shades & Specters
Blue Kingdoms: Zombies, Werewolves, & Unicorns
Martian Knights & Other Stories
This and That and Tales About Cats
Under the Protection of the Cow Demon

**Walkabout Publishing**
**S.D. Studios**
**P.O. Box 151**
**Kansasville, WI 53139**
**www.walkaboutpublishing.com**

## Official Home of the Blue Kingdoms.